THE SEXUAL OCCUPATION OF JAPAN

ALSO BY RICHARD SETLOWE:

The Black Sea
The Brink
The Experiment
The Haunting of Suzanna Blackwell

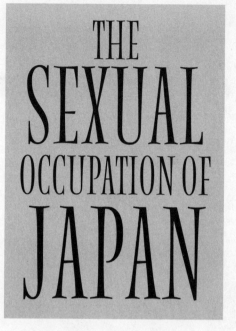

THE SEXUAL OCCUPATION OF JAPAN

A NOVEL

RICHARD SETLOWE

■ HarperCollins*Publishers*

HarperCollins books may be purchased for educational, business, or sales promotional use. For information please write: Special Markets Department, HarperCollins Publishers, Inc., 10 East 53rd Street, New York, NY 10022.

FIRST EDITION

Designed by Elina D. Nudelman

Library of Congress Cataloging-in-Publication Data

Setlowe, Richard.
    THE SEXUAL OCCUPATION OF JAPAN: a novel/ Richard Setlowe --1st ed.
        p.   cm.
    ISBN 0-06-018393-4
        I. Title.
    PS3569.E78S4   1999
    813'.54--dc21   98-54269

99 00 01 02 03 ❖/RRD 10 9 8 7 6 5 4 3 2

For my wife Beverly,
whose love nurtures
the light by which
I write

Fear has an odd seduction. Fear and the sense of sex are linked in secret conspiracy.

—GRAHAM GREENE

CONTENTS

The United States military occupation of Japan began in September 1945, when General Douglas MacArthur landed at Atsugi Air Base, climbed into a waiting staff car flying a four-star flag, and sped up Highway 1 to his new headquarters in the Dai-Ichi Building directly across Hibiya Avenue from the Imperial Palace.

The military occupation officially ended in April 1952, when the peace treaty went into effect. But there is no documented date on which the American sexual occupation of Japan ended.

FOREPLAY

1999: Death at the Love Hotel

The evening I landed at Tokyo's Narita Airport from Los Angeles, Matami Okamatsu—the senior official at the Ministry of International Trade and Industry with whom I had scheduled a critical meeting—checked into a love hotel in the Roppongi district with a young blonde the desk clerk later told police looked like the actress Sharon Stone.

The love hotel, named Dreams Castle, has an elaborate stucco facade of rococo battlements and fairy tale turrets—a Japanese designer's fancy of a European medieval fortress. But the small, barren lobby with the unseen desk clerk behind darkened glass features only illuminated photographs of the hotel's fantasy suites. Okamatsu had already reserved the chamber named Malibu Nights. The blond carried an elaborately wrapped package, possibly a gift from her admirer or a costume for the tryst.

Malibu Nights is decorated in Art Deco furnishings of black and gold, with matching black and gold statuettes of Erté-styled nudes. The large circular bed covered in gold-dyed sheets rests on a raised platform with mirrors on two sides and on the ceiling. There are no windows, but large photographs of the California coast are backlighted in recesses framed by stylized fake palms. Hidden speakers emit a recording of surf.

The sound is controlled with a remote control by the bed, which can switch the track to love themes from Hollywood movies, soften or raise the lighting, or turn on the TV to the porno movies that run continuously on the hotel's private channel.

The decor is stylish, deliberately designed to make lovers feel as if they are not really at Malibu but movie stars on a set—an erotic pretense that is larger, more tumescent, than real life.

According to the Tokyo Metropolitan Police coroner's report, it apparently worked for Okamatsu-san. Either before or after having sex, he and the blonde drank two-thirds of a bottle of champagne chilled in a black and gold enamel ice bucket near the bed, and the Sharon Stone look-alike departed shortly thereafter, at the doorway slipping out of fleece-lined sandals and back into the flat shoes young Western women wear in Tokyo so as not to loom taller than their Japanese escorts. She left the spent Okamatsu-san naked in the still-vibrating bed to nap—as the MITI official was not a young man—or perhaps contemplate the possibility of AIDS—as he had not used a condom in a city where there is a seldom-spoken-of miniepidemic.

Within a few minutes of the blonde's exit, a young man with short-cropped hair bound with a black *hachimaki*, wearing a black T-shirt, black jeans, and Adidas running shoes, stole through the unlocked door. He carried in front of him a gleaming *katana*, the two-handed samurai sword.

Suddenly abandoning the stealthy ninja approach, he shouted "Keep Japan pure!" and rushed forward, warning the dozing Okamatsu, who instinctively threw up his arms to block the blow.

The razor-edged blade nearly severed both of Okamatsu's forearms, and blood splattered the golden sheets, the spotless mirrors, and the attacker. Okamatsu screamed.

"Traitor, traitor," the swordsman cursed, and thrust the blade into Okamatsu's stomach. But the stabbing, rather than killing the old man, only seemed to heighten the pitch of his screams.

The young man lowered his sword, stunned. The assassination attempt had degenerated into a noisy, gory mess, and shame overwhelmed the assassin. But with the humiliation, a wave of loathing for the old man washed over him. "Traitor," he shouted again, and chopped at Okamatsu's unprotected neck. The sword fatally hacked through the carotid artery, spurting blood all over the killer's hair, face, and arms.

Revolted, soaked, and dripping with the murdered man's blood, the young assassin bolted out the door, still gripping the *katana* with both hands. He careened into the hallway of the Dreams Castle, where a dozen couples, interrupted in their amours by Okamatsu's screams, gaped at him from the doorways of their fantasy chambers.

Part 1

THE JAPANESE LADY'S KNIFE

1

A Very Dangerous Game

"What the hell happened to Okamatsu?"

Ozu looks startled. "Excuse me, please. I do not understand."

The Mitsubishi limousine eases away from the portico of the Imperial Hotel and briefly skirts the tree-lined moat of the Imperial Palace itself, then yaws into the skyscraping stone canyons of the Marunouchi financial district.

"Matami Okamatsu at MITI. In charge of communications and electronics. Had an appointment with him. But I can't get through to him. I don't know if it's a language problem or what, but his office tells me he's no longer there. That someone else will assist me. And then they hang up."

"Oh yes, please, someone at MITI will contact you."

"What happened to Okamatsu?"

"He is no longer there, I think."

This surprises me. Japanese bureaucrats are always there, for life. "I just talked to him a week ago. And confirmed our meeting."

"It is his health, I think."

At my first mention of Okamatsu and the Ministry of International Trade and Industry, Hara had glanced up but now stares out the window, as if the conversation is of absolutely no interest. But there's a tense silence, not comfortable at all.

The glaring neon kaleidoscope of totally incomprehensible calligraphy that surrounds the limo now, at night, feels vaguely threatening, buzzing with a sharp electric hum, the high-tech hieroglyphics of an alien culture.

After the cordial greetings and bowing at the hotel, we ride in uneasy silence for a while. The Japanese, I had been briefed, are very comfortable with silence in business negotiations. But I'm not.

Then Hara says something in Japanese. Ozu translates, "Today's talks went well, I think, Mr. Saxon?"

I turn to Hara, who sits next to me. "I think we understand each other's positions better, Kenji."

"It was a productive reconnaissance flight for you?" Ozu asks without being cued in Japanese by Hara. The translator sits strapped into the jump seat facing me, a small man with close-cropped hair and round rimless glasses, but I can't read his expression in the dark cab. Ozu is a second-level executive whose English is fluent but schoolbook. "Reconnaissance flight" is an odd but telling phrase.

"It was informative, not productive." The fact that they know so much about me personally puts me on edge as much as Ozu's casual arrogance about his knowledge.

He translates, and the question comes back, "Why not productive?"

I smile at Hara. "Kenji, you are not taking the merger proposal seriously. You think it's a ploy, a maneuver to get a higher price. You still believe we are going to sell you the company, the studio, except, of course, the TV stations. We're not. We're here to buy, not sell. Our plan is *quite* serious."

The limousine stops at a traffic light. Crowds pour across the intersection from four directions, and Japanese faces stare into the dark-tinted windows of the limo, squinting to discover whatever tycoon, politician, or pop star is inside. A girl in her twenties, black feathers of hair framing a delicately lovely face, smiles hesitantly into the windows, seemingly looking right at me, and that face momentarily mesmerizes me. It strums a haunting, poignant cord that all but draws me out of the limo into the street.

"Universal sold. Columbia sold," Ozu asserts, yanking me back to the present.

The Japanese are tap-dancing. There is no way Kuribayashi Electric can finance a buyout. The company is sound, but the collapse of the Asian market has dragged down their sales and income, and their stock is at an historic low, along with the rest of Tokyo's Nikkei index. The Japanese banks are shuffling a trillion dollars in bad debts on the books. But still Hara and Ozu tap-dance, as if they had secret billions to slap on the table.

And I buck-and-wing along with them because to state the truth will offend the Japanese. And I am here to make history.

"Universal was owned and sold by a seventy-seven-year-old agent who wanted to cash in and make the biggest deal of his lifetime for a grand finale," I say. "Six-point-six billion. And he's regretted it every day since. Even after Matsushita bailed out.

"Columbia," I continue, "that was owned and sold by Coca-Cola, a very old and conservative company from our deep South. The good old boys in Atlanta thought they knew all about show business because they spent six hundred million a year on TV commercials with rock stars to sell Coke. But they didn't know dreck from drama."

Ozu looks bewildered. *"Dreck?"*

"Shit," I translate. "They didn't know shit about the movie business. Their MBAs were projecting steady growth and profit curves and suddenly found themselves on a roller coaster coming round a curve and staring straight down into a fiscal black hole."

"Oh yes," Ozu nods and launches into a long explanation in Japanese.

Hara listens with head cocked, eyes darting from Ozu to me. He repeats the words "roller coaster," but the *l*s fade to "ro-wah coastah."

"Do you know what a roller coaster is?"

"Oh yes," Ozu nods. "We have this amusement at Disneyland. Mr. Hara's wife and children like it very much."

I wonder just how hair-raising the roller coaster at the Tokyo Magic Kingdom is. "Coca-Cola wanted off the wild ride. They were ecstatic to sell to Sony for three-point-four billion. And Sony immediately took another two-point-seven billion in write-offs on top of a half-billion in operating losses. And now Sony is on that exciting, heart-stopping ride up, and down again. Do you like roller coasters, Mr. Ozu?"

"Not so much," Ozu acknowledges politely. "Very banging up and down too much, I think. This up and down makes me a little sick." He goes back and forth with Hara in Japanese, then adds, "Mr. Hara also."

"Then very definitely Kuribayashi Electric should not get into the movie and TV business. It's always a roller-coaster ride. There are no steady market shares and profits here. Always very banging up and down too much. Never a smooth ride." I smile broadly at both Ozu and Hara.

The translator frowns and in the harsh glare of the pulsating neons looks startled but apparently repeats what I said. To my surprise, Hara laughs. "Yes, yes. I think you enjoy riding roller coasters very much, Peter," he says, suddenly switching to comprehensible English.

Kenji Hara is a handsome man with a strong, almost aquiline nose and straight, thick black hair that—I note somewhat enviously—shows no hint of receding from a broad ivory brow.

I rather like him. Behind the austere politeness of the Japanese executive in a large corporation, there is a genuine cordiality, and on this the second day of my negotiations with the Kuribayashi Electric Industrial Company, Hara has invited me to his home for dinner.

He lives in the Sanbancho residential area, not far from downtown, and as we pull up, there's a tense flurry of conversation between Hara and Ozu. The white-gloved driver springs out and opens the door, but Ozu doesn't move toward the house.

"It is a pleasure to meet you and work with you today, Mr.

Saxon." He bows deeply. "After a pleasant evening, the limousine will take you back to the hotel."

"You're not joining us?"

"Mrs. Hara speaks English very capably and will serve as your excellent translator." Despite Ozu's almost rigid formality, there is still a hint of his surprise and unhappiness at this apparently sudden decision, and he looks back and forth from Hara to me with a strange intensity.

Michiko Hara is poised on the threshold, as though she has been standing there waiting for hours. She's a beautiful woman, perhaps in her late forties, early fifties, in an elegant shawl-collared dress of off-white that perfectly matches her skin tone. I mention this because from the very first moment there is the quality of an apparition about Michiko Hara, something almost ghostly that I can't quite grasp.

She studies my face—this gaijin bearing gifts now before her—with a smile of nervous expectation. "Mr. Saxon, it is a pleasure to welcome you to my home. You are our honored guest." Her voice has a soft, breathless quality, and accents, not necessarily Japanese but exotic, that seize your attention.

I had been briefed at length in Los Angeles by our consultants on the protocol. The Japanese place a great deal of importance on establishing personal relationships with those they do business with, and invitations to meet the wife and family are to be taken very seriously.

"You have been to Japan before." The lilting intonation makes it neither a question nor a statement.

"A very long time ago, I'm afraid. It was another world, an entirely different country."

"Ah . . ."

I remove my shoes and am ushered down a few steps into the main room. In a stark recess of the far wall—an alcove to itself—stands a small cabinet of Japanese cedar, which in distant memory I recognize as a family shrine. There is something disturbing and familiar about it—the brass gong and incense burner, the scroll, the faded photographs of a Japanese woman and an army officer.

But it isn't the shrine with its pagoda roof that shrivels my scrotum and flashes a chill up my spine. It is the two matched daggers like offerings on an alter—the lady's knife, the *kai-ken*, and the *wakizashi*, the short sword, both with blood-red silk hilts and delicately carved ivory handles now yellowed as old bones, in sleek black lacquered scabbards. They are the knives of my nightmares.

When I look up, Michiko Hara is watching me carefully, her lips parted in some breathless anticipation, her eyes widened in alarm, as though she is about to bolt—or so it seems to me in my muddled, alien perception.

"My wife is from very old family," Hara says, indicating the shrine with a nod.

Suddenly two curious, grinning kids materialize, a boy about seventeen and a girl a few years younger, eager to inspect the creature from Hollywood and practice a few shy phrases of English. For the next several minutes there is a politely awkward settling down. Michiko, assisted by her daughter, serves cocktails and steaming dumplinglike hors d'oeuvres I do not recognize, while Hara himself says little but merely sits smiling, radiating a quiet pride in his wife, his family, his home.

The boy, it turns out, is not a teenage high schooler, a deception of the smooth Japanese complexion and slight build, but a student at the University of Tokyo. He soon asks the question festering on his tongue. "Do you know Madonna?"

No one admits to not actually knowing somebody, so I say, "I've met her at functions. But I don't really know her. Nobody does. Not even Madonna. That's the secret of her success."

Michiko Hara lets out a delighted chime of laughter. I have not heard her laugh before, and yet it is a hauntingly familiar sound, a throaty peel that resonates in memory.

We sit down to dinner. Throughout, Michiko Hara quietly moves through a sliding frame-and-paper door into what must be the kitchen to appear a moment later with each new steaming, fragrant course. I hear the whisper of servants on the other side, but I never see them.

Polite questions are asked about my wife, my children, my home in Pacific Palisades, as if all the momentous issues that have brought me to Tokyo are to be assiduously avoided. And I sense, or perhaps just imagine, a tremulous undercurrent in Michiko Hara, a certain eagerness to hear the answers.

"Have you spent much time in the United States?" I ask. Her English indicates she has.

"Oh yes. Eight, sometimes twelve hours a day," she answers. She enjoys my confusion for a moment or two, then laughs. "I worked at the American embassy in Tokyo. That's officially part of the United States, isn't it? International law." Like her laughter, there is something haunting about Michiko Hara's voice.

"I guess it is."

After dinner the children excuse themselves, deeply bowing ceremonially, and Hara leads me out into a cloistered garden off the dining area to smoke Havana cigars.

From the way he fumbles with the stogies and matches, apparently this is not a normal after-dinner habit with him but something for my benefit.

"You like cigars?" he asks.

"On occasion."

"This is an occasion, yes?"

"Hopefully an historic occasion."

Hara takes a long, contemplative draw on his cigar, as if waiting for something. In a moment I hear the gentle sliding hiss of the door as Michiko enters the garden.

Hara looks directly at me but speaks in Japanese. "This deal is extremely important to you?" his wife translates.

"Yes, of course. Of great importance."

"To me also it is important. But I do not understand your position very clearly. You are a lawyer. You do not work for the company at this time."

"I have a private practice, and I represent them."

"But if you make this deal, you will become important in the company." He speaks with confident, persuasive hand gestures, making a point with a full palm and then, when he wishes to be translated, ending the sentence with a polite *dozo* (please).

"I will probably become one of the directors, yes."

Hara shakes his head. "I still do not understand the motion picture and TV business."

I laugh. "And you never will. That's one of the rules. Nobody knows anything."

Hara's eyes go wide. "That is very frightening to us."

"You think that's frightening. Wait until you have a hundred and fifty million tied up in production, prints, and advertising for just one movie that's going against six other blockbusters, all opening within days of each other at Christmas or the Fourth of July. And you have to do that a couple of times a year to stay in the game. Look, there are no guarantees. As I said, there is no projected market share or growth in profits here. Don't let the current grosses of *Love Songs* or *Nebula* deceive you. It will always be the same financial roller coaster ride that Matsushita and Sony took."

"You negotiate in a very strange way, Peter Saxon."

"Kuribayashi must stay out of the movie business. When you believe that, we can begin the real negotiation." It was time to let the cat out of the bag. "I'm here to put together the first Japanese-American *keiretsu*."

Hara does not appear surprised but merely nods, as if he has anticipated this. "The cross-ownership of Japanese companies by foreign companies is not accepted," Michiko Hara translates.

The Japanese financial bubble had burst years ago. The banks are bankrupt and the country in the worst recession since World War II. Los Angeles real estate speculators are buying portfolios of distressed

Tokyo office buildings for ten cents on the dollar. But to detail this will insult Hara. So I say merely, "The game has permanently changed." And in that phrase there is a world of repercussions.

"This is a very dangerous game, Peter." Hara says it in perfect English, as though he has practiced saying the phrase many times. "Very dangerous."

I nod. "But a small price to pay for control of the world in the new millennium."

From the shadows, Michiko Hara's soft laughter lilts, reverberating sharply, familiarly in my memory like old chimes.

2

Strange Fruit

When the limo drops me off in front of the Imperial Hotel that night, I am still much too wired to sleep. It is early morning yesterday in Los Angeles, alarm clocks are just going off. My biological clock still lags the jet and is puttering somewhere between Oahu and Guam.

Back in my hotel room, I pour a tumbler of neat Haig & Haig from the minibar and sit in my underwear sipping it in the dark.

I coax sleep with Scotch, something I seldom do at home because I never want Joan or the girls to see me as a solitary drinker. But bring an old boy back across the Pacific to bygone haunts, and he effortlessly falls back into the dissolute ways of his youth. Exhausted, drowsy with Scotch, I doze off in the chair.

I awake with a start. There is a pop, like the shot of an air rifle, and then a second pop, in the corridor just outside my hotel room, and the door shakes. A heavy thud against the door brings me bolt upright. I listen intently, but there is only the faint, fading tread of someone rushing away down the hall. I check my watch, and the phosphorescent arrows glow spookily in the dark—4:20 A.M. Tokyo time.

I'm awake again now. The sound bothers me or rather rouses my curiosity enough so that I cannot fall back to sleep. I shuffle to the door, just stick my head out, and look up and down the corridor. There is nothing and no one there.

As I step back into the room I see it on the door, pinned there by a dagger. I stare, at first in confusion, at the gray-pink pendulous mass hanging there like a small bouquet of a grotesque fungus. It takes a moment or two to recognize what it is, and then I stagger back and slam the door shut to block it out.

It isn't just the obscenity of it, although that's terror enough, but all the horror of this place from a distant time that it carries for me. It is totally irrational, this chill that suddenly grips me. It starts in the groin, at the testes, and rapidly spreads through my body like a shudder. It has been more than three decades, but still the fear is there, as involuntary as a fever.

I can't just leave it there. At any moment people will be leaving to catch an early jet to New York or Singapore, the bullet train to Kyoto. I put on a robe and open the door wide so that anyone passing by will be less likely to see it unless they look directly into the room. I reach for the dagger, recoil at the thought of touching the obscenity, and go back for a hand towel from the bathroom.

I pull out the small dagger, but the fastening still hangs there. I inspect it more closely. It is held by two staples. *Staples.*

I work the tip of the dagger to loosen the staples, but as I lean in close to pry the blade I catch a strong whiff of formaldehyde. I gather it all in the towel, shut the door tight, bolt it, and dump the towel on an end table. I just stare at it.

Who the hell stalks the halls of the Imperial Hotel at four in the morning with a staple gun in hand to tack human mutilations to someone's door. Not just any door, but *my* door.

The obvious thing is to act rationally in the face of an irrational act. Or is it?

I dress quickly, then call the front desk. "This is Mr. Saxon in suite twenty-seven-oh-nine. Would you please send the manager to my room immediately. There is a serious matter for the police, but I don't want to talk about it on the phone. Yes, either send the manager or the police to my room as quickly as possible." I hang up before the desk clerk can ask any more questions.

Then I call room service and, queasy as I feel, order a pot of coffee, orange juice, and toast. It's going to be a long morning.

There is apparently an assistant manager on duty all night, and it's only minutes before there's a polite knock on the door. A young man in his twenties in a dark business suit presents his card with a slight bow, little more than a nod of his head. "Is there a problem here, Mr. Saxon?"

I glance at the card. "Yes, Mr. Motomoto. A few minutes ago I was awakened by a banging on my door. Someone hung a strange fruit there." I point to the small staple holes and the chipped paint where I had pried it off.

"Strange fruit to door?" Motomoto repeats in confusion. He fingers the small holes.

"Nailed, attached." I make a stabbing motion. "Also with a knife."

"With a knife. Ah yes. What is it?" He looks very concerned and frowns at me, as if I am the culprit who damaged the Imperial Hotel's door.

I gesture him into the room, ease the door shut, and lead him to the end table. Motomoto stares at the dissections. He hisses audibly like a snake, his eyes widening perceptibly, his ochre skin paling.

"They are a man's sexual organs."

"What?"

"A prick and balls."

Motomoto looks up at me, astonished. "Who would do this?"

"I don't know. It may be a random act of American bashing. I suspect a Japanese did it. But it's possibly any Asian or short European."

"A Japanese?" Motomoto again frowns at me, as if I am somehow at fault.

I walk to the door, open it. It had not occurred to me until I saw Motomoto finger the splintered wood. "An American or European of average height like me would have stuck the knife *here*." I stab my hand down and point to a spot almost a foot above the holes.

I shut the door. "I want you to listen to me very carefully, Mr. Motomoto, because what you do in the next hour is very important to the reputation of this hotel and your career. Do you understand me?"

"Yes, Mr. Saxon."

"Good." I continue in the same slow, deliberate tone of voice. "I am here in Tokyo representing a major American corporation in a very private negotiation with a major Japanese corporation. This may be a random act, or it may be the very deliberate act of a Japanese competitor to embarrass and frighten me. Or it may be an act of political terrorism. But in any event I believe it is an act by a Japanese against an American executive." I want to deflate real fast the idea that this is some barbaric act that the gaijin has brought on himself.

"Yes, Mr. Saxon." This time he bows his head, then reaches for the dagger.

"Don't touch the knife," I order, and cover the hilt with the hand towel. "The police will want to dust this for fingerprints."

"The police?" He looks alarmed.

"This is a distinguished hotel, and you have many important international guests. I'm sure you have an arrangement with the Tokyo police to keep certain occurrences confidential."

"Yes, Mr. Saxon." His bow is now down to twenty degrees.

I poke at the shriveled genitalia with the knife point. "These are very old and pickled. They smell of formaldehyde. Probably from a university anatomy class. But I don't think this is just a medical school prank."

"Prank?"

"A bad joke. But it doesn't have to be a police matter."

"I must discuss this with my superiors."

"Of course you must."

There is a knock at the door, and Motomoto starts. I cover the pickled genitals with the towel and go to the door. It is room service with my breakfast.

"I have a car coming for me in a few hours," I say to Motomoto. "And then I'll be tied up all day in meetings. I'll be available here until then."

Motomoto says something quickly to the waiter and unobtrusively picks up the check. He silently waits for the waiter to leave, then turns to me. "This is a very terrible business. And you have my deepest apologies. The hotel very much regrets this, and we will see that nothing like it happens again and that you are inconvenienced as little as possible." He looks as if he is genuinely ashamed.

"You will be our guest, Mr. Saxon, for the rest of your stay here. I would like to move you to another, a nicer, quieter accommodation. It will be at our expense. And there will be no inconvenience. With your permission, we will move you when you are out. Everything will be settled when you get back."

"Thank you, Mr. Motomoto. That's not necessary, but whatever you think is best."

He bows to leave, and this time his bow is forty-five degrees deeper than when he arrived.

"Mr. Motomoto." He turns back at the door.

I gather up the towel like a small sack of meat and hold it out to him. He noticeably pales, but he takes the sack with him.

But at the door, Motomoto turns and shuffles a moment, looking embarrassed. "Mr. Saxon, I am very sorry. But I must ask you this."

"Yes, go ahead."

"Maybe you have girlfriend who warns you not to leave?"

I have to smile and shake my head. "No, I don't have a girlfriend. I just arrived in Tokyo."

I point to the sack, which he gingerly holds at almost arm's length. "Is that still a romantic tradition here in Japan?"

"Oh yes, very romantic. One lady tie it on a string and wear like necklace when police come." He gives a slight smile. "Never sleep last night with girlfriend after saying good-bye." He exits, closing the door very quietly.

I stare down at the knife. I deliberately have not given it to him. It is a woman's dagger with a hilt of faded silk, a *kai-ken*.

It is about one in the afternoon in LA, but unless he has a business lunch Rufus Ready is generally at his desk with a sliced turkey sandwich. He is a man of set, efficient habits.

"Rufus Ready here." The way he drawls his name in a southwest-accented baritone makes it sound like "Rough 'n Ready," an affectation cultivated over the course of a career in the FBI. "What brought you to Tokyo?"

"I came to Tokyo for the cherry blossoms."

"The cherry blossoms? What cherry blossoms? There are no cherry blossoms in Tokyo. They're in April."

"I was misinformed."

Ready grunts. "It's—what?—four or five in the morning there." His voice takes on an alarmed edge. "Anything the matter?"

"I have jet lag. Can't sleep."

Ready grunts again. "Well, it's your dime, Mr. Saxon. I could suggest a shot of brandy in warm milk to make you drowsy. It works for me when I'm up all night on a stakeout, swigging coffee, too wired to sleep. But I don't think you're calling thirteen thousand miles for advice on how to slumber."

Ruff Ready is retired from the FBI, the ex-bureau chief in LA, a former subdirector in Washington. Rufus Ready and Associates, a management and investigative consulting firm, is very thorough, high tech, and expensive. They are retained by Levy, McGrath and Saxon, but the five-figure fees are paid by our clients.

"Certain Japanese business associates seem to know a great deal about me. How do they find that out?"

"The same way you do. They hire a firm like mine."

"I wondered why you were so familiar with time zones and the ripening of the cherry blossoms."

"I said 'like mine,' Peter. It wasn't mine. We have certain ethics about the confidentiality of our clients."

"But you do investigations for Japanese firms."

"It's down considerably nowadays, but income-wise just a few years ago it was over fifty percent of our business."

"I'm shocked. You a pensioned U.S. public servant."

"It's my contribution to the balance of trade. Except that which I've paid out in German cars and Japanese electronics. What do they know about you that they shouldn't?"

"I don't really know." I'm hedging. "Just minor stuff that's slipped out. Like what I did in the navy."

"You were a navy pilot. You flew in Vietnam in the early part of the war. That's in PR bios."

"Yeah, but not specifically that I was photo-recon."

"Was it a secret?"

"No. I just don't talk about it. No one's really interested in what my job was."

"Yeah, but it was hairy. Did you get any citations?"

"Nothing exceptional. Presidential Unit Citation, Air Medal, Purple Heart. I mean we weren't personally killing anybody or blowing things up. We went in and out before and after raids. If you survived X missions, you got an Air Medal. And if you were hit, a Purple Heart."

"Well, if it's no dark military secret, it might have been on some school or employment application still on file somewhere. Or if they did a background check, they might have picked it up as trivia from a friend. I'm not saying you can't get into military records, but it's a lot of trouble and you've got to call in favors."

"What about things here in Japan?"

"What kind of things?"

"If something happened back in sixty-four, sixty-five."

"Is it on record?"

"Yeah."

"Military or civilian?"

"Both."

"Japanese police?"

"Yeah."

"What the hell did you do?"

"I didn't *do* anything. I was just in the wrong place at the wrong time."

Ready grunts. "And it's come up *now*?"

"Maybe, I'm not really sure. But it was thirty years ago."

"Was it serious?"

"Yeah."

"Then there'd still be a record of it. The Japanese are meticulous with records."

"Why would anyone even think to look in old police records?"

"Hey, who does this sort of work? Former cops and G-men. It's what we do. It's the first place we look. If nothing's there, that tells you something. But if there is a record, then you've got old acquaintances, old addresses, places of employment, maybe a couple of photos, and a professional account of the subject's walk on the wild side. You going to tell me what's going on?"

"I wish the hell I knew."

"From the broad strokes you've already painted, you might consider practicing electronic paranoia."

"I hear you."

"Public pay phones are private. And you can use just about any credit card now. There is a firm over there that I'm associated with. If you need any on-the-spot help, I mean. They're very professional, and honorable. Only blue-chip clients. None of the *burakumin* crap. They're all ex-government pros, and they don't come cheap."

"What does, over here?"

"Yeah, well Lieutenant Pinkerton can't buy Madame Butterfly for a hundred and eighty yen anymore for a three-week marriage."

"I didn't know you were an opera buff."

"I'm not. It's something a Japanese client once said. The way he said it, they didn't like you latter-day Lieutenant Pinkertons very much."

"Well, there were millions of us for a long time."

"That's reason enough."

"Ah, the wild seeds of our youth have sprouted thorns."

"Believe it. A whole generation of Japanese men—the ones now in power—deeply resent our sexual occupation of Japan."

"What a phrase."

"Hey, what do you think fueled all that reckless, overpriced buying of America a couple of years back? Not just Columbia and Universal, but Rockefeller Center, real estate, golf courses. These guys are normally shrewd, tough traders. But they were whipping their cocks out on the table to be measured."

"Now you're a Freudian."

"No, just a good listener when my Japanese clients get drunk."

Back in 1989, and again in '91, when Sony bought Columbia and then Matsushita Universal, both at outlandish prices, I participated in a minor way, negotiating clients' contracts and stock buyouts, all the while knowing there was more to the takeovers than just the inflated yen.

After I hang up, I stand in the bay window in this tower above Tokyo and stare at the pale rising moon. It is still dark, and a mist creates shimmering halos around the streetlights in the shrouded streets below. The ghosts I have banished for so long—I'd exiled them back to the Far East because they had no part in my life home in America— have clamored at the twilight edge of my consciousness since I landed at Narita, and now they surge about me.

Lilli, her sooty lashes and hair and eyes as black as original sin, teases me, crooning in a husky whisper,

"Underneath the lantern
By the barracks gate,
Darling, I remember
The way I used to wait . . ."

I stumble into the bathroom to shower and shave but then stare at the image in the mirror, the face now etched with cobwebbing about the eyes that no amount of cold water erases, the graying hair cut by a stylist to camouflage the bald spot at the rear, the thicker flesh about the waist that sit-ups, tennis, jogging, and laps in the pool never trim.

And I marvel at the memory of the young navy officer with washboard muscles and hair so thick the Filipino ship's barber had to thin it with special scissors. And yet that face had not been innocent, for the younger man had known passion and horror more intimately than the dulled middle-age guy in the looking glass that now examines me so intently.

I push it all back, shower, but then, drawn by the whispers of ghosts, I return to the window and gaze down into the still dark warrens of Tokyo twenty-seven stories below. At this hour streetlights and the headlights of the trucks that feed this congested megalopolis map out the city streets, and I wonder where among its twenty-six million souls Lilli might now be. What has become of her? Given the violence and passion that haunted her life, is she still alive?

3

1964: My Lilli of the Lamplight

"Was there that you whispered tenderly
That you loved me,
I'd always be
Your Lilli of the lamplight,
Your own Lilli Marlene."

Lilli smiled at me, lips glistening faintly with smeared light and unspoken suggestions. "It is old English lesson," she said.

"An English lesson?"

"Oh yes. When I little schoolgirl, I have teacher to speak English. She is wife of GI, and she teach us this song. It is very popular song, yes?" Her mouth was exceptionally wide, impudent, teasing.

"A few wars ago, yes, it was very popular."

She nodded, reassured. "Teacher of English, she say if you sing this song, you never have problems to speak *l*s. *L*s are very difficult for Japanese."

"How do your friends say your name?" Cochran asked.

"They do not," Lilli said, and her lips pursed in a slight cryptic smile.

"What's your real name?"

"It is not important," she said quickly and looked away, out the window of the cab onto the blazing neon-walled Broadway of the Ginza.

About us were cascades and bubbling fountains of lights. A cylindrical glass-walled department store glowed, incandescent as a colossal candle. A gargantuan globe whirled in the night sky, a band of mirrors flashing at its equator. And on a 100-foot-high pedestal, one of the new made-in-Japan sedans rotated above an intersection, its headlights blazing like beacons. As the cab traveled through the Ginza, the walls of lights pulsed and changed, and we rode through an eerie, constantly shifting aurora borealis.

Lilli, Tommy Cochran, Junko, and I were all crammed into a tiny Toyota cab bouncing from the Ginza to the Roppongi district to check out a new American rock band the girls were excited about.

"This is very romantic song, bittersweet, I think," Lilli said, taking another tack. "*Bittersweet* is right word?"

"Yes."

"This is bittersweet love story of Lilli Marlene and soldier. Very beautiful, very sad. Very Japanese."

"Except that the Japanese cannot sing, 'My Lilli of the lamplight, my own Lilli Marlene,'" I crooned to her.

And that, of course, was the point. Lilli was a romantic fabrication only for Americans. Most Japanese men could not pronounce her name.

"I tell story, and I practice English," Junko suddenly spoke up, as if challenged.

Junko, Cochran's *cho-san*, was a dimpled, pretty girl with a fetching Asian-doll face framed by straight black bangs. Her pidgin English tumbled out with great inventive energy and humor. "Little, very old nun with head no hair . . ."

"Shaven head, a Buddhist nun," Lilli translated for Cochran and me.

"She dies, goes up, up, up." Junko's hand rose in a fluttering ascent like a dove taking wing.

"To heaven, paradise," Lilli explained.

"To Buddha is there," Junko nodded earnestly.

"'Are you good woman?' Buddha say. 'Oh yes. All time pray, fast, pray, fast. Never men. Virgin. Die virgin,' old nun with head no hair say. Buddha, he smile. 'Here is gold key to'—how you say again?—" and she pronounced a Japanese word.

"Paradise," Lilli translated.

"Ah so, paradise. Buddha say, 'Here is gold key to paradise.'" She looked at Cochran and me to make sure we got this spiritual point.

Cochran was sardined in the backseat between Junko and Lilli, and I squeezed in the front beside the driver, constantly jabbed by his frenzied shifting. The Japanese cabs in '64 were still miniature cars—with half the space of a low-cost Ford—sized for smaller Asian physiques, maximum fuel economy, and navigating and parking in streets little wider than alleys.

The cab took a sharp left and now wended through a narrow street, passing by packs of young men about college age with white cloths about their heads and carrying signs in Japanese.

"Next, old fat woman go to Buddha. 'I good wife,' she say. 'Very good wife. Only sleep with husband. Never butterfly. Work hard. Three little children. All grow, marry. Cook, clean very good for mother of husband.' Buddha smile. He say, 'You good woman. Here is silver key to paradise.'"

Again Junko grinned and fixed us with a look. I twisted about in the front seat and glanced at Lilli. From her expression, she had apparently heard this story before and didn't like it very much.

The cab was slowed by the crowd in the street. Guys in white saucerlike World War II British helmets blew whistles like traffic monitors.

"Next very beautiful young girl go to Buddha. 'Who is this?' Buddha say. 'I am not good woman. I am hostess at Black Rose cabaret,' beautiful girl say. 'All time play, dance, laugh, have good time, make love with handsome men.' Buddha frown.

"Beautiful girl say, 'I tell truth. Every night I make men happy.' Buddha frown more. He say to beautiful girl, 'You not good woman. Here is wooden key . . . to *my room*.'"

Cochran and I laughed, as much at Junko's breathless, bubbling delivery as at the punch line. She grinned back happily.

Lilli's expression remained reserved, and I sensed the story offended her. But she said nothing.

The crowd outside had thickened, slowing the cab to a crawl and finally bringing it to a dead stop. The driver gripped the wheel, glanced nervously at me, and then stared intently out the windshield. From my sense of direction we were somewhere south of the Imperial Palace, near the Kasumigaseki area of Japanese ministries and foreign embassies.

"I was going to be a priest," Cochran said.

Junko let out a peal of laughter and immediately covered her mouth with her fist.

"No, true story," Cochran insisted. "I was an altar boy when I was a kid. The pageantry, the ceremony, the mystery of the Mass all awed me. I heard the calling. And we Cochrans had a tradition of our best and brightest entering the priesthood."

"What's that all about?" I asked Lilli, gesturing at the crowd outside, but she was intent on Cochran's story, or pretending to be, and did not answer.

"You like girls too much, I think," Junko said.

"You're right, it was a girl." Cochran nodded.

"Maybe we should try turning down a side street," I said to the driver. If he understood me, he made no reaction.

"I was still in high school, and I went to Father Doyle and confessed my carnal sin. He counseled me, 'Thomas, my boy,'" and with this Cochran slipped into an easy brogue, "'when you fall and break a bone, it will heal stronger than ever. Faith is a grand thing, like that bone.'

"And I said, 'No, Father, you don't understand. I want to do it again. And again. And again.'"

Everyone laughed. "And again and again and again," Junko said, and made a fanning motion over her thighs with both hands, as if to cool herself.

One of the signs parading through the street was in English: YANKEE IMPERIALIST GET OUT.

I squeezed around. "Hey, guys, I think we're in the midst of an anti-American demonstration."

Lilli glanced at me, and I had the impression that she had known it all along but some Japanese sense of decorum had prevented her from saying anything.

The driver continued to stare straight ahead, but now I saw the fear in his eyes and in the fierce way he clutched the wheel, as if for protection.

"What the hell!" Cochran said, looking about. "What do the signs say?"

"Americans, you get out," Junko translated.

"Of where?"

"Vietnam. Japan."

"Vietnam gladly, Japan never." Cochran laughed and gave Junko an affectionate hug. If he was at all intimidated by the situation, he gave no hint.

At that moment, one of the scurrying demonstrators stopped to peer into the cab. I had a flash of a young, curious face that suddenly contorted in rage. He screamed and started pounding on the cab, all the while shouting in Japanese.

"Let's get the hell out of here," I ordered the driver.

The cab was instantly surrounded. Angry faces pressed against the windows, then began shouting, pummeling the cab's doors and roof.

"What the hell are they screaming?"

I turned to Lilli and Junko. Whatever it was had turned them bloodless with fear.

"What do they want?" I shouted at Lilli.

Her eyes were downcast, her voice terrified and hardly audible over the din. "They do not like Japanese girls with Americans, I think."

Whatever they were screaming in Japanese galvanized the driver. "You must get out of taxi, please," he said to me.

"Are you crazy? Drive!"

"You get out of taxi!" the driver shouted back, his own fear now generating rage.

The crowd now engulfed the cab. As if on command, they suddenly stopped pounding on the doors and roof. The cab started rocking as they shoved it back and forth. They were trying to tip the car over.

They weren't yet in rhythm, with the mob on each side pushing against the other. But in a beat or two, through some subconscious mob telepathy, they would get in synch and the tiny cab would instantly crash on its side with us trapped inside. It would only take a spark to ignite the spilled gas.

"OK, let's get the hell out," I barked.

"Are you crazy?" Cochran yelled behind me.

I reached across the driver and opened his door a moment before he realized what I was doing. Then I shoved him with all the weight and force I could muster in that tight space.

He frantically tried to shut the door with one hand and clutched the wheel with the other. I brought my fist down like a hammer on his hand. He yowled and let go. A dozen hands yanked open the door and dragged him out, as I shoved him from inside.

As the mob seized the driver, I slammed the door. Fingers gripping the edge were crushed, and over the howl of the crowd, I heard screams. But the men outside managed to yank their mangled hands free, and I locked the door.

Now behind the wheel, I shoved the shift into low gear.

"Easy," Cochran cautioned behind me. "Shove them out of the way easy."

I stepped gingerly on the gas, at first inching the cab forward, but steadily faster, as if hauling a trailer with dead weight.

One young guy in a white helmet flung himself across the hood, his face pressed against the windshield, ineffectively pounding against the glass, trying to punch me.

On both sides others in the mob jumped on the cab but could not find strong handholds and slid off.

I felt the car bump as it rolled over feet and the hands and limbs of the fallen.

The crowd beat at the car with their signs and poles. A side window splintered into a cobweb of cracks, but the safety glass held.

I gathered speed. Bodies now slammed off the car rather than being shoved aside. The crowd scurried to get out of the way. Cochran was bent halfway into the front passenger seat, shouting instructions.

I could hardly see around the guy with the helmet still hanging on across the hood. His eyes, inches from mine, stared at me. And whatever he now saw frightened him. I stepped on the gas a bit more, and he let go, struggling to shove himself off the hood and fall free of the car.

Ahead, a demonstrator started to get down on his hands and knees as if to lie under my wheels. At the last second he scurried on all fours out of the way, the impulse for self-sacrifice giving way to the instinct for self-preservation.

And then we were suddenly on a broad, well-lit avenue. "Go right," Cochran ordered.

I didn't look behind me, but I sensed that was where the larger demonstration was gathered.

"Well done, Saxon," Cochran said excitedly. "Now let's get the hell away from here and ditch this cab before the police grab us."

Both girls were absolutely silent.

Cochran turned to them. "Where's the nearest subway station, so we can get far away from here?" He sounded as if making getaways were a standard procedure.

The girls conferred in hushed voices. Then Lilli said, "Kamiyacho station a little way, I think. From there go to Ginza or Roppongi."

We parked in front of the station. Lilli insisted on taking the keys and locking the cab but first writing down the driver's name and address from his license and registration.

"What'll happen to the driver?" Cochran asked.

"They will not hurt him. He is just a Japanese working man," Lilli said.

"What about you and Junko? They wouldn't have hurt you?"

Neither girl said anything. But I had seen a murderous rage in the faces of the men beating against the cab windows that had gone beyond politics, that had welled up from deeper, more primal fury.

The Roppongi district was only a stop away, but no one could track us down in the jammed, narrow, neon-glittering ways of bars and nightclubs, cinemas that played French films, music stores, boutiques, and all-night restaurants. Rock blared into the crowded street. A pack of young Japanese men parted before us, but now beneath the averted eyes and hostile side glances I sensed the anger that had surrounded us earlier that evening, seething to tear us limb from limb.

We opted for a quiet bar that played subdued jazz over high-fidelity speakers in the walls. Lilli persisted in getting writing paper and an envelope from the manager and writing a brief note to the driver with the cab's location. She enclosed the car keys, then a thin packet of thousand-yen notes.

"Why the hell are you sending him money? He would have gotten us killed!"

"It was not his fault," Lilli said. Without comment, Junko handed Lilli a few bills to enclose. If there were amends to be made, she and Lilli apparently shared them. The girls had been extraordinarily quiet from the moment we ditched the cab, but there had been something else in their silence and downcast eyes that evening, a sense of shame.

At the next table there were three Japanese stags. As I looked up, I caught the looks of flat anger, then quickly averted eyes. I nodded toward the table. "What the hell's going on?"

Lilli looked puzzled by my question and glanced discreetly at the next table. "Oh, they are jealous, I think."

"Jealous?"

"Oh yes. Japanese girls think Americans a little glamorous."

"*Glamorous?* What a word."

"It is not the right word?" she asked with great concern.

"It's a terrific word. I just don't think I can live up to it." It was Lilli, exotically lovely, who radiated glamour. Even in the darkened bar she seemed to catch the light. Her hair was cut in a loose style that framed her face in black glossy feathers, and her long sooty eyelashes alternately veiled and revealed eyes that glittered like chips of anthracite. Her makeup of mascara and glycerine was a delicate art that gave her a subtle lush dark beauty that made other girls look as if they sprang from drabber stock.

I glanced about the club. The patrons were almost exclusively pretty Japanese girls with young Americans, obviously military from their age and trim haircuts. Few young Japanese men could afford the imported liquor and cover charges, priced in American dollars. At the next table, there was again that flash of resentment, then the dodging eyes. If being with Lilli made me the focus of two decades of burning jealousy, it was, there in a bar in Roppongi, a price I accepted.

Cochran and I were still hopped up on adrenaline, as if we had just landed after a hairy combat mission. "Saxon, you've done it again. Right into the guns."

"*Under* them, under them," I insisted. "There's a big difference. When they throw one of those new SA–2 missiles at you, the technique is to turn into and *under* the SAM. Trust me on this."

Cochran laughed, and the girls stared at us with uncomprehending eyes.

Cochran raised his glass. "To the guns of Phuc My Luc."

"To the guns," I toasted.

"What is this?" Lilli asked.

"Ah, Phuc My Luc is that key railroad bridge where the missiles are as big as telephone poles and the flak so thick you can taxi on it," Cochran explained carefully with that bravado he acquired after a few drinks.

"Or it's a small, insignificant road junction where a single antiaircraft gunner gets off a lucky burst into your engine or hydraulics," I said.

"A place of doom and disaster," Cochran intoned.

"Oh, it is—how you say?—a myth."

"Oh no, it's very real," I insisted. "But the guns keep moving around, and you don't know you're there until it's too late. That's what identifies the guns of Phuc My Luc, you see—that they nail you."

"And you make little offering with drink?"

"Yes."

"Then you must not make joke," Lilli said, that beautiful face now solemn, her eyes flashing with reproach. "You must be very sincere, with much respect." And she pressed her palms together and bowed her head over her drink.

"Oh yes, this way," Junko nodded solemnly, and repeated Lilli's invocation.

In another life I stand in a tower of the Imperial Hotel. "To the guns of Phuc My Luc," I now whisper aloud, and as I say it I feel the dull pain of old wounds, long healed, I thought, stir me.

Above the horizon, beyond Tokyo Bay, the darkness erodes to an oily peach color and gradually shifts to a smoky pink. The rising sun quavers in the layers of Tokyo's air pollution as if afraid to ascend.

I try to envision Lilli's face. But I can't. Instead I conjure up Michiko Hara, transformed into a younger, more sensual woman thirty years ago. And I hear the echo of a distinctive low chime of laughter, but not in distant memory. I had heard it just that evening. By some strange transference of time and place, Michiko Hara has somehow taken possession of Lilli in my memory.

4

Taking Over the World

The limousine shoulders through the crowded Ginza to the morning meeting at the Kuribayashi corporate offices. At street corners swarms of young, pretty office ladies and salesgirls obediently freeze at the traffic lights as if deliberately posed there for my obsessed study, and I stare out the tinted windows, searching for another vision of Lilli to call up. But no other face, however lovely, resonates in my memory. Michiko Hara now possesses it.

There is a deafening blare of martial music. A dark van draped with banners of orange Rising Suns, its panels painted with red calligraphy, drives alongside the limo. Roof-mounted thousand-watt speakers broadcast tsunamis of sound.

"What the hell is that?" I shout at Ozu.

At first he doesn't hear, but then the music suddenly cuts out and a voice bellows in Japanese at a no less ear-splitting volume than the music.

"Oh, Yakuza," Ozu waves at the truck and nods. "Make trouble." And we drive by, neither he nor the driver giving it a second glance, as if it is as routine an annoyance as garbage collection.

"What do the signs say?"

"They are patriotic."

"What do they say?"

"'Love the country.' 'The Emperor is divine.' 'Keep Japan pure.' Like bumper stickers in America."

"Do they give you any trouble?"

"Oh no, we have arrangement. *Sokaiya*."

"What's that?"

"They do not make trouble at our stockholders' meetings."

"They own stock in Kuribayashi Electric?"

"Oh yes. Own stock in many companies. Nippon Steel, Nomura Securities, Mitsui Kinsoku. If no *sokaiya*, they make trouble." For some reason he find this amusing, turns to me, and smiles. "It is like your Mafia, I think."

"No, like our trial lawyers. They run the extortion rackets in the United States."

"Ah yes."

But before I have a chance to pursue a definition of *sokaiya*, the limo pulls up and the liveried driver yanks the door open with a white-gloved hand.

"Kuribayashi Building," Ozu announces.

Aluminum louvers and glass panes open onto the lobby, which functions as a glitzy high-tech showroom for Kuribayashi products. A carousel with an animatronic horse, lion, and giraffe merry-go-rounds in the window, exhibiting their electronic innards and intricate steel skeletons through Plexiglas skin. At one side of the entrance, an electronic games arcade already buzzes at that morning business hour with a handful of businessmen and high school students playing computer games displayed on large hanging video screens. An attendant with a clipboard circulates among them, apparently taking down consumer data.

The way to the elevators is flanked by pedestals displaying Kuribayashi camcorders, TV sets, CD players, each with a brief promotional video on an overhanging screen. At the rear of the showroom, by the elevators, is an historic exhibit—an army field radio from the age of tubes with World War II photos of Japanese troops in the Solomon Islands. Half-century-old aircraft navigational instruments, framed by dramatic paintings of Zero fighters with blazing Rising Sun insignia, confront my eye, before the elevator door slides shut and hurtles me to the executive suite.

I wait while Ozu announces my arrival in the conference room where Hara has assembled his staff. The reception area, with its atrium lighting, is a gallery for several oils. They are French expressionists, originals. A fish with blazing wings playing the violin, and a grandfather clock float above a river. *Time Is a River without Banks.* In the lower left corner is the artist's signature, and in the right corner the lovers—the sketchy figures of the artist and his wife that are as much Marc Chagall's signature as his name—embrace on the riverbank.

"And what is the artist saying, do you think?"

The man is almost as tall as I am, but there is an aggressive fitness about his stance and figure not cloaked by the expensively tailored suit. He wears an Armani tie with a discreet red pattern.

"The artist is saying that love and passion make time a river without banks."

"Ah yes," the man nods, a half-smile pursing his lips. "America, it seems, is the farm where the Japanese make money, but"—he gestures to the other paintings—"Paris and London are the boutiques where we spend it."

The man in the Armani tie glances away from the Chagall and straight at me. "This should be very interesting, Mr. Saxon. I understand you are something of a warrior."

"I don't believe I've had the pleasure . . ."

But before I finish asking who the hell he is, he strides into the conference room. Ozu is at the door, and from the depth of his bow—his crew cut bobs down to knee level—the fellow is a high-status pooh-bah.

"Have you spoken to Kyoto yet?" I ask.

Ozu looks startled, but before he translates, Hara responds at length in Japanese.

"Mr. Hara wants to hear more of your thinking and long-term

strategy before he discusses the details of your proposal with Mr. Kuribayashi."

The fact that he has not yet communicated with headquarters pisses me off. But I put a cork in it—American impatience has blown more than one negotiation. The Japanese look for long-term relationships, not deals, and that is certainly the scenario here.

We hunker down about the conference table. Hara stands. "I am sorry, but I first say something in Japanese."

"I understand." I smile at Hara. But my mind immediately wanders to how I might later broach the subject of his wife. The thought no sooner bubbles into consciousness than the lunacy of it strikes me.

It is, of course, not possible that his wife, Michiko, is Lilli. She is the right age, with two children about the same age as my own. And that, rationally, is why my nostalgic ramblings have latched onto her image. She had no doubt been a similarly beautiful young woman, and my faded thirty-year-old memory has unconsciously reinforced itself with her face. It is a crazy delusion.

With deliberate effort I force my attention back on the business at hand. While Hara speaks, I study the group about the table—all in dark suits, white shirts, and ties so indistinctive that you can't spot the pattern at five feet. The wardroom of a U.S. Navy carrier has less regimentation—at least the marines and aviators dress to deliberately stand out.

Hara's comments are brief, and then he introduces me formally in English.

"Thank you, Mr. Hara. Gentlemen, I assume most of you already know the broad outlines of what I am about to propose. We plan to take over the world."

Hara laughs, a chuckle really, and as Ozu translates, there are a few more nervous twitters.

"This meeting is of the utmost delicacy, and it is certainly not to be discussed with the press or competitors. We would consider that a breech of good faith. Even within your own company it must be kept confidential, on a need-to-know basis. At InterNatCom we are exercising the same corporate security on our side of the Pacific. My own daughters think I'm in Tokyo negotiating a multimillion-dollar Pocari Sweat commercial for Arnold Schwarzenegger."

At that there is an easier laughter about the table, except for the man in the red Armani tie.

"Mr. Ozu, are you familiar with everyone present?"

"Yes, Mr. Saxon."

"Would you do me the honor of briefly introducing everyone."

Ozu is bewildered by the request. He glances first at Hara, then at the man in the Armani tie. The latter gives him an almost imperceptible nod.

At Ozu's introduction by name and title, each man formally rises and bows, with the exception of the man in the Armani tie, who in apparent indication of his status remains seated but acknowledges the introduction with a nod and a sardonic smile, as if in appreciation of the ploy. He is Matsu Yurikawa, the only one present not an executive of Kuribayashi Electric. He is with MITI, the Japanese government Ministry of International Trade and Industry.

"Gentlemen, our plan is quite simple. What will happen in the next five years—what is happening as I speak—is that a handful of multinational conglomerates—seven, possibly eight—will control the entertainment and communications industry worldwide." I pause for Ozu's translation.

"We are highly financed, deep-pocketed, vertically integrated companies, now able to play this game on a much different level than it's ever been played in the past. Our company, InterNatCom, is currently one of those players. And we have mapped out a long-term strategy to become the major player. We invite Kuribayashi to join us in a partnership to form the world's number one entertainment and communications organization."

This time I pause for dramatic effect as much as translation. There is a collective exclamation about the table—sounds of audible "Ah so," grunts, and sighs like the lowing of a herd.

I plunge back in. "In very broad strokes, gentlemen, we are on the brink of the biggest revolution in television broadcasting since the introduction of color in the nineteen-sixties. It's HDTV—high-definition television. It's digital television. There are going to be an estimated five hundred channels of it, and it's going to be interactive to a certain degree.

"We're still waiting for the dust to settle on the FCC requirements—the U.S. Federal Communications Commission—for high-definition television. But it is a digital system that delivers four times the resolution of the current analog system.

"More importantly, the new equipment to make that technical conversion is tremendously expensive. There are some fifteen hundred television stations in the United States alone. And the best economic projections and studies that we currently have estimate that the cost to convert many of these television stations is more than they are currently worth."

I pause again for the translation, then repeat, "The cost of conversion is more than many are worth.

"And our cable and satellite systems have the added problems of delivering not just one channel but a possible five hundred—many of which will be interactive for home shopping, movies on demand, education, and video games.

"There are, in fact, gloomy projections that the cost of this conversion may take anywhere from twenty to forty years to earn back. Rather obviously that will put many stations, networks, and delivery systems in a very vulnerable debt position. The decades of the eighties taught us all how dangerous that kind of debt can be . . . *how dangerous*.

"The reality is that all our competitors are still struggling to pay off mergers. Time Warner and Viacom each have debts five or six times their cash flow, and Disney's acquisition of ABC has loaded Mickey Mouse with a thirteen-billion-dollar debt. And that's a lot of cheese for even a very big mouse to digest."

There are polite laughs at the translation. I glance at Yurikawa of MITI. He smiles faintly. He has a small falcon beak of a nose, which gives his eyes a predatory glint, and I have the sense that he is sizing me up rather than the proposition.

"The economic turmoil in Asia and South America has depressed sales of merchandise and videos. The devaluation of currencies has cut income from movie rentals, even where ticket sales are at all-time highs. That's true of all the players I've mentioned.

"We've analyzed all this in some detail at InterNatCom—the stations and cable systems we now own, our strategic investments in other systems, and our network. Our present cash flow and debt load—I might point out—is still very healthy. And we've come up with a strategy to leapfrog—jump way ahead of—our competitors."

I have now set the stage and wait for the translation and note-taking to catch up. During the wait I am busy looking about the table, catching each man's eye, not long enough to be threatening but just making contact.

"Our ideal partner will be a company that can manufacture and supply the very equipment—the video relays, videotape recorders, cameras, monitors, switchers, etcetera—that will be the major capital investment in this HDTV and digital conversion."

As Ozu translates, Hara smiles and nods vigorously. "Very sound, very sound," he says in English, as though hearing the proposal for the first time. This is a dog-and-pony show for the division heads.

I look at a young Japanese exec who is busily scribbling notes as I talk. "That's my first point. Number one. Are you getting all this?"

"Oh yes sir, Mr. Saxon."

"Very good. Right now our FCC estimates a ten-year transition—which again parallels the introduction of color. This creates a great opportunity for growth for both of our companies. Kuribayashi Electric would, of course, have automatic access to a tremendous developing market—worth tens of billions of dollars. And as InterNat-

Com manages, and essentially underwrites, this conversion of TV stations and cable companies well ahead of their competition, they will form partnerships with us. That will also open up markets in which we are not currently represented. Quite simply, together with Kuribayashi, we will become the major players, not just in the United States but around the world."

I look around to see if they are getting it. There is a palpable tension in the room, almost a fear. I note several of the Kuribayashi executives glancing cautiously at Yurikawa, the man from MITI.

It is time to wrap. "Over the last fifty years the value of broadcasting properties has gone only one way—up, up, up. And the cost of new technology has, historically, always come down. When these two curves cross, the broadcasting industry around the world will race to convert. It is our strategy to move five years ahead of these curves. That's our timetable." Again I pause for the translation.

"The high cost of the new technology—digital, high-definition, five-hundred-channel television—will present a crisis for many TV stations and cable systems—especially those already overburdened with debt. And especially in the countries whose banking systems are already overwhelmed with bad debts and near collapse." I'm deliberately needling the Japanese here, but from the stoic expressions about the table I have no idea how the point is taken.

"Gentlemen, I don't write or speak Japanese. But I understand that the kanji calligraphy for *crisis* is made by combining the symbol for *danger* and the sign for *opportunity*. The structure of mergers, joint ownership, and strategic investment we have on the table minimizes the dangers and creates historic opportunities for both our companies in the twenty-first century."

There is a dead silence about the conference table. "If any of you have questions, I'll try to answer them."

All heads swivel toward Hara. He speaks in a low voice to Ozu, who nods intently, then turns to me. "Your company would acquire a controlling interest in our Phoenix Electronics divisions, is that correct?"

The question is polite, but there are decades of tension behind it. American companies simply have not been allowed to acquire control of major Japanese companies.

I hedge. "Only those divisions that manufacture and sell television equipment for stations and cable systems. The reason is that American law does not allow foreign ownership of broadcasting, and the control of these stations and systems is our goal." This is the crux of the merger.

The high yen and depressed sales worldwide have Kuribayashi and other Japanese manufacturers struggling. The slowdown and their devalued stock have made the young Turks in the company receptive to the proposal. "But we have no interest in Kuribayashi's line of consumer products, as successful as they are: the TV sets, VCRs, cassette and CD players, radios, home entertainment consoles.

"Not incidentally, the American market alone for high-definition television sets is estimated at over a trillion. That's *trillion* with a *T*, and dollars not yen." There is a smattering of smiles. It is, as the comics say, a tough room.

"Consumer electronics is not our business. We do, however, have a keen interest in developing and owning that little black box that sits on top of the TV set and decodes the signal from the cable, microwave, or satellite systems. That is a key link in the distribution system. And our primary business is the creation *and distribution* of movies and TV—entertainment, music, news, and sports—whatever you want to call it. We are involved in all forms of distribution, whether in theaters or TV networks, cable systems or stations, because, frankly, that's where the money is."

I pause, and after translating, Ozu says, "We understand the American law regarding ownership of TV stations." He appears to be reading from notes or a question someone has handed him. "But your company has"—here Ozu gropes for the right word—"*resisted* the cross-ownership of the motion picture and television studio. Both Sony and Matsushita have owned American studios."

I glance at Hara, who is regarding me with sharpened interest, almost as if warning me. "Yes, they have," I agree. "And does Kuribayashi want to repeat both Matsushita's and Sony's experience?" I let the question hang for several moments. "Motion pictures are, by their very nature, a volatile, irrational business. And yet . . . at the core of each one of the seven, eight major conglomerates that control the entertainment and communications industry is a Hollywood 'dream factory'—an established studio that makes this volatile, irrational product. And they have been manufacturing it and distributing it successfully for three-quarters of a century. Why?"

In the silence I answer my own question. "Because movies—especially hit movies—drive all the delivery systems: cassettes, laser disc, cable, and direct satellite broadcast. The American studios didn't really care if the customers saw their movies on Beta or VHS. They let Matsushita and Sony fight it out and made money, even on their flops, on both systems. But as Matsushita and Sony painfully discovered when they took over studios, movies and television are chaotic businesses. At their very centers there is chaos."

I am deliberately trying to frighten them away.

"But to level out the chaos, the ups and downs, we also own TV stations and cable systems. We show everybody's movies and programs and make money all the time . . . even if we have a year, or even two or three years, in which our own movies and TV pilots go in the toilet."

However Ozu translates "go in the toilet," it gets my biggest laugh.

"And as an economic base, the TV properties also give us a more solid line of credit with banks, which allows us to finance movies at lower interest rates. Our TV stations—which are all in major markets—give us advantages in advertising and promoting our films. And our cable systems exploit our movies to their maximum, so that even the box office flops have greater exposure and revenue than they would have had if we did not control this distribution outlet."

I take a breath. "And this maximum exploitation in the United

States in turn increases our worldwide television sales and syndication—which is basically underwritten by a group of stations we either own or have large investments in. That's our vertical integration and synergy."

Hara nods and smiles with approval. I decide to quit while I am ahead. "And that, gentlemen, is the more *stable,* more *rational* business in which we invite you to participate with us in these very troubled economic times—but a time of transition, one that creates great opportunities for both our companies." For the moment I have finessed the minefield—the Japanese will not set foot in the studio except as sightseers.

When we break, I buttonhole Ozu. "Your people are taking detailed notes. I would appreciate the transcripts, both in English and Japanese, if that's possible, so there's no misunderstanding in language. What do you think?"

"I think it is an excellent idea."

Then, almost as an afterthought, "I'd also like a list of all the people you introduced, their exact positions, and a sentence or two about their responsibilities."

"Yes, Mr. Saxon."

I intercept the man from MITI at the door as he is leaving. "Ah, Mr. Yurikawa, thank you for taking the time to attend. I hope we'll have an opportunity to get better acquainted." I give him my concerned smile. "By the way, what has happened to your colleague Matami Okamatsu? In the conversations and correspondence I had with him, I rather liked and admired him. I found him a very wise man."

Yurikawa's hawkish face is expressionless. "Ah yes. I'm afraid his health failed."

5

The Tale of the Prince and the Geisha

Back at the hotel I am immediately intercepted in the lobby by a tall, aristocratic looking man in a black blazer, pearl gray vest with lapels, striped tie as wide as a cravat—the formal morning dress of a diplomat at court. He introduces himself with a stiff bow as the hotel's general manager and presents his card. Just behind him hovers a thin man with sunken cheeks that he introduces as the director of hotel security, who also presents his card, with a considerably deeper bow.

"I suggest we talk in my suite, if that's acceptable to you."

"We have moved you to a much nicer, quieter accommodation," the manager says on the elevator. "You will not be disturbed again." His features are almost European except for the cast of his eyes and skin tone.

"Thank you."

We get off at a different floor, and the manager leads me past a plainclothes security man in a dark suit who immediately drops his newspaper, springs to his feet, and bows as we pass. This new suite—in the older section of the hotel directly overlooking Hibiya Park and the Imperial Palace—is larger than my original one.

"This is very nice." I nod to the manager.

While the security director takes detailed notes, I repeat everything I told the assistant manager, Motomoto, earlier. "Have you notified the police?"

"We conducted an investigation, but no one saw any suspicious person. Do you wish us to notify the police?"

I shake my head. "No. My business negotiations are very sensitive and private. I believe the people who did this want to create an embarrassing incident. They wanted your other guests to see that . . . obscenity before I did. Luckily, I had jet lag, trouble sleeping. But to bring in the police might make this very ugly incident public. I'd prefer not to do that."

"Yes, Mr. Saxon." The manager nods, as if complying with my request rather than doing exactly what he wants.

I turn to the security man. "What did you do with the decorations?"

"Please, I do not understand."

"The prick and balls they nailed to my door. What did you do with them?"

"They are in a refrigerator."

"A refrigerator?" The manager is appalled.

"To keep for the police."

"Very good. Please keep them in case there's another *incident*." The pickled genitalia speared to my door are beyond any coincidence.

"Another incident?" The manager looks even more worried.

"I'm sure your excellent security will prevent anything."

The man with the sunken cheeks nods vigorously. "Please, Mr. Motomoto said there was knife. We did not find knife."

"I have it. I didn't want the fingerprints disturbed in case we have to turn it over to the police."

"Please, to see it."

"Yes, of course." It is tucked in my briefcase, wrapped in one of the plastic bags in which the laundry returns my shirts. But now I retreat to the bedroom, quickly check the closet and drawers to see that my clothes have been moved, retrieve the knife from the case, and return with it to the sitting room. The whole charade is to flimflam sunken cheeks that the knife has been there all the while, overlooked by him and his staff. I'm not letting it out of my hands.

"It's a *kai-ken*, I believe."

"*Kai-ken?*" The manager looks confused.

"A lady's knife. In olden days samurai ladies carried them to protect their virtue. I understand they were very popular at the end of World War Two, just prior to the American occupation."

The manager looks at me and blinks. Sunken cheeks reaches for it.

"Please don't take it out of the plastic," I order, placing my hand on it. "I'll hold onto it. If the police don't need it, I want it." I smile. "A souvenir of Japanese passion, *neh?*"

The manager and the security man glance at one another in confusion, apparently neither having a ready objection. After reassuring me that I will not be disturbed again, they leave.

I don't know why I keep the *kai-ken*. In its plastic wrapping the glinting blue steel blade looks watery, an illusion that might dissolve away. But the hard hilt, covered with sharkskin and silk, is something I can grasp, the only tangible link to a past that had faded into dreams and the occasional nightmare but has now, without warning, materialized again, suddenly conjured up to haunt me.

"In the life of each of us, there is a place remote and islanded and given to endless regret or secret happiness"—my wife, Joan, had once quoted that line, probably in a subtle attempt to draw me out. It is from a nineteenth-century novelist whose name escapes me, but her sensibility burned itself into my memory. At the time, I had with great will islanded a hunk of my life. Now, in this remote place, the dark regrets and secrets stream back . . .

> *And there 'neath that far-off lantern light*
> *I'd hold you tight,*
> *We'd kiss good-night.*
> *Your Lilli of the lamplight,*
> *Your own Lilli Marlene.*

Lilli had an obscure recording of "Lilli Marlene" by Marlene Dietrich—lord knows where she got it—and she sang along in an imitative husky whisper as she brushed her silky raven hair.

Then she knelt on the bed, holding up a small dagger as a child presents a cherished object.

"Where did you get the knife?"

Smiling with some secret mischief, she slipped the blade from its black lacquered scabbard and held its blood-red silk hilt with her fingertips as though it were a paintbrush. "I tell you a very beautiful story," she said. "Once upon a time—that is how you begin stories in English, *neh?*"

I nodded. "Once upon a time."

She smiled, pleased that she had gotten it right.

"Once upon a time there was very famous geisha, very beautiful, very sexy. Her name is Ono-no. All men very crazy for her. You understand?"

"She was the Lilli of once upon a time." I caressed the golden bow of her hip. We were both naked after lovemaking.

She smiled again to acknowledge the compliment. "The Lilli of once upon a time," she repeated, savoring the words. There was always something a little poignant about Lilli's smile, as if once she opened herself to an emotion, however pleasant, it tapped some deeper, darker well.

"Did she have a dagger like this?"

Lilli held the knife in front of her face, contemplating its razor edge. "All the men court her—is *court* the right word?" she asked, not to be sidetracked in her telling. "They visit her and give her rich presents, but she loved only young prince."

"*Court* is a very good word for this story."

"They have princes in Japan in old time. Not so much now."

"Once upon a time."

"Yes. The prince and Ono-no very happy. He visit her every night, and each time he brings her beautiful presents."

From the bed, I surveyed Lilli's room, which had a classic Japanese austerity to it, and wondered what presents ancient princes or their latter-day counterparts brought to their ladies.

"But then he does not come to visit Ono-no for many nights. Ono-no very sad. Then a man who courts her says that prince is to marry a woman from a very important and rich family." Lilli's voice now took on a low, tragic note. "And Ono-no is very sad. Men come to court her with rich, beautiful presents, but she sends them away. She not see them. And she thinks very much she will kill herself."

Lilli traced a line with the dull edge of the blade across her throat, the red silk and bone of the hilt flashing like an opening wound.

"But *then* the prince comes back with a very beautiful present," she continued without a break, her voice now registering heightening excitement. "He says he loves her very much, but he must marry this woman for his family. Or else he will dishonor them. It has been arranged since they are little children. You understand the honor of his family?" Lilli studied me, assuring herself I understood the stakes here.

"Yes."

"That night they make love. It is very beautiful, very sad. It is the last time they will make love." Lilli paused, eyes downcast with the bittersweet image of this final meeting.

"Then they sleep together. But Ono-no not sleep. For long time she looks at the prince sleeping in the moonlight. It is little silver light. She raises the knife maybe to kill herself. Kneels over the prince. *And cuts off his prick!*" Before I realized it, Lilli had made a swipe over my groin with the dagger.

I yelped and grabbed her wrist. "Jesus!"

"Now the prince will never make love to another woman." Lilli dramatically wilted into my arms, the knife dropping from her limp hand onto the bed.

"It is a very beautiful story, romantic, *neh?*" she asked.

"That's a romantic story in Japan?" My tone was incredulous.

"Oh yes, very famous story, very beautiful."

I looked at Lilli's solemn, awed face, the glint of tears in her eyes, then at the razor-edged dagger, and silently vowed never to say goodbye to Lilli. Apparently Madame Butterfly was a Western male fantasy.

In Japan, the true romantic heroine did not commit hara-kiri when her lover left.

As if taunting me, Lilli now knelt, straddling my thighs. She drew the dull edge of the dagger across my bare belly, from left to right, but then instead of giving the edge a quarter turn upward toward the heart, tracing the disembowelment of seppuku, she paused and turned the dagger downward, etching a white line on my flesh to my groin.

The blade flashed a bluish light. "Jesus, careful with that." The light touch of the tip felt like the scratch of a fingernail. As chilling as it was, it excited me tremendously. It was a moment before I noticed with horror that where the needle point of the dagger had barely touched my flesh there was an angled red scratch oozing blood.

I howled, and Lilli immediately bent forward and put her lips to the cut, kissing it clean of blood. Her hair fell across the perfect ivory flesh of her shoulders and breasts like a headdress of black feathers. Then she raised up, impaled herself on me and fell forward, her breasts burning my chest, her mouth feverishly smothering any other cry, as if the whole narrative and drama with the knife had been part of an elaborate foreplay.

Afterward I asked, "Why do you have that knife?"

"It is a *kai-ken*, very old," she said, as if that explained everything. She retrieved it from where it had dropped onto the tatami. "Lady keep *kai-ken* close to breasts. If enemies maybe rape lady, she stab them." Lilli made an alarming underhand thrust.

"Hey."

"But if too many or if samurai lady is prisoner, then she must keep honor." Her gleaming black hair was loose and disheveled from our lovemaking. She pushed it aside with one hand, held up the *kai-ken* with her right, and again made that slow, ceremonial slicing motion across her carotid artery.

"Jesus, be careful with that thing."

Lilli gave me a faint ironic smile. "But first lady ties legs together with a silk cord, so people know she dies with virtue. Is that right word?"

I nodded. "Virtue, right." Something about her reverence struck me. "Is this *kai-ken* in your family?"

"Oh yes, it is my mother's, for Americans' invasion."

"All Japanese women have these knives?"

"My father was an officer," she said, and by her tone indicated that cutting one's throat was clearly a class privilege.

"What about the other women, the ones who didn't live by this samurai code of virtue?"

"They get little bitter almond pills."

"Cyanide?"

"Oh yes. My family have factory make parts for airplanes. All factory ladies get little bitter almond pills."

"But the daughters of the samurai didn't really tie their legs together with silken cord."

"*Hai*, we have opened our legs for you, have we not?"

Something in her voice and expression warned me not to comment. I remained silent.

Lilli replaced the knife in a small cabinet of *sugi*, the Japanese cedar wood, and within it I saw a second, much larger black lacquer sheath, of a short sword.

"What's that?"

"It was my father's." She closed the doors and knelt with her back toward me. Closed, the cabinet resembled a miniature shrine with an upward-curving pagoda roof. Despite her nudity, there was something reverent in her posture, as if in momentary prayer before it.

Her skin had a golden perfection—no freckles, blemishes, or sunburned swimsuit lines, the abrupt changes in hue that define our public and private parts. But there at the small of her back was a wide, wrathful scar where the flesh had been so cruelly wounded that it would be forever thickened and dead. Like a child, I wanted to reach out and touch the hard, slick gristle of the scar with my fingertips, but I didn't. Not yet.

Then Lilli turned and smiled sadly at me and sang in a soft
1whisper,

> *"Time would come for roll call,*
> *Time for us to part.*
> *Darling, I'd caress you*
> *And press you to my heart."*

Somewhere, through the grapevine, she had heard that my carrier was sailing south to Vietnam.

But I never really said good-bye to Lilli before we sailed. The
story of the prince and the geisha and the way she had traced the
gleaming blue blade of the *kai-ken* across my loins had, frankly, sent an
icy stab of fear right into my groin.

Thirty years later, in a tower in the Imperial Hotel—which had been
the headquarters for the U.S. army of occupation at the end of World
War II—I study the *kai-ken* in my hand and think of that knife Lilli's
father had given her mother.

Those of us who were once the pawns of history and survive
often become buffs. It is our midnight reading when memories
become haunted and we cannot sleep. And in that history, war and sex
are linked in secret conspiracy, leaving a trail of black footnotes that
leads to the Japanese lady's dagger I now grasp.

For instance, during the war in China in 1937, Evans Carlson,
then a U.S. Marine captain operating behind the line as an observer
with the Chinese 8th Route Army, reported back to Washington that
the Japanese forced the cities they occupied to supply women for their
troops' pleasure. Three thousand women was the order for the provin-
cial capital Taijan.

Beyond the infamous atrocities—the rape of Nanking with its
three hundred thousand victims—the Japanese occupation armies in
China, the Philippines, Korea, and Indonesia routinely abducted Asian
and Dutch women at gunpoint and forced them into sexual slavery, the
euphemistically tagged "comfort women."

The Japanese had expected no less from the American army. On Okinawa, as American troops battled across the savage smoking ridges, fathers slew their own daughters to spare them from the advancing "devils."

Lilli herself had not yet started school, and the older children had terrified her with stories that Americans choked little girls to death and strung them up with wires through their ears.

Emperor Hirohito, in announcing the surrender to the Japanese people, had told them that they must endure the unendurable and suffer what was insufferable.

And the Japanese had prepared their women for rape with cyanide pills and *kai-kens*. But they had not prepared for thirty years of seduction.

6

The Black Rose

I have to report to Stan Greenwald, InterNatCom's CEO. He's off schedule, not in New York but in Los Angeles at his studio office, but his New York secretary switches me directly.

"What's happening?"

"I'm getting a lot of mixed signals. There's major opposition to this deal."

"In Kuribayashi?"

"In the company. Other companies in the *keiretsu* that holds heavy shares of Kuribayashi. The banks. Probably in MITI."

"The government?"

"That's a delicate point. They can't openly be against it. That's all the White House or Congress has to see—the Japanese deliberately blocking an American company from making the same acquisitions that they've made freely in the U.S. for the last two decades. Across-the-board trade restrictions will hit the fan."

"Hey, it took twenty-five years to get Washington Delicious apples into the Japanese market. For chrissakes, what's more American than an apple?"

"That's apple pie."

"You tell them the pie will hit the fan?"

"Not yet. I've set up a lunch with the man from MITI to diplomatically inform them the Black Ships have sailed into Tokyo Bay."

"What the hell are the Black Ships?"

"Commodore Perry's gunboats. About the time of our Civil War, they forced the Japanese to open their ports to trade. Japan was a hermit kingdom, keeping all foreigners out."

"So what's new? How do you think they'll react?"

"I honestly don't know. They just nod politely to this gaijin and say, 'We'll think about it.' Which can translate to 'Fuck off' in Japanese. Or it can mean they are thinking about it."

"What's a gaijin?"

"A non-Japanese. A foreign devil."

"Sounds like goyim. Not one of our tribe."

"You understand it perfectly."

"They still talking about buying *us*?"

"It's a stall. Their stock is too depressed. And no Japanese bank can afford that kind of loan, especially to buy an American film company. But they really believe Sony's and Matsushita's problems were management."

"After all these years, they still don't get it," Greenwald says with a sigh that resounds over 5,500 miles and into tomorrow. "It's like the Stage Door Deli's New York pastrami sandwich. Their stomachs aren't conditioned to digest it."

"Neither is mine. That much pastrami, I mean."

There is a thoughtful pause on the other end, and I envision Greenwald's brow screwing up into a worried frown. "You still want to fly solo on this deal?"

"Yeah, convinced. I don't want a task force of lawyers, investment counselors, *shtarker* CAA agents—each with their personal agendas—confusing the Japanese with a lot of buzzwords and projections. There's no way to keep that sort of negotiation under wraps. Our only realistic shot is to work this in secrecy as long as possible. The way Eisner wrapped up ABC."

Now Stan is nodding. "You're right, you're right. Especially the investment guys and agents. They're so focused on playing matchmaker and walking away with their fortune in fees, they don't really care if the marriage works. That's the Columbia and Universal deals all over."

I jump to agree, "You make this a team play, and you'll be dodging reporters in your steam bath. Reading fictionalized play-by-plays on the front page of the New York and LA *Times, Wall Street Journal, Variety*—followed by daily sidebars with every smart-ass showbiz and financial writer—quoting unnamed sources—second-guessing, speculating, and raking over the Matsushita and Sony disasters. The smartest thing we can do is fly under the radar."

"No argument here," Stan acknowledges. "We've seen that scenario before. Turner, Diller, Viacom, Bertlesmann—you name 'em—all suddenly pop up. They don't really want to buy. Just fuck up our trade."

We've discussed all this before, but it's part of Greenwald's genius to constantly review the strategy and bidding, never wedded to the plan but only to the long-range goal. "That kind of publicity puts the stock prices on a roller coaster, so nobody can get a fix on the company's worth," I remind him.

"I know. Just double-checking if you wanted to revise the game plan now that you've run a few plays against them. Maybe bring a player off the bench—Levine, for instance—to run interference, pass the ball off for an assist, whatever. I mean I love you like a kid brother, but I know your moves before you make them. You have this thing about flying solo. Then afterward you bring the rest of us along for the ride and con us that it was our idea that we take off in the first place."

I laugh. "Am I that devious?"

"Hey, I'm not complaining. It's put me in the Forbes Four Hundred. You pull this off, and we move up in the league standings to the top ten. But who's keeping score?"

"I am, in yen. Because the final play has to be me and Kuribayashi sitting down head-to-head."

"When are you going to see the old man—where is it?—in Kyoto?"

"It's not set up yet. Hara and I are still romancing."

"Well, just keep hitting the ball back to them so they can return it. Feel out their game, and don't go for any of your down-the-line winners and scare them off."

"You play this weekend?"

"Yeah, a foursome with Schneider and the *shleppers*. I didn't work up a sweat, but I still played badly. They throw my stroke off. I need to hit with a boomer like you. Schneider was relieved you weren't there. He says you're always trying to drive the ball into his stomach when he's at the net."

"At his groin, actually. He's got a racket to defend himself."

Greenwald laughs. "That's my negotiator. You pull this off, and I'll be working for you."

"I know my limitations. I can't run a studio and a network."

"You won't. You'll be president. But I'll have my lawyer put it in your contract that you absolutely cannot make any creative decisions."

"I'm your lawyer."

"See, it's done already. That's why you're over there now. That, and the Japanese asked for you."

"*The Japanese asked for me?* You never told me that."

"What's to tell? During the prelims it was suggested to Levine we send someone who'd been to Japan before. So they wouldn't waste time adjusting. Had perhaps been a military officer, so they had a sense of protocol and rank. Somewhat comfortable with technology. So who else?"

"It's really amazing the way they do their research on whom they're negotiating with. I haven't been here in thirty years."

"Yeah, but I've heard your war stories. And you read up on it and watch all the PBS specials. You're not starting from scratch. We go to the Mandarin or Fung Lum's, you handle the chopsticks like Toshiro Mifune, and I'm still using a fork. Me, I hate sushi. I mean I really can't eat it. With all due respect, to this Jewish kid it's *treif*. And somewhere along the line I'm going to inadvertently offend Kuribayashi if I go over there."

"You're shitting me, Stan."

"No, I'm dead serious, kiddo. According to the scouting reports, Kuribayashi's an old samurai family, and that stuff's important. You're the designated Pac-rim player. I'll get into the game in the play-offs over here, where we'll have the home court advantage. We'll dazzle them with our passing off. Just get them on the court on our terms."

"I'm getting a little nauseous from the food and sports analogies."

"Hey, what's a Jewish kid really know—food and sports. And movies."

"Don't be so colorfully ethnic with the Japanese. They don't understand it. It doesn't relax them, just confuses them."

Greenwald is silent a moment. "I hear you, counselor. What the hell time is it there? Are you ahead of us or behind us? Grosses and participations, even stock swaps I can figure to the penny in my head, but time changes always confuse me. I never got London straight, and now I've got to go the other way."

"It's tomorrow here. Tokyo's sixteen hours ahead."

"No kidding. Quick, look in that tomorrow's paper. How's our stock going to finish today over here? More importantly, what're the Lakers going to do? What was the point spread?"

"The stock finished at thirty-nine, down five-eighths. And the Lakers took the Bulls by six."

"Wait, I'm going to put you on hold while I call my bookie to make up my stock losses." Greenwald's rich chuckle reverberates over the phone, undiminished by the satellite transmission.

"While you're making a fortune, I've got terminal jet lag. My bio-clock's still somewhere east of Midway Island."

"Force yourself to get up at seven and go for a jog. It'll shock your body onto the new clock. That's what I do when I go to London."

"This is the other direction. I already jogged, and it's having some dire reverse effect. What do you do when you get home from London?"

"Hell, then I go out and have a nice dinner, a bottle of wine, get laid if I'm lucky, and I'm asleep in thirty seconds."

"I like the east-to-west routine a lot better."

"Me too. But be careful. Remember, Paramount changed the ending of *Fatal Attraction* for Japan. For screwing around, the guy ends up in prison for murder. Anything else I should know?"

I wait a beat.

"What?"

"I saw the Chagall."

I hear the deep intake of breath across the Pacific. "Fuck me. That anonymous buyer in London was Kuribayashi."

"It's hanging in the foyer of the executive conference room of the Tokyo headquarters, along with a modest Utrillo. While I was admiring it, this senior official from MITI comes up and says to me, 'America is the farm where we make our money, but London and Paris are the boutiques where we spend it.'"

"This MITI character said that to you?"

"Yep."

There's another trans-Pacific pause. "Hey, kiddo, forget diplomatic. Take a pound of flesh."

A messenger arrives with the transcript of the meeting at Kuribayashi and the personnel notes I had asked Ozu to assemble for me. But as I go over them my eyes burn, and I finally drop the packet and let my heavy lids close.

I doze fitfully, awake sweating, then, reassured it is only a dream that evaporates like vapor, I slump back in the chair, still hovering between past and present with a sad, plaintive longing and desire.

It's with a certain astonishment that I realize how long ago it all happened—over a quarter of a century. I've lived an entire life since then.

I'm still haunted by the image of Lilli, or rather now the face of a younger Michiko Hara, conjured up from the clouds of memory, her lips curled in a teasing smile.

The mottled Tokyo night lights seep through the uncurtained

window of the hotel room. I heave to my feet, punchy but now awake, and peer at my watch. It is not quite midnight, but I feel the compulsion to get out, at least for a walk.

Across the wide boulevard from the hotel, the grounds of the Imperial Palace with its encircling stone-walled moat look forbidding, and I restlessly stride off in the other direction, toward the Ginza.

I've wandered only a few blocks when I find myself in Yakitori Alley, the cluster of food shops under the tracks of Yurakucho station. The din of the train overhead and the sweet, cloying aroma of soy-soaked charcoaling sticks of meat call up long-forgotten pathways. Nothing in the great neon way of the Ginza looks familiar, but moving on automatic pilot I turn into a narrow side street of now darkened shops, illuminated only by the occasional electric sign of a bar or restaurant.

The streets are murky with a threatening rain, and behind me I hear muffled footsteps, haunting my own. I turn, but there is no one there in the misty darkness. The ancient imperial planners of Tokyo plotted their streets with baffling turns and enigmatic dead ends deliberately to confound any foreign invaders, but in five minutes I am standing before a red neon sign in English stylized to look like calligraphy that announces the Black Rose. It is still there.

When I enter, a tuxedoed maitre d' immediately pounces on me. "Hello, sir. Our foreign guests will enjoy the balcony."

I do not really see the club—the roped-off entrance, the glittering chrome and ebony bar, the lounge with its coveys of pretty young hostesses cooing together—I don't register it as it is so much as try to remember how it had been.

"Our foreign guests will enjoy the balcony."

"What? Excuse me."

The maitre d' smiles faintly and gestures to a staircase. "Foreign guests go to the balcony, please."

I search about the tables and dance floor. The men are Japanese. But I notice that almost all the girls at the tables are Caucasian, the majority blond.

The maitre d' offers me an unctuous smile. "Hostesses here speak no English. On balcony speak English."

My anger flares, but at that moment a hostess, unusually tall for a Japanese girl, materializes behind the maitre d' and smiles at me. She has a broad, sensual face, almost Polynesian, with prominently modeled cheekbones, perhaps deliberately chosen to appeal to more exotic gaijin tastes. The maitre d' again gestures to the staircase.

I shake my head, "No, thank you," and retreat back into the street.

Two guys, their faces looking tough and belligerent in the red neon, are about to enter the club and are startled by my abrupt exit.

A light drizzle now mutes the neon, muffling the street sounds and obscuring reality. Dark specters suddenly materialize out of the mist. A Japanese face glances up, momentarily unnerved by the hulking gaijin stalking the Ginza after midnight, and floats by.

The visit to the Black Rose had been one of those really rotten ideas to revisit the past, or rather an old address, that leaves you irretrievably depressed. But of course there had been that subconscious, totally irrational expectation that time had somehow miraculously bypassed the floating world of the Black Rose, and Lilli might still be there. You can buy a first-class ticket from Los Angeles to the other side of the world, but never back to the past.

Now again I hear dull footsteps tracking my own, following me around one corner, then another. I am as much curious as alarmed. I step into the entranceway of a camera shop by an overhead streetlight.

Two guys emerge out of the mists into the halo of light and then stop in confusion. They are the same two toughs I almost crashed into leaving the Black Rose. From the cut of their suits and the dark sweaters they wear underneath their jackets, they do not look like businessmen out on the town. One growls in Japanese and gestures down the street. He lights a cigarette with quick, angry gestures, bringing the match to his gaunt, pockmarked face, and in the flare under the streetlight I see that the backs of both his hands are tattooed with dragon heads and sense that under the dark sleeves spiny serpents' bodies snake up the length of both arms to his biceps.

He suddenly sees me in the doorway, starts, hisses something in Japanese. The other, a bigger, beefier man, glowers at me, then turns his head to the right and left in an almost theatrical way, checking to see if anyone else lurks about. The top of his head, either bald or shaven, gleams in the streetlight, and the long black hair at the side is pulled back in a short ponytail like a samurai.

With another deliberate, stagy motion, his right arm reaches across his body, then suddenly whips back. A short sword materializes in his hand, held low but pointed upward to disembowel me. He holds the black scabbard tight against the dark cloth of his left leg, where in the dim light I never noticed it. The blade glimmers with a blue-white intensity that is more than just the reflection of the street lamp.

He suddenly shouts, makes a short, startling lunge, the blade swiping up within inches of my belly and chest, and then steps back.

"Jesus!" I instinctively reel back into the doorway of the camera shop. But now I'm trapped on three sides by the display windows of Nikons, Canons, and Pentaxes, with no place to run.

If these two muggers playing samurai outlaws are trying to scare me, they have totally succeeded. "OK. OK. Here. This is all my money and credit cards." I take out my wallet and toss it on the sidewalk in front of the swordsman.

He scowls at it, as though deeply insulted. "No money," he growls, a deep rumbling sound. He bends and contemptuously taps the wallet with the edge of the blade, a quick snap of his wrist that produces a bell-like *ping* on the pavement.

I stare in amazement. The leather wallet with its several layers of plastic cards lies split in two halves.

"I cut you," he snarls. Then, as if to dramatize his intentions, he makes a slow choreographed movement with the sword. The son of a bitch is enjoying himself.

I'm defenseless against that sword and not going anywhere,

trapped in the entranceway with my back to a locked door. The lenses of two dozen expensive cameras showcased on plastic pedestals and life-sized cutouts of exquisite Japanese models are the only witnesses. At least they are protected behind plate glass and an alarm system.

The idea flashes with instant clarity. I cower against the display window on my left, then bounce off it, make a quick step across the entranceway, and kick hard at the window opposite. It shatters into great shards of glass.

The two thugs jump back and stare at me in astonishment, but just for a moment. Then it slams them. The wail of the camera-store alarm system is, in itself, loud and piercing enough to shatter glass.

The big, beefy samurai looks at me with a hurt expression, as if I have offended him yet again. But the other grabs his arm, shouts something that has the tone of a warning, and yanks him away. The first guy allows himself to be pulled away with no resistance, but glares back at me with reproach.

They disappear around a corner. I jump in the opposite direction, stop, scurry back to retrieve the halves of my wallet, then run like hell.

When in the safety of the wide, well-lit avenue Harumi Dori, I slow down, not wanting to attract attention, and immediately hail a cab to get off the street.

Should I go to the police? What can I say? Two samurai bad guys sliced my wallet and credit cards in half with a sword and in self-defense I kicked in the window of a camera shop. It is a comedy, and the press will love it. After all, Japanese tourists and students are mugged and murdered with alarming abandon in America.

I'd have to explain my business in Tokyo. The publicity would undoubtedly shoot down the deal. And that, for me, is the bottom line. The cab drops me at the entrance of the Imperial, and I pay the cabby with the unsliced bills in my pocket.

I check my watch and immediately head for my room. Ready, of Rufus Ready and Associates, confidential investigations, is at his desk in LA.

"I was mugged tonight."

"What happened?"

I describe the incident. To my surprise, Ready laughs, a deep, hearty sound that booms over the Pacific. "Goddamn, who the hell else would think to kick in a camera shop window to set off an alarm, then actually do it. In the middle of the Ginza, no less."

"You don't think it's unusual?"

"Hell yes."

"No, I mean the swordplay."

"Naw, standard Yakuza MO. They wave samurai swords around to intimidate people just to make collections. Guns carry long jail sentences in Japan. They were probably two soldiers making their rounds, spotted you at a club where you can drop a couple of thousand just buying drinks, and followed you down a dark street."

"That wasn't too bright of me."

"Nooo," Ready says. "Tokyo's a hell of a lot safer than LA. Normally Americans aren't hassled by Yakuza. You just got unlucky."

"Did I? I tossed them my wallet. All they did was use it to demonstrate the sharpness of their blade."

"Peter, I gather you have reason to believe it was more than a random mugging?"

Two sensational incidents in two nights, both meant to terrorize me and call in the police, seem beyond coincidence.

Ready reads silences perfectly. "Local security might be compromised," he says.

"Levy will brief you." Bob Levy is my partner in Levy, McGrath and Saxon.

"Anything else?"

"Yeah. Wait a second." I retrieve the notes from Hara.

The bureaucrats of MITI are collectively all-powerful but individually faceless. In Japan, the nail that sticks up is to be hammered down. But Yurikawa had worn an Armani tie to a meeting with a Beverly Hills lawyer. He had offered a subtle insult while viewing a Chagall and dropped a reference to my personal background as if throwing down a gauntlet.

"I need all the background your contacts in Tokyo can get on a senior bureaucrat of the Japanese Ministry of International Trade and Industry." I spell the name.

"Matsu Yurikawa," Ready repeats. "You know, you can call my associates there directly. It might be quicker, if you have specific questions."

"I don't want this inquiry to come from me. I don't know what the hell I'm getting into. This guy's a high pooh-bah. Your Tokyo guys know you and hopefully trust you. They'll tell you more, especially if they think the inquiry is from LA rather than from an unknown gaijin in their own backyard."

"Your instincts are probably right on this. That's why the good Lord gave us fax machines." A pause. "Peter?"

"Yes."

"Watch yourself. Remember, despite their London-tailored suits, the high tech, the rock 'n' roll, you're still the foreign devil in a devilish place."

I know that more painfully than even Ready suspects.

7

Taking a Pound of Flesh

The two young waitresses in full-length kimonos exit as they entered, sliding along the tatami on their knees, heads bowed in our direction, until they scoot out the door and silently close the shoji.

Yurikawa gestures toward the steaming dish with his chopsticks. "It is *gindara,* black cod I think you call it in English. It has a very strong flavor. We Japanese enjoy a fish with a strong, oily taste. Whereas Americans seem to like white fish like halibut or mahi-mahi, which we Japanese think have no taste at all."

We sit on tatami mats across a low lacquered table from one another in a small private room of paper walls and light polished wood. A window opens out onto a small garden of bonsai and polished stones.

I chew a piece of *gindara* that tastes like ginger-flavored cod-liver oil. "Yes, it certainly does have a distinctive taste," I nod.

Matsu Yurikawa, senior bureaucrat of the Japanese Ministry of International Trade and Industry, is telling me something—he doesn't give a Japanese pickle if I gag on this meal or not.

The restaurant is in the Kasumigaseki area of government offices just a few blocks south of the grounds of the Imperial Palace. There is no apparent sign outside the restaurant's discreet entrance, and if the driver had not known exactly where it is I would have never found it. The restaurant exists for just such meetings—perhaps it has for centuries—and I have the sense that the steel girders of the present sky-scrapers have risen up about this traditional Japanese inn—a *ryokan* in which intrigues of the Edo era shoguns had been plotted—without altering a timber.

"What does your government think of this Japanese-American *keiretsu?*" Yurikawa asks with exquisite politeness.

I take a chopsticks bite of the boiled *ebi-imo*, a kind of potato, to clear the cod oil taste out of my mouth. The moment to launch the Black Ships has come.

"We have not discussed this with the White House. Our government does not exercise the same control, or cooperation, with business that MITI enjoys in Japan."

"Oh, I am surprised. We understood that Mr. Greenwald had . . . influence in Washington."

"Your intelligence is entirely accurate. Mr. Greenwald is, of course, a personal friend of the president. And *influence* is a very good word."

I take a lingering sip of sake. "But it's really *more* than influence. Both his company and our law firm make considerable campaign contributions. Perhaps more important than the money is our ability to organize fund-raisers in Los Angeles, produce galas in Washington. We arrange for the celebrities, the entertainers, for a rally in, say, Houston. The star power to stump through the snow in the New Hampshire primary. Add to that, of course, the *influence* of our newspapers, magazines, TV stations, network . . ." I pause to allow Yurikawa to absorb this, contemplate this web of influence.

"It's not a matter of politics, or even power. It's our business. We don't even know what to call it anymore. Show business, communications, multimedia, the electronic information superhighway . . ." The phrases hang in the air for reflection.

"Every day there is some . . . change before the Federal Communications Commission, a bill before Congress, a prospectus to the Security and Exchange Commission. So as a purely business matter, we cultivate our influence in Washington. But no, we have not said any-thing about *this business*."

I look down, then up, shrug, feign a slight embarrassment. "Frankly, we're very afraid the Japanese will embarrass us."

"I do not understand. How could we embarrass you?"

"I've been very straightforward with you, Mr. Yurikawa. But the fact remains that direct investment in Japanese companies by Ameri-cans is practically nonexistent. The cross-ownership of shares by other Japanese companies, the members of the *keiretsu*—manufacturers, suppliers, the financial institutions—effectively keeps any American from buying in. It locks us out."

"We are studying this matter."

"You've been studying it for twenty-five years now." There is an edge to my voice that startles Yurikawa. "And there are still no Ameri-cans even sitting on the boards of major Japanese corporations. The total of *all* direct foreign investment in Japan is less than one-half of one percent. In the United States, large as we are, foreign investments make up over seven percent of our economy, in Europe thirteen per-cent. Japan remains the most closed industrial economy in the world. And the most closed market in the world."

"And you are going to change all that."

I take another fishy bite of *gindara* to achieve the proper look of distaste. "Not me. As you're aware, Congress and the president—one of the few things they agree on—have become increasingly aggressive about a level playing field in our trade with Japan. Matsushita bought Universal, then Sony bought Columbia. If the reverse is not allowed—if an American communications company cannot now acquire Japanese electronic companies—then . . ." I smile faintly at Yurikawa and again shrug.

"Please, what will happen?"

"I'm afraid this time there won't be two years of trade negotia-tions followed by a face-saving whitewash, as there was with automo-biles. Or a year-long study as in the Kodak case. Time has run out. This is it. This is what they call at the Harvard Graduate School of Business the specific case study."

"And if it does not succeed?"

I shake my head.

"Please, Mr. Saxon, I value your counsel."

"I expect there will be trade sanctions for Japanese electronic and communications equipment. In past years, American companies endured long delays in getting Japanese patents—during which time Japanese companies studied the American patent applications and copied our technological advances. There is a school of thought among engineers that the last real Japanese invention was sushi. Patent infringements, or suspicion of them, might have customs inspectors stopping ships from unloading Japanese-made electronics at the docks. Even products made in Mexico by Japanese-owned corporations."

Yurikawa's face is impassive, expressing neither anger nor alarm.

"Please understand, we realize Japan is the economic engine that drives Asia. And we experienced the worldwide ripple effect of that in ninety-eight. But the protection, the creation of American jobs and industries is a highly emotional political issue. And a practical one. We are, after all, talking about what will be the dominant industry of the twenty-first century.

"As for my company, we would seek other strategic partners— probably in Europe, possibly Korea—to follow through on our plan. And we would, of course, use our influence to protect those interests."

"In short, Mr. Saxon, you are telling me that the shit will hit the fan."

I laugh at Yurikawa's use of the idiom. "Well, we have a very close working relationship with both the shit and the fan. But I'm not telling you anything your own excellent intelligence hasn't already."

Yurikawa smiles. "It is interesting that you use the military term—intelligence. But then you have a military background, I under-stand. A former jet fighter pilot."

There it is again. Why are the few years I spent between college and law school such a point of interest? I look down at the fish and poke at it with my chopsticks.

War as a macho metaphor—for business, politics, or football—offends me. Perhaps because my piece of the real thing was so brutal, even surreal, beyond any analogy, and therefore terrifying. My closest friends were annihilated, forever MIA, without ever having set foot in Vietnam.

"Mr. Yurikawa, may I be bluntly honest?"

"Please."

"Possibly insulting?"

He is silent but looks at me challengingly.

"Business is not war removed to another field. Although I understand that idea is very popular in Japan. It's especially pursued among your generation, who grew up after World War Two. And a lot of old men who are obsessed with refighting that war by other means. It makes for a glib strategy. Protect the homeland from any invasion and dominate foreign territories. But it's a policy that will only end in economic disaster for your country. I'm here trying to create a merger in which both sides win, and flourish."

"Perhaps, but this mission you are on in Japan is very dangerous, Mr. Saxon."

There it is again, the polite but direct warning.

8

Yankee Station

On August 6, 1964, in retaliation for an alleged attack on the U.S. destroyer *Maddox* in the Gulf of Tonkin, planes from the aircraft carriers *Ticonderoga* and *Constellation* bombed and rocketed North Vietnamese PT-boat bases at Quang Khe and Hon Gai. President Lyndon Johnson declared, "We seek no wider war," but the carriers *Kearsarge* and *Ranger* immediately steamed toward the Tonkin Gulf. By the winter monsoons, they were joined by the *Coral Sea* and *Hancock*, and then the *Midway*, *Independence*, *Bon Homme Richard*, and *Oriskany*.

The carriers and their squadrons first broke in on Dixie Station, east of Saigon, launching strikes in the South Vietnam war zone, where air defense was at a minimum. The green attack pilots launched their bombs and rockets at suspected Vietcong positions, and the fighters strafed and patrolled with relatively little antiaircraft fire while the ships' crews worked out the backbreaking daily combat operations. Then the carriers rotated north to Yankee Station off North Vietnam, where there were MiGs, missiles, and the guns of Phuc My Luc.

The northeast monsoon swept across the South China Sea into the Gulf of Tonkin, at first trucking in billowing clouds and a hangdog persistent drizzle. The warm moist wind beat against the mountains to the west, where it clashed with the colder polar air out of Siberia and China funneling southward through the mountains. The clash generated a clockwise swirl that fed on itself, churning the polar air and monsoon into the *Crachin*, layers of dark, thickening clouds that exploded into torrential rains and shrouded the sea down to five hundred feet.

Lytle, the lieutenant in charge of the carrier's photo reconnaissance detachment, looked up from the intercom in the ready room. "Hawkeyes report a break along the coast and inland to Thanh Hoa. It's show time."

He looked down and then up again and held my eye. It was a bitch. An alpha strike, the whole air group over the target. And then when they finished their attacks—and the North Vietnamese antiaircraft gunners were boresighted in—I had to fly in behind them, a lone RF–8 Crusader, low and unarmed, to photograph the bomb damage for assessment by air intelligence.

The five-hundred-foot ceiling and mile visibility were breaking up, but rain still splashed against the canopy by the time I strapped in and, bowels knotted with dread, taxied forward onto the port catapult. A metallic clang vibrated through the aircraft as the shuttle yoked the plane to the steam-driven catapult.

I cycled the controls, checked their movement. Just off my wing, the catapult officer in his identifying yellow jersey stood bent over into the gale that blasted straight down the carrier's deck. He made a whirling motion with his arm, and I shoved the throttle to the stops and clenched the catapult grip with my left hand. With my head jammed into the headrest, I snapped the catapult officer a salute.

Then I stared straight down the track. Ahead, the carrier's bow dipped down into a trough. There was a splash of slate-gray sea, and the bow heaved up again. The catapult officer lunged forward, his right knee touching the deck, like a fencer making a sword thrust toward the bow. At that moment the catapult exploded, and I was mashed into my seat. The jet rocketed straight toward the sea ahead. The troughs of gray water and whitecaps were instantly beneath me and then melted together in a blur. I flipped the landing gear up. The air speed indicator hit 175 knots, and I reached down and threw a lever that adjusted the pitch of the jet's truncated wing for flying speed. The nose of the Crusader came up automatically as if instinctively climbing away from the dark sea, only sixty feet below, toward the stratosphere for which it was designed. The plane was immediately enveloped in a gray soup of low-lying clouds.

I eased back on the stick and steepened the climb, and finally broke through at eighteen thousand feet, raising my eyes from the instrument panel to sail through white islands of condensation. I checked in with Tommy Cochran, who was leading a pair of heavily armed F–8 fighters riding shotgun on me overhead.

Over the coast it was almost high noon, and I could see the swept-wing shadow of my own Crusader leading me like a darkling guide across the glittering surf and the sandy beach into North Vietnam.

"I'll start the run from the north, lining up on the railroad tracks," I radioed Cochran.

"Roger, Kodak Nine. Got you covered."

It was a choke point, an enfilade between mountains through which the railroad and road south from Hanoi had to pass, but then so did I. I could see the columns of smoke from the attack and, more terrifying, the black blossoms of flak hanging in the air. The strike had done everything but aim their guns for them.

I circled to the north and jinxed parallel to the railroad tracks, but my little serpentine dance didn't fool anyone. They were ready and waiting for the lone recon they knew would follow right behind the bombers to take pictures.

I watched the 37-millimeter antiaircraft bursts coming up to punch me, black poisonous puffs of flak that instantly flared from a red point of fire. At the last second, when the concussion shook the plane, I pushed down, as if embracing the black clouds, and dove under them into the maws of the guns themselves. I leveled off at an oddball uneven altitude before they had a chance to re-aim, and ran parallel to the tracks.

At the end of the enfilade I broke off the photo run, jammed to full throttle, straight up and out, the Gs of the pull-up crushing me into the seat, draining the blood from the periphery of my vision. I focused on the target combat air patrol circling over me and climbed toward them.

"OK," Cochran radioed, "let's head home."

I double-checked my panel lights. *Shit!* Shit! Shit! Shit! "Black Knight One-Oh-Seven, this is Kodak Nine. I've got a problem here."

"You hit?"

"No, camera problem." In my frenzy to outflank the flak, I simply forgot to turn it on.

I had a whole air group, the admiral's staff from Task Force 77, even the Pentagon waiting to see the pictures. I couldn't fake it. "I've got to go back."

I immediately peeled off and dove, back down into the guns. I was running on adrenaline, and in the pit of my stomach was the cold certainty that a hundred 37-millimeters were now converging on me and in the next moment would splatter me in flaming wreckage all over the Vietnamese foothills. In that certainty I didn't think. If I'd thought about it for two seconds, I'd have been paralyzed with fear.

I didn't even bother to jinx, but swooped straight in at the south end, reversing the path of the previous run. This time not a single black blossom of flak rose out of the pall of smoke hanging over the road and tracks. I flew straight down the railroad, clicking off photos, without a shot being fired. Then, suddenly, I was at the pass, and I had to haul up, climbing steeply with the tree-covered sides of the ravine rushing by both wings.

When I leveled off, two Crusader fighters immediately joined me on my right wing. "OK, I'm really impressed," Cochran radioed. "Now can we go home?"

My irrational second run had not only surprised Cochran, but it had apparently taken the gun crews below totally by surprise. Not expecting a second pass, they had stood down to reload after my first run.

I was delirious with my escape, sky-high on adrenaline, but in the cramped, electronics-jammed cockpit of the RF–8, all I could do was whoop and holler. I whooped and hollered halfway back to the carrier

By the Christmas truce of '65, the carriers of Task Force 77 had flown a total of 57,000 combat sorties and lost 100 aircraft, with 46 men rescued and 82 captured or killed, and I became a statistic in all but one of those columns.

9

Fire Scars

"What's she like?" Joan asks.

"What's who like?"

"Who the hell are we talking about?" What infallible sonar do wives possess that allows them to ping off the silent dense masses submerged in our consciousness from even eight thousand miles away? "The Haras at whose home you had dinner."

"His wife is rather chic in a Japanese exec wife sort of way."

"What's a Japanese exec wife sort of way?"

"Well turned out but polite and self-effacing. She speaks English very well. In fact, she served as translator between Hara and me."

"That sounds awkward as hell."

"Not really, after you get into the rhythm of it. Hara speaks and understands English well enough, but he's not fluent. A translator is a face-saving sort of thing. But I don't really trust our working translator, this guy Ozu. He's an executive just below Hara, and I have this sixth sense he's working on his own agenda. The output doesn't always equate with my input."

"As soon as you get into a negotiation, you start getting paranoid."

"Remember what Freud said, 'Paranoids putting together billion-dollar deals have real enemies.'"

"That was Mike Ovitz."

"Whatever. How are the girls?"

"Erika hasn't called in yet from Stanford. You know, your first daughter. And Beth came home this weekend to keep me company. She had a date on Saturday, and he drove out and back from SC."

"It must be serious."

"Guess what? He's Howard Frankel's son."

"I keep hoping she'll meet some nice jockstrap at that school, one going to sign a ten-million-dollar pro contract in his senior year."

"She wanted to know where Daddy was."

"What did you tell her?"

"I used the cover story."

"God, I hate lying to Beth."

"You didn't. I did. But if you want to keep your mission to Tokyo under wraps, you can't tell Beth. You know that."

"How'd we ever get a daughter whose stated ambition is to be Mary Hart?"

"You know she's your favorite."

"She just tries so hard to be lovable."

"Well, what can I say, Erika takes after you."

I think of my oldest daughter and the impasse that has developed between us. "She asked me why I kept my old flight school picture in the study, and not any others. I told her it was because it was taken the first time I had flown solo, been truly alone, and I wanted to remind myself how it felt. She asked if I was frightened, and I said no, I was too exhilarated to be frightened. Too thrilled to be doing it."

"What did she say?"

"'Wow!' Just 'Wow!' I remember it because it's the only time I've made contact with her since puberty."

"She was amazed. You know, Peter, it's the only thing I know you to be inarticulate about. You never talk about it."

"It was all a long time ago."

There is a moment of silence, then Joan says, "Well, you make contact with your firstborn a lot more than you think. Trust me."

"Why are we talking about our daughters' quirks? I'm calling from halfway around the world—it's tomorrow here."

"Because they transcend time and space. And so do yours."

"Meaning?"

"Don't get paranoid about this translator Ozu. Or start obsessing. You know how you are sometimes."

"It's the secret of my success."

"You're not cutting deals with CAA or Midwest Cable now. It's the Japanese. They're a subtler but very exotic culture."

"You've been reading up again."

"I always read up. So what did you have for dinner? What did the polite and self-effacing but chic Mrs. Hara feed you?"

"A beef thing."

"A beef thing? I didn't know the Japanese ate much beef. Was it sukiyaki?"

"No, it was more like *shabu shabu*, thinly sliced, with shrimp."

"Turf and surf teriyaki."

"More subtle but exotic than that. The shrimp was sliced into the shape of waves on the sea. And there were these almost transparent vegetables cut into flower shapes."

"Now you're intimidating the hell out of me. We're going to have to reciprocate when they visit the U.S."

"Yeah. The boys are taking me out to dinner tonight."

"Oh." Joan's "Oh" echoes with all the articles she has read about Japanese business entertainment. "What's this? A male bonding playing goosy-goosy with geishas?"

"Don't I wish. We'll probably just drink too much and conspire to wire the global village for Hollywood sex, violence, and adolescent humor."

"How about universal peace and enlightenment in the new millennium."

"Isn't it pretty to think so?"

"You sound tired, Peter."

"Just jet lag. It's tomorrow over here, and I still haven't caught up with yesterday's sleep."

But it's not just jet lag. It's this haunted time warp into which I have been suddenly thrust and from which I cannot escape.

Once, when delayed stress syndrome was very much in the news, I attended a counseling group for Vietnam vets at the VA Hospital in Westwood. I arrived at the meeting late, straight from the office, a clean-shaven Beverly Hills lawyer in his thousand-dollar suit and seventy-dollar haircut. There hadn't been time to change. I sat at the edge of a group punctuated by guys with open flannel shirts over T-shirts taut across swollen beer guts, middle-aged hippies with bald crowns and ponytails held by rubber bands, thick mustaches, muttonchops, gaunt haunted junkies, edgy angry alcoholic blacks with blood-flecked eyeballs, and even the more normal workaday guys glanced at me and wondered what the hell I was doing there.

An ex-marine in long-range recon recounted in tears a patrol in which his squad had set up firing positions along a suspected supply trail. A group of kids from a nearby village had materialized, smiling, gleefully accepting candy and rations from the marines, until this particular marine noticed one of the older girls, maybe twelve or thirteen, very carefully pacing off the distance from his M60 machine-gun position to a tall, prominent tree.

The girl suddenly looked up, saw him watching her, and bolted. Instinctively, he cut her down with the M60 before she disappeared into the jungle.

The other kids scattered. Within fifteen minutes the position was hit with a pinpoint mortar barrage that wiped out two-thirds of his patrol.

I had been in-country less than an hour. What comparable horror did I have to unload on these guys? I never went back. Lilli had already absolved me of my secret sins.

Sometimes, in my nightmares, I woke Joan. The next morning

she said, "You were moaning in your sleep. What were the nightmares about?"

"I don't remember."

After a while she stopped mentioning it.

Sometimes the nightmares woke me, and unable to sleep, I would get up—mumbling to Joan that I was going to read. I stumbled to the study to court sleep with a history book and a couple of shooters of Scotch. I drank until memories dissolved, but I had done that as a young pilot before I was ever shot down. It was not a problem. I still woke to the clock radio in time for a three- to five-mile jog before breakfast.

I didn't have a problem really. I worked compulsively and exercised to combat the occasional depression, and I flourished. On occasion, Joan tactfully inquired about Vietnam or my tendency to limp when I had worked too long or played too much tennis. It was her way of saying that if I wanted to talk about it, she was there to listen. But I couldn't really talk about it without talking about Lilli.

Joan and my daughters thought it somewhat glamorous that I had been a navy pilot. But in conversations with their friends, they quickly added that I took photos, implying that I was some sort of jet-borne war correspondent who took the film at eleven.

Lilli held no such illusions.

There are times, after an affair, when the carnal, moist, musky odors and touch of sex haunt you, teasing in the lonesome hours of the night. With Lilli, I too often remembered that fire scar. Sometimes, in perversity, I touched the slick, leathery gristle of it when we made love, and late at night, after she had fallen asleep, it conjured up that nightmare vision of Hell itself.

"How did you get that?" I ran my fingertips along the shiny thickened flesh of the scar at the base of her spine, but then, feeling her stiffen slightly, I leaned over and gently kissed it.

"Very bad burn when little girl." She regarded me with no

expression whatever on her face, then added, "When Americans burn Tokyo."

"The Americans burned Tokyo? You mean an air raid during the war?"

"Oh, much more than air raid. I was only little girl but I still remember," Lilli said in a now hushed, awed voice. "The fire is so high it is like million tongues that lick at the American planes. And this terrible noise like animal that wants to be fed. And the American planes are so low—you could see them in the fire—so low. Never so low before. And never so many. And more American planes fly into the fire and drop more bombs. They keep feeding this terrible animal."

There was a single lantern in the room, and its red light eerily illuminated Lilli like the glow of that wildfire itself. Her eyes were wide and awed, removed from the horror, as if she were retelling a terrifying story that she had often heard, and not reliving a memory.

"Everybody crazy. They run into streets, screaming, clawing each other, trying to escape. Little children and old people fall down and people run over them. Arms, legs torn off. I see a man naked, no clothes, no arm. People just drop dead. There is no air." She clutched her own throat. "Just grab throat and drop dead. Fire burns up all the air. They die. So they all run to the river. You know the Sumida River?" She gestured vaguely toward the east. "All the people run to the river to escape the fire. They so many, they cannot move or fall down. Everybody squeezed together. Then the fire comes to them and burns all the air, and they die. All still standing up. The next morning, they still standing in the river, all dead, but so squeezed together they cannot fall down."

"Where were you? Where did you get hurt?"

"I am there. My clothes catch fire, and my mother beat fire out with bare hands. My mother carry me and my sister in blanket, and she runs through the fire and over the bridge. My brother—he is oldest—he runs back to get my grandparents. We never see brother or grandparents again. My brother, my grandparents, all burned up in fire."

The story came out in one breathless rush, and then Lilli stopped and stared at me. There was in her eyes and face, not fear, but a heightened awareness of horror, the extraordinary vulnerability of a beautiful young child. She could not have remembered all that horror. The images and details were too exact. Hundreds of B–29s feeding the flames with incendiary bombs of magnesium, napalm, and white phosphorus. The clawing, stampeding, frenzied mob panic to escape. Someone must have described them to her later, in the harrowing years that followed, or she read them, and she had incorporated it all into her own personal tragedy.

Just a few weeks later, at Yankee Station just south of the Gulf of Tonkin, there was a time I could not sleep. I wandered down into the wardroom lounge for a grilled cheese sandwich to settle the heebie-jeebies in my stomach about that morning's prestrike photo mission. A commander in the air department sat hunched over a burger after his late night work of rearranging the planes on the flight deck for the morning launch.

Lilli's story weighed on me, and I recounted it to this senior officer, who had fought in World War II. He nodded and shrugged. He was familiar with General Curtis Lemay's firebombing of Tokyo. The wood and paper homes had instantly blazed into the funeral pyres of the families within. At the time, March 1945, the commander had been on the carrier *Enterprise* off Okinawa fighting off kamikazes, and the dread in his own heart justified the air force strategy. But one fact in his story that night obscured all the others. When the B–29s' bomb bay doors had swung open to drop the F–46 and M–69 bombs and canisters, the stench of a hundred thousand people burning to death five thousand feet below had brought the bomber crews to their knees, puking on the planes' steel decks. And as the black reek of it permeated the cockpits, pilots vomited over their controls on their flights back to the Mariana Islands.

My God, I could not imagine what black stench of her family and playmates burning had filled Lilli's nostrils and her nightmares. And yet as Lilli told me the story that night, it was not with bitterness but with the tacit acknowledgment that our lives, a generation later, were somehow unalterably interwoven.

"Even now, I hear airplanes, I am very frightened. I want to hide, but there is nowhere to hide." The terror had transferred to an irrational adult fear. Did it also, in some perverse transference, fuel a passion for American pilots? But I held my tongue.

As if reading my thought, she gave me a strange smile. "And now we are lovers, and you are my protector," she said.

I simply smiled back at her. I did not tell her that my own childhood memory of that time was of playing on the living room rug with my Jack Armstrong bombsight dropping toy bombs, darts that impaled targets on a map board of Tokyo—all sent to me from General Mills for a couple of Wheaties box tops and a quarter. In addition to incendiaries and atomic bombs, a generation of kids stuffed with the breakfast of champions worked voodoo on the Japanese.

Lilli knelt on the bed next to me, a bronze nude sculpture. Her arms were cradled beneath her breasts as if holding a bunch of flowers. Then she reached out to me, as if offering those blossoms.

The black, sooty feathers of her hair framed her eyes, hauntingly intense, almost irrational, compelling me to readily agree to any fantasy she had.

10

Return to the Black Rose

"Your wife is a lovely woman," I say tentatively. I'm suddenly aware that I don't know the etiquette in Japan for complimenting another man's wife.

"Oh yes, from very old family."

Some men all but dismiss their wives at required business social gatherings, presenting them perfunctorily, and others introduce them with a pride that proclaims their wives to be one of their major fulfillments. From the invitation to Hara's home, the way he deferred to his wife throughout dinner—partly because her English was considerably better than his—and now the way Ozu translates his reply, I sense that Hara has in some significant way married above his place.

"She's very knowledgeable. She worked at the American embassy?"

"Oh yes, knows English very well. She is very helpful to me."

Hara, Ozu, and I are dining at a French restaurant in the maze of the Akasaka district, just west of the American embassy. The restaurant is *intime* despite the white wood and Scandinavian furniture. There are over a hundred selections on the wine list, and I wonder where the hell they keep them.

"Will you learn Japanese, I wonder?" Ozu asks.

"The pessimist studies Japanese. The optimist studies Chinese," I say. "And the visionary works on his computer skills."

Ozu translates but looks totally bewildered. Hara thinks about it a moment and then laughs and slaps the table.

Ozu, still baffled, says, "Mr. Hara thinks what you say is very funny, and he is memorizing it."

"And what do you study, Peter?" Hara asks.

"Computers . . . and a few cautious words of Japanese."

"Why are you cautious?"

"The cross-ownership of a Japanese company's shares by *keiretsus* has, to date, effectively blocked Americans from directly investing in companies like Kuribayashi."

"The Japanese market is not as closed as Americans claim," Ozu says.

I give them both my rueful negotiator smile. "My father used to have a saying—'Throw a puppy in the river. If it swims, good. If it sinks, well, life is tough. But don't tie a rope round its throat, weight the other end to a brick, and then say the puppy wasn't strong enough to make it.'

"The bottom line—since the mid-eighties, the Japanese have bought controlling interests in some seventy American electronics firms. Americans have acquired major stakes in only a handful of Japanese companies. It's a one-way transfer of technology that's extremely disturbing to my government.

"Fortunately that technology is now obsolete. And if you're not on the cutting edge, you're not in this game. As all media become increasingly digital—and especially high-definition television—the computer software and technology developed in America will define the cutting edge. The Japanese genius has always been to develop American technology into marketable consumer products."

Again I pause, but this time for dramatic effect rather than a comment.

"In the future the Japanese won't have the same access to our licenses, or our markets, as they have in the past."

"Mr. Kuribayashi does not like *gaiatsu* . . . foreign pressure," Ozu says. Significantly, Ozu states this on his own, not translating anything Hara has said.

"To be perfectly honest, your *gaiatsu* is not from Washington, it's from Paris. I'm flying there in two days."

Both Hara and Ozu look at one another in surprise.

"As you're aware," I continue, "Philips, Thomson, and Euro-Media are actively developing high-definition TV with American consortia. And we're exploring our options in Europe. There are great advantages, and disadvantages, to playing these European cards."

"Playing these European cards," Ozu repeats, as if savoring the phrase. "Please, what would be the advantages of playing these cards, may we ask?"

"Obviously, it gives us entrée into the European Common Market. There are always trade barriers or restrictions springing up there. We already have a major distribution company and investments in two satellite broadcasting systems, but nothing in hardware. That's the first advantage."

"And the second?"

"Europe, and France in particular, is emerging from the worst recession since the Great Depression. No one foresaw the degree of this recession; even Euro Disney is still hurting. European companies have undergone major devaluations, and French real estate is still in a slump."

Hara listens very carefully, nodding. "And your company is cash rich from your European movie and TV income and now eager to make strategic investments and acquisitions at recession prices," Ozu translates for him. He's done his homework.

"Especially at this time, before the next explosion of media technology."

"And what are the disadvantages? Why are you now in Tokyo and not in Paris?"

I give my best imitation of a Gaelic shrug of dismay. "One must deal with the French."

Ozu nods gravely, but Hara laughs and slaps the table again. "Yes, yes, one must deal with the French."

Then he falls silent and studies me with half-opened eyes. Ozu does not speak either.

I fork my fresh trout with chilled butter sauce. In negotiations with the Japanese, the silences are as meaningful as what is said. I have been warned by consultants in Los Angeles not to impatiently fill that silence with new pitches, proposals, or pressure but to just quietly wait them out. I sip the Romanee-Conti Montrachet from the delicate crystal and hold Hara's eyes with a slight smile.

When he finally speaks, Ozu seems caught off guard. He starts to say something, but Hara's peremptory tone brooks no argument. Finally he translates, "Mr. Hara says he understands your impatience with the progress of our discussions. They are an internal matter within our company. If you could accommodate him by postponing your flying to Paris for a few days, he will fly immediately to Kyoto to personally confer with Mr. Kuribayashi and arrange a meeting for you."

I nod and say, *"Hai,"* the noncommittal Japanese yes that only means you have heard what was said and understand it. Then it is my turn for silent contemplation.

"My priority has always been to speak with Kuribayashi-san," I finally say directly to Hara. "If that can be arranged, then I will certainly stay in Japan. But in case the meeting cannot be set up in the next day or two, I will keep to my schedule. First-class reservations from Tokyo to Paris are very tight."

"Yes, we enjoy Paris very much," Hara smiles, then speaks sharply to Ozu in Japanese.

"Do you play golf?" The blonde named Debbie smiles at Ozu. "You look like the outdoor type."

"Blond bombshell," Ozu exclaims to Debbie. "You look like movie star Sharon Stone." And before she can respond to the compliment, he turns to me. "All American girls," waving his hand to sweep in the hostesses of the Black Rose. "Different when you here long time ago. Then only American men and Japanese girls." He grins at me with a manic intensity.

After dinner, Hara, true to his word, left to fly to Kyoto that night, insisting that Ozu entertain me. I tried to beg off, but it was apparent that Ozu would lose face if I did not accept his hospitality for the evening.

To my amazement Ozu has taken me directly from the restaurant to the Black Rose, rather than to one of the trendy hot spots in Akasaka closer to where we had dinner. As though by prearrangement, the manager immediately assigned Ozu the blond hostess and an unusually tall Japanese girl to me. Except for the aborted visit the night before, I have never been back to the club or mentioned it to anyone.

"You have been to the Black Rose before, Mr. Saxon? Maybe when you were in the navy?" Ozu asks.

I look about. The wooden dance floor has been replaced by Plexiglas lighted from beneath, and a multifaceted mirrored ball rotates overhead, splashing beams of light. The stage set for *Saturday Night Fever* ends there. This crowd doesn't boogie. The girls are all in their twenties—most of them blond—but the clientele, all Japanese men, is middle-aged, with the oldest pushing seventy. All the fine young American warriors are gone.

The small band plays rock arranged for the elevators of office buildings, so quietly that no one at the tables has to raise their voice. There is no one on the dance floor.

I turn back to Ozu, as if to answer his question. "Let's drink to foreign affairs," I toast. There is a bottle of Johnny Walker Black Label, bottles of soda, and a bucket of ice on the table.

Both girls laugh and clap their hands. "To foreign affairs," Debbie repeats and laughs again, as if she has made the joke.

"You two in government?" she asks.

"No, just into foreign affairs."

Ozu blinks.

Mari, the Japanese hostess, whispers to Ozu, and then he laughs loudly. "Foreign affairs. It is double sexy meaning."

"A double entendre," Debbie says. "That's French. French is the language of love."

Ozu grins at her and fingers the long tress of blond hair that falls calculatingly across her shoulder onto her breast. "Blond bombshell, like Sharon Stone."

Debbie is, perhaps, twenty-seven, but with her mane of evenly dyed loose blond hair, a chain of heavy gold links about her neck and another on her wrist, heavy gold earrings, and glossy semitheatrical makeup, she looks like a teenager, all dressed up in a hot pink party dress.

A waiter pops up to ask officiously if the girls need another soda or snack—at fifty dollars a pop. Ozu magnanimously orders a round of everything.

"You have Japanese girlfriend here?" he persists, his eyes bright with booze and desperation. The alcohol is rapidly dissolving Ozu's discretion—or perhaps he imagines me to be as tipsy as he is—and his English is not subtle enough for him to be clever.

"Absolutely. A sailor has a girl in every port," I say. "It's part of the job description." I smile at Ozu, wink, and lift my glass. "To all the beautiful women of the Black Rose, past and present."

The girls giggle and applaud. I drain my glass, and Ozu has to match.

"You a butterfly," the Japanese girl, Mari, accuses.

"Not so. I was true to every one of them sequentially."

"I do not understand that," Mari says. "Sequencha—I want to understand English." There is a yearning in her face that seizes my attention. Her eyes are wide, almost round, with only a slight fold. In the smoky light her skin seems a shade darker than the pale ivory of the other Japanese hostesses. She smiles at me with lips that are full, sensual, with a slight pout.

"In sequence. It means one thing after another in order," I

explain. "*Sequentially* means the same thing. It's just a different form. Remember *in sequence,* one thing after another in order."

"In sequence. One thing after another in order," she repeats.

"Riiight!"

"You are true to one girl after another in order."

"You have it."

"Thank you very much for the English lesson. I learn new expression. *In sequence.* But you are still a butterfly." She has a wonderful smile that lights up her face. She leans toward me intimately, her hand on my arm, and whispers, "I help you get him drunk, OK?"

"Just a little bit more," I say aloud.

"What is name your Japanese girlfriend?" Ozu asks.

"Mari," I say, patting her hand.

"No, no, old Japanese girlfriend," Ozu says, shaking his head truc-ulently. "When you navy pilot."

"Japanese girlfriend back in sequence," Mari says.

"Very good. You've definitely got it." I turn back to focus on Ozu. "Lilli. Her name was Lilli."

"Lilli," Ozu slurs, having difficulty with the name, as though the *l*s were dissolving in Scotch on his tongue. He frowns and shakes his head again. "Not Japanese name."

"Not a Japanese name," I agree. "But she was a very Japanese girl from—" I am about to echo the phrase "from a very old family" that Hara had used earlier to describe his wife. And I remember again the knives in the Hara family shrine that seem, in memory at least, identical to the bloody blades before Lilli's altar.

"It's a work name," Mari says.

"Lilli," Ozu worries it. "Not Japanese name."

"Mari is my Japanese name. It sounds like famous American name, yes?"

"Yes, a very popular American name."

"Mari Midori. That is my true Japanese name."

"Mari Midori. It has a pretty sound." I turn back to Ozu and reach across the table in friendly confidence. "Masahiro-san, how come you want to know about my old girlfriend Lilli? You want me to get you a date?"

Ozu can't contain his excitement. "You know her?"

I laugh. "It was a long time ago, and she is now an old woman."

"You are not an old man," Mari says.

"You see her?" Ozu is visibly sweating.

"Yes, I have seen her."

Ozu rises half out of his chair. "Who is she?" His shoulders and hands on the table quiver in anticipation. I study him, trying to translate that desperate, drunken Japanese body language.

"I have seen her"—I turn and lightly touch the cheek of Mari with my fingertips—"in the face of the beautiful Mari. In the faces of"—I turn and gesture expansively to the room at large—"all the lovely Japanese girls here. And in the chic, stunning girls on the Ginza."

Mari laughs and applauds. Ozu sinks back in his chair and continues to sag, as if all his alcohol hits him at once.

"Masahiro-san and I are embarked on a great business venture, right, Masahiro-san?"

Mari catches my eye. "We will drink to your great success," she toasts. Debbie obediently raises her glass. Mari has already unobtrusively filled ours from the bottle, and from the difference in the hues of the drinks that Ozu and I hoist, she has obviously belted him harder.

"Banzai," I say.

"Banzai," Ozu echoes, draining his glass.

"Masahiro-san is a man of great honor," I say. "He loves Japan, and he is deeply troubled by our business."

Ozu smiles at me uncertainly and nods.

"Masahiro-san thinks it is treason to sell or merge Japanese companies with Americans, and I understand his very deep feelings about this."

Ozu continues to nod, but tears fill his eyes and stream down his cheeks. His lower lip thrusts out, as though he is about to bawl, but then his eyes suddenly become unfocused, and he bolts from his chair.

I'm apparently more concerned than the two hostesses, who both giggle. "Should I go after him?"

"Oh no," Mari insists. "He be very embarrassed. Japanese not so good drinking whiskey. They get drunk, sick. You say nothing. You forget. It is after work good time. You say something, very embarrassed."

"Thank you, Mari-san, for your very sage advice."

"Sage advice?"

"Very wise." I tap my temple. "Very smart."

"Ah, sage advice," she parrots. "Thank you for second English lesson, Peter Saxon-san. I think he too much drunk to tell you business things now."

I nod. But he has already told me.

"You know, more business is conducted here than at most offices in Japan," Debbie says. "I mean big business."

"I'll bet."

"I'm learning a lot."

I regard the gold chains of her necklace and bracelet. "I'll bet you're a hell of a negotiator."

She smiles. "You know it. But it's not as good as it was."

"What is?"

"I mean a good-looking blond could make a thousand dollars a night easy, just, you know, talking, flattering these guys. And that doesn't count all kinds of gifts. Jewelry . . ." She delicately touches the gold chain about her neck with her fingertips, indicating that it was a gift from an admiring patron. "I mean Porches, even condos. I haven't been so lucky in that department. But it's still good, you know. Still big money around."

She is talking one Yankee trader to another, here to sell the rich Japanese American goods, as if Mari is not there.

"They all Americans?" I ask, indicating a table with a half-dozen blondes jollying three middle-aged Japanese.

"Forget it. Brits, Australians, Swedes, Germans, even Russians. The Russians are the worst. Give new meaning to the word *slut*. But they all pretend to be American. It's kind of laughable. 'Yah, I yam California gurl,'" she parodies in a thick, nonspecific mock-European accent.

"You navy pilot in Japan?" Mari suddenly interrupts with some eagerness.

"A long time ago."

"You know Bobby Jackson? He is in air force. He is from Detroit in Michigan."

"I was here a long time ago."

"Also Bobby Jackson. Nineteen seventy-two."

"I was here in sixty-four, sixty-five."

She seems very disappointed and falls into a moody silence.

"The Japanese guys want American girls," Debbie continues. "They're crazy for us. Blond American girls are a big status symbol for Japanese men, you know."

"I'll bet."

After a few minutes Ozu reappears, still looking a bit queasy, although his hair is wet and combed. He bows and apologizes several times.

"No apology necessary," I insist.

He remains standing. "I must go now. Much work to do tomorrow before meeting. But you must stay, enjoy yourself. Have a good time. You are our complete guest. It is all taken care," he insists.

I'm ready to leave, but Ozu is so insistent I stay that a polite interval after his departure seems called for. He moves away unsteadily, with Debbie supporting him as far as the entrance.

"We may go somewhere else if you like," Mari says, as if it is a textbook phrase she has practiced. "It is arranged."

"Arranged?"

"You are Mr. Ozu's guest."

I nod. The hostesses are paid an hourly fee plus exorbitant prices for anything they eat or drink. If a patron wants to hit another club or a restaurant with the hostess, the club is paid for her time and a generous premium. Ozu, at some time or other, has taken care of it.

"That's very nice. But it's late, and I have to be up very early tomorrow."

"It is arranged," she repeats. The look on her face is perhaps all the more poignant for being without expression, disappointment cloaked by a mask. It isn't that she loves my company; it is the shame of having her time paid for and the customer still abandoning her sitting there.

"Do you like yakitori?" I ask.

Her face instantly breaks into a wonderful smile.

The cab lets us off alongside a great embankment, the raised railroad of the Yamanote line that separates the Ginza from the Palace district. In the alley under the tracks of Yurakucho station, a dozen motley food shops, long and narrow as train compartments themselves, compete wall to wall. At the front of each shop, skewers of the soy-soaked meat, chicken, and vegetables that give Yakitori Alley its name grill over glowing charcoal, the hibachis casting up a sweet, cloying smoke that scents the air.

Unlike the Black Rose, Yakitori Alley has escaped the onslaught of postmodern neo-Tokyo. Even at that hour the tables are crowded, and I automatically steer Mari into a cramped restaurant.

As we settle at the tiny table, Mari flashes a sly smile. "You come here with girlfriend Lilli."

"How did we get on that subject?"

"Ozu-san want very much to talk about your old girlfriend."

"Do you think that's peculiar?"

"Peculiar?"

"Unusual. Strange."

"Ah . . . yes, very *peculiar*." She savors the new word.

"Why?"

"Japanese men don't talk about Japanese girls and American GIs."

"Oh?"

"Yes. You see separate balcony for foreigners? American business-men call it the gaijin ghetto. Only special girls work there. They paid less money."

"But they have to speak English."

"Yes, I like to work there. Speak English with American business-men. Practice my English. It is very good for me."

"Is it less . . . status if you work in the gaijin ghetto?"

She hesitates a beat, avoiding my eyes. "Yes, I think so." Then she adds quickly, "Americans are very nice. They are kinder than Japanese men. Many are old GIs like you who come to Black Rose in *old days,* they say."

The thought of a stream of middle-aged American businessmen searching for their bygone youth in the gaijin ghetto of the Black Rose is depressing as hell. "Was Bobby Jackson from Detroit in Michigan looking for his old girlfriend?"

"Oh no, I never meet Bobby Jackson."

The quiet note of alarm in her voice catches me. I had missed the connection in the subdued lighting of the nightclub, but in the bright glaring light of the yakitori booth, surrounded by paler Japanese, men to whom she stood eye to eye, the brown eyes more feline than Asian, the thicker curly hair, and the full lips she now licks nervously under my scrutiny are all a history. "I'm sorry. I've been stupid. Bobby Jack-son was your father."

"Yes." The rest of what she says is drowned out by the din of the train passing overhead. She fishes in her handbag and withdraws a pho-tograph, a black-and-white snapshot of a young black man in a civilian windbreaker smiling broadly into the camera. It is encased in plastic as if it is a official document to last a lifetime.

"When was this taken?"

"Nineteen seventy-two. The year before I was born, I think."

"Where, here in Tokyo?"

"No, my mother work in Tachikawa."

"The air force base." It is just west of Tokyo.

"You in air force?"

"No, in the navy. In Yokosuka." She nods, only dimly absorbing the logistics of the American military presence in Japan a quarter-century before.

"Did you ever try to contact him?"

"My mother write, but letters come back."

"He probably moved. And I expect there are a lot of Bobby Jacksons in Detroit. It's a common name." The air force undoubtedly did not help in tracking down her father.

She nods, a sad resignation that is all the more poignant because she is so young.

"Has it been difficult for you?"

"Difficult for me?"

"Has life been hard for you?"

"Oh yes, very hard sometimes. Not so many friends." Another overhead train roars through the silence. She suddenly smiles brightly. "But I practice English. I study very hard. Maybe I get good job with American company."

"Do you study English formally?"

"Oh yes. I go to Rikkyo University."

"You go to college?"

"College. Yes. I study business and economics. Not—how you say—full-time. I work long hours, so I study—how you say—part-time."

"That's how we say it."

"I graduate maybe two years more. You think I maybe get job with American company?" I marvel at her game plan, but the idea of her working for a Japanese company is apparently unthinkable.

"Why don't you come to the United States?"

"Not so many job there, I think. Very hard."

"Yes, but it's gotten much better. And you'd have an edge."

"An edge?"

"A woman who is half-black, half-Japanese who has studied business and economics in Japan, knows the system, and speaks the language fluently would have an advantage."

"It is advantage to be a half-black, half-Japanese woman in America?" There is an unbelieving wonder in her voice.

"Yes, it could be." How do you explain the paradoxes of affirmative action to a foreigner, who is practically an untouchable in her own country? "You don't believe me."

She stares at me in silence, then looks away at the Japanese men crowding the adjacent tables. "An American businessman say same thing to me one time, but I think he make a joke of me same as Japanese, and I say nothing." She turns back to study me. "But you, I think, are a sincere man."

"Yes, I am. The key is having an education and being an American."

"But I am not American."

"That's not a problem. If you want to be, that can be arranged. It's not very hard to prove your father was an American serviceman."

The thunder of the Yamanote line once again stuns us into silence. This Black Rose is a college girl the same age as my daughter Erika, but how different their lives have been. But then their lives would have been entirely different if Mari had grown up in Detroit, except then she would have had a lot more friends. Perhaps that, ultimately, is what gives her her edge, growing up an outcast in the world's most homogeneous country.

"I went to American school in Tachikawa," she says, as a point of pride.

"Really."

"Yes. Very hard because my English is not so good. But Americans are much nicer. In Japanese school I have only one friend. A boy who has American GI father, but he is white. He killed himself. Japanese make him feel so bad, he cut throat. I am very sad, depressed, you know?"

"Yes."

"I don't go to school. My mother very worried. She goes to air force officer and says, 'GI boy kill himself.' So I go to school on base with air force angels. It is better."

"But not terrific."

She gives me a polite smile.

"Talk to me. Tell me about your life."

"Japanese do not like to talk about self. Not like Americans."

"Talk to me," I repeated. "It's important for me to know how the Japanese think."

"How Japanese think," she repeats. "Japanese men rich now, so they keep Americans out of Black Rose, except for gaijin ghetto, unless special guest like you. Many American girls at club. You see them?" Mari asks with some passion.

"Yes. My friend Ozu-san made a point of pointing them out."

"Not so nice now. Japanese men treat own women like toilets. So I work in gaijin ghetto and practice English with very nice men like you."

I take out a business card and hand it to her. "Write me from time to time," I say. "Practice your English letter-writing. No promises. But when you graduate, we'll see . . ." I leave it unfinished.

She carefully examines my card, then looks up. "Thank you, Peter Saxon. You are very nice to me." In a way it is a question.

"You're Bobby Jackson's little girl."

"In Japan I am *kuronbo*."

"What does that mean?"

"Black. But it is not a nice word."

"We have words like that. Look, I'm not saying it would be totally wonderful for you in the United States. Hell, it's getting tough for a white middle-aged man. But if you speak English well and have an education from a Japanese university, there will be more opportunities for you there than here. Get your degree and keep your grades up, even if it takes longer. Later, you might want to do graduate work. That would give you another advantage."

She smiles beautifully. "You are a very good advisor, Peter Saxon-san."

"That's what I do."

She again studies my business card. "Attorney at law. You advisor?"

"Mostly I make business deals, as with Ozu-san tonight."

"He not think so much business tonight, I think."

"But why?"

"Japanese men same age as my mother, they have much *kenbei*. You know *kenbei*?"

"No."

"Ah, Japanese word you should know. It mean very much not like Americans"—she gestures with her hands over her stomach—"in guts. So later they treat Japanese women who have American boyfriends like . . . *kuronbo*."

Apparently the ultrapolite Japanese, who have no conversational word for no, have all sorts of words for hidden nastiness. "That happen to your mother?"

"Yes, I think so. But also Japanese girls with white American boyfriends. Sometimes girls make suicide."

I don't want to ask about her mother, and Mari senses it.

"My mother is OK. She save money and open coffee shop in Tachikawa. Very popular. Play all the time Motown music. You know Motown music?"

"Yes. Aren't things better for you in Japan?"

She looks at me, and there is something in the sadness of her smile that breaks my heart. "In Japan, buildings all change, new modern." She gives a little wave of her hand to embrace the unseen glass towers that surround us. "Clothing, music, all the time change, very fashionable." She lightly touches her breast. "In heart, Japanese never change."

"What about at college, at Rikkyo?"

She shakes her head, a discreet side-to-side nod of confusion. "I have a teacher in school in Tachikawa, Mrs. Shapiro. She is very nice. She says I am a very good student, and I should go to college. Then I can get a good job with an American or foreign company and have a better life. Also, Mrs. Shapiro says I am very pretty. Japanese all the time say I am black and ugly. But Mrs. Shapiro says I am black and beautiful." She says it matter-of-factly, not in a way that begs for confirmation. Perhaps working at the Black Rose—outside whatever caste system still permeates Japanese universities—has by now confirmed Mrs. Shapiro's appraisal.

"God bless Mrs. Shapiro."

We finish the yakitori.

"My evening is all paid for," she says.

"That's very generous of Ozu-san and the Kuribayashi Company, but it's late, and I have conference calls to make to Los Angeles."

"You work now?" she asks, not quite believing me.

"Yes, it's this morning in LA now, or yesterday morning. My colleagues are just getting to their offices."

"You are a very nice man, Peter-san. A very handsome man. I like you very much." She is Bobby-Jackson-of-Detroit-in-Michigan's abandoned love child. And she is looking for her father's love in all the wrong places.

"And you are a very beautiful girl. So if anyone asks, you say I drank too much and almost passed out. You just dropped me at my hotel and had to help me to the door. That way you keep the money and Ozu-san saves face."

As we stand, two men at a nearby table watch us intently. One is gaunt, with a pockmarked face and crew cut. The other bigger, beefy, with a bald dome but his side hair pulled back in a brief ponytail, making him look like a misplaced samurai. It had been dark, misty, and my memory of the nuances of Japanese male faces is at best uncertain, but they are the two thugs that had followed me from the Black Rose several nights before.

Without alarming Mari, I quickly exit Yakitori Alley and commandeer the first cab that passes.

At the Imperial I pay off the driver to take Mari home.

"You're a lovely girl, Mari Midori." I kiss her lightly on the fore-head. "Take care of yourself. Finish college. And if you want to come to America to work or establish American citizenship, write me."

Part 2

ADRIFT IN THE
FLOATING WORLD

11

The Floating World

I call Sadie at the studio. "Hey, Saxon, I miss you. Not having you here to schmooze with. What the hell, you're what?—sixteen thousand miles away. I miss you."

"Hey, you're Sadie, Sadie, married lady now."

"Yeah, but I was once Sadie, Sadie, shady lady. You know what amazes me? You're my only heterosexual male friend, real friend."

"How's it going?"

"OK, I guess. Terrific. How's marriage supposed to be? I really don't know. I was too young when I was married before, and I totally fucked that one up. Never had a chance. I want this to work."

"Then give it a chance. It's not easy for him either, you know, with you now head of the studio. Married to Wonder Woman."

"You know better."

There is a silence, and I can hear her blow her nose in a tissue from the marble dispenser on her desk. "Shit, in two minutes I've got to kick-ass a director who's going ten million over budget, and my mascara is running." Then she suddenly changes tack. "Hey, I got a letter from Erika."

"My Erika?"

"Very much your Erika. She's part of a student-faculty committee that's invited me to speak at her commencement. That's cool. Did you put her up to that?"

"I can't put Erika up to anything. She's her own lady. She did ask me about it, though, and I said I thought you might think it was cool."

"Well, you were right. I do think it's cool. Though an audience of Stanford girls like Erika scares the hell out of me."

"Trust me, the rest aren't as tough as Erika."

"I swear when she sets her jaw and looks straight at me, I think I'm looking at you in drag, maybe twenty-five years ago."

"Please don't ever tell her that. You'll devastate her."

Sadie laughs, a deep, throaty sound rich with innuendo. "You know I always find you sexiest when you're being a daddy. It must be biological or something."

"Hey, what's this about?"

"I don't know. Maybe it's about my not having kids. A daughter like Erika someday. Maybe not like her exactly, but you know what I mean."

There is nothing to say, and the silence vibrates for sixteen thousand miles. "Hey, let's talk big business. Am I going to be under you? Let me rephrase that. Are you going to end up president of a megagiant international communications conglomerate?"

"It's not about me."

"I know. That's why everyone's so comfortable with the idea, especially Greenwald."

"You talk to him?"

"We had dinner. He wanted to bring me up to speed and have me confirm how the studio fits, the synergy. If one and one really add up to three-point-five."

"He's still computing how high a price he's willing to pay. What did you tell him?"

"Exactly what I told you before you left. You beam five hundred channels of high-definition digital TV by satellite into a yurt in Outer Mongolia, it's still American movies that will make it pay. Expanding the cable and television operations only makes sense if you have the original product that excites viewers. Gets them to tune us in, not the other networks, not rent a video. Otherwise the whole high-tech *megillah* is just very expensive hardware.

"And the stuff we make here isn't software. That just confuses everybody. Makes those nerds in Seattle and Silicon Valley think they can be moviemakers. Software is that logical digital stuff that runs computers. Our stuff isn't logical. It's irrational, emotional stuff that moves people. Makes them laugh, cry, love, hate, lust, fight, whatever. And the Japanese haven't a clue how to make it. They are truly clueless. At least as far as the rest of this planet. If they could, they would, and they don't. Never have. Forget all that ooohing and aaahing about Kurosawa. That's strictly art house. And if we let the Japanese into the studio, we'll end up like Universal and Columbia, spending the next ten years finessing them out. That cannot be on the table. If it is, *I'm* out of here."

"You told Greenwald that?"

"In so many words, yeah. No, those exact words."

I laugh.

"Why are you laughing at me?"

"I need you here. To kick ass."

"So what's Japan like?"

I hesitate. "Very different. We're not the young conquistadors here anymore."

Sadie catches the hesitation and says softly, "It must have been exciting for you when you were."

"It's not politically correct to say so. It was another time, another world, Sadie."

"*Politically correct!* When the hell did you ever worry about being politically correct? You refused to resign from the Tailhook Association, for chrissakes."

"I cannot and will not cut my conscience to fit this year's fashions."

"My God, now you're quoting Lillian Hellman to defend a bunch of drunken ass-grabbing sexists."

"No, to defend loyalty to comrades."

"Your politics have always confused the hell out of me."

"Actually they're pretty straightforward. I believe fervently in peace on earth, goodwill toward . . . persons. And I sip white wine and generously support liberals working toward warm, fuzzy goals. Show business being what it is, of course, that's much better for business than reverting to my natural fascist tendencies. But if we go into combat—and that's sometimes necessary in this wobbly, volatile world—I want a solid conservative, ready to die for God and country, on my wing, covering my ass."

"I wonder. You're so glib. But there's always that secret part of you—like the picture of Dorian Gray that reveals his hidden sins, his soul—locked away somewhere."

"You're making me into a bad old movie."

"Am I?"

How do you translate another time, another world to the politically correct sensitivities of the millennium?

By August 6, 1964, when Crusaders, Skyhawks, and Skyraiders from the carriers *Ticonderoga* and *Constellation* blasted over the Gulf of Tonkin to attack PT-boat bases along the North Vietnamese coast for the first time, Japan had become the United States' major military outpost.

After World War II and the Korean War, the last U.S. Army ground troops did not actually withdraw from Japan until 1958. But throughout the Cold War that followed and the pell-mell muscling up for Vietnam, the U.S. Navy, Marines, and Air Force remained and expanded their bases. There is, as far as I know, no official figure for the millions of young American men stationed in Japan during the three decades of military buildup.

Navy and air force squadrons swept into Atsugi and Tachikawa, trained for a while, then deployed to Korea, Vietnam, or Thailand. Great armadas of aircraft carriers, cruisers, and destroyers sailed into

Yokosuka and Kobe, operated from those ports for six, seven months, then sailed on, returning year after year.

Just across from the main gate of the U.S. Navy base in Yokosuka, the headquarters for the Seventh Fleet, a red and blue Statue of Liberty crackled at the center of a neon arch spelling out Broadway Avenue. It spanned the narrow street like an electric rainbow.

Sailors and marines swaggered under that neon Arc de Triomphe, walking the walk of conquistadors, as though the blood victory of our fathers were still ours. This was the entrance to the Floating World.

The street, known to sailors as Thieves Alley, was a bawdy carnival midway with cooch shows and bars named like amusement park rides—the Playmate Pen, Heaven & Hell, the Jet, the H-Bomb, San Francisco. Hand-lettered sandwich boards advertised HOT SEXIEST GIRLS, BIGGEST DRINKS & BIGGEST BOSOMS IN TOWN, BROWN BAGGERS, COME IN & SUFFER! And many sailors wandered from concession to concession, spent all their money there, and never ventured further. There was a Thieves Alley outside every U.S. base.

But this randy, hell-bent Floating World extended from "underneath the lantern by the barracks gate" to the trendy clubs of the Ginza and Roppongi, only a commuter's train ride north, up the murky shore of Tokyo Bay. It was there, to the Black Rose, that Tommy Cochran led me.

Cochran was two years my senior, an Annapolis man, and by tradition he had served a tour of duty aboard a destroyer in these Asian waters salting down his ensign bars before volunteering for flight school.

> "Up, up the long delirious burning blue
> I've topped the wing-swept heights with easy grace,
> Where never lark, or even eagle, flew;
> And, while with silent, lifting mind I've trod
> The high untrespassed sanctity of space,
> Put out my hand, and touched the face of God."

"This is poetry. It is very nice," Lilli said solemnly. "But airplane is not for touching face of God. When little girl, I walk for days through ruins, piles of dead people, all burned, killed by airplanes."

Cochran was silent a moment, glanced at Junko, then said, "No, you're right. I'm a samurai, not a priest. I serve God and country. But not in that order."

"A samurai," Lilli repeated and studied the dark, lean, handsome face. "Yes, I think so." She was fascinated by Cochran, the dark, moody, poetic outbursts to which the Irish are often wont after a few belts.

"Almost became a priest but went to Annapolis instead. A compromise." He squeezed Junko's hand and smiled slyly at her, as if it were she who had led him astray.

"This is a *compromise?*" Lilli pronounced the word carefully, the way she did when she was adding another word to her vocabulary.

"Oh yeah, Annapolis is a monastery. Discipline, ceremony, even celibacy, but without the vows."

The Black Rose's Filipino dance band had segued into "She Loves You," and the whole band suddenly chanted out the chorus, "She loves you. Yeah, yeah, yeah," with a sniggering glee.

I led Lilli to the dance floor, and we embraced for a foxtrot. She ran her forefinger over my lapel pin of gold navy wings, testing the sharpness of the point of a wing with her fingertip, as a child tests the prick of a pin. She gave a quick, pained intake of breath and sucked her finger.

"Airplanes frighten me very much," she said, staring at the pin as if it were the plane itself.

"They scare the hell out of me, too."

There was a rough tap on my shoulder. "Mind if I cut in."

My immediate impression was of dark scrappy features and the pug nose of an adolescent kid, his hair clipped to the skin at the temples with a short sandy brush on top. He might have been the apple-cheeked all-American marine, but now he was flushed and mean with booze.

I glanced at Lilli, but she was silent, expressionless. I smiled at the guy, "Sorry. I'm signed up for the evening," implying that there was a formal arrangement here.

"That's OK. I'll take care of the hostess fees. Lilli here and I are ol' friends." The smile was smug and lewd.

Lilli looked from me to the other guy with bright excited eyes.

"Sorry."

"The hell you say! You *golf balls* just float in?" He slurred the marine's term for navy men with heavy contempt. The guy was beefy, perhaps an inch taller than I was. He reached for Lilli's hand, but at that moment I swung her away and boogied off to the beat.

In seconds I had maneuvered two or three couples between us. He just stood there, frustrated and angry, then embarrassed at being on the dance floor alone.

"Who's your old friend?"

"His name is Brannigan." She didn't volunteer anything more, and we danced in silence.

"She loves you. Yeah, yeah, yeah," the Filipino musicians chanted up on the bandstand.

"It's late," I said in a quiet voice.

Lilli leaned back to look up at me. "We may leave when you like."

Bad-ass Brannigan was stalking us in the smoky gloom at the edge of the dance floor, stoking his frustration with alcohol. I joined up with my wingman. Cochran and Junko were still at the table.

Lilli excused herself to cash in her pay chips, instructing me to meet her at the door in five minutes.

"We're going to grab a bite."

Cochran waved a boozy benediction. "*Pax vobiscum*. And rock 'n' roll."

Outside, jazz blared from a club across the street. There was a cab at the curb. We had no sooner pulled away when Brannigan burst through the door of the Black Rose into the harsh red glare of the neon sign. He glowered up and down the street, coiled to attack in either direction, spotted the cab, jogged a few steps after it, then savagely hurled the glass in his hand. Over the accelerating whine of the cab engine, I heard the glass explode against the pavement.

The car careened to the right around a corner, and Brannigan was gone—Lilli, busy instructing the driver, had not seen him—and then the cab took a sharp left out of the narrow side streets onto the glowing neon-walled Ginza.

At Lilli's command the taxi let us off under the tracks of Yuraku-cho station. A dozen or more little yakitori booths, each with a large fuming hibachi, were wedged side-by-side in the alley alongside the railroad rampart. Despite the lingering winter chill, the outdoor tables were crowded. Packs of Japanese men, apparently office workers, each in a dark suit and loosened tie, huddled over their food, beer, and cigarettes in a yellow pall of cigarette and soy smoke.

"It is a little bohemian, I think," Lilli offered, as we crammed knee to knee at a table inside one of the train-car-sized shops.

Her precise schoolgirl English with its shy Japanese intonation had its own allure that made me lean forward to hear her. Unlike, say, Junko's pidgin, there was a grammatical base to Lilli's English, learned in school, but she spoke carefully as if measuring her phrasing, and every now and then an odd literary phrase, picked up in her reading, popped out.

"Have you read this F. Scott Fitzgerald?" She pulled out an American paperback copy of *Tender Is the Night* from her handbag.

"Only *The Great Gatsby*." It had been required in an English class.

"But this is a novel of increasing popularity and reputation," she said, probably quoting the jacket.

"With people who read novels. I don't read a lot of novels."

"Why is that? You are educated at a very good university. You are an officer. But you do not read literature."

"There's not that much free time," I defended myself. "And I read mostly nonfiction."

She ignored my excuse. "This is a very beautiful story. Very beautiful and sad. Bittersweet, I think."

The clamor of a train braking into Yurakucho station on the railroad overhead broke the conversation. As the noise receded, a voice thick with a husky southern slur came from over my left shoulder, "Well, looka here now. It's ol' Lilli of the lamplight. Our own sweet-ass Lilli . . . what-the-fuck."

Lilli looked up startled, then frightened. She looked back at me expectantly.

I turned to Brannigan, who loomed over me menacingly, his dark face flushed and his eyes thickly veined with blood. "Can I do something for you?"

"Yeah, golf ball," he said in a mocking voice. "I want to dance with Lilli-san here under the lamplight." He reached forward to grab her hand.

I caught his wrist. His arm jerked, as if he had expected to shake off my grip by an easy flip, but I held fast. We locked, straining and trembling in a frozen arm wrestle, glaring at one another.

"Outside," he said and yanked away from the table. I followed him through a side door into an alleyway piled with garbage cans and wood crates.

I had no sooner stepped out the door than Brannigan whirled and swung on me. It was a wild roundhouse, and the force almost bowled me over. But Brannigan had been too rushed and too aggressive and swung without looking when I was right behind him. The blow went around me and pummeled me on the back. His charge carried him right into me, and we both went crashing into garbage cans and boxes that tumbled and splintered about us.

Brannigan's size and frenzied power panicked me. A moment before I had planned cagily to take advantage of a big guy with a few drinks too many under his belt, dance inside and pound his alcohol-queasy guts. But now I was flopping around in garbage, fighting for my life against a madman.

Garbage cans banged between us. Brannigan flung a can out of the way, spewing trash and chicken bones, and came charging at me again. I backed up and, more by instinct than skill, blocked a vicious right and then a left. I fell against a brick wall, bounced off, and tied up Brannigan's flailing hands. He drove me back into the wall, slamming me against it as if he were trying to crush me to death against the bricks in his wildness.

His knee came up sharply to kick me in the groin, but he was off balance, and his knee stabbed painfully into my thigh. I felt him slip in the garbage, and I drove off the wall, shoving him back. He skidded, stumbling for footing, and I hit him low, one, two, with all my desperate, ruthless fear exploding into his belly.

He let out a hoarse bellow and crouched so low he might have dropped to his knees, covering up with both hands.

I stepped back, blindly grabbed a garbage can, and swung it. The can slammed Brannigan broadside in the head and shoulders and knocked him sprawling face down in the dirt. Even then, his arms and legs were churning to heave him back up.

I still had a hold on the can, and I brought it down like a sledgehammer on the back of his head and back.

He was still only a moment or two, then got his elbows under him and started to rise up, but his muscles did not quite have the strength.

I stepped forward with every intention of kicking him in the head. It was sheer survival. The next time he got up he would kill me.

At that moment Brannigan raised his head and looked at me, as if expecting the kick. He was hurt, and the pain was in his eyes. The madness was gone.

I hesitated, and he let out a breath, then pushed himself and rolled over, face and belly up, like a dog signaling submission. The fight was over.

I was not about to give him a hand up. I stumbled back into the yakitori shop, shoving through the silent, awed crowd gathered at the backdoor. Lilli was not among them but still sat at the table by herself. She looked up at me with anxious eyes and, I'd like to think, a pleased smile playing on her lips but did not say anything. I shook my head, attempted a grin, then took her hand and led her out of the shop as quickly as I could move.

In the cab the pain began. My scalp was bleeding where Brannigan had banged me against the bricks. "I've got to go somewhere I can get fixed up."

"You break something?" she asked, very concerned.

"The conduct of an officer and gentleman."

"I do not understand."

"A bad joke."

"You joke, you not hurt very bad, I think."

I started to laugh, but my ribs hurt. I groaned. "Actually I hurt all over. But you ought to see the other guy." The ugly truth was that I was terrifically excited. I had not been in a fistfight since high school, and here I was having a knock-down-drag-out back-alley brawl over a beautiful Japanese cabaret girl.

In the backseat Lilli stanched the blood from my scalp wound with a handkerchief, ran her hands under my jacket, her fingers tenderly probing my bumps and bruises, convincing herself by touch that I was really not badly hurt, then announced, "I will be your nurse."

She directed the cab to a Japanese-style hotel with private baths, actually a large room separated into stalls by wood partitions. The quiet voices, soft laughter, and the sound of splashing water of others unseen echoed off the intricately tiled walls and ceiling.

Lilli, as unself-conscious as any nurse, insisted on undressing me. Then, as I sat on a low wooden stool, she gently lathered and massaged me, mewing and sighing sympathetically at my scrapes and now purpling bruises. I administered my own old home remedy of alcohol and aspirin to ease the charley horses and swellings and sat sipping hot sake as Lilli then bathed herself from a large ceramic bowl.

"Do you know who Circe is?" I asked.

"Circe?"

"In Greek mythology, in the story of *The Odyssey*, she's a beautiful enchantress who turns the young warriors—returning from the Trojan War—into rooting pigs. You didn't even drug us with a magic potion, but you had us brawling in the garbage." I ran my fingers across her belly. "It's just a spell you weave."

"Circe, the beautiful enchantress from *The Odyssey*," she repeated thoughtfully. It was another English lesson to be memorized. But then she favored me with a radiant smile and kissed me lightly on the lips.

Then she turned away and bent forward, washing her thighs with a large yellow-flowered cloth. Her bare spine made a graceful bow, her breasts hanging free, amplified in their fullness, her hair tumbled loosely about her face and shoulders. At that moment, in spite of my pains, I understood Brannigan's panic and rage at losing her.

She rinsed herself, then led me into a deep, steaming pool. The steam, the hot water, and the alcohol dissolved every throbbing ache but one, and I pulled her to me. But she pushed me away with a playful gentleness. "Not in hot water. You feel nothing," she whispered, then stroked my cheek and kissed me in a way that told me all that had gone before was merely foreplay.

Later, after my nerve ends had exploded for the second time, I rose and groped my way down the hall to the small communal toilet.

Returning, I stood for a moment looking out a window into the dark, narrow street below. The sudden flare of a match caught my eye. The man below in the street brought the cupped flame up to his face to light a cigarette, and in its glow I saw Brannigan's tough blunt features.

I watched for several minutes, but he didn't move. He simply stood there smoking, staring up at the hotel, as if searching for some sight of Lilli.

It occurred to me for the first time, what if Brannigan had been the one who had returned from the alley? Would she be here with him? It was a question that arose in my mind several times over the next months, but I never dared ask it.

I returned to the room. She was asleep, curled on her side like a baby. I peeked out a corner of the window. The street below was deserted, Brannigan gone.

I lay back down on the hard tatami, now restless with the sharp aches of my brawl. Beside me under the silken quilt Lilli breathed softly. I caressed where her hip curved into its voluptuous swell. She stirred and fell asleep again. My fingers glided over the velvet of her flesh to the angry slick fire scar near the base of her spine, that intimate deep wound only a lover dared to explore.

In January of 1992, Yoshio Sakarauchi, the Speaker of the Japanese House of Representatives, quipped to the great laughter of the Parliament that he was sorry the American sailors in Yokosuka no longer had money for good times in Japan. It was, perhaps, the Speaker's way of announcing that the American sexual occupation of Japan was over. The dollar was then plunging to its post–World War II low, worth only 79 yen.

Reading the story in the *Los Angeles Times* over granola, nonfat milk, and black coffee in my breakfast nook in Pacific Palisades, I heard the half-century of bitter jealousy echoing behind the Parliament's laughter, and the gloating.

Today the Japanese no longer gloat. The yen fluctuates nervously. On a given day it takes 119 to 147 yen to buy the stable dollar, and Tokyo's Nikkei stock index spasms up and down around a thirteen-year low.

But that year of '64—when our aircraft carriers shuttled from Yokosuka to Yankee Station in the South China Sea—the dollar bought 360 yen, and the United States recorded its first trade deficit with Japan, as Japanese autos and television sets invaded our markets.

As we struck across the Gulf of Tonkin to bomb North Vietnam, the dominant explosions in Tokyo were the boom of pile drivers and the clang of steel girders as workers labored through the steaming nights to raise office buildings, elevated expressways, and stadiums in time for the Olympics in October.

The gleaming new Olympic Express Highway from Tokyo International Airport to the National Stadium traced the old Highway 1 on which MacArthur's motorcade had entered the charred ruins of the city nineteen years before. The red and white candy-cane spire of the Tokyo Tower rose up, beam by beam, until the metal-framed spike pierced the sky a self-congratulatory forty feet higher than the Eiffel Tower.

I have a purpose in making this economic report. These great currents of history created the eddies and swirls in which Lilli, Junko, Cochran, and I were caught up like so much flotsam and jetsam to work out our individual passions and survival in the Floating World.

Americans did not invent the Floating World. We simply occupied what had traditionally existed in Japan, commandeering it from the middle-aged, married Japanese men whose domain it had been, inflating prices beyond their reach, and without intention, expanded it.

For instance, Japan was the most prosperous nation in Asia in '64, but the young office ladies who spent ten hours a day making tea and answering phones or the salesgirls endlessly bowing to customers in department stores made about eighty-two dollars a month.

However, in the clubs of the Floating World, the prettiest of these excruciatingly bored working girls and struggling college students could earn many times those impoverishing wages acting as hostesses at a continual party.

Lilli seldom talked about her family, but I picked up that she was the main support of a younger sister and an aunt who had raised them after their mother's death.

One night Lilli, Junko, Cochran, and I had gone out for tempura, a favorite after-hours snack. Lilli studied the four bowls of rice, hardly touched, sitting on the table, shook her head, and sighed. "That was our ration—my mother, my aunt, and my sister—for a week. We had to mix it with soybeans and barley, weeds even, not to starve."

Junko sighed also, nodded solemnly, and said something in Japanese, from her expression and tone briefly sharing her own memory of privation with Lilli, to which Cochran and I were not privy.

In the three decades following World War II, the Floating World became a way of bursting their childhood shrouds of wartime poverty and deprivation for many Japanese girls, a rite of passage. The clubs were where the American boys were—single men in their twenties, selected for their health and sense of adventure by the Pentagon and made relatively wealthy by the exchange rate and Japan's long postwar impoverishment.

But we were invested with more than money. We arrived glamorized by American movies and music, cast in our own artful mythologies. And we actually jitterbugged, boogied, then rock 'n' rolled and discoed, to the delight of Japanese girls. Let the good times roll.

For three decades Japanese men looked on and seethed. In that bitter brickbat that resonates to this day, we Americans were overpaid, oversexed, and over there.

The median age of marriage for Japanese women rose from twenty-two at the official end of the occupation in 1949 to twenty-eight by the end of the Cold War in 1989. Sociologists cite several reasons, but with typical Japanese evasion, no one has yet mentioned the seductions of the Floating World inhabited by millions of American servicemen and Japanese women.

In our carrier's wardroom lounge there was a well-thumbed issue of *National Geographic* dated October 1964, with a lead article headed "Tokyo—the Peaceful Explosion." The writer, a former foreign service officer, reported on the great changes occasioned by that month's Olympics and included interviews with geishas and hostesses.

"What Tokyo's thousands of nightclub hostesses lack in formal training," William Graves reported with apparent surprise, "they make up for in beauty and brains. Many are better read and better informed than the average university graduate."

I met girls working in the bars of Thieves Alley who hungered to discuss Camus and Dostoyevsky. Lilli's own reading tended toward American novels. It was her canny way of studying English. She would first read a Japanese translation, then, if she liked the story—invariably a romance with a tragic ending—she would reread it in English.

"Do you know this book?" she often asked. "This is very beautiful and sad. Bittersweet, I think."

When I first met Lilli, I left Tokyo with a book list to be filled with paperback editions from the Yokosuka PX. I returned with two of the titles, plus a selection of my own, Hemingway's *A Farewell to Arms*. "It's very beautiful, very sad. Bittersweet," I said.

Lilli oohed and aahed over the books, fingering them like jewels, carefully unfolding the wrappings. I had taken the trouble to have the three paperbacks artfully gift-wrapped in the Japanese manner by a Thieves Alley shopkeeper.

Then she jumped up and kissed me passionately. My small present endeared me to Lilli infinitely more than beating Brannigan's brains out had done.

"You know *sayonara*? This word, not this book," Lilli later asked me.

"Good-bye."

"It is a little sad, very delicate shade. It means 'If it is so, we must part.'"

The arrivals and departures of squadrons and ships circulated through the Floating World as rapidly as at ComPac headquarters.

"Your lady Lilli is a still water that runs very deep and dark," Tommy Cochran said. "Not a party girl like Junko. And not a lady to trifle with, boy-san." We were on the train back to Yokosuka. "Tread gently and be on guard, for we are strangers in a strange land, with our pants down."

Cochran, two years older, with the experience of his west-Pac cruise aboard a destroyer, was given to pulling philosophical rank. He sat slumped back with his eyes shut, and for a while I thought he was asleep. Then he suddenly recited in a whisper,

"Nor law, nor duty bade me fight,
Nor public men, nor cheering crowds,

A lonely impulse of delight
Drove to this tumult in the clouds."

"What's that?"

"'An Irish Airman Foresees His Death' by William Butler Yeats."
Cochran laughed, then continued,

"I balanced all, brought all to mind,
The years to come seemed waste of breath,
A waste of breath the years behind
In balance with this life, this death."

Our leave in the Floating World had ended, and we sailed the
next morning on the tides of war for Yankee Station and the guns of
Phuc My Luc.

12

The Skeletons in Japanese Closets

I awake sweating from dreams and nightmares I'd hoped I had forever vanquished. And as in the past, whenever I have dreamed of Lilli, Tommy Cochran, or Vietnam, there is always this astonishment that a lifetime has passed, and I lie there in the bewildered twilight between past and present, slowly registering that I am now this middle-aged man who has somehow survived, even flourished. But this morning, after the particulars of the dream evaporate, there remains a disturbing feeling, a conviction that I can still reach out my hand and grasp it.

I rise and will myself to exercise—a morning discipline of push-ups, sit-ups, and stretches—then stumble out to an early morning jog.

The bumper-to-bumper morning traffic belching exhaust into the Marunouchi business district does not make the avenue the healthiest place to jog, but the dark greenery of Hibiya Park just across from the hotel offers a more serene path. I slog through the black pine groves and fountains surrounding the Imperial Palace. My biological clock has not yet reset to the sixteen-hour day-for-night time change, and exotic food and alcohol at bizarre hours are confusing it even more. It is a matter of faith with me that exercise reorients the body, focuses the dark labyrinthine workings of the mind.

There's an overcast with a dank chill in the air, and I run stiffly, heavy-footed, laboring, under a canopy of dogwood trees, across a medieval moat lined with irregularly shaped dark stones, then along the moat onto the broad lawns of the outer palace grounds.

To my left, beyond forbidding stone walls, the inner moat, and dark stands of towering evergreens, is the sanctuary of the Imperial Palace itself. Even at that early hour there are groups of Japanese tourists assembled in chattering, grinning phalanxes for snapshots with the Nijubashi, the landmark double bridge, in the background.

I pass other joggers, all decked out in designer warm-up suits, who smile at me, fellow travelers from other luxury hotels along Hibiya Dori. This is apparently the trendy place to jog when in Tokyo.

I circle around the Imperial Palace Plaza, now following another, inner moat. I sweat, but I'm still tight and breathing heavily, working hard, running with resolution rather than rhythm.

The rough, steep black granite walls of the moat are oppressive, brooding fifteenth-century bulwarks to keep out invaders. Then a memory hits me. I turn and run back to the Imperial Palace Plaza and, breathing thickly, stop to stare at the double bridge that is the main approach to the palace.

It was here in this plaza that Lilli's father had knelt, faced the palace, bowed his head, slipped the short sword from its black lac-quered scabbard, and plunged the nine-inch blade into his left side. With an insane will he forced that silk hilt from left to right, disemboweling himself, but in his agony still had the strength to give the blood-soaked hilt a final quarter turn and force the blade up into his heart. He had been one of the many who committed ritual seppuku that day in 1945 on this spot.

I now watch the groups of giggling Japanese tourists line up in front of the Nijubashi and then—what I had missed before—their faces transform, become dead serious and reverent for the photograph.

Preoccupied with my own personal history, present and past, I had forgotten all that. Did I dare?

I trudge back to the hotel and into the lobby. *"Mr. Saxon."* The urgency in the voice turns me.

I don't recognize the girl at first. The thick wavy hair is pulled back into a ponytail, a leather jacket thrown over her shoulders to ward off the morning chill, the long slender legs now clad in jeans and boots. She looks like any college girl on her way to class the world over, even totes a book bag across her shoulder. But she wears wraparound sunglasses as though there's a glare here in the lobby to be avoided.

"I am so sorry to disturb you. I called first, but you were out. So I come to wait for you. I am so sorry if I disturb you. Are you hurt? You are—how you say—lame."

"I'm limping. Limping is temporary. Lame is more serious, usually permanent. It's an old . . . injury. Bothers me when I don't get enough sleep or am under tension or out of shape. And all three conditions apply now."

"Thank you again for the English lesson, Saxon-san." Mari Midori makes a slight bow of the head and smiles, but there's something tremulous and frightened in her voice. "Maybe I should not be here," she says in a nervous whisper.

I wonder myself what the hell she's doing there. Then I notice a slight discoloration along her cheek that the sunglasses do not quite hide.

"I've been jogging. I'm thirsty and hungry. Have you had breakfast?" I take her arm and lead her down into the lounge just off the main lobby. It is as intimate as Grand Central Station but only half as large, with great pale gold pillars that ascend and disappear into recessed wells of subdued light.

"Thank you very much. Not eat so much early. Maybe a little juice of fruit."

We sit down at a table veneered in pale gold wood to match the pillars. I reach across, and before she quite realizes what I am doing, I slip off her sunglasses.

A puffy welt runs from her eye along her cheek. "Let's put some ice on that before it swells up and discolors more," I say. "I'm an expert on minor injuries. I'm always getting them."

She quickly puts the sunglasses back on just as a waitress materializes. "Two large orange juices, whole wheat toast, and coffee, please. Anything else?" I ask Mari.

"Yes, coffee. That is very nice."

"Oh, a bowl of ice, please. And an extra cloth napkin." I point to the side of my head. "I banged into a cherry tree when I was jogging. Want to put a little ice on it."

"You hurt?" the waitress asks with great concern, examining my face.

"Not serious." I gingerly touch my temple.

"Oh yes, ice very good," the waitress agrees. "I bring very soon."

"Thank you." To Mari, "What happened?"

She doesn't answer right away, as though collecting herself. "This morning two men come to my apartment, wake me up. They say they are police, but they are not police. They maybe Yakuza, gangsters. They ask questions about you."

"About me? What kind of questions?"

"They want to know if I have good time with you. What we do, maybe sex?"

"You never saw these guys before?"

"No. I am very frightened."

"With very good reason."

"So I say what you say. You drink too much, and I help you to hotel."

"They laugh, make fun of me. Insults. Say you do not like *kuronbo*, a black girl. Bad things like that. Then they ask question about your old girlfriend from Black Rose. What did you say about her? I say you say nothing about old girlfriend. One hit me and say I lie. I am very frightened."

I nod, pushing down my rage. "You should have told them everything I said. It didn't really matter."

"I say her name is Lilli. They do not speak English. They cannot say it. They say it is not Japanese name and I lie again. He makes motion to hit me again, and I cry, 'Is true. It is work name for Americans.' Why they want to know these things?"

"I don't know. I don't know what the hell's going on."

"I very frightened, so I tell make-believe story."

"What did you say?"

"We go to Yakitori Alley like you and old girlfriend Lilli, and you tell me story. Very romantic story, very sad. A beautiful Japanese girl and a tall, handsome American airman live in Floating World where everybody laughs and dances rock 'n roll. Good times every night. And the handsome American is rich, and you bring her beautiful presents. And money. And she gives money to family so they are not so hungry and poor. She and other beautiful girls live alone, not with family like other Japanese girls. And it is their world—how you say—private?"

"Yes, private."

"Yes, their private world, this Floating World. And in afternoon, they go to American Hollywood movies and eat ice cream. Eat all time in very nice restaurants. And in April you and beautiful girl go for walks in rain of cherry blossoms. You find beautiful secret place and make love on carpet of cherry blossoms. You love her very much. You say you will marry her and take her to America. But air force sends you back to America, and you have new life and forget her."

Her tears touch me. I wonder if they touched the Yakuza hoods, or if they had a clue that she had recounted the story of her own mother and father. I marvel at Mari, ripped from her bed at dawn by two goons, spinning this romantic fable, like Scheherazade, to save her head.

"Did they believe you?"

"Oh yes, I think so."

Of course they did, because she herself totally believed this romantic vision of luxuriant rock 'n' roll love among the cherry blossoms. Was it a story that her own mother had told the shunned and abused half-caste bastard to make her feel she was the heir to a romantic legacy? My own memories have darker shadows.

"And these Yakuza get very angry, maybe jealous."

"Is that when they hit you?"

Her eyes turn downward, as though it is her personal shame. "They very angry. They say Ishii-san must know this."

"Who?"

"They say Ishii-san. I do not know this name."

"Write it down for me."

"Please, I am not so good to write Japanese names into English."

"Write it in Japanese characters and what you think it might be in English."

She takes a pad from her purse and writes.

It still has no meaning for me. "I have a favor to ask."

"Yes," she nods.

"I want you to write me a long, detailed letter about what happened. What the two men said and did. Write it in English or Japanese or both, whatever is the most accurate. If they said something like this name Ishii that is not accurate in English, then please write it in Japanese. I can have it translated."

"Is this important to you?"

"I don't know. Why do you think they were Yakuza?"

"All the time shout, make threats. One have—how you say—skin pictures."

"Tattoos?"

"Tattoos. Yes, one very bad. Yakuza have tattoos on arms, on body. Never see, only when take off shirt. You understand?"

"Yes."

"This bad Yakuza have tattoos on hands. Head of dragon. Right hand, left hand. Everybody see he is bad Yakuza."

"Dragon heads?"

"Oh yes."

"The other one. Was he bald?" I run my hand across the center of my scalp and grip the ruff at my neck. "I mean no hair here but a ponytail?"

Mari's eyes go wide. "You know Yakuza?"

"These two were following me the other night."

Mari lets out a low exclamation like a moan.

"Are you in any danger? Will they come back?"

"Why they come back?"

"I don't know. I don't know what the hell's going on. You should go to the police."

She is silent.

"Why not?"

"I am a *kuronbo* who work in cabaret, maybe owned by Yakuza. Police not help me. I maybe get into big trouble. At work. At school."

"But you haven't done anything."

Again Mari is silent. Obviously that isn't the point. A half-black cabaret girl working her way through a Japanese university has to keep her head down.

The waitress arrives with our orange juice, coffee, and a bowl of ice. She hovers about, curious to see what I am going to do with the ice. I thank her with the universal nod of dismissal.

I've deliberately taken a table against the far side of one of the thick golden columns so that it effectively blocks being seen from the lobby. I wrap the ice in a cloth napkin, making a pack, and press it against Mari's cheek.

She shakes her head.

"No one can see you from here. It'll prevent swelling. Put ice on it several times today, twenty minutes each time. Understand?"

"You are very kind to me."

I sip the orange juice. "Are you in any danger coming here?"

"This is important to you?" she asks.

"Yes, very."

She nods, privately confirming something. "You give me advice on coming to America and maybe becoming American citizen. You say there are opportunities for me, where in Japan doors are closed. You give me business card and say write to you how I am at school." She lays down the ice pack, reaches into her bag, and pulls out my card, delicately holding it in her fingertips as though it is something very fragile. "You are sincere, I think. And all night I do not sleep very much, and I think about this. A different life. I know it is very hard, much work, but it is possible for me, yes?"

"Yes, it's very possible. And I'll help you where I can. Now put the ice pack back on." I raise it back to her temple and cheek.

She studies me with the ice pack partially covering one eye. There it is, that Japanese exchange of obligations. Does she really feel indebted to me for a small kindness, or is she now deliberately putting herself in harm's way to bond my debt to her?

She rises. "You have business to do. I must go now." She glances at her watch and lifts a shoulder bag stuffed with several books.

"You have classes this morning?"

"Later. It is better to study at the university."

"You took a chance coming here?"

"I do not think so." But she glances warily about the lounge and lobby, casing who may be watching her.

"Do you think I should look up my old girlfriend Lilli?"

The question catches her by surprise. She lets out a low breath and shakes her head.

"Why not?"

She shifts the book bag. "My mother owns coffee shop, plays Motown music with big posters of Michael Jackson, 'retha Franklin on wall. Very popular. No big deal if old boyfriend, American GI, visits her. Because that is her"—she gropes for a word—"place in Japan. You understand this *place*."

"I think so."

"I am sorry. If old girlfriend Lilli is married to Japanese, your visit maybe bring shame. Maybe she never tells her husband she work as hostess, she has American boyfriend. You are old skeleton in closet."

In spite of myself, I laugh at the solemn way in which she delivers this.

"Oh yes, lots of American skeletons in Japanese closets."

"Why exactly?"

"Japanese men think if Japanese women sleep with American, they are ruined. Always shame. It is all bullshit in men's head." Then she flashes a professional seductive half-smile. "Don't look for old girl-friend Lilli. You visit me at Black Rose."

For Mari, there is no army of handsome, rich young Ameri-cans—just the occasional gray-haired veteran of the blossom-dappled Floating World.

"If I have time. Mari, you are golden and beautiful. But you're going to have a black eye if you don't keep the ice on it."

As she leaves the lobby, this tawny hybrid beauty, even in her jeans and leather jacket, catches eyes, and both foreign men and women turn to glance at her, but not the Japanese, who seem to avert their eyes.

"Ah, good morning, Mr. Saxon."

In Mari's wake, Ozu suddenly materializes out of the glare of the golden pillars.

13

High Tech, Low Blows

If Ozu has seen Mari, he gives no indication. His face is chalky, and his red-rimmed, shadowed eyes squint, as though the bright lights of the lobby cause him physical pain.

"What's happened?"

"I am to take you on tour of our advanced research center in Tsukuba. You know Tsukuba Science City? It is the future."

"I've read of it." I study Ozu. He moves and talks reluctantly, as though bruised. They are the torpid movements of a man in the throes of a throbbing hangover. But apparently he's been commanded by Hara to entertain me. And aching eyeballs or not, he is determined to be my tour guide to Tsukuba.

He peers at me through hooded, bloodshot eyes. "I came here to wait for you. I called your room, but manager said you are out jogging."

He seems astonished by my exercise. And it is information to me that in a hotel with several thousand guests, a manager is now answering my calls and keeping track of my whereabouts.

I smile. "They take very good care of me here."

The limousine speeds along the Joban Expressway to Tsukuba, the city northeast of Tokyo that is totally devoted to high-tech research. Ozu gingerly sips hot green tea from a thermos. I wait until he carefully sets down the cup and his consciousness is again painfully focused inward on his queasy stomach.

"Ozu-san, why is your faction against this merger?"

"Americans must not own Japanese companies." It comes out as a hiss, even before he realizes what he has said.

"Why not? A great many Japanese have owned American companies?"

He turns to me with an unhappy face. "It has not been decided. It requires much more study." I have caught him totally off guard, and he is desperately backpeddling to retract what he has revealed. He is hurt that I have taken unfair advantage of his condition.

Back at the hotel I had been sympathetic, at first trying to beg off from the tour. But when Ozu insisted that it was Hara-san's invitation, I understood that he would lose face if I did not accept. With Hara in Kyoto, I had no plans for the day other than to catch up on the contract work I had brought along for just such lulls. But this tour of Kuribayashi's advance research facility might be useful background. My work often requires the pretense of familiarity with gigabytes and bandwidths.

Ozu had had telephone calls to make, and I'd suggested that he would be more comfortable in my hotel suite. I'd urged him to eat some breakfast, and he had ordered tea, boiled rice, and miso soup, apparently the Japanese treatment for a hangover.

But he had deliberately waited until I was under the shower to make his calls, and when I had emerged to dress he was still on the phone making arrangements with Tsukuba, judging from the few international words of English and my name that I overheard.

"We have carefully studied the situation, Mr. Ozu." Nothing in Japan is obvious. And I talk to Ozu with the design that whatever I say will be dutifully relayed. "Your country is in a long recession. The only growth area in the Japanese economy is beer sales, which I believe went up three-point-five percent last month. Not necessarily a good sign. What we foresee down the road—say five years from now—

Japanese firms like Kuribayashi that don't have strategic partnerships with American companies may find themselves left in the dust."

I carefully bait Ozu—taking advantage of whatever is troubling him to break that Japanese facade of politeness. "For one thing, you don't have a large enough domestic consumer base to finance the new technology. Japan isn't wired with fiber optics, and your satellite capability is a question mark. Your electronic superhighway is still a dirt road, a bypass. Bypasses are often quaint and interesting, but seldom prosperous. You always need entree to the U.S. market."

Ozu turns to me. During the course of breakfast and the ride, his color has returned. He looks levelly at me and says, "I believe that is *Yankee salesmanship,* Mr. Saxon." From the way he spits the phrase, he means "bullshit." "The Japanese economy will quickly recover its great strength and then lead Asia into the next century. Asia will be our most important market, not the United States, in a few years." He states this as an article of faith.

The limousine now drives through the same haphazard, prefabricated, tilt-up factories—punctuated by an occasional startlingly ultramodern high-rise block—that have transformed the verdant plum and apricot orchards of the Santa Clara Valley into the smog-choked, paved-over sprawl of Silicon Valley.

"You have a place like this in the United States?" he asks.

"We have electronics and chip factories." What I don't see are the shaggy-haired, bearded twenty-somethings in plaid shirts and jeans commuting on motorcycles.

"Like Tsukuba?" Ozu gestures with a proud, all-encompassing sweep. Tsukuba Science City is the high-tech creation of Japanese bureaucracy, whose ethos is that central control is good and total central control is best. Forty miles out of Tokyo, at the northeast edge of the Kanto Plain, at the base of two peaks of the Tsukuba Mountains called Male Mountain and Female Mountain, are crammed together some seventy-six government, university, and private laboratories—a third of the national research institutes.

"Oh no, not all in one place. We like to spread out more. San Francisco, Seattle, Dallas, a belt near Boston, at dozens of universities like Cornell, SC, MIT."

"It is very disorganized in the United States," Ozu says with some smugness. "Here we set goals and all work for them."

Apparently the Japanese theory is that a critical mass of research brainpower in one spot will have some sort of chain reaction, accelerating a technological explosion.

"America operates on our founding fathers' belief that creativity needs a lot more slack," I say. The concept that creativity, by its nature, requires a certain unbuttoned chaos is not just alien to the disciplined, industrious Japanese, it is anathema. This, in fact, is the heart of the matter. But how can I tell that to Kuribayashi and still pull off this deal?

Actually Tsukuba depresses me. It is as if some ironic karma has brought me there. In 1964 I had been a recon pilot—essentially a scout for the nuclear-propelled armada, Mach 2 aircraft, guided missiles, electronic countermeasures, and computerized Integrated Operational Intelligence Centers that had been the spearhead of American technology. Our electronics industry never recovered from that intense military diversion.

The Japanese dominate the key areas, particularly Kuribayashi, which has developed the technologies originally invented in garages in Silicon Valley. And we need them now to seize the strategic advantage.

The limo follows a parklike drive between sleek windowless structures that mushroom up from manicured, almost treeless lawns. It is the setting for a sci-fi movie in which the grubby rebels with a week's growth of beard battle high-tech storm troopers of the future for mankind's soul.

The Kuribayashi Advanced Research Center is five stories of alternating dark rectangles of glass and white concrete slabs that resembles a vertical gridiron of chips—no doubt a conscious intent of the architects. The mall to the entrance is flanked by rows of black pines as studiously placed and clipped as bonsai. It is a design meant to be miniature and elegant, constructed to overwhelming dimensions.

A tight phalanx of managers, all neatly barbered and uniformed in gray suits, white shirts, and regimental ties, greets us. And after the handshaking, bows, and exchange of business cards, we immediately don baggy white nylon jumpsuits, caps, and booties.

Ozu conducts the tour himself, calling on the accompanying executives in Japanese for an explanation here and there, which he translates. Through the corridors of chilled, filtered air, anonymous drones in spanking white dust suits and hoods flurry about us with hurried efficiency.

We trek through a gleaming laboratory in which an electron beam etches patterns exceeding a street map of Tokyo in their complexity on silver-gray flakes of silicon the size of a baby's fingernail.

An ethereal purple-rose colored light pulses at the end of the room, emanating from a circular glass window as high and wide as a man. A quavering alarm buzzes through the lab.

"What's that?"

"Oh, very interesting," nods Yamaguchi, a gaunt man with sunken cheeks who has eagerly but incomprehensibly been explaining the electron-beam lithography. "We fry chips."

The glass window proves to be a hatch set in a heavily instrumented stainless steel wall. A technician in a white robe and hood intently monitors the instruments as an eerie glowing gas, like a mist concealing a violent sunset, floods the chamber. Yamaguchi points, and I peer at whatever it is. Through the gas I make out a rack of silicon wafers the size of salad plates.

Ozu and Yamaguchi confer in Japanese. "The xenon is superheated to two thousand degrees," Ozu explains. "Great heat permanently etches the circuits on the silicon chips."

The gas, superheated to incandescence, glows and wavers in and out of perception at some threshold of the visible spectrum, at once awesomely beautiful and deadly. "Is that glass strong enough?"

"Oh yes, double strong glass," nods Yamaguchi.

We move on to an assembly line of glowing, vibrating monitors and exposed circuit boards. Women in white head coverings and robes like surgical nurses hover over electronic microscopes. At a musical tone over the address system, they all suddenly stand as one, face the front of the room, and massage their eyes with white-gloved pinkies for ten seconds, then promptly sit down again.

At the end of the tour, the squad of managers all shake hands, smile broadly, bow again, and promptly disperse. Ozu excuses himself to call his office, leaving me alone with Yamaguchi, whose English is considerably rougher.

I smile at him and say something like, "Ultimately it comes down to producing a black box that can process five hundred channels of four thousand pixels per nanosecond on demand."

"Oh yes, Kuribayashi is number one," he boasts enthusiastically, and I'm not sure if he means that as a measure of quality or some specific market that the company now dominates.

There is no doubt that Kuribayashi can develop and efficiently produce the next generation of digital television processors. But it still takes that free-floating Hollywood conspiracy of neurotic bearded writers, megalomaniac auteurs with rubber-banded pigtails, pumped-up narcissistic thespians, and hustling barracudas in Armani suits to concoct the spectacles, mythic fantasies, and day-to-day soap operas that, ultimately, will drive the technology. In a way the grubby rebels have won.

Three technicians in white jumpsuits and hoods, their faces hidden behind surgical masks, briskly stride down the corridor, each carrying some sort of staff. Yamaguchi peers at them as they pass by.

Suddenly the three lunge at us—a movement I detect only out of the corner of my eye. My head reels from a whack that drives me to my knees. Another blow sends me sprawling.

I am stunned and too shocked to move, but not out. I instinctively lie still, not to invite a third hit.

There is a deep guttural exchange in Japanese. My feet are seized by several hands, and I'm unceremoniously dragged across the floor for some distance.

I am conscious only that my neck throbs and the jolting sends shooting stars across blackness. I all but pass out.

A metal door like a hatch on a ship opens, and I am heaped on a hard, unyielding low table. Then the hatch clangs shut. The air has a warm, acrid smell that makes me cough violently, rousing me from my stupor. A buzzer sounds, and the alarm has a familiar ominous sound that brings my head up.

I am sprawled across a metal rack holding a dozen and a half round silicon wafers—inside the chamber where the intricate microscopic circuits laid down by computers are permanently etched on those quartz-hard silicon chips. The buzzer is counting down to the instant when two-thousand-degree incandescent crimson gas shoots into the chamber and vaporizes my flesh.

In one movement I pull my legs under me and hurl my shoulder against the glass—and bounce off.

I brace against the tray and kick frantically against the hatch, but my panicky kicks lack any force.

I yank the metal frame by its rim. To my surprise it is merely lying on its pedestal, unattached, and comes loose. With my back to the glass, I swing it in a semicircle like a hammer thrower building momentum and slam it into the glass hatch.

The metal frame hits on a corner. The glass cracks but holds. The alarm suddenly stops. I freeze, expecting in the next instant to be incinerated in a red vapor hotter than fire.

Nothing happens, at least in the next two seconds. I swing again at the glass, and again, now aiming the metal frame directly at the crack. The glass splinters into jagged shards.

Suddenly there are several men in hooded white suits all shouting and jabbing at the hatch on the other side. It swings open, and I stagger out. Still dizzy from the blow to the back of my head, I'm moving on adrenaline and fear.

The first face I recognize is Yamaguchi. His white coveralls are stained with blood from a still bleeding head wound, and he is being half carried with his arms draped about a technician on either side.

When he sees me, his face contorts in some mixture of relief and grief. He lurches free of his two attendants and clutches at my jacket. "I so sorry. I so sorry."

Ozu stands to one side staring at me with a bloodless, stricken face.

"We must call the police," Ozu says.

"No, you must not call the police," I insist for the third time. "That's what they want. To create an incident that will make us call off this deal. At the least, get it into the newspapers in a way that terribly embarrasses Kuribayashi. No one must answer any calls from the press."

"Who are they, Mr. Saxon?"

"They're your people, Mr. Ozu. You tell me. Who are they?"

Ozu is silent.

We're in the research center's medical clinic. A company doctor has finished his examination. I'm luckier than Yamaguchi, who has a concussion and requires stitches. The blows missed my skull and caught the thick nape of my neck. An inch or two higher and they might have shattered the fragile lower edge of my skull, paralyzing or killing me.

The doctor has given me a painkiller and muscle relaxant, and a young company nurse holds an ice compress to my neck as I sit there.

"Somebody in your company tried to kill me—fry me alive at two thousand degrees. They had access to high-security research areas. They wore your company's protective suits. But most significantly, they were familiar with the workings of your gas chamber."

"I feel a great shame that this happened to you, Mr. Saxon." There is a film of sweat on Ozu's brow and upper lip, and he is visibly shaken. "Perhaps they only meant to frighten you."

"They meant to kill me, Mr. Ozu." The combination of the muscle relaxant and the adrenaline rush makes me high, aggressive. "They thought they hit me harder than they did. They were going to make it look like an accident. That I was snooping around for your technical secrets where I should not have been. The superheated gas wouldn't have left enough of me to examine for foul play."

"Engineers say the chamber is fail-safe," Ozu insists in a low voice. "There are motion detectors inside that shut down operations. Also, after alarm sounds, a technician right outside chamber must initiate the gas flow. Maybe it is, as you say, only to create incident for newspapers, not kill you."

"Did you know about the fail-safe before this?"

"No, only now engineers tell me."

"Maybe they didn't either—whoever they are."

Ozu shakes his head. "I feel great shame."

"Where was everybody, for chrissakes?"

"They are all working with great diligence in their offices. Because there are so many bosses around for your tour." But if Ozu sees any humor in his workers' sudden diligence, neither his voice nor his expression betray it.

"What about the technicians?"

"There was no etching of silicon chips scheduled, so they are also in their offices."

"What the hell did they hit me with?"

"It is hardwood kendo sword, I think."

"Kendo? That's pretty exotic."

"It is very popular to practice traditional sword fighting. Many patriotic sports clubs compete."

"Patriotic sports clubs?"

"Yes."

In three days I have had pickled genitalia nailed to my door with a *kai-ken*, been attacked in the Ginza by Yakuza with a samurai *wakizashi*, and been belted with a kendo hardwood. Now, tradition be damned, they have tried to vaporize me with two-thousand-degree xenon.

If either Ozu or Hara knows about the other assaults, they have given no sign. And if I tell them, it may embarrass or alarm Kuribayashi enough to call off the negotiations.

"Who wants to terrorize me, Mr. Ozu?"

"I do not know. I only feel great shame that this happened," he says for the third time.

On the drive back, Ozu is at first silent, sitting with a pale, stricken look. "Excuse me, please, Mr. Saxon."

"Yes."

"I admire you very much."

"Admire me?"

"Yes. If someone had attacked me, I would be very frightened. I would call police. But you are very calm. You think always, 'What is best thing to do?'"

"*Shikata-ga-nai*, Mr. Ozu."

He looks startled. "What?"

"*Shikata-ga-nai*. It cannot be helped. We must be resigned to what happens."

"Yes, I understand, but I am very surprised to hear you use this Japanese."

At that moment the car phone next to Ozu buzzes. He picks it up as though expecting the call.

The conversation is long, but terse at his end, punctuated by a brief, obedient *"Hai"* every few sentences. He hangs up and turns to me. "You will be very pleased, I think. That was Mr. Hara. The trip to Kyoto to confer directly with Mr. Kuribayashi has been arranged." He bows his head slightly as if in respect, but his face becomes a mask that displays anything but pleasure.

The limousine slows to a crawl in the jammed expressway traffic leading to downtown Tokyo.

"Why are your headquarters in Kyoto?"

"Kyoto is old capital of Japan. Very important center of Japanese culture, and it was not bombed. Mr. Kuribayashi went to Kyoto after the war to build new business to make radios, then televisions. All factories in Tokyo were destroyed by bombing."

He makes a gesture that embraces the gritty industrial area now flanking the expressway and the approaching skyline of Tokyo. "This all ashes."

To the west, the spired twin towers of the new Tokyo City Hall and its surrounding cluster of glass and stone skyscrapers rise above the thriving Shinjuku district. And yet some dark cerebral fold conjures up an image of this area as that ruin of ashes and bombed-out hulks of brick. The shops of Shitamachi, the old downtown, stretch to the Sumida River. The bodies had been packed so tightly in the river to escape the firestorm that they could not fall down, even in death. That was how Lilli had once described it to me.

Ozu's eyes study me, the thick lenses of his glasses focusing his attention like rays of sunlight to one hot combustible point.

"Do you remember the bombings and the fire?" I ask.

"It was a very long time ago, Mr. Saxon."

"But do you remember them as a child?"

"Yes."

"*Shikata-ga-nai*, Mr. Ozu."

I look at Ozu. This time he understands.

Yes, this was all ashes. From this spot you could see for miles. The industrial areas with the factory workshops dispersed in homes had been deliberately razed, two-thirds of Tokyo destroyed. The population of seven million people reduced by half. The conversation has suddenly veered. Or has it? Is this always the subtext? How many others with whom I now negotiate grew up, like Lilli, with the stench of ashes and burning flesh in their lungs and this landscape of smoking ruins searing their eyes?

The flames of that funeral pyre had reached 2,000 degrees—remarkably the temperature of the superheated xenon in which I was almost cremated two hours earlier.

In Japan, "the war" has only one meaning. And at the end, it had taken place right here. In the United States, each subsequent generation has had its own war, a foreign adventure abroad—Korea, Vietnam, the Persian Gulf.

"When I was here in sixty-four, sixty-five, this had been totally rebuilt."

"Oh yes, this was all rebuilt."

One Sunday morning, Lilli had roused me early for a "little pilgrimage" to the Sensoji Temple, whose Buddha was reputed to bestow powerful grace. I certainly needed all the grace I could get, because the carrier sailed back to Yankee Station in three days.

The temple was in Asakusa Park, which flanks the Sumida, and afterward we caught a sightseeing boat downriver to the Hamarikyu Gardens at the mouth on Tokyo Bay. But en route the wrathful ghosts that haunt the Sumida stole whatever grace the Sensoji Buddha had bestowed on me that morning.

Now, as then, they are trying to kill me.

14

The Guns of Phuc My Luc

On March 8, 1965, thirty-five hundred marines of the 9th Marine Expeditionary Brigade landed at Da Nang, the first American ground troops to enter Vietnam.

In April a photo recon from the *Coral Sea* snagged the first shots of surface-to-air missile sites in the North, and the same month MiGs shot down two air force F–105s.

By June there were five carriers in the South China Sea, and our interdiction strikes ranged along the entire North Vietnamese coast to within seventy miles of Hanoi. A couple of F–4B Phantoms off the *Midway* ran head-on into a flight of four MiG–17s south of Hanoi. Closing at a thousand miles an hour, the Phantoms fired radar-guided Sparrow missiles and shot down two MiGs, our first aircraft kills of the war.

"This air war is getting challenging," Tommy Cochran blustered with his Annapolis bravado. Cochran was stoked about bagging a MiG.

Cochran and I weren't in the same squadron. I was with the specialized four-plane photo reconnaissance detachment that was aboard each of the carriers. Cochran was in a fighter squadron. But we flew the same aircraft, the F–8 Crusader. Mine was unarmed, equipped with five cameras instead of the four 20-millimeter nose cannons, Sidewinder missiles, and belly pack of 2.75-inch rockets with which Cochran's warbird bristled.

His squadron was usually assigned as fighter cover for our recon runs, and Cochran worked the flight schedule so that he often rode shotgun for me. The truth is that I would have preferred someone with more experience covering my ass, say a lieutenant commander with a combat tour in Korea, but I couldn't say anything.

The North Vietnamese were now setting up early-warning radar sites along the coast and surface-to-air missiles as fast as they could truck them. In August a couple of A–4 attack planes from the *Midway* were shot down by SAMs.

Our strike tactic was now to fly in at low level and high speed, outside the performance parameters of the SA–2 Guideline missiles but unfortunately in range of the radar-directed antiaircraft guns. According to the senior pilots, the North Vietnamese flak was now thicker and more accurate than that over Germany in World War II.

The photo recon planes were taking hits out of all proportion to our numbers. With the restrictions out of Washington, we had to accompany the strike force and fly in immediately after the bombers had passed over the target, exactly when the North Vietnamese radar crews and ground gunners were alerted, zeroed in, ready and waiting for the lone unarmed RF–8 photo plane they knew would be coming in right behind the strike.

Each launch, with my gut tied in a knot, now felt like a suicide mission. A little military secret here—we were experimenting with chemistry just to climb into the planes. Shaken out of bed at two to suit up for the predawn mission briefing, we immediately guzzled navy coffee, black and thick as tar, to wash down tranquilizers bought over-the-counter at Subic Bay in the Philippines. Between the time I exploded off the catapult and the time I radioed "Feet dry" over the coast, the heavy adrenaline rush, tranquilizers, and overdose of caffeine had chemically combined to create a hyperalert buzz, buffering the terror of the 37-millimeter flak and SA–2 missiles to a fine combat edge.

Over Van Hoi I barreled in right behind the attack of A–4 Skyhawks, paralleling the lineup of railroad boxcars, which were now in flames.

Cochran's element wove above me, hunting for MiGs.

Fortunately the antiaircraft gunners stayed on the last few attack planes, and the tracers parted ahead of me like a shimmering red-beaded curtain. I shot the length of the railroad, getting the target coverage for the carrier group commander without getting hit, and then darted straight and low for the sea. It was a mistake.

The radar-directed antiaircraft below had had the returning strike to calibrate on. The guns of Phuc My Luc nailed me halfway to the coast.

I saw the burst out of the corner of my eye—a fireball that slammed into the wings behind me. The plane shuddered and bucked, then yawed to the left.

"I'm hit!" I wasn't wounded, but the plane was. It kept dropping off to the left.

"You're pouring smoke," Cochran reported.

I could see the coast ahead—the thin pale line of dunes and beach, a faint line of breakers rolling in.

"Pete, can you make the coast?" Cochran queried.

"Roger, I can make it."

The escort Crusaders were now jinxing around the sky to keep the radar confused, but I was too busy to notice.

I stared at the distant surf as if I could will the plane to it. But I was already too low, and the plane barely responded to the stick or rudder. The gauges scarcely registered hydraulic pressure. The blast had blown out the lines. The out-of-control aircraft was now descending, paralleling that shoreline. In another moment I would veer back inland, back toward the guns and railroad at Van Hoi.

I heard Cochran screaming for the rescue combat air patrol on the radio.

The plane suddenly dropped off on its left wing. *"I've lost all control! I've got to punch out."*

"Roger, Kodak Nine ejecting. We've got you covered. Rescap will be here in a second." A beat or two, then Cochran's solemn prayer, "God protect you, Pete."

The plane was a crippled bird falling out of the sky to its death. I groped about the cockpit, dropping everything—speed brake, flaps, landing gear—to slow the jet down. Then I reached up and grabbed the two candy-striped rings above my head that activated the ejection seat. God, indeed, protect me. I yanked.

There was a deafening blast of wind that whipped me with tornado fury as the cockpit canopy jettisoned. A moment later the five-inch cannon under my ass went off and shot me out into the maw of the cyclone. Rain like ice pellets lashed my neck, chest, arms, and legs—and I fell, a senseless blind tumbling, not a sensation of dropping, really, but of being batted about and hurled like a ball. I just rode the whirlwind, because there was nothing else I could possibly do.

There was a sudden jolting yank at my crotch and a queasy vertigo in which I whipped back and forth above a white heaving cup. Then the world rotated 180 degrees, down became up, and I was suspended from a parachute, drifting in eerie silence between a dripping smoke-gray sky and mud-brown fields and trees below.

For several moments there was a sense of wonder that I was still alive. I twisted around, but I couldn't spot Cochran or the other Crusader.

Below I made out a road and village. I had to get as far away from them as possible, but the wind was carrying me in that direction. I yanked on the risers, trying to slide the chute to the right. The chute descended more rapidly, and I panicked, eased up, and again drifted toward the village.

It was a choice of dropping too rapidly into what looked like a flat muddy field from which I might get hauled out by helicopter or tumbling right into the village and, at best, immediate capture. I jumped on the risers again.

I drifted now toward a grove of trees, yanked harder on the parachute to clear them, but a gust caught the chute and dropped me right into the branches.

I hugged myself, digging my chin into my chest, and crossed my arms and feet. *Keep tight. Arms and knees together.*

I crashed hard into a thick limb and spun about. Branches tore at my legs, flailed at my head and body. The collapsing chute snagged, snapped limbs, ripped, and dropped me savagely to the ground. The pain in my right leg was an electric bolt that slammed the breath out of me.

It took me a minute or two to get it together. I was on the ground, my face in the mud, but at least the chute wasn't dragging me. It hung in tatters above me in the tree, fluttering white battle pennants signaling anyone on the ground exactly where I was. I listened intently, but the sounds were all muted. I still had my helmet on. I took it off and now heard the sound of an overhead jet.

I heaved to my feet, but my right leg collapsed under me with a pain that drove blood into my eyes.

I had to get the hell out of there, and I could not walk. I tried to examine my leg, but I couldn't tell whether it was a fracture or a terrible sprain. I twisted around, unstrapped the parachute harness, and crawled away, each touch of my dragging right foot sending a fireball of pain through me.

There was the sudden roar of a jet close to the ground and the explosion of 20-millimeter cannons.

I couldn't see anything through the trees, but Cochran was strafing somebody nearby. Seconds later his wingman roared in and repeated the strafing run.

I huddled against a tree trunk for cover and in a frenzy clawed in the pockets of my survival vest for the emergency transmitter. It had suffered no apparent damage. "Black Knight One-Oh-Seven, this is Kodak Nine. Do you read me? Over."

"Pete, that you?" Cochran's voice on the small tinny speaker was a deliverance. "You in one piece?"

"Maybe two. My right leg isn't working."

"Where are you? I lost sight of your parachute."

"The bad guys won't. It's hung up in the trees like a goddamn beacon."

"The angel's on its way. So is a rescap."

"What was the shooting?"

"A group of the bad guys. Militia or farmers."

"Jesus. How close are they?"

"I don't know where you are." Cochran had to be very low on fuel.

"Should I send up a flare?"

"Negative. You'll only be flagging the bad guys. Wait for the angel or rescap. Can you work your way out to a clearing where they can cover you? It looks like paddies all around."

"I'll try." I started crawling again, each little jar shooting stabs of pain up my leg. Bite the bullet.

I stopped and slipped a .45 slug from the extra clip, popped it into my mouth, and literally clenched down. It didn't help. There was a steady drizzle seeping through the trees, and I was now soaked, cold, and shivering.

"Pete, there's a squad of soldiers and farmers headed for this grove of trees. It may be where you're at. I don't know. I only have fuel enough for one more pass, and then they'll have to rescue me. The rescap will be here in five. You're going to have to stay low and hang on."

I checked on my gun and knife. They hadn't gotten ripped away in my thrashing gauntlet through the trees. I started to cock the Colt automatic, then stopped. The last thing I needed was to accidentally shoot myself with a .45 as I crawled through roots and mud.

Suddenly Cochran zoomed in right over the trees, so low that the jet blast churned the branches overhead. The blast of the 20-millimeters sounded much too close. Cochran, with his last run, was pointing out to me exactly where the bad guys were.

I squirmed on my belly and elbows in the other direction, clutching the .45 in one hand, the radio in the other.

"Hey, Pete, you still there?"

"Roger, you practically landed on me."

"Right. I figured that's where you were. Work your way to the paddies to the east, if you can, so the chopper can pick you up. Pete, I got to go, or they'll be picking three of us up. My fuel's critical. The rescap will be here in a few minutes."

That's what he had said five minutes ago. I heard the jets fade away to the east like distant thunder.

And that terrible silence sucked something right out of me. I heard myself sob in fear, pain, and abandonment. The pain was a constant now, and I knew with certainty that it was the edges of a broken bone grating against each other each time I attempted to move.

I sprawled face down in the mud. Let them find me and shoot me. I heard a voice and shouts somewhere behind me. *Like hell!* I shoved up on my hands and elbows, groaned with the electric shock of pain up my leg, consciously clenched the .45 slug between my rear molars, and squirmed on my belly, elbows, and knees.

I grabbed a small sapling, hand over hand pulled myself upright to one leg, and then hopped from tree to tree, collapsed against each one for support, waited for the searing red paralysis of pain to fade, and then hopped again.

The pain fueled a burning rage, and for a brief explosion, it drove me to the edge of the wood. Beyond was an open plain of flooded rice paddies separated by raised earthen banks. I searched the leaden sky and listened intently, but there was no sight or sound of a rescap or chopper. I collapsed, sobbing, lowering myself to the ground hand over hand, as I had crawled my way upright.

There was a call and then an answering shout behind me. From the sound of it, they were closer. In a few minutes they would be in the trees and spot the parachute. I was in a bright orange flight suit, the flashiest color American science and technology could create, so that I could be instantly spotted from the air, only the bad guys were going to see me first.

I cowered behind a thick tree, but it wouldn't hide me. Beyond it the land sank down into reeking paddies, and even in my pain, the stench of the night soil—a black noxious muck of pig shit and human offal used as fertilizer—gagged me.

The voices were in the trees now. And then there were excited cries and jabbering. I did not have to understand Vietnamese to know they had found my chute.

I slid down the bank into a paddy, but at the last moment I had the presence to lodge my radio and .45 high if not totally dry in a crevice on the bank.

The paddy was not quite waist deep, and I scooped handfuls of the black reeking mud and shit of Vietnam and plastered my face, working it onto my neck, ears, and brow, then crouched down against the bank, waiting, sighting the .45 barrel at the woods.

A Vietnamese came out between the trees, an old farmer in a coolie hat, awkwardly carrying an ancient hand-bolt rifle.

"Kodak Nine, this is Dog Meat Five Eleven on guard, can you read me? Over," the radio on the bank suddenly blared out.

The Vietnamese started and then froze, his eyes wide and frightened, staring in the direction of the voice. He had not yet spotted me, crouched in the paddy right below him, awash up to my nose in shit.

"Kodak Nine, Dog Meat Five Eleven. We'll be in your section in a minute. Do you read me? Over. Give me a ten-second blast of the beeper if you can't talk."

Somewhere in the distance I heard the sound of a piston aircraft engine. At any moment the other Vietnamese would burst from the woods, and I would be butchered meat.

I lurched for the radio and clicked on the homing beacon for a count of ten. I could now see other figures searching through the trees about fifty yards away. I searched the sky frantically for the aircraft.

It was about two miles away, not a chopper but a lumbering prop-driven AD Skyraider.

I clicked on the radio and turned down the volume to a whisper.

"Dog Meat Five Eleven, this Kodak Nine. Read you loud and clear. Over."

"I hear you, Kodak Nine. Roger your beeper. I'm in your reported area. Can you send up a flare?"

"Negative. There are hostiles just thirty yards away. I'm at your nine o'clock, about two miles."

Twelve tons of engine, guns, ammo, bombs, and fuel immediately wheeled into a vertical bank toward me. The aggressiveness in that response gave me a surge of hope.

"Have they spotted you yet?"

"Negative. I'm hiding in a paddy about twenty yards out from the trees you're now heading for. The hostiles are in the trees looking for me."

"Roger that. Identify yourself. Over."

I took a deep breath to try to steady my voice, but it still came out a breathless groan. "Peter Henry Saxon, Lieutenant JG, six-one-four-oh-seven-six."

"Roger, copy ID. Authenticate your favorite sport."

"Football."

"Your favorite team?"

"Stanford Indians."

"You call that football?" Before the AD pilot called in the helicopter, he had to authenticate my identity with the personal code questions kept on file for each airman. I might be a North Vietnamese with a captured radio luring a rescue chopper into gun range.

"Keep your head down and watch your ass. I'm going to hit the trees and keep them busy. Can you give me a better fix on you?"

"I'm a hundred yards to the right of your current flight path."

The brawny single-engine attack plane, looking like a relic of World War II, roared in at one hundred feet and blasted the trees with its four 20-millimeter canons. The roar of the big 2,700-horsepower radial engine at full throttle at tree top and the cannon explosions were deafening. The Skyraider labored up to altitude and circled back for another run, creating an eerie stunned silence in its wake.

Then another Vietnamese, dressed in a ragtail uniform and army cap, skulked out of the woods and stared up at the AD. He gazed about the rice paddies but in the direction from which the attack had come, then disappeared back into the trees. All the while I gripped the .45 with both hands and watched him over the barrel. But I would be lucky to hit a water buffalo at twenty-five yards with the .45.

"Dog Meat Five Eleven, this is Angel Three. Do you have the pilot in sight? Over."

"That's negative. But I have his area. We're in radio contact. And there are hostiles around."

"Roger. Kodak Nine, Angel Three. Over."

I grabbed the radio. "Loud and clear, Angel Three."

"Lieutenant Saxon, how bad are your injuries? Can you get into the hoist, or will you need assistance?" The chopper pilot's voice was calm, solicitous, like a doctor on his rounds.

"I can handle the hoist, but I can't run for it. My leg's broken. You'll have to drop it right on me."

"Roger. I'll need a flare to mark your position."

"You'll have to move fast or the bad guys will get me before you do."

"This is Dog Meat. I'll go in first to keep them down. Angel, follow me in. Pete, do you read me? Over."

"Roger."

"Fire your flare as soon as I pass."

"Roger flares." I laid out the flares and all my bullets on the bank. Then I waited.

I could now see the helicopter flying in low against the distant hills. The Skyraider circled and set up for its run.

I could hear the Vietnamese calling back and forth in the trees, apparently convinced that I must be hiding somewhere near the telltale chute.

The Skyraider's strafing run was going to miss me by almost a hundred yards again. I fired the flare in front of it. It exploded in a bright red puff, but the wind almost immediately blew it west. The Skyraider slightly corrected his run, but he was already too low and committed to make a sharp turn toward me. This time it spewed its 2.75-inch rockets in a fiery stream ahead of it.

The angel followed him, but from the line of its flight path, they did not see me. I dragged myself up onto the bank, pushed myself up onto one foot, and waved frantically. The pain was searing, but fear and adrenaline drove me through it.

The helicopter banked away along the tree line, still not seeing me. Glancing down at my shit- and mud-smeared body against the bank, I could hardly see myself. But the Vietnamese, drawn out of the woods by the meandering chopper and the flare, did. They pointed at me and shouted.

I dropped to my knee and fired at the closest one. I missed, but the bullet smacking a tree near him frightened him enough to make him sprawl on the ground.

I fired wildly at the next Vietnamese I saw. Now they all dropped down or crouched behind trees, shouting back and forth. One fired back.

I fell back into the paddy for cover. Suddenly the mud and water churned in a whirlwind. There was a deafening shriek of jet turbines and the thump of rotors. A hurricane of dirt, grass, filthy water, and pig shit blinded me. The green metal fuselage hovered right overhead, the rotor wash beating down.

The hoist unreeled and swung back and forth, salvation out of reach. I poked at it, lunged, hooked it, and slung one arm through.

Now all the Vietnamese were firing, not at me but the helicopter. I fired back, then struggled into the harness, fiercely gripping the cable with both hands. A helmeted crewman, his face covered by a visor, peered down at me, shouting, but I couldn't make out a word.

The helicopter did not bother to haul me in but just took off, banking away from the trees in a climb, with me spinning below it, battered about in the violent downwash. I sensed, rather than heard, bullets whipping by.

The hoist operator seized my hand and swung me aboard. "We made it," the crewman shouted, a big satisfied laugh splitting his face. Deliverance was in that laugh, and at that, all my strength evaporated and I collapsed onto the aircraft's deck. Both my hands were bleeding from where I had gripped the hoist cable.

"Hey, we've gotcha. It's OK. You all right?"

"My leg's broken."

"Which one?"

I gestured to the molten agony that was my right leg.

"You're shot," the crewman said.

"No, it's broken."

"No, you're shot. There's the wound." He was cutting away the leg of my flight suit.

Sprawled on the deck of the helicopter, I couldn't see what he was pointing at.

I must have passed out because I have no memory of the flight to the carrier.

In sick bay, they doped me up on painkillers, and I kept nodding off. I remember Cochran, that gaunt, handsome, black Irish face unusually solemn, always present in the chair next to my rack, sometimes in a flight suit, other times in his khaki working uniform, the fragments of conversations over days segueing into one.

"How are you doing?"

"OK. Probably terrific when you consider the alternatives." My leg was in a full cast and suspended to reduce the swelling. So I was flat on my back, practically immobile, and alternately sweat-soaked or shaking with chills from a fever and infection.

Tommy's shoulders slumped, and he stared down at his feet as though avoiding my eyes. His expression was contrite, even ashamed. "It was the toughest thing I ever did, man. I hated it."

"What? What are you talking about?"

"Leaving you there. If I had been alone, I would have covered you until my fuel ran out and taken my chances. But I had White with me, and I was responsible for him. As it was, we got back to the carrier on the vapors. I didn't have enough for a go-around." Tommy Cochran, the ex-altar boy and Annapolis grad. His doleful eyes now found mine, searching for some absolution.

"What the hell are you talking about? You saved my life. Your last fire runs kept them at bay. You called in the angel and the rescap and steered them right to where I was. Another minute out there, and I was dead. Everything you did saved my life."

I remembered being nervous about his insistence on covering me, but a more experienced pilot, with whom I would have had only a nodding acquaintance at best, would not have made those last two gun runs, burning his fuel down to fumes. Cochran had not even asked his wingman to take that risk.

Out of weakness, or gratitude, tears came to my eyes, and I grabbed his head and kissed him.

He jerked away, embarrassed. "Hey, what are you doing? You're going to give me that shit you picked up."

"You saved my life. Nothing less."

Cochran grinned. "You're delirious. But write it up. A medal's always a terrific career move."

"You weren't there. You don't know how close it was. It's Indian territory out there. Peasants with hunting guns, militia. God knows what they'd do if they captured me. Another minute, and they had me. Those last two suicide runs of yours were my margin."

"That scary, huh?"

"I just remember the pain." I gestured to my foot. "If they caught me, the pain was going to get worse. And if I was rescued, it would get better. The pain made everything absolutely clear to me. I would have chopped off my own leg if it was necessary. That's how crazy it was. But not a moment of indecision."

"Wow, the Zen of pain."

"Even if I had been killed or captured, you did everything right. Don't doubt it."

Cochran laughed. "Oh, you're magnanimous now"—he nodded to my suspended leg—"with a gold ticket home."

"Maybe not. Lytle is pushing the flight surgeon to ship me to Yokosuka." Lytle was the lieutenant in charge of the reconnaissance detachment.

"Why?"

"I might be able to rejoin the ship before the deployment ends. If I'm shipped to a San Diego hospital, I'll end up in some officers pool."

Either way, the ship's flight surgeons wanted me off. Even through the fog of painkillers and fever, I sensed their uncertainty. My gamboling about the woods and paddies had compounded the fracture, and they wanted it reset by an orthopedic surgeon. I had not felt the bullet—my leg was already too traumatized—when I was shot dangling from the helicopter. But it had been the bullet that had injected into my bloodstream all the corruption of the pig shit, human offal, and piss of Vietnam in which I had wallowed. And the infection and fever were complications the ship's doctors wanted out of their sick bay.

Cochran grinned. "Well, from now on your log is one of the rare books that reads less landings than takeoffs. Not many walking around can say that."

"I'm not exactly walking yet."

"I saved your knife," Cochran said at one point.

"What?"

"When they stripped you, you kept insisting the corpsmen save your knife. Like your life depended on it. What was that about?"

I shook my head. "I don't know. I was out of it."

"They gave me the knife. The flight suit went in the garbage. It smelled like shit. But I cleaned the knife for you."

"It was shit. Thanks for cleaning the knife."

I never told Cochran why I had to have the knife. I didn't even tell the intelligence officer who debriefed me on my flight and especially grilled me on every detail of my escape and rescue.

Navy pilots, especially of reconnaissance flights, were increasingly getting shot now in the North. A few were rescued, but more killed and captured. Radios and survival equipment were being constantly updated and modified, helicopters stationed on destroyers in the Gulf of Tonkin, rescap patrols intensified. But my own salvation had narrowed down to the point of that knife.

15

Wanted for Murder

"Mr. Saxon."

The two waiting in the hotel lobby wear the dark, shapeless suits and dark ties of mid-level bureaucrats the world over. The youngest can get away with it, as he's still trim, but the older man is meaty and thick, and he should have bought a size larger off the rack. But there is a dull meanness in his face and a scar that make me glance down at his shoes. They're scuffed, worn, unpolished, with the thick rubber soles of a man who spends a lot of his day on the street and doesn't give a damn about appearances, except, perhaps, for the scheduled morning inspections.

I glance at the front desk, and the assistant manager watches us with obvious nervousness. I'm surprised that the hotel has called the police several days after the incident, but perhaps they have had second thoughts.

The younger man makes a slight bow and presents his card. "I am Detective Hiroshi Yuasa of the Tokyo Metropolitan Police, and this is Inspector Goto."

I inspect the card, printed in English on one side and Japanese on the other. Goto stares at me without even an attempt at a smile. Good cop, bad cop. But why? I'm the victim here.

From his expression, Goto, like the hotel manager, appears to have the attitude that this gaijin must somehow be responsible for a weirdo using a dagger to pin pickled genitalia to his hotel room door. Is the original horror still in their files, I wonder?

"What can I do for you?" The less I say, the more they'll tell me what they know.

"There is a serious matter that we must discuss with you," Yuasa says, looking properly grave.

"Would you like to discuss it down here or up in my suite?"

The younger man glances at Goto, who indicates upstairs with a barely perceptible lift of an eyebrow, as if he communicates telepathically.

In the elevator Yuasa asks me, "Mr. Saxon, what is your business in Tokyo?"

"I'm a lawyer."

"Yes, a lawyer," Yuasa repeats, and Goto mumbles something barely audible in Japanese.

"And what is your business here in Tokyo?"

"I'm representing an American company in a negotiation with a major Japanese corporation."

"Ah yes," Yuasa says. Neither of the cops says anything further until we enter the suite.

"Can I offer you something?" I indicate the small refrigerator and bar service. I'm trying to be cordial. "Or we can order coffee, tea, or food from room service, if you like."

"Mr. Saxon, please come this way." Yuasa gestures toward my bedroom. When I look at him in confusion, the older cop grips my elbow and steers me through the door.

I stagger back. "Oh my god!" The girl is sprawled on the bed, stark naked, her legs spread at an acute angle, muscled into that unnatural position after death to expose glistening, moist sex.

"What the hell's going on?" I whirl on Goto. He studies me impassively, taking secret measure of my surprise. "Who is she?"

Suddenly two more men step out of the bathroom into the bed-

room, and behind Goto the drawing room suddenly fills with uniformed Japanese cops.

"Do you know her, Mr. Saxon?" Yuasa asks. His voice, amazingly,
still has that polite intonation.

"No!" I protest. "What the hell's going on here?"

"She was not here with you?"

"No."

"You will please look closely at her, Mr. Saxon. You cannot make
identification from here."

I step toward the head of the bed, moving with dread. The girl
has been beaten, her mouth bloodied. The jaw is agape in a loose, odd
way as if unhinged, and blood cakes the long black hair, thicker and
curlier than most Japanese women's.

"Oh no!" I shake my head to ward off tears. "They killed her."

"Do you know her, Mr. Saxon."

"Yes."

"Who is she, please?"

"Her name's Mari Midori. She's a . . . student at Rikkyo University." In death I give her the status she sought in life. "She works . . .
worked at the Black Rose nightclub in the Ginza, as a hostess."

"This is where you meet her?"

"Yes, last night."

"And she sleep here with you?"

My head suddenly clears of grief with a sharp stab of alarm. I
look from Yuasa to Goto. "She was never here with me. I've never had
sex with her. I've been gone all day on business. But they killed her and
dumped her here. To create an incident."

"Who are they? Who killed her?"

"I don't know. Two guys. They've been following me for a couple
of days. She said she thought they were Yakuza."

I look back at poor Mari Midori, so exposed and abused in death
as in her life, while a squad of Japanese dicks gloat about her. There is

little clinical detachment in their interest. I start to get angry. It is the wasting of that spunky, striving life that outrages me, more than the atrocity itself.

The hotel manager, uniformed in his formal morning dress, materializes in the sitting room. "Where the hell was your security?" I rail at him. "Did you tell the police about someone nailing a prick and balls to my door?"

He starts as if jabbed with the *kai-ken* itself. "Yes, Mr. Saxon." He looks frightened.

I turn back to Goto. I do not know much about Japanese criminal justice, but I know enough not to get arrogant with their police. I take a breath, then speak very slowly. "Mr. Goto, you are a very experienced police officer, and I believe you know this is a setup. I left this morning with an executive of the Kuribayashi Electric Industrial Company, Mr. Masahiro Ozu, who had breakfast here in this room. We spent all day at their research center in Tsukuba. If you don't want to start World War Three, I would suggest we talk quietly."

Apparently Goto understands English well enough because he grunts, and Yuasa commands, "Please come this way, Mr. Saxon."

The hotel suite two doors away has already been commandeered by the police. From the thick cigarette smoke and the butts in the ashtrays, it is where they were staked out waiting for me to return.

For the next half-hour, while Yuasa scratches away taking lengthy notes, I tell the two cops about meeting Mari Midori the night before, her dropping me at the hotel in a cab—which presumably they can check—and her appearance that morning with a black eye and a tale of being interrogated by two Yakuza thugs.

"Look, since that incident with somebody nailing that genitalia, the sex organs, to my door, the hotel staff has been monitoring my coming and going. Check with them. And how the hell did they get into my room? It's an electronic key."

Goto grunts again, and Yuasa scratches another note.

"How did *you* know the girl was in my room in the first place?"

"We will ask the questions, please, Mr. Saxon."

"Well, with all due respect, may I politely suggest that whoever tipped you was the one who killed her and left her body. Was she killed in my room or somewhere else?"

I catch a glance that darts from Goto to Yuasa.

"Maybe you should establish that before you move the body. However you do that sort of thing."

"We are still conducting our investigation." Yuasa checks his notes. "You said you were with Mr. Masahiro Ozu of Kuribayashi Electric Industrial Company."

"Yes, last night—but he left me with the girl at the Black Rose—and this morning he came by to take me to their research facility at Tsukuba, as I said. I had been out jogging, so he came up to my suite while I showered. He had some breakfast, and then we left."

"When did Mari Midori come to see you?"

"She was waiting in the hotel lobby when I came back from jogging. She apparently asked for me at the desk, and they told her where I was. You can check with whoever manned the hotel desk this morning."

"Why was she so loyal to you?" Goto asks. It is the first question he has asked directly.

"Because the Japanese treated her like shit. She's the daughter of an American serviceman, a black man named Bobby Jackson. We talked about her working in Los Angeles after she graduated."

"You know her father?"

I shake my head. "She just told me his name." And now he would never know that he had a daughter named Mari, who honored his memory.

"Your black people riot. Why would it be better for her in Los Angeles?" Yuasa asks.

"We value our diversity," I say, sounding in my own ears like a Rebuild LA slogan. "It's practically the law."

"When do you leave Tokyo?" I'm impressed by the way Yuasa and

Goto work, the younger man, as if by intuition, asking the routine questions without being prompted by the tough old detective.

"In a few days. But I'm scheduled to go to Kyoto tomorrow for an important business meeting."

"You will please give us your passport," Yuasa directs, almost with apology. "It is a formality. You will please not leave Japan."

16

A New Translator

"Ruff 'n Ready here."

Rufus Ready and Associates, the investigative consulting firm, and I have played trans-Pac phone tag until I catch him at home at seven in the morning.

While the cops and forensic technicians comb the suite, the hotel has moved me into a third one. Yuasa and Goto search my shirts, toilet articles, and suits as they were packed. A plainclothesman is now stationed outside my door.

"Something has come up. It's rather critical," I tell Ready. "I need whatever you can find out about a guy named Ishii." I spell it the way Mari had. "That's the way it sounds, but I'm not sure of the spelling. I'll fax you the Japanese characters as soon as I hang up." I'm conscious that the police probably have my phone bugged.

"Can you give me a hint where to start?"

"Yakuza. Or someone who would hire a couple of thugs to beat a nightclub hostess to death for information about me."

"Jesus, what the hell are you into?"

"I wish the hell I knew. But I've got a couple of local hoods with tattoos following me around."

"Tattoos?"

"One of the guys has dragon heads etched on the back of his hands."

"He's a *chimpira*," Ready says with derision, "which literally means a 'little prick.' Regular Yakuza might have a complete body suit of tattoos, but nothing that shows under a business suit. This guy wants to tell the world he's a badass."

That's what Mari had said, but her insight had not saved her life. "Why?" I ask.

"Why? Hey, let me give you the facts of life. Contrary to the profitable Hollywood portrayals, bad guys are criminals because they're basically stupid as anteaters, twisted, and total losers to begin with. That's why."

"Well, this anteater probably killed a hostess I was with. It has something to do with a deal I'm trying to put together, but that's as much as I know."

"The police on it?"

"Yep."

There is a long pause, then Ready says, "Look, Peter, you're a good client. More than that, I like and respect you. I can be on the next plane if you need me."

"I sincerely appreciate that. It's an option I'll keep in mind. Thanks. But I don't know what the hell's going down. I mean that."

Ready is smart, resourceful, but at six feet three with shoulders wide as a door, he would stand out in Japan like Godzilla.

"Ishii's a common name. It's not much to go on, but I'll work it. You asked me to double-check Kenji Hara."

"And?"

"Really not very much. He's a straight arrow. Joined the company right out of Keio University, then married very well."

I don't even pretend to be cool. *"Who is his wife?"*

There's a pause on the line while Ready reads over his notes. "Maiden name—Michiko Kuribayashi. She's the top honcho's niece. You didn't know?"

"No. Not a clue. I just spent an evening with her and Hara. She acted as his translator. There've been hints dropped about her family but nothing specific. The Japanese are nothing if not subtle."

"Yeah, you could say that. I also have a preliminary report on that Matsu Yurikawa you asked about."

"What?"

"Just boilerplate. According to my Tokyo associates, he's a senior official of the Japanese Ministry of International Trade and Industry. Considered a blue-blooded bureaucrat—Tokyo University and then graduate school at Harvard."

"Harvard, that's interesting."

"Why's that interesting to a Stanford man?"

"Explains his attitude. I thought he was a Japanese asshole, but he's just being Harvard."

Ready's laugh comes across the Pacific as a bark. "He's considered a traditionalist but a pragmatist, not a right-winger."

"What the hell does that mean?"

"Those are the labels, but what they mean in Tokyo where the Liberal Democrats are the conservatives is murky."

"I guess I'm going to find out."

"His primary area is electronics. Been active in the long-range policy of Japanese companies expanding overseas. And he's a leader of the faction that's resisted opening Japanese markets to U.S. manufacturers. Remember blocking Motorola out of the mobile phone market a few years ago?"

That doesn't bode well. "Anything else?"

"Well, he's lost influence. Apparently his faction had Japanese manufacturers commit heavily to a high-definition TV system that's already obsolete."

"An old analog system versus the digital system the U.S.—and the world—is adopting. It's given us back the technical lead."

"And it's pissed away over half a billion—that's dollars, not yen—that Japanese TV makers invested. And billions more down the line, if they lose the market to U.S. licensees. It could blow away the Japanese electronics industry." Ready recites this, not to convey information but to clue me that he knows the stakes involved.

"You've really done your homework."

"I figured it was an area in which you had an interest. You're not involved in anything that might piss off the ultraright in Japan, are you?"

"I don't get involved in politics like that. You know that."

"You're making inquires about the Yakuza."

"What's that got to do with politics?"

"Everything. The Yakuza and the ultranationalists are joined at the hip, have been for centuries. The gangs organize as *uyoku,* fanatic right-wing political parties, to exempt themselves from taxes. They've a long history of strike-breaking, corporate extortion, intimidating politicians, even assassinations. Government doesn't crack down, because the Yakuza back right-wing politicos, run labor unions, and—most importantly—can deliver blocks of votes."

"You're unusually well informed."

"Hey, remember? Before I became an overpriced corporate consultant, I was FBI. In LA, especially, we had to be on top of it. Our liaison at the Tokyo embassy regarded the Japanese ultraright and Yakuza as the same beast. Five prime ministers in five years resigned in scandals—mob related. It's the water they swim in."

There are several beats of trans-Pacific silence. "Look, Peter, I know you have this penchant for flying solo. But there you're operating in a different world—"

I interrupt him—conscious of a police tap. "Brief Levy. What I said, what you said. And make security arrangements. A fighter patrol covering my ass."

Ready gets it immediately. "Roger Wilco."

I leave the suite to hunt down Goto. The bodyguard at my door does not stop me, and I resist looking back to see if he is following.

"Inspector Goto, I'm scheduled to leave for Kyoto for a business conference first thing tomorrow morning," I politely remind the gnarly old cop.

"Hai," he nods. It is the Japanese yes that acknowledges hearing what I say, not necessarily agreeing with it.

I walk toward the bedroom door. Mari Midori's remains are already gone, but the rumpled bedclothes retain the imprint of her body, and two young men wearing clear plastic gloves search through them. One suddenly plucks up something with his tweezers and holds it up to the light to examine.

"Please, you will leave the room now for our investigators to work," Yuasa, the younger detective, cautions behind me.

This time I head for the lobby to test how long my leash is. I stride off the elevators, through the square golden pillars of the lobby, and out the front entrance. A lineup of taxis, engines idling at a purr, waits at the curb.

It is now night, and the headlights of the cars that crawl along Hibiya Dori, then suddenly veer to unload strangers at the hotel, dazzle my vision. Across the avenue, rainbow-lit fountains in the park cast spooky shadows in the groves of dark trees. I retreat back into the hotel.

The daughter, Yuki, answers the phone, and when, in English, I reintroduce myself and ask for her father, Michiko Hara takes the call.

"Yes, Mr. Saxon, my husband is home. I can have him call you right back." Hara has had only an hour's sleep, if that, to fly to Kyoto that morning and then back. He's probably taking a nap.

"It's extremely important that I see him immediately. Some critical matters must be arranged before I leave for Kyoto tomorrow morning." I call from a pay phone on the hotel mezzanine. "If it is convenient, I could come right to your home. Absolute privacy is necessary."

"I understand." Does she really? In Los Angeles, the biggest deals are negotiated in the living rooms and on the patios of Bel Air and Beverly Hills, away from the buzz of studios, law offices, and agencies. "You are always welcome in our home."

For a moment I think she has hung up, but then I hear her soft breathing on the other end of the line, and she says, "Are you enjoying this visit to Japan? I believe you said that you found it an entirely different country than when you were last here."

"Yes, it is. An associate of your husband took me to a club that was very . . . well, significant when I was here in another life."

"Yes."

"The Black Rose."

There is a sharp intake of breath, a silence, then, "Wives do not go to such clubs in Japan. They are for the entertainment of businessmen."

Voices are unique, distinctive as fingerprints. Long after the sex appeal of their faces withers and bodies are smothered in suet, the voices of actors and actresses retain their quality to intrigue us. Is it Lilli's voice I hear on the phone after a quarter of a century? Or is Michiko Hara's merely a similar Japanese voice that time and romantic memory transform.

"But when we were young, it was where Japanese girls and Americans . . ." I don't finish the thought. What is the word? *Fraternized?*

"Yes, it can be very disturbing to revisit the past." She has heard something in my voice. "Perhaps even destructive."

"Time is a river without banks."

"Is that English poetry?"

"It's the title of a painting in your Tokyo boardroom. A French expressionist."

"Time is a river without banks," she repeats in a soft, musing voice, almost inaudible, then in a stronger voice says, "That seems to me very dangerous, Peter. A river without banks will flood and again sweep away your home, your family, all you have built in a lifetime."

It is the tragic note in her voice and the word *again* that electrify me. Lilli had had her home, family, all she had ever known swept away in a firestorm.

But before I can respond, she says, "My husband will be waiting for you." This time she does hang up.

In the taxi, I struggle to think rationally. I am in danger of making a great fool of myself. It's too extraordinary a coincidence, beyond chance, that out of the millions of women in Tokyo, the one into whose home I had been invited by her husband is Lilli. What are the odds? Thirteen million to one?

Michiko Hara cannot be Lilli. Fantasy plays tricks with memory, and Lilli is an image that has faded and fragmented through the years, until now—this absurd middle-aged obsessing with the past—that ghost has taken possession of the flesh-and-blood Michiko Hara.

From the first moment I alighted in Tokyo, I have been subconsciously seeking Lilli in the fleeting glances of young girls glimpsed in the Ginza or, perhaps more realistically, in middle-aged women like Michiko Hara, who are now Lilli's true age. Do I even seek Lilli, really, or my own lost, reckless youth, that passion that existed only for itself without any hint of a future? And ultimately, do I still seek absolution from the one person who might give it to me?

There have been years when I have not thought of Lilli. But now she manifests again in vivid, compelling dreams, and when I awake in the predawn blackness, it is always with that same amazement that it was all so long ago. I have lived this entire life since then, quietly, diligently doing business, acquiring what is regarded as power as the deals became more ambitious, not because I am necessarily ambitious but because the new technologies require expanding capital, conglomerations, and mergers. I have simply understood that.

If I was cool, somewhat fearless in negotiations, what was there to fear in mere business in light of what I had already survived? So I made money, bought bigger houses, indulged my wife and daughters.

When we traveled, it was ski vacations with the girls, except for brief jettings to Europe tagged onto business trips. But I have, until now, avoided the Far East, vaguely haunted by the foreboding that there was a karmic debt still to be paid here.

Michiko Hara cannot be Lilli. And yet, of all the gin joints in in all the towns in all the world, Ozu had walked me into the Black Rose. And the twisted, brutalized body of Mari Midori, my hostess there, has materialized in my hotel room bed. That is neither an obsessed middle-aged memory nor a coincidence, but a murderous reality.

Michiko Hara meets me at the door, and there is something tremulous in her greeting, a quavering in the cordial, extravagant formality of her welcome. "Oh, Mr. Saxon, I am so very delighted to see you again. You got here very quickly. My husband is working in his study. I will tell him you are here."

But she lingers for a moment, her eyes studying me. I have only seen Michiko Hara once before, on that first visit, surrounded by home, husband, and two children. I had not recognized her as Lilli then. But I had been immediately seized by a disquieting sense of an apparition from the past.

Her hair is less luxuriant and sensual than Lilli's, a more subdued frame for her face, suitable for an executive's wife and a mother. That alone will dramatically change a woman's appearance, even if there has not been a passage of more than thirty years. Despite two children, Michiko Hara has retained an essentially slender figure.

She studies me now with shining but apprehensive eyes.

"I'm sorry," I say. "I wasn't sure. I didn't recognize you at first."

Michiko Hara visibly pales.

"And who is my wife, Peter?" Hara enters through a shoji that silently slides shut behind him on polished wood runs.

I glance at Michiko. She looks faint.

I grope about, hesitate, then stammer, "Kuribayashi-san's niece. His brother's daughter. I did not realize that I was already dealing directly with the family. If I acted impatient . . . well, I apologize. I am honored by your hospitality, and your confidence."

Hara makes a slight bow of the head and a subtle gesture of dismissal. He is dressed in jeans, neatly pressed as slacks, an oxford shirt, and a tweed jacket, an outfit less formal than a business suit but as calculated in its casualness.

"This business is of the gravest family concern, Mr. Saxon," Michiko suddenly interjects. "Our children are my uncle's only heirs. And it would be great harm to their future, my husband's career, if there were any embarrassment."

Hara looks curiously at his wife, as if wondering why she is warning me.

I nod. "That's why it's imperative that we talk tonight."

Michiko immediately translates, and I can only speculate on what spin she is giving to what I say.

"I would tremendously appreciate your assisting me as interpreter so that I make no mistakes in communication. I need to talk to Hara-san quite seriously."

Michiko smiles yes—somehow, without saying it, conveying that her attendance is subject to his approval. She disappears behind a shoji, suddenly leaving Hara and me alone.

It is apparently the fashion to furnish a major room or two in Western style, but behind that facade, the intimate regions of the home behind the delicate paper walls remain Japanese. It is there that Michiko has retreated. But there is one traditional furnishing in the room where we now silently wait. In the *tokonoma*, a recess in the far wall, stands the cedar cabinet with its pagoda roof that had seized my attention during my first visit to this house: the family shrine, with its faded photographs of a woman in a kimono and an army officer, the gong, incense burner, scroll, and behind them, in the shadowed sanctuary, the matched woman's dagger and the short sword with its nine-inch blade, both with red silk hilts and intricately carved ivory handles in shining black lacquered scabbards.

They are the blades of my nightmares. I stare at them. Are they the same cabinet, relics, and knives that inhabited Lilli's room in another life? Many traditional Japanese families have this ritual altar. Do I accurately remember the knives any more than I remember Lilli? What do I truly recall, and what do I impose on the past from the present?

Hara silently stands next to me, following my gaze. "I am admiring the *wakizashi* and *kai-ken* in your family altar."

"Oh yes, they are my wife's family. Very old, very fine," he says. At first I'm confused about whether he is referring to his in-laws or the knives, then realize by the nod of his head—a bow toward the altar—that the family blades, blood, and history are one and the same.

Once, back in the seventies, I had with morbid fascination looked into collecting Japanese short swords—*objects d'art*—as my personal guilt-edged investment. They could still be had then in Los Angeles—souvenirs of the great war—but the Japanese were quickly buying them back. My wife, Joan, immediately vetoed the idea. With two kids and their friends rampaging about, my wife would not allow razor-edged blades in the house, any more than she would my navy .45.

I am about to recount this to Hara to fill the uncomfortable silence, when Michiko reenters carrying a tray. She pours green tea and sets out small plates of dainty pastries, as exquisitely arrayed as flower arrangements.

I do not know whom the police have contacted, and I don't want to derail my negotiation with lurid revelations of dead nude women in my hotel bed. If either Hara or Michiko knows of it, there is no hint in their behavior as we sit down.

Hara smiles and nods at me, inviting me to speak.

"Mr. Hara, I have strong reason to believe that factions are actively trying to destroy our negotiations, and they will go to any length, including murder, to stop them."

To my surprise there is neither shock nor protest in Hara's receipt of this information but merely a grave nodding of his head. "Yes," he says.

I glance at Michiko, and here again she is neither startled nor upset but speaks with the hesitancy of one repeating something awkward, somewhat embarrassing.

"But why?" I ask. "Why does this deal threaten them so? There have been other U.S.-Japanese partnerships."

"But not in the interlocking way you are proposing, a Japanese-American *keiretsu*. It threatens the other *keiretsu*, the way the Japanese have done business with each other for over a century."

Hara pauses for his wife to finish the translation. "More than that, it also threatens the government, the power of the bureaucrats. What your newspapers refer to as Japan, Inc. They can't control you, or any American company. So this deal undermines their all-powerful authority over Japanese industry."

"You're saying that I landed in Japan with powerful enemies already in place."

"Yes."

"Matsu Yurikawa?"

Hara is silent.

"And there are people within Kuribayashi who strongly oppose this merger."

"They do not agree to selling control of our companies to an American corporation."

"Ozu?"

"He does not make these decisions."

"Do you trust him?"

"He is a very hardworking and loyal executive who has been with Kuribayashi his entire career."

An American would ask why I am asking about Ozu. "Is he your man?"

"He is from Kyoto headquarters. I have not worked closely with him before."

I nod. "Then he's not your man or your choice. I have strong reasons to believe he is working with whoever is trying to sabotage this merger."

"He does not have that authority."

"No, but he will be the translator conducting my negotiations with Kuribayashi-san. By his choice of words, his emphasis, he could easily influence the negotiations, even have me offend Kuribayashi, and I would never know it."

As Michiko translates, her husband nods, *"Hai, hai,"* as if I am confirming his worst suspicions.

"Ozu cannot conduct the translation," I insist.

"We cannot dismiss him."

"If I don't want him?"

"It would offend him and those in Kyoto."

"What if he agrees? I think I can do that without insulting him. But first I must have another translator to accompany me to Kyoto. One who is trusted by Kuribayashi-san, familiar with my speech and with the situation. Someone who is absolutely loyal to you."

I see the fear rise up in Michiko's eyes as she translates for her husband. She catches it, and it terrifies her. Hara does not yet get it. "I have no one like that available."

"Yes, you do."

Ozu waits for me in the hotel lobby, fretful and worried at having been summoned in the middle of the night. "We have a very serious problem," I state immediately. "One with grave consequences for Kuribayashi Electric, both our governments, and the economy of Japan. You are very directly involved, Mr. Ozu, possibly responsible."

Ozu's eyes go wide behind his magnifying glasses, and he blinks rapidly, puzzling out if he understands me correctly. I stride off toward the open elevator.

Ozu follows at a trot. "Mr. Saxon, please, I do not understand."

I hold up my hand, cautioning him not to say anything, and glance purposely about the elevator as if searching for hidden devices. At my floor, a plainclothesman loiters in an alcove, pretending to concentrate on a newspaper.

"Good evening," I nod to him.

He startles, stares a moment at Ozu and me, comes to attention, and performs a stiff bow, muttering something in Japanese.

"I've had to change my suite—this is the third time, actually—and now have twenty-four-hour security, since an incident this afternoon." Again I do not give Ozu a chance to respond, and once in my suite I go directly to the minibar and pour two stiff Haig & Haigs on the rocks. I hand one to Ozu, who now stands silently, waiting for me.

"The hostess at the Black Rose to whom you introduced me last night, do you remember her?"

Ozu frowns, smiling nervously, as if having difficulty remembering.

"A beautiful girl, half black, half Japanese. Her name was Mari Midori."

"Yes, I think I remember her a little." He shakes his drink with a sheepish smile. "I am a little drunk."

"She was murdered today. Beaten to death. Somebody, a Japanese informant, called the police to tell them that I had spent the night with her. They were here this afternoon to interrogate me."

"Oooh!" Ozu gives a passable exclamation of astonishment.

"You ran into her leaving the hotel when you came to pick me up this morning."

"Ah, I don't think I remember this."

"Too bad. You would have been one of the last people to see her alive."

Ozu lets out another long audible breath, a Japanese expression of concern.

I sip my Scotch, and Ozu politely joins me. "But she did not spend the night here." I gesture toward the hallway. "A security guard verified for the police that I was alone."

"Ah yes."

"And the cab driver—when the police traced him—also verified that he just left me off and that he drove her home."

Ozu nods again, absorbing all this with deep seriousness. "This morning, she came back to warn me. That's when you saw her."

Ozu stares at me, hesitating to contradict.

"What she warned me of was that two thugs—probably Yakuza from her description—had terrified her. They slapped her around to make her tell them about our business dealings. Do you understand what I've just said?"

Ozu nods vigorously. "Oh yes."

"Now they've killed her. And they are trying to implicate me. Who is behind this, Mr. Ozu?"

Ozu's eyes again go wide, and he shakes his head, denying any knowledge.

"One of Kuribayashi's competitors may know of this negotiation and want to kill it at any cost."

Ozu looks at me warily, acutely alert. "Yes . . ."

He says nothing else, but nods and regards me with hooded eyes.

I rise and freshen both our drinks from the bar. "I feel, Ozu-san, over the past few days of working with you—and our socializing—that you've become more than a business associate. You are a friend I can trust."

"I am very honored, Mr. Saxon."

I take out the card that Inspector Goto of the Tokyo Metropolitan Police had presented to me and hand it to Ozu. He examines it with great curiosity.

"First thing tomorrow morning, I want you to go to the police and explain all this to them. I don't want to involve the American embassy, start World War Three over this."

"World War Three?" His eyes again go wide behind their lenses.

"A figure of speech. If my government finds out about it, they might think this was some sort of Japanese conspiracy just to stop this deal. Then there might be trade sanctions, especially against Kuribayashi. I don't want that to happen."

"I don't understand."

"Ah yes, well, you should discuss that with Matsu Yurikawa. But first thing tomorrow morning, I want you to go to the police. Explain that I was with you most of last night and all today. That I had just met this girl during a business entertainment with you."

Ozu starts to protest, but I hold up my hand. "And you should also refer the police to Yurikawa at MITI."

Ozu is astonished. "Yurikawa-san?"

"You must impress the police with the sensitive nature of our business. First thing tomorrow morning. Before this gets out of hand. Only you can do this."

"But I am to go with you to Kyoto this morning to meet with Kuribayashi-san."

"That has been taken care of. I will miss your excellent English translations, your expert knowledge of this business. Certainly your acquaintance with Kuribayashi-san would have been very valuable. But we have arranged for an excellent translator who knows Kuribayashi-san at least equally well."

"May I ask who?"

"Mr. Hara has generously allowed his wife to accompany me to Kyoto to translate for her uncle."

No matter how hard he tries, Ozu is not successful at deception. It is his glasses, mainly, the lenses magnifying and exaggerating every squint of suspicion, each widening in surprise. He hasn't seen it coming. Ozu looks dumbfounded, but there is no legitimate way he can object without embarrassment.

"We are catching the bullet train to Kyoto this morning." I give him my most heartfelt, sincerest smile. "And I really need you to take care of this terrible business with the police. Only you can do it."

"Yes, yes," he nods, but the lenses magnify the panic in his eyes. He glances at his watch. It is too late for Ozu to report to whomever is giving him his marching orders.

After Ozu leaves, I stand again gazing out the window, across Hibiya Dori toward the massive gate tower on the Imperial Palace wall, now blurred and hidden in the night mists. But my mind still pictures—

imagines is the word—the great fortress with its steep curving roof.

In time, memory blurs into the mists. Every day the war fades inside me, and Lilli a little more. And there are only attitudes where there was once pain, fantasies where there was passion. But the way we were shapes who we are today.

17

Dark Secrets of Two Wars

I hobbled into the Black Rose, leaning on Cochran and a cane, a walking cast to my knee. My arrival caused a stir among the hostesses at the booths and tables near the entrance.

But I didn't see Lilli about. Perhaps she was at one of the far tables with a new patron. I eased onto a bar stool and ordered a Scotch to ease the fire in my leg. Stoked with antibiotics and codeine, I wasn't supposed to drink. But the opiates scarcely worked, and I was developing my own painkilling pharmacology.

Cochran eyed me with concern as I washed down a couple of pills with the Scotch. "You OK?"

"Yeah, sure. Just a pill to keep the fever down."

He reached over and actually dabbed at my forehead with a bar napkin. "You're sweating."

Suddenly Lilli was standing there, her face drawn, her dark eyes searching my face and then, implacable, sweeping down my body to the cast encasing my right leg, the thick hospital-issue cane leaning against the bar.

"A boyfriend of Sumiko—he is navy pilot like you on *Midway* ship—he said you are shot down in Vietnam. I go a little crazy. Sumiko mixes up message with her very bad English, and she does not know if you are dead or prisoner or maybe hurt."

"Who is this guy?"

"I do not know him. He said he is your friend, and he sees me with you, maybe. You shot down in Vietnam, that is true?"

I nodded. "I was very lucky." I nodded to Cochran. "I had a good friend watching over me."

Her eyes never left my face. "You are so thin. You do not eat?"

"I'm in the hospital. The food's not very good."

"He's got a fever," Cochran said.

"He's my nurse."

"You need real nurse, I think. Why are you here?"

"I wanted to see you again." It wasn't enough for her. I leaned forward and held both her hands.

"Wounded in a paddy
Far behind the lines,
Even though we're parted,
Your lips were close to mine,"

I whispered in a singsong baritone, husky with Scotch.

"You wait where the lantern softly gleams.
Your sweet face seems
To haunt my dreams,
My Lilli of the lamplight,
My own Lilli Marlene."

Her mouth dropped open, and she stared at me with total astonishment.

I shook my head. "Look, this is a mistake. Maybe I should have just kept the fantasy."

For the first time the stiffness in her face softened. She reached up and touched my cheek with just her fingertips. "You are so thin," she said with concern. "What—" she started to ask another question but then stopped and looked around. The other girls were watching her.

She turned back. "You buy my time. We go somewhere."

"Gladly. Happily."

She took a twenty and was suddenly all business. "You please wait outside. It not so good if they see me leave with you. OK? I will not be long time."

"You constantly fucking amaze me," Cochran said. "An Annapolis man could . . . would never have done that."

"And he would have lost the girl." I took a slug of Scotch. "Actually, neither could I. Thus doth the poppy make poets of us all."

"The poppy?"

"Codeine. An alkaloid of opium—$C_{18}H_{21}NO_3$—but where's the poetry in that."

"Amazing!" Cochran was much too upbeat. He gave me a sidelong glance. "You're not taking too much of that dope, are you?"

"I don't know, what's too much? What difference is it going to make one way or the other?"

He was silent. Somehow, bullying the doctors, Cochran had signed me out of the hospital on a pass after practically dressing me himself, then loaded me into a cab, onto the Yokosuka to Tokyo train, and into another cab to the Black Rose. I was in pain and soaked with sweat by the time we arrived, but Cochran was determined that the condemned man was to have a last night out on the town, even if it killed him.

Now I waited outside like a thief, shivering more from the fever than from any chill in the night air. I had not lied to Lilli about constantly thinking about her. In the hospital I had fixated on luxuriant images of her beauty, the glossy ebony hair flowing across moist golden skin, and that silken flesh molded into breasts, voluptuous hips, and thighs. The pixy mischief of her smile and, even in her anger, the haughty elegance that revealed secret breeding. These were the pictures that I deliberately forced to mind as an act of will when I bolted awake, feverish, in the middle of the night from the nightmare of the gaping blackened face of the dead man and sensed I was surrounded by specters of vengeful peasants, slowly encircling me in the shadows.

The throbbing daylight held its own terrors, as the navy doctors greeted me with funereal cheer, then conspired in dark frowns. I didn't know what the numbers on the chart meant, but the carrion stink of my leg terrified me more than the pain.

The thought of seeing Lilli again became an obsession stoked by the fever. Perhaps it wasn't love, but in my weakened, drugged condition, it certainly wasn't lust.

Now I hunched my shoulders against the chill, lit another cigarette, and checked my watch for the fifth time with a sinking feeling in the pit of my stomach. I had been waiting outside for almost fifteen minutes. I was being played the fool. She had had me wait outside merely to get rid of her crippled, brawling ex-boyfriend.

She had also done this to Brannigan, the lovelorn marine with whom I had ended up battling among the garbage cans. I was too weak, too wounded to sustain anger, only humiliation. I was debating whether to venture back into the thorns of the Black Rose to gather Cochran or just to hobble off into the cold dank Ginza and catch the night train back to Yokosuka, when Lilli burst through the door. She fumbled with her purse with one hand and dragged her coat with the other, as if she had not had time to throw it on. "I make big deal with manager," she said, a little breathless. "He not so happy I leave customer."

She waved for a cab parked outside the club and awkwardly tried to help me into it. I didn't really need help, but I had apparently aroused some instinct in her, and I wasn't going to fight it.

"Did you really dream about me?" she asked.

"In the hospital—when I have nightmares—I think about you. You keep the nightmares away." It was a partial truth, because she didn't keep them away. "How did you get off?"

"I make big deal with manager." She settled back, then immediately sat up and interrogated me. "Is that how you say it, 'make big deal'?"

"It's one way. Another word is *negotiate*. You negotiated with the manager."

"I *negotiated* with the manager, *neh?*"

"Right."

"I negotiated with the manager," she said, and favored me with a sly smile. "Not so many customers tonight. So I tell him you will pay for my time, and we get nice hostess, who not working, for customer. So manager makes two times money. Now he very happy."

"You're a terrific negotiator."

"When I little girl, I negotiate everything. Food, rooms, medicine. Or maybe we die. My mother cannot do it. She is sick. Everything crazy after the war. No food, homes all burned down. People die from burns, bleeding. No doctors, no hospitals. Long time things very crazy."

It was as much as Lilli had said about her childhood, and apparently she felt she had perhaps said too much because she now became silent.

I looked at Lilli, a sad smile fleeting on her lips, and imagined her as a child, the impoverished daughter of the samurai, bartering among the ruins of Tokyo for her mother and sister. The privation, the suffering had in some way tempered her beauty—it was there in the line of her cheekbone, in the poignancy of her smile, the way she never looked away but held your eyes as if defying you to read the secrets of her soul.

That night I needed her strength, and I was naked before it. "Where are we going?"

"Kanko." A hotel with private Japanese baths.

"I can't get my leg wet."

"Not soak in bath. Just maybe wash. Hot water, cold water. You feel better."

With my constant feverish sweat, I was getting a little rank. In the confines of the cramped Toyota cab I was conscious of my smell of sweat and decayed flesh, and I cracked a window.

At one point, after a brief dialogue with the driver, Lilli directed the cab to a side street of dark, ancient, musty shops, bypassed, it seemed, by the avenues of larger modern stores. Lilli jumped out, returning quickly with a small cloth bag, which she pushed to my nose for inspection. There was an earthy herbal smell of dried leaves and roots.

"What's that?"

"It is very good. You drink like tea." Again she fell silent, offering no further explanation of what drinking it like tea was exactly good for.

At the Kanko, Lilli insisted on undressing me—something she had never done before, carefully folding and arranging my clothes like a valet.

The tiled baths were empty. It was too late for the regular workaday customers and too early for lovers. Lilli wrapped my leg in a towel to keep it dry, then soaped me down with a large natural sponge that scraped my skin and made it tingle.

"You are so thin," she exclaimed, and then made her first act of affection, gently kissing my shoulder. "Almost like a Japanese."

"That skinny, huh?"

"Skinny?" she questioned.

"Very thin. Just skin and bones."

"Ah." She ran her fingers across my chest. "More muscles, I think, but very thin."

I was sitting on a low wooden stool. She stood in front of me, her head bent forward, as though inspecting my shoulders. I hugged her fiercely, burying my face in her soft breasts, and something in her touch released all the grief in me. Tears began flowing, and once they started, I was powerless to stop them.

Lilli said nothing but just leaned over me with her arms around me, my head literally to her bosom.

"I'm going to lose my leg," I said finally. "They're going to cut it off. They can't stop the infection in the bone, so they're going to have to amputate before the blood poisoning spreads and kills me. I've got all the shit, piss, and corruption of Vietnam in my leg. It'll kill me if they don't cut it off."

She nodded, as if she already knew. Perhaps Cochran had told her, and that, not negotiating, was why she had kept me waiting at the Black Rose.

Back in the room we lay on the mat, naked, my arms about her. "The doctors, they tell you this thing?"

"They're talking about it, easing it to me." My fingers gravitated once again to that strange slick weld of flesh on her lower back, the childhood fire scar too deep to ever dissolve, and caressed it.

"I killed a man," I said. To not tell her made my own mutilation a lie. "He was just a little peasant, no bigger than you. I was face-to-face with him when I killed him. With my hands."

And I told her that part of the rescue I could not tell the air intelligence debriefer, or even Cochran.

The Vietnamese came out between the trees, an old farmer in a coolie hat awkwardly carrying an ancient bolt-action rifle.

"Kodak Nine, this is Dog Meat Five Eleven on guard. Can you read me? Over," the radio on the bank suddenly blared out.

The Vietnamese started and then froze, his eyes wide and frightened, staring in the direction of the voice. He had not yet spotted me, crouched in the paddy right below him, awash up to my nose in shit.

"Kodak Nine, Dog Meat Five Eleven. We'll be in your section in a minute. Do you read me? Over. Give me a ten-second blast of the beeper if you can't talk."

The scrawny little farmer tiptoed to the radio and stared down at it as if hypnotized, his back now to me. Then, as if the comprehension of what he was looking at suddenly flashed, he bent down to grab the radio.

I didn't think about what I did next. It was instinctive, galvanized by both the maddening pain and the panic about being captured.

I exploded out of the shit, lunging up on my good leg, tackled the Vietnamese around the neck, and dragged him down into the paddy.

The mud and water drowned his cry. I was on his back and drove him face down into the muck, my knees now on his back and my hands groping about his throat.

He squirmed and struggled under me, but small and slender as a teenage girl, he was totally pinned down by my weight. His splayed out arms and legs were unable to get any leverage in the mud that sucked him in and smothered him.

Somewhere in the distance I heard the sound of a piston aircraft engine. At any moment the other Vietnamese would burst from the woods, and I would be butchered meat. Holding his head down with one hand, I groped at my leg for the sheathed survival knife there, reared up, and drove the blade into his back. It hit a shoulder blade or rib, deflected off, and stuck between his ribs.

He squirmed with the agony of the stab, exhaling a big black bubble of air. I grabbed the knife handle with both hands and fell on it with all my weight, driving it up to the hilt. I felt the convulsion of his body under me, then he went dead, releasing a final black bubble.

Another Vietnamese, dressed in a ragtail uniform and army cap, skulked out of the woods and stared up at the approaching plane. The dead farmer's rifle, an old single-action bolt, was on the bank where he had dropped it. It was probably used for hunting and had good range. I eased back the bolt. There was a single long round in the breech. Where were the rest of the bullets?

I fumbled around in the muck for the body. Something that felt like a cartridge belt was about his waist. I rolled him over to unhook it. The ghastly shit-and-mud-smeared face, eyes open and teeth bared in his final agony, rose out of the water, inches from mine, as if he were going to tear my throat out. I cried out and shoved him back under, falling on him to bury that horror again in the reeking mud. My hand hit the knife handle, and I yanked it out and stood, crazed, with the blade pointed, waiting for him to rise up again.

The pouch on the dead man's cartridge belt held a dozen bullets, which I piled out on the bank next to the rifle and the flare gun. Then I reloaded the single shot and waited.

Suddenly the chopper was right overhead, a deafening roar of turbines and splashing downwash. The hoist unreeled and swung back and forth, out of reach. I poked at it with the rifle barrel, hooked it, lunged, and slung one arm through.

Now all the Vietnamese started firing, not at me but the helicopter. I fired back with the peasant's rifle, grabbed another of the bullets, reloaded quickly, fired again, dropped the rifle, and struggled into the harness, fiercely gripping it with both hands.

Lilli listened to the story without saying a word, her face expressionless.

"You understand what I'm saying?"

"You killed him with a knife?"

"When we fly, we always carry a survival knife, sort of a hunting knife. It's regulation survival equipment."

"It is necessary you kill him?"

"That poor son-of-a-bitch was between me and the radio, between me and being rescued. He had a gun—an old farmer with an old hand-bolt rifle to protect his land. They were some kind of militia, and in another minute they would have shot me. An American plane was firing rockets at them. And Cochran had already strafed them with his twenty-millimeters. I don't think they were in any mood to capture me. They shot me in the leg as the helicopter pulled me out. That's how close it was. That's the bullet that started the infection. Or maybe it was the fracture. I don't know. I broke my leg when I hit the ground. And then I compounded the fracture jumping around trying to escape. Do you understand what I'm saying?"

"Yes. What does your friend Cochran think?"

"I haven't told anyone this, not even Cochran. I don't know why. I just can't. Maybe if I had just stayed where I was in the first place I would have been easily captured. The leg would have set and healed."

"I don't think so." Lilli sat up. For the longest time she stared down, until I could hold her gaze no longer and looked away. She rose and went to a hibachi, where the roots and herbs she had bought earlier were brewing in a flowered enamel kettle. She poured a small cup and brought it to me. "It clean shit from your blood."

The steam carried the aroma of dark, bitter roots, but Lilli seemed so intent that I sipped it without a fuss. I have drunk navy coffee no less bitter that promised a great deal less.

Lilli smiled faintly. Then, as if coming to a heavy decision, she said in a very solemn voice, "I tell you a story. It is about my father. I also tell no one this story. Not my sister. Only you know. And you will tell no one. It is only for you to know."

I nodded. I thought she was offering a confession of her own in some grave Japanese exchange of obligations for the trust I had just accorded her. I did not know until later, perhaps weeks, that what she was giving me was my life.

The World War II firebombing of Tokyo that had scarred Lilli had burned to death her brother and grandparents, consuming them in that horrendous pyre. Her mother was deranged by the holocaust. Lilli's father, at this time, near the end of the war, was a major stationed at the Western Army District Headquarters in Fukuoka, just north of Nagasaki on Kyushu, the southernmost of the islands that make up Japan. The American B–29 bomber crews shot down on the raids over Japan were imprisoned at that garrison. And it was there that Lilli's father received the news of the death of his son and mother and father.

He grieved for several months. Then on August 9, 1945, a bomb named the Fat Man incinerated Nagasaki. Two days later Lilli's father and a group of other officers loaded eight of the captured B–29 crewmen into a truck and transported them to a field south of Fukuoka. The American POWs were lined up, stripped to their shorts, and one by one they were dragged forward, beaten to a kneeling position, and formally beheaded with a gleaming *katana*. The Japanese officers took turns, and by the fifth execution, her father's turn, the dulling blade required two butchering blows to sever the prisoner's head.

The sword's failure enraged the Japanese officers and shattered any sense of ceremony. The sixth airman was dragged out to be killed with bare-handed karate punches. But the first blow to the stomach only brought him to his knees. Lilli's father and another officer held him up while the executioner hit him two, three, four times, and still the American did not die. He was then badly decapitated with the dull sword.

The seventh American prisoner of war also survived the karate beating, and the angry, frustrated executioner kicked him in the groin, then chopped him through the lungs with the sword.

There was one man left. And again the American was forced to his knees. But this time a Japanese officer brought out a bow and arrow and sighted on the kneeling prisoner. The first two arrows just missed his head. The third struck him just above the left eye, but it did not kill him. Tiring of the torture, the army officers then cut the American flier's head off with the sword.

Four days later, the Emperor of Japan went on national radio to proclaim the surrender and tell the Japanese to endure the unendurable and suffer what was insufferable. At the Western Army Headquarters, Lilli's father and fellow officers listened to the Emperor, then herded the remaining sixteen B–29 crewmen still imprisoned onto trucks. They drove back to the same field south of the garrison. There, without the formalities of the previous executions, the American POWs were dragged into the woods, and in an insane frenzy the Japanese officers hacked them to pieces with swords.

Afterward, at headquarters, Lilli's father helped burn the records. Then he changed his blood-soaked uniform and returned to Tokyo for a tragic reunion with what now remained of his family, his wife and two small daughters.

The next day, in full uniform, the major went to the Imperial Palace. In the Kokyo Gaien, the Palace Plaza, crowds knelt and offered eternal allegiance to the divine rule of the Emperor. The major knelt among them, opened his uniform tunic, removed the short sword from its lacquer scabbard, and disemboweled himself, seppuku-style.

Lilli told the story in extraordinary detail in a hushed voice. Although she had not actually witnessed any of these scenes, once again—as in the story of the firebombing of Tokyo—I was impressed by how much the story had become personally her own. She did not narrate it as an account of atrocities but as the second and third acts of a drama that had begun with the firebombing that killed her brother, grandparents, and a hundred thousand others. Although I don't pretend to fully understand it, her father's hara-kiri was the symbolic act by which he accepted full responsibility so that no retribution would be visited on his family.

"In Vietnam they kill you just like that," Lilli whispered. "There is no price to be paid for this man you killed. It is not your leg for his life. It is the way it is. *Shikata-ga-nai.*"

"What's that?"

"Very old Japanese expression. It means 'It cannot be helped.' But more than that. It is resignation to what happens, when you cannot change it."

She arose, brought me another cup of the healing bitter herbs and roots, and commanded that I drink it.

Then she took off her robe, lay down next to me, and kissed me. "Do not give your leg for his life. He would kill you. I know this." The heat of her flesh flowed over my skin like a balm.

I was shy with Lilli that night, not at all sure of what I was capable of, or even what was appropriate. But as we lay on the futons naked and cleansed under a silk quilt, for the first time in many weeks I felt the warm surge of life and desire flow again in my blood.

When we made love, Lilli mounted me at her initiative, and she moved at first in cautious, gentle undulations, fearful of jarring my leg. As her heaving, and my own thrusts into her, became more insistent, demanding, any distinction between the pleasure and pain she was creating blurred into one searing frenzy, her half-shut eyes fixed on mine, her lips pulled back against her teeth in a smile that was at once a gasping. Her excited movements drew out in long slithering retreats in which I almost slipped from her, and then shoved shivering down again, knowingly holding me in a thrall where searing pain and ecstasy had become one, and I could not let go of it.

When I at last exploded, the release came almost like death itself, the mating of a spider whose head is bitten off at the moment of climax. I almost fainted.

But even then Lilli did not let me go, her hips rhythmically stroking, as if easing herself down through a series of gentler but still violent aftershocks. When finally spent, she simply slid off to one side, her wet thigh still thrown over my hips, an arm across my chest, her mouth at my cheek.

She never said a word, but just lay there catching her breath, her breath a warm moist pant in my ear. Then I fainted.

18

The Bullet to Kyoto

The two black guys are young, around twenty, barbered in a fashion that gives away their status despite the trendy mufti. The Japanese girls with them wear candy-colored lime and coral minidresses of skintight neoprene that flash yards of tawny legs on four-inch stiletto heels.

About them surges a tsunami of commuters inbound from the suburbs, all seemingly outfitted in navy blue or gray suits and attaché cases. The two girls formally shake the young men's hands and, letting go, are immediately swept off in the wave pouring through Tokyo station toward the office buildings of the Marunouchi district.

The two Americans gaze about the station, bemused by the early morning flood of commuters.

One catches my eye and, seeing a friendly gaijin face, nods in greeting.

"How you doing?"

"I'm doing fine, sir. Unbe-lieve-ably fine. Not to be be-lieved."

The other guy laughs, as if to confirm how fine things really are.

"That good, huh?"

"Un-fucking-believable. We are accessories."

"Oh really, to what crime?"

"No no, not accessories to a crime. Accessories, ya know, like a handbag, or gloves." He tugs at an earlobe. "Earrings. Shit like that. We are their accessories. These Japanese bitches—that's what they call us. Ya know what I'm saying?"

"Really."

"Hey, man, I mean they pay for everything. Everything. They take us around to the clubs, you know, as their accessories. That's what we are."

"Cool."

"It's something else," the second guy says. "I mean here these Japanese girls, they're waiting on the docks at Yokosuka, and they pick up on the brothers coming off ship. No white guys, you understand."

"No white guys at all?"

"Well, maybe if a guy's blond and like a surfer type. But they definitely dig the brothers. For accessories, y'understand what I'm saying. It's a thing with them. And they pay for everything. Shee-it, the way things cost here, I couldn't buy a Coke. But these bitches got the money."

The other nods. "That's how it is."

"Going back to Yokosuka?"

He gives a broad grin, entertaining a private joke. "We're going to Disneyland."

"That's what you do when you score big, right?" And they plunge into the horde, pushing toward the Yaesu exit.

This side of Tokyo station facing the Yaesu district accommodates the bullet trains. Michiko Hara and I are to rendezvous here. I have maneuvered her into accompanying me to Kyoto as the emissary to her uncle. Three hours alone with her on the nonstop *shinkansen*, isolated from past, present, and future, to transform her back into Lilli, as if I can then undo and redirect the past. There is middle-aged madness here.

The unending swarm of commuters surges by me. Tokyo station is five times busier than Grand Central, and I am beginning to gravely doubt we will connect.

Searching anxiously, I catch a flash of a familiar darkly menacing beefy face under a glistening bald pate, which immediately ducks and is lost in the crowd. My heart lurches, but the fear is not for myself. In my obsession I have now exposed Michiko to the assassins who murdered Mari Midori and stalk me.

I start after him, when Michiko, flustered and apologizing in a breathless voice, materializes out of the flood of bodies, and, oh Jesus, she grips her daughter, Yuki, by the hand.

I look from Michiko to Yuki, forcing a smile.

"Kyoto is the ancient capital. This trip will be very educational for Yuki," Michiko explains as we settle down into our seats. Yuki has been suddenly yanked from school—a serious matter for a Japanese teenager preparing for her exams—out of some delicate sense of propriety, as Hara himself is not accompanying us. There will be no revelations of Lilli and of love lost, in the presence of her daughter.

In the train, a middle-aged woman, perhaps fifty, struggles through the car, lugging a suitcase, burdened with several packages, a shopping bag hanging from her arm. She jostles through the crowd and collapses into the last empty seat. After a few minutes a businessman saunters onto the train, only a newspaper in his hand. The woman rises and with a little bow relinquishes her seat, which he immediately occupies, reading his newspaper, while the woman—apparently his wife—sways in the aisle, clutching her packages and bags, as if preparing to stand at least to the first stop two hours away.

Both Michiko and Yuki avoid my eyes.

I study mother and daughter as they discuss some school text Yuki has brought along. The beauty of the older woman and blossoming girl opposite me overlie the poignant image of Lilli that teases my memory. The flickering sunlight and rushing landscape in the window behind them lend their dual presence a hallucinatory quality—as if Lilli were splintered and misplaced in time.

Michiko notices me watching and flashes a tentative, nervous smile.

"Your daughter is very pretty," I say. "She will be a beautiful woman."

Michiko smiles "Thank you," taking it as a compliment. "She will have a very nice life."

"And does her mother have a nice life?"

Michiko is startled by the question but then answers quite seriously, "I was born during the war. It was often very difficult when I was young. We had to endure many hardships."

"When did you work at the American embassy?"

"I worked there from August nineteen sixty-three until I met Kenji, in May nineteen sixty-six. Even after we were married, I worked there. Four years total, I think. It was a very good job. At that time it paid much more than any Japanese job for a woman."

The time frame perfectly covers the year I knew Lilli. And Michiko recites it with a certain intensity. But is it Lilli giving me her cover story—fixing me with a silent plea in her eyes—or Michiko Hara noting her qualifications for our mission?

"That's terrific. Your experience will be a great help during the negotiations. But we should take this time as an opportunity to talk, so that you're familiar with my speech patterns and way of phrasing. Ask me questions."

"What kind of questions?"

"Business or personal. We Americans are less private than the Japanese, so I won't be offended. And the better you know me, the better it will be. As your husband may have told you, I have a tendency to be blunt and direct. I might offend Kuribayashi. I trust your discretion and tact to rephrase what I say if I do that."

"That is a great responsibility."

"I trust you with it, certainly much more than I do Ozu."

Michiko bows her head. "Thank you."

The *shinkansen,* the bullet train from Tokyo to Kyoto, silently whizzes at 130 miles an hour along rubber-cushioned steel rails that are welded together rather than bolted, never echoing back the clickety-clack of the blues in the night. The electrically propelled ride is, in fact, so smooth that only the blur of the Japanese suburbs through the windows indicates its speed.

"Do you have trains like this in America?"

"No, in many ways we're still playing catch-up after the Cold War. In Southern California, the factories that built the warplanes I flew a long time ago are only now struggling to convert to build trains like this."

There is, perhaps, a dark personal irony here. This bullet train was inaugurated in '64—in time to showcase Japan's modern emergence during the Tokyo Olympics—and Lilli had eagerly suggested taking this excursion, a high-tech ride to the mystical ancient temples of Kyoto. But the escalating war had intruded.

Suddenly the flash of an image on flesh, just at the periphery of my vision, makes me turn. A gaunt man with a crew cut strides up the aisle, his retreating back now to me so I don't have a look at his face. But his arms swing behind him in the energy of his stride, giving me a quick glimpse of a dragon's head tattooed on the back of his hand.

"But personally you have been very successful."

I turn back to Michiko Hara. Is it the polite comment of the wife of an executive with whom I am conducting business, or Lilli asking me about my life in the thirty years since I left Japan, terrified of losing my leg, perhaps more frightened of her?

"Strangely, that wasn't really my goal."

"In Japan, everyone works so hard to be successful."

"It's a very formal system. In rigid systems people must work harder to rise. There is less room for luck."

"And you have been lucky?"

"Very. Success is often just doing what hasn't been done before. You catch a wave like a surfer. To ride it you don't have to be a great surfer, just stay up on the board."

"A wave?" she questions.

"A new, rapidly expanding industry—in my case, cable TV and satellites. The truth is, the better lawyers in the firm I joined right out of law school were intensely bored by anything technical. I was a very junior associate, and they just dumped it on my desk—'Here, you know about this stuff'—because I had been a navy pilot. I didn't, really. But I learned enough to put together deals."

Michiko laughs softly, and her eyes flash. "But you must have daring to be a surfer."

She's flattering me. The truth is that I had surfed that wave from the law office to executive offices through the mergers and acquisitions of the eighties. It had not been daring so much as lack of fear of new technology. Rosenfield, the senior partner who first tossed the cable TV/satellite transmission files on my desk, had had the right instinct after all.

Most lawyers—even business executives, unless they are engineers—are confused, even frightened by anything technical. My survival had depended on technology for several years, so I was a quick study. Rosenfield would tout my expertise to our clients. He unwittingly sold Greenwald on recruiting me as his VP of strategic planning.

"I don't invent or design any new technology. But I do design financial and corporate structures to successfully exploit it. That's why I'm here."

Michiko Hara studies me, perhaps reading between the lines of what I am saying. I smile. "That's probably more than you want to know."

"No, no. It is very interesting to me. You have been very successful."

"Lucky. Truth is, if I hadn't fallen into communications at the right time, I probably would've become a third-rate legal drudge who hates his work and drinks too much. With all the other attendant vices."

Michiko stares at me but remains silent. Why did I say that? I am compelled to account for my life—not to Michiko Hara but to this ghost of Lilli who haunts me—to reckon my extraordinary good fortune where friends have died or spent years of torture in POW camps.

"Did you always want to be a lawyer?" Yuki suddenly asks.

For a moment the question disorients me. It is, I realize, something Lilli and I never discussed. The future beyond the arrival and sailing of the carrier from Japan to the South China Sea did not exist. If law school had been a serious ambition, I would never have volunteered for navy flight school and the extension of service it mandated.

I shake my head. "No, not really. When I was discharged, the Vietnam War was still going on, and I was . . . disoriented. Most veterans were. Very disoriented. I had no pressing ambitions really. Law school was a refuge from the world for three years. An escape from having to make a decision about what to do with my life. People study law in the United States often with no intent of practicing. It's like getting an MBA, a master's degree in business." I smile at Yuki. I realize that I have never discussed this with my own daughters.

Does Michiko Hara have a memory of me at twenty-five?

"It was the late sixties, an extraordinary time. A lot of us were waiting for the world to somehow change. I thought a law degree might help. Perhaps I was right. Here I am to marry the United States and Japan in the electronic global village."

Michiko smiles, and there is something enigmatic in the purse of her lips. But then, suddenly embarrassed, she looks away and smoothes some unseen wrinkle on her daughter's dress.

"Do you meet many movie stars?" Yuki asks.

"Rarely. Mostly I meet their lawyers. My partner Stan Levy handles our clients who are actors."

"Yuki's generation is very much infatuated with American movies and music, your pop culture."

"Does that disturb you?"

"A little bit. It is very important to remain Japanese, but I understand this fascination with Americans. It is part of growing up, I think."

"And for your generation?"

"It was very different. We were born either during the war or right after it. Our feelings about Americans are very confused. There was also the movies, the music. Perhaps not so much as there is today, but many American young men were here. So our experiences were more personal." Michiko's gaze remains steady. She glances at her daughter, who is following the conversation with interest.

"And what do you think?" I ask, turning my attention also to Yuki.

The girl at first glances out of the corner of her eye at her mother, then suddenly very bold says, "I think Americans are glamorous." Then she immediately dissolves into an embarrassed giggle.

"Glamorous. Gee, you can't do any better than that. And how does Mr. Kuribayashi feel?" I ask Michiko Hara.

"I do not know what is in Kuribayashi-san's heart." She speaks very slowly, in that precise, polite way that holds its own charm. "What might seem insignificant or forgettable to you might be devastating." She holds my eyes for a beat, then adds quickly, "To your negotiations, I mean."

I nod. "It is very important that you told me that. Thank you." Are there always two levels to this conversation, or do they exist only in my imagination?

For the next hour I stick to business, going over my briefing for Kuribayashi, a pitch really. At one point I note Yuki avidly taking it all in without a hint of the usual teenage ennui.

"Oh no, I find it all very interesting," she insists.

"You should meet my oldest daughter. She's planning to be president."

"Of the United States?"

"Of whatever there is."

"She must have her father's mind," Michiko says.

"No, she's much smarter than I was at that age. And wiser. But then women are always wiser."

Michiko laughs. "Does she favor you or your wife in appearance?"

"Probably me, poor thing. Her features were always too strong to ever be cute as a teenager. But she seems to be growing into them in some strange, wonderful way. By about the time she graduates from law school, she's going to mature into a very striking and attractive woman. I can see it in her."

"She wants to go to law school, like her father?"

"Don't tell her that. She's very much into being her own woman. It's her religion."

"Ah yes, I have read that about American girls," Michiko says and laughs softly.

An hour out of Tokyo the snow-capped volcanic cone of Mount Fuji looms up in high relief above mist-cloaked tangerine groves and trimmed tea bushes, the sun spotlighting the 12,389-foot peak, an ancient icon framed in the window of the bullet train.

There is a quiet contemplation of the sacred mountain. "I've only seen it from the air before," I say.

"You flew an airplane over it. What was that feeling?" Yuki asks with that rapturous intensity teenage girls have.

"Spooky." Was it a sacrilege or a blessing to parade over a sacred mountain in warplanes?

We had taken off from the U.S. naval air station at Atsugi, just west of Yokohama, then circled in formation over Fuji—the white nipple thrusting through the cottony layer of scud, glistening moistly in the sunlight. We climbed out over the Sagami Sea to search out the carrier steaming south.

"Spooky?" Yuki questions.

I try to smile. "Everything spooked me then. I was going back to Vietnam, and the way things were there, I wasn't at all sure I was coming back."

Who am I talking to? Is Michiko's daughter my imagined picture of Lilli at that age, yet innocent, without that grave beauty the war had etched in her face or the seductive makeup of the Black Rose?

I excuse myself on the pretext of the men's room. I have to ascertain if I have placed Michiko and Yuki in harm's way. The train is an express, two hours from Tokyo to Nagoya, with forty-eight minutes more to Kyoto. The Yakuzioso with the dragon-head tattoos—if that is indeed who I have seen—isn't going anywhere. By now he is reasonably relaxed, perhaps dozing.

The woman with the packages is still standing in the aisle, hanging on next to her husband, who now intently examines a magazine. I amble down the aisle, trying to keep the search as unobtrusive as possible—a tall white man on a train, peering into the homogeneous faces. There are very few white, let alone Filipino or black, faces in the crowd.

But Dragon Hands has not gone far. He is in the very next car, and I spot the dragon head carrying smoke and fire to his mouth. He is talking with the beefy bald man with the ponytail when, as though some street sixth sense alerts him, he looks up and stares right at me. I quickly retreat back to my own car and duck into the men's lavatory.

The seats on the eighteen-car bullet train are reserved. If they are in the very next car, then they had known where Michiko Hara and I were seated before they boarded.

This betrayal hits me just as the bathroom door bangs open. Dragon Hands and the samurai quickly enter and slam the door shut behind them.

Dragon Hands smiles evilly, as if in greeting, and the other shakes his head. "Stupid, stupid Yankee no go home."

He carries a black briefcase, and from it he withdraws a short sword in its scabbard. He holds it up in front of him, one hand on the sheath, the other gripping the hilt, and stares levelly at me, as if about to perform a solemn ritual.

Behind him Dragon Hands turns to lock the door. But it suddenly bursts open with a force that shoves Dragon Hands aside, banging him into the samurai.

A huge man stands there, his girth totally filling the doorway.

Then he steps into the compartment with the swift authority of a sumo wrestler wading into the ring of combat.

In one movement he slides by both men and pivots to place his great back to me, embraces the two thugs, one in each arm, and seemingly without struggle pushes them out the door into the aisle.

There is a harsh, guttural exchange in Japanese. Then the man reenters and says something in almost incomprehensible English. It is a moment before I decipher "They leave next station Nagoya."

He bows and presents his card. "Taiyo Security and Investigations," it reads on the English side. This sumo wrestler with a crew cut in a black business suit is Nakabe Ichiro.

"Very good. Very well done, Mr. Ichiro. *Arigato gozaimasu*," I blurt out in my dismay, the words awkward and thick as tofu on my tongue.

He nods. "Oh yes, very welcome." He backs out the door but cautions me with a gesture to wait a moment before following him.

Neither thug is evident when I step out. Ichiro moves down the aisle, totally filling it yet somehow easing his way with a ponderous grace. He passes Michiko and her daughter without glancing at them and takes a seat at the end of the car from which he overlooks the length of the compartment.

Ready had been right. His Tokyo associates were pros. Huge as he was, I had not spotted Michiko's and my bodyguard, nor apparently had the Yakuza thugs. What other security, or assassins, are about us?

Fuji still shimmers in the flashing windows as I work my way back to my seat. According to my guidebook, it last erupted in 1707 and spewed black ash six inches thick on the Imperial Palace seventy-five miles away as the ash flies, making the Tokugawa Shogun wonder what had evoked this anger from the gods. Dark omens are also giving this wayfarer pause.

But I smile at Michiko Hara. "It's interesting that I was in Japan about the time you worked for the American embassy," I say offhandedly.

Michiko's gaze is even. "Did you enjoy Japan?"

I smile. "Well, it was a very disoriented, emotional time for me."

"It was emotional for you?" Again there is that Japanese way of repeating what I say, not a direct question really, but tactfully inviting me to elaborate.

"There was the war. And I was in love. With a Japanese girl named Lilli, a hostess at the Black Rose cabaret."

At that moment Michiko Hara loses it. Tears flood her eyes. She shakes her head as if to deny them, then quickly rises and bolts down the aisle.

19

Disorders for Sailing

Orders came for sailing
Somewhere over there.
All confined to barracks
Was more than I could bear.
I knew you were waiting in the street.
I heard your feet
But could not meet
My Lilli of the lamplight,
My own Lilli Marlene.

Flaming Dart, Rolling Thunder—the bombing campaigns calculated to bring the North to the peace table—had only escalated the
war. By the Christmas truce of '65, the carriers on the line began
rotating home, first the *Coral Sea*, then *Midway, Independence, Bon
Homme Richard*, and *Oriskany*.

There was a formidable armada in port in Yokosuka. At the
end of the pier at which the carriers berthed, Cochran and I
caught one of the tiny Toyota cabs that shuttled sailors from the
docks across the sprawl of the navy base to the main gate. As the
cab careened along the waterfront, the heavy prows of cruisers,
amphibious assault, and supply ships loomed alongside in gray steel
battlements. Beyond them nests of destroyers—tied up side by
side—ceaselessly stirred, sighed, and rubbed against each other as

if for warmth in the black choppy water. The ships were heading south, to the war.

But our carrier was departing for the continental United States at week's end, and I was not sailing home aboard it. The flight surgeons did not want me back aboard with a septic infection they didn't comprehend, constantly reinjuring my leg hobbling up and down steep ladders, banging through narrow passageways, and tripping on the raised sills of fire doors. Whatever the medical prognosis for my leg, my war was over.

Cochran helped me pack my gear and carry what I might need to the naval hospital. "Junko's morose at our leaving," Tommy said, "so I invited her down for the squadron party."

I didn't comment, but I had my misgivings about the invitation.

My infection appeared to be abating, and aside from cleansing the wound, the doctors had now apparently decided to hold off with anything more drastic. After the morning examination and change of bandages, against doctor's orders, I immediately hobbled out of the hospital on my cane and caught the commuter train to Tokyo, as if by fleeing the surgeons and their scalpels I might avert amputation.

In Tokyo, Lilli and I went to the movies, the flamboyant all-female Takarazuka Theater, and made a second pilgrimage to the incense-fogged Sensoji Temple. She was convinced that the grace of this particular Buddha, bestowed on our previous visit, had saved my life, if not yet my leg.

She continued to ply me with her teas of bitter herbs from the Asian alchemist. The baths at the Kanko became a nightly rite, with its stripping away, its ritualized cleansing, its naked intimacies, and shared confessions. I had, in the end, come to Lilli for absolution. And she had washed me clean—if not totally, she had at least purged me of horrors by revealing greater ones of her own and by sharing the darkness in her own life.

And my leg slowly healed. The navy doctors in Yokosuka, of course, took the credit with their regimen of antibiotics. But I am con-

vinced it was really Lilli. She brought me alive, caused my blood and
hormones to throb in a surge of life force. I can make too much of this,
but cures have been effected with much less than herbs, absolution,
and sex.

And yet there was a melancholy sweetness in our lovemaking
because Lilli knew that I would be following the carrier home as soon
as the navy surgeons were convinced they had checked the infection.

It wasn't until several years later—when the first POWs were released—that I became painfully aware how few had survived the years
of torture and imprisonment with injuries like mine. Many perished in
bamboo cages before ever getting to prison camps. My own salvation
had narrowed down to that runty middle-aged peasant whom I had
smothered in night soil and stabbed in the heart with a hunting knife.

I was practicing law by then, married, and I would look at my
daughter and at Joan, pregnant with our second, and know that I had
not just been spared, but delivered in an extraordinary way. I have
never known to what end.

Yet there were more appalling events waiting in the wings.

During our carrier's last in-port stay in Yokosuka, Cochran's fighter
squadron threw a sailing party. From all accounts, it was not particularly different from the all-hands brawls—i.e., egalitarian affairs
attended by both officers and enlisted men—that each squadron and
division aboard a carrier held sometime during a deployment to the
Far East. But the timing was tragic.

Junko entrained down from Tokyo to the navy port, and by the
time she and Cochran arrived at the banquet room of the restaurant
just off Thieves Alley, the party was well under way. They could hear
the noise a block away. Master Chief Avionics Electrician Dannemeyer, red-faced, sweating, and tolerably drunk, stood weaving near
the door, his arm about a girl whom he introduced as Sugar-san,
warmly grasping each arrival's hand in his moist paws to solemnly
thank them for coming.

Cochran had mentioned in passing that all the officers in his squadron would be there, and Junko—despite his warnings—had conjured up the fantasy of an elegant cotillion of officers and their ladies. She had gone out and bought a new dress and had her hair elaborately done. And as soon as they arrived, she took off for the girl's room, apparently to freshen up before being presented to his superiors. Cochran grabbed a drink and settled down at one of the tables ringing the dance floor, next to a civilian technician of an aircraft parts manufacturer, who was attached to the squadron.

Just then the four-piece band struck up "Blue Velvet," and a stripper sashayed onto the dance floor. It was instant strip and no tease, and as she dropped the seventh veil, there was an audible gasp from the tech rep.

"Terrific what they can get away with over here," he said to no one in particular, taking off his glasses to wipe them.

"Be careful they don't fog up on you now," Cochran said.

The tech rep looked startled, his eyes went wide, and he broke out into a high unnatural whooping laugh that attracted the stripper. She slithered toward him like a snake to a bird, flaunting her nakedness, taunting him with it. He grinned stupidly at her, his eyes blinking nervously behind his glasses, transfixed as she leaned forward and mischievously shook her breasts in his face. The crowd cheered.

Egged on, the stripper grabbed him by the ears, pulled him forward, and made bumping and grinding motions, his nose inches from her pubis. He suddenly lunged forward, grabbed her about the hips, and shoved his face into her pubic hair, rubbing back and forth with choked, blubbering sounds. The crowd roared.

The girl screamed and tried to push him away, then beat on his head, but he had a tenacious grip about her waist and hung on.

After a brief struggle, he let go and emerged red-faced, his glasses now hanging off one ear, and gasped, "I've always wanted to do *that*." He again let out that high whooping laugh. "All my life, yes, to do that."

Cochran hilariously pounded him on the back, almost knocking him out of his chair. "You dirty old man."

"I'll drink to that."

At that moment Cochran glanced up and saw Junko standing by, frowning, absolutely devastated.

"This party for your squadron officers?" she inquired in a stricken voice. She now looked about at the other girls, seeing the Seventh Fleet camp followers for the first time.

"I told you it was not going to be a black-tie reception," he said.

But she did not hear him. She touched her hair and smoothed her new dress, as if determined to be the lady here.

Another stripper materialized on the dance floor, but Junko haughtily ignored the show and silently studied the dissolute crowd of sailors and the girls.

The stripper on the dance floor reached her finale, retaining her G-string.

"Take it off! Take it *all* off!" the high-pitched whooping voice next to Cochran sang out. The cry was taken up by the crowd.

The girl hesitated a moment in confusion, then hurriedly fled from the floor. A sailor reached out, grabbed at her, and in a quick cat-like swipe ripped off her G-string.

The girl shrieked, tried to recover the garment, then, as if suddenly conscious of the flushed, leering faces pressing in at her, stood stunned, her hands now covering her loins and breasts in the classic pose of startled nakedness.

Master Chief Dannemeyer lurched onto the floor next to her and hauled off with a boot that sent the offending sailor across the dance floor, upsetting a table. "This is one of the Class B strippers, damn it," he roared. "They keep their G-strings. And we're going to treat the entertainment with respect. Remember, we're guests in this country."

He turned to the terrified girl. "Sorry, Miss, the boys didn't understand the contract." He bent to retrieve the G-string, but the girl fled from the floor through a gauntlet of groping hands.

"Hey, we'll have no more of that shit," a red-faced Dannemeyer bellowed, "or I'll stop this here entertainment. I kid you not." With that he nodded to the band, which exploded into "A Hard Day's Night."

The dinner was served. Junko regarded the sukiyaki balefully and instead picked at a plate of steak and French fries. The band was too loud for conversation, the dance floor too crowded with bruising, bumping, jostling drunks, both arms wrapped around a girl, hugging pelvis to pelvis, shuffling in vague syncopation to the music. And Cochran drank too much.

By the time the first enlisted men staggered out of the room, their arms beerily draped about girls, the evening was an irretrievable disaster. Cochran led Junko by the hand, picking their way through the tangle of disordered tables with dead drinks and empty bottles, cold bowls of sukiyaki gone thick and sticky, plates of congealed steak juice, grease, limp French fries, sodden napkins, and pyres of squashed cigarettes butts.

"Howzit goin'?" The tech rep sprawled in a chair, his arm dangling about a chunky moon-faced girl. He grinned up at Cochran, and as Junko passed he tipped forward to give her a swat on the behind, but his foot caught and he crashed to the floor, pulling the girl on top of him. They both lay there laughing. Junko never said a word, which for this normally ebullient girl was ominous.

Nor did she speak much on the train back to Tokyo, after adamantly refusing to spend the night in Yokosuka. Her normally animated, impishly beguiling face was set in an expressionless yellow mask.

Yet as late as the hour was, she insisted on dropping by the Black Rose, apparently to let the other girls admire her new dress and hairdo and regale them with an extravagantly fantasized and bowdlerized account of this final soiree. Tommy shook his head as he quietly filled me in on the squalid details.

Then Junko led Cochran to the Kanko baths, as though to ritually cleanse away whatever corruption still clung from that descent into the seedy fleshpot of the fleet.

Lilli and I had our own private rites to perform.

"Orders came for sailing.
Time for us to part.
Darling, I'd caress you
And press you to my heart."

She knelt beside me, naked, her feet tucked under her, combing her long sleek black hair with slow sensual strokes, a self-conscious tease that was more foreplay than grooming, and sang in that husky, affected Marlene Dietrich whisper,

"And there 'neath that far-off lantern light
I'd hold you tight.
We'd kiss good night."

The single low lamp reflected that tint of red in her black hair, as if revealing a concealed fire. It made me strangely edgy, insinuating some danger that seethed about us.

"Talk to me, please," Lilli said. "I want to practice my English."

I pulled her to me. "I am kissing your bare shoulder."

"It is also my naked shoulder."

"Yes, technically that's correct. But generally we say your arms are bare, your legs are bare"—I moved lips and fingers lightly over her limbs—"your bottom is bare, but your whole body is naked or nude."

"That is not my bottom. My feet are my bottom, *neh?*"

"Yes, that's right. But when we talk about a person's bottom, we usually mean *this*. It also is your ass, but that's a harsh word. It's not polite."

"*Bottom* is polite?"

"It's humorous, or funny." Just above her bottom, at the small of her back, I felt the leathery fire scar, that welt in the otherwise satiny, unblemished skin. "A polite or formal word is *buttock*."

"So many words in English with very small difference in meanings," she sighed. "I never learn."

I turned her around to face me. "That's why we must study very hard. These are your breasts, and this part is the nipples." I kissed them.

"They are also my tits, *neh?*"

"*Tits* is a vulgar word."

"Don't tell me vulgar words for anything. I don't want to know them. Only polite or poetic words."

"We don't have poetic words for sex in English. Only scientific medical words or dirty words. The trick in English, I guess, is for lovers to make the vulgar words poetic. But to everyone else, they are harsh and dirty. And what does that tell you about us?"

"That is sad," she said. Her head tilted back, and her teeth suddenly seized the lobe of my ear, a sharp little bite, then her tongue licked it as if to soothe the pain.

After we made love I fainted away. I don't know how long I slept with Lilli draped over my chest, but we were both jarred awake by a fierce, anguished howl from the next room. Then a series of deep, gut-wrenching moans through the paper walls made us sit bolt upright.

Cochran suddenly burst through the wall, shattering the fragile rice paper. He staggered through the great tear, stark naked, his face contorted with pain, eyes wild with fear and madness. They focused only momentarily with recognition when he saw me. "Look what the bitch did to me," he croaked in a voice that was unrecognizable.

Blood gushed down his legs from the open wound in his groin. Then his gore-covered knees buckled, and he sprawled against me in a faint. Behind him, framed in the rent in the paper wall, stood Junko, naked, motionless as if carved in ivory, holding a bloody *kai-ken* in one hand and the obscenity of Tommy Cochran's butchered prick in the other.

Part 3

KYOTO—TIME IS A RIVER WITHOUT BANKS

20

The Flight of the Phoenix

Kyoto is a holy city with eight thousand ancient temples, spared by American bombers during World War II in return for Japanese assurances that there were no antiaircraft guns or military installations in the city. The headquarters of Kuribayashi Electric Industrial Company is well south of those eight thousand temples, off the highway that leads to the heavy industry of Osaka.

The corporate headquarters is a modern sprawling structure with pyramiding tiers of dark glass and concrete slabs like ramparts that to my brooding eyes looks at a distance like the profile of a World War II battleship stripped of its guns. The vertically spouting fountains at the entrance do not soften the effect.

I am to meet Michiko Hara there for our late-afternoon conference with Akira Kuribayashi, the chairman of Kuribayashi Electric and the major stockholder of its subsidiary electronic companies. Michiko and Yuki are staying at a family residence Hara maintains outside the city, while I quarter at a luxury hotel downtown.

On the brief ride earlier from Kyoto station to my hotel, Michiko had profusely apologized for her bolt from the train compartment, explaining it as a sudden seizure of travel sickness, and nodding emphatically at Yuki, as if seeking to confirm her delicate stomach.

Michiko was nervous, more remote than on the *shinkansen*, speaking little. But as the limo pulled into the hotel's formal carriageway, she turned to face me directly, her lips teasing into a smile but the dark eyes, for a moment, misting. "Peter, your story of Lilli touched me. It is like a novel. Sometimes lovely, sometimes painful. Bittersweet, I think. Is that the word?"

"Yes, *bittersweet* is the word."

The white-gloved driver opened the door and stood at attention, waiting for me to depart.

"But it can be very disturbing to dwell on the past," Michiko said, her eyes never leaving mine, "even destructive, when the present is so critical to so many."

Rather obviously, if this meeting is to succeed I have to stay focused on the business at hand, not distract her with my bemused, obsessive probing of the past.

Michiko is already waiting in the formal conference room. Perhaps a stable marriage and two children will transform a haunted, wild soul—and I can testify to that—but the woman who now smiles and examines me with curious eyes is not the Lilli I knew.

At that moment Kuribayashi himself enters. A spare man, reedy as bamboo, with hair—surprisingly full for a man of seventy-nine— the same battleship gray as the building. And he conveys the same austere impression. His suit and tie are earth tones of that gray, and the quarter-inch of white handkerchief in his jacket pocket is so precise it might have been folded in with a carpenter's level.

He smiles politely, but behind the oversize black-framed glasses his eyes reveal neither warmth nor anticipation. A bad sign. According to the PR, he enjoys golf, but I get the distinct impression that he probably plays only with other members of the *zaibatsu*, the clique of family-dominated holding companies that controls Japanese business, and never for the pleasure of the game.

Without a word Kuribayashi sits at the middle of the table, flanked only by two other senior executives a few years younger but dressed almost identically. He gestures for Michiko and me to sit opposite him, signaling by our positions that this is to be a head-to-head discussion, not a one-sided presentation.

The old man seems intrigued that I have come alone, accompanied only by Michiko as the interpreter and without a staff. He keeps glancing with keen interest from his niece to me, even before she begins interpreting.

"I don't know to what extent Kuribayashi-san has had time to study our proposal," Michiko translates.

Kuribayashi nods at the question. "We are to have a strategic investment in your company, a share of profits but no say whatever in the management of the studio and production companies."

"We greatly value your advice, counsel, and research for the Japanese and Asian markets. And we certainly need it in the implementation of the new technology."

"No ownership whatever in the TV stations," Kuribayashi continues. In two sentences he has cut directly to his bottom line.

"This is not allowed by American law. But you will be partners in the subsidiary companies that supply the stations and cable systems with all their high-definition television equipment. They will, of course, be your best customers. That market alone will be in the billions."

"But under the reorganization you would own the majority interest in these Japanese manufacturers."

"We would have to, yes, if they acquired the major equity in U.S. broadcasters." I can feel myself start to sweat.

"And have proportionate seats on the board of Kuribayashi Electric."

"Yes." And we are immediately at the issue that is more than the deal-breaker; it is a point of nationalism for which some are willing to kill. The old man sitting across the table from me will be criticized, even called a traitor, by many.

The conference room and table are identical to the one in Tokyo, or rather the reverse is true—the designer in Tokyo had not deviated from the corporate headquarters. And in that there is a message.

"And you believe that Kuribayashi will be left in the dust if we do not agree to this merger?"

Left in the dust. That is the expression I had used with Ozu on our ride back from the research center.

"No, I believe that Kuribayashi will still be a prosperous and inventive electronics manufacturer. The transition to high-definition television and five hundred channels—if that is what the market eventually dictates—will take perhaps ten years, perhaps more, depending on the economy. The question is to what extent Kuribayashi will participate in it." It will offend the old tycoon if I detail his company's depressed earnings or Japan's bankrupt banks.

"Are you familiar with the DuMont Television Corporation?" I suddenly ask Kuribayashi. "An American company that briefly flourished right after World War Two."

Kuribayashi takes in the information, neither acknowledging nor denying that he knows of DuMont.

"It was owned and managed by a brilliant engineer named Allen DuMont. They were the leaders in making the first TV sets, and they set up studios to produce many of the first shows. But they did not successfully organize a network of other stations. CBS and NBC did, using their radio stations as a base. There was then only room in the market for one more network. It became ABC—which had formed a strategic alliance with their radio stations and Paramount Theatres. DuMont eventually went out of business, not only broadcasting but manufacturing as well.

"There are times, Mr. Kuribayashi, especially at the start of a new mass communications technology, when even the most brilliant engineers and manufacturers must reinvent their companies. And there is that necessity at this moment in history. The future, Kuribayashi-san, belongs to those who identify the unmet needs of our new world and then figure out profitable ways to meet them."

The old man smiles faintly as Michiko translates, then says in a soft voice, "You are traveling to Paris."

"Your company was kind enough to arrange for my flight." Apparently my bluff about the French consortium has grabbed his attention.

"What of Philips?" The giant Dutch electronics conglomerate.

"They, of course, have been very active with NBC in developing high-definition TV. They are also pioneers in the area of interactive compact discs. They've recently sold off their motion picture interests . . ." I shrug and gesture with my hands. "There are many areas where we interface very neatly."

I wait until Michiko finishes translating. "But the downside is that it is like marriage to a eight-foot Dutch woman. You can go to bed with her, but you're going to be overwhelmed. And you have to do things her way."

Michiko looks startled, blushes slightly, glances at me slyly, then translates with an expressionless face without a giggle or fist in her mouth. There is a beat after she finishes, then Kuribayashi laughs and slaps the table. "Yes, yes, Hara-san said that you had a sense of humor. But that is very good point, very good."

"But the point is not about control, not in an economic or business sense," I continue. "It is about the soul, the spirit of what we do. Without it, all your TV sets, CD players, switchers, chips, circuit boards, cameras, our studios, cable systems, TV stations, satellites, fiber-optic networks are just dead hardware."

"Yes, it needs software."

"Software is programming that run computers. It dictates in what sequence circuits go on and off. It is confusing to use it to describe motion pictures, television programming, or music. What I have learned over the years, Mr. Kuribayashi, is that I represent a concentration of the talents that create dreams, fantasies, romances, adventures—for want of a better word, entertainment. These stir people, make them laugh and cry, feel passion and anger and, more often than not, hope." I turn to Michiko. "Am I laying this on too thick?"

"Thick?"

"Does it sound like bullshit?"

"Perhaps in English. In Japanese, it is very poetic. Spiritual."

"Terrific. Poetic and spiritual are good." I watch Michiko speak in that soft breathless voice to Kuribayashi. Is this the woman who in another life once taught me that there were no harsh, dirty words for sex in Japanese? Suddenly, as if she has been hearing my thoughts, she pauses and cocks her head toward me with a slight pleased smile before turning back to Kuribayashi.

"We make such movies in Japan," he replies.

"Yes, you do. And so do the French, the Swedes, the Italians. And the Chinese, Indonesians, Mexicans, Russians. A dozen countries have film, TV, and recording industries. But American product dominates all these markets." I pause for the translation.

"I don't have the exact figures, but I would make an educated guess that the combined international income of all Japanese films— outside Japan—for the last twenty-five years does not equal the international gross of just one of the blockbusters from our studio this year."

From Michiko's slight frown, I wonder if I have offended Kuribayashi, but he merely nods and grunts as she relays this information. I wonder how she has tactfully phrased it.

"And how long do you believe that Americans will continue to dominate the world market for software? You dislike that term, but you know what I mean."

Michiko is apparently translating word for word.

"How long will Americans dominate . . . ? A good question. We have for almost a century now. Since the first invention of movies, radio, recordings. And our market share and audience have increased. And it would be even more if it weren't for government regulations, as in France and Spain. We're now developing significant markets in China, India, Eastern Europe. What do you see in the future, Kuribayashi-san, that would reverse this trend?"

When Michiko translates, his lips purse in a bulldoggish expression that might be interpreted as a smile.

"The center of our communications industry is Los Angeles—a city that is Hispanic, Asian, African-American, and Caucasian. The Caucasians are in the minority now, but they include Jews, Italians, Irish, Iranians, Armenians, Arabs. Many Japanese see this as a weakness, a source of violence, and perhaps it is.

"But our films, television, music, and our writing have been nourished by this mix from the beginning. We're a city of immigrants in a nation of immigrants. Perhaps we don't create American . . . software. It's universal. It just emanates from the west side of this city on the Pacific Coast, a few hours' drive from the Mexican border. That's why, I believe, we'll continue to dominate international communications for the next century.

"Under GATT, the General Agreement on Tariffs and Trade, the Europeans are trying to limit their TV programming to fifty percent American shows. And the French—who invented movies and are so proud and protective of their own culture—have to tax our films to subsidize their own. Is it America they are trying to keep out, or the rest of the world? Maybe the future? I don't know. And, of course, the next question is—what is Kuribayashi trying to keep out?"

Kuribayashi smiles faintly. "Hara-san said that you often negotiate in a very strange way." Michiko allows herself to reflect Kuribayashi's smile.

I don't know quite how to respond, so I just smile back. "Even by American Wild West standards Los Angeles has always been a strange, rootless, disconnected town—not even a city really, but an urban sprawl where people come to reinvent their lives. Maybe that's why it's the perfect place to make movies and TV shows. Now it's a megalopolis, at once a city in the twenty-first century and a mongrel Third World country—"

"A mongrel?" Michiko questions.

"A street dog that's a mixture of many breeds."

"Ah so."

I look at Michiko. "Does this make any sense?"

"It does not have to make sense to me." She talks at some length to Kuribayashi. "It is something we discuss often, but we do not understand."

I nod. "Nobody understands it. It's not something you can analyze and create a formula for, although a lot of people pretend to."

"You do not think we can learn this international language?"

"Do it! You make movies and television. Create something here in Japan that will capture a world audience. You have actors, writers, directors, producers. You have the financial and technical resources. Do it! Don't buy Universal or Columbia or our studio. Do it here!"

I look at Michiko and wonder how she is translating this challenge, but at the end Kuribayashi merely nods again and emits his faint grunt of acknowledgment.

Finally he says, "You refused our offer completely. Why?"

"Mr. Kuribayashi, you don't want to be involved in a motion picture or TV studio. Look at what happened to Matsushita and Sony."

"I understand there were management problems."

"And there always will be. But when an executive vice president of Sony announced at a Tokyo news conference that *Last Action Hero* was going to be the company's *last failure*, Sony demonstrated at its highest level that it did not understand the motion picture or TV business. There will *always* be failures. Total bombs. It's an irrational business."

"You do not think that prudent management can eliminate these costly failures?"

"Prudent management guarantees failure. The most economical and profitable movie you can make is a hit. And in today's market that may cost two million or two hundred million dollars. You can't be afraid of failure or consider it a disgrace. You must be willing to accept it. To be frank, I think there's something in the essential Japanese character that's not able to do that. The Japanese are too acutely sensitive to the possibility of failure. And a high degree of failure is inevitable."

"But businessmen like yourself manage your entertainment companies."

I shrug. "Today's communications business requires cutting-edge high technology for its production and electronic distribution, sophisticated international financing, elaborate real estate development for its exhibition, theme parks, and merchandising venues. And all this sophisticated technology, finance, and real estate development seduces successful businessmen into thinking they know what's going on. And we don't understand a thing. Because it's still irrational dreams, fantasies, and entertainment that drive everything. That's always what the consumers are buying."

I watch Kuribayashi's gestures and listen to the softness in his voice. "The Japanese now dominate the electronics industry. We have had great success in business and financial power." The hesitation is echoed in Michiko's words. "But I do not know if we as a people can have great success in this business."

I nod gravely. "No, I don't believe you can achieve that success by yourself at the present." I wait for Michiko's translation. "Perhaps you never will."

She stares at me, pale and a little frightened.

"Please translate."

Kuribayashi's eyes narrow with interest. Apparently she has taken the edge off the affront but conveys the meaning.

"You are a nation, a race, of incredibly refined sensibilities. It is expressed in your unique language, calligraphy, food, art, theater, ceremonies, and even in your movies. There is nothing else in the world quite like Japanese culture. Even your religion is distinctive."

Michiko looks startled, but she keeps translating in that hushed, breathless voice. From Kuribayashi's raised eyebrows, I guess that she has devised suitably elegant Japanese metaphors.

"As a people you were isolated for centuries. In spite of a century of being exposed to the rest of the world, conquering other countries, being occupied in turn by the United States a half-century ago, you have remained essentially Japanese. There is something about you as a people that does not easily translate to the rest of the world."

Kuribayashi's response is again a grunt that seems to rumble deep in that frail chest, and an emphatic nod.

"Do you enjoy Kyoto, Mr. Saxon?" he asks after a moment.

"I haven't really had an opportunity to see it."

Kuribayashi gestures. "It is the ancient capital. Twelve hundred years ago, the Imperial Palace was built here. Twelve hundred years ago. This is the soul of Japan." There is a timbre in the old man's voice; he isn't just reciting a history lesson. I glance at Michiko, and her dark eyes dart to me with a furtive warning.

"In nineteen forty-five, our home and Kuribayashi Electric, our family business—a small engineering firm—were ashes. Ashes."

"But I understood Kyoto was never bombed, because of its historical treasures."

"Kuribayashi-san's home, his family and business, were in Tokyo," Michiko answers, not translating my question. Then she continues his narrative. "So I came to Kyoto, and in a very small old building I made radios from spare parts. That was fifty years ago."

Kuribayashi looks directly at me. "Do you know why our brand label in America is named Phoenix?"

"The phoenix was a magical creature that was reborn and rose from its own ashes," I say, realizing it for the first time.

"To be a victor, Mr. Saxon, when you are already powerful is not very difficult. To rise from the ashes requires greater strength."

The negotiations have suddenly taken a dark turn. They are no longer about movies or communications.

"Our wealth and power are something we have created, Mr. Kuribayashi, not an inheritance. And we continue to recreate it. We invite you to join us in this creative process."

"Yes, young executives in my company have recommended this

merger. And officials in our government think this is a proposal that we must study very seriously. We will study it. Thank you very much for coming. This has been very entertaining."

Entertaining. I stare across the table at Kuribayashi and then at Michiko Hara. The tone of her voice is devoid of conviction, and the color has drained from her face. The old man is dismissing me.

He has taken the meeting not because the younger faction in the company, led by Hara, has recommended it but because MITI, the Ministry of International Trade and Industry, pressured him. There will be repercussions from Washington if he does not at least go through the motions of a negotiation.

We will study it. Kuribayashi stares at me, his lined, hooded eyes burning with an intense glint. I understand him perfectly. The old man will cut his guts out before he merges or sells one of the companies that have risen from the ashes of American bombs. From its moment of conception, the whole deal had been dead.

21

Rough and Ready

The limo drops me off at the hotel entrance, and I slink into the lobby. I have spent months romancing Kuribayashi and come halfway around the world, all to consummate a deal that has never existed.

"Mr. Saxon, I presume."

My heart lurches at the voice right behind me. Rufus Ready is six feet three, well over two hundred pounds, with shoulders that block out the light.

"What brings you to Kyoto?"

"I came for the Fire Festival."

"The Fire Festival? What Fire Festival? There's no Fire Festival in Kyoto now. We're in the rains."

"I was misinformed."

I stare at him. Ruff 'n Ready would never hop a jet to Japan on his own initiative. "Greenwald sent you."

"Mr. Greenwald and I had a conversation about your security and your inclination for flying solo. But that was only *after* I found out what had happened to your friend Okamatsu at MITI. And the late Mari Midori—whose association with you has caught the serious attention of the Tokyo police. You failed to mention to me that they dumped her body in your hotel bed." Ready looks pissed and tired, as if he has not slept for two days.

"What happened to Okamatsu?"

"Can we go somewhere and talk?"

"My room."

Ready gives me his flat-eyed cop's look. "That may not be a good idea."

I give that a moment's reflection. "You think it's bugged."

"The thought would certainly occur to me if I wanted to keep tabs on someone moving about without any obvious security. But hey, I have a certain criminal mentality." Ready glances about the hotel lobby and points to a cocktail area where a harpist strums background music. "Let's chat over there. It's public, yet meant for clandestine conversations."

Ready is high-priced, and one of the things for which his clients pay—besides his professionalism and a network built up over his three decades with the FBI—is the theatrical flair with which he debriefs us.

We sit down, leaning in toward one another over a cocktail table. "Okamatsu?" I repeat.

"Yes, well, my associates in Tokyo could only get incomplete information. I had to personally contact old friends in the National Police that I'd worked with in the FBI." He shrugs. It's Ready's way of saying he's had to call in old debts.

"And?"

"A young 'true believer'—that was the term the police used—chopped him up with a classic samurai sword. In a *love hotel*. It was—coincidentally, or possibly not—the night before you arrived in Tokyo."

Ready apparently enjoys my expression, and his eyes never leave my face.

"Who? What? Nobody said anything when I checked with his office. We were scheduled to meet."

"Yeah, well, the Japanese find assassinations acutely embarrassing. They don't like to talk about them much."

"*Assassination? A samurai sword?*"

"The Yakuza like to flash them to scare extortion out of people, remember? But they're hardly ever used as a weapon."

"This was Yakuza?"

"Probably political. The kid was a member of an ultranationalist group."

"They caught him?"

"Running around the halls of the love hotel, soaked in blood, waving the sword, threatening to slice up the clientele. Okamatsu's screams apparently disturbed everyone's trysts. Love hotels have very discreet entrances and exits, and this clown couldn't find his way out. He panicked, was going to kill himself, but somebody whacked him with a Scotch bottle as he was on his knees attempting to ream himself."

"What do they know about him?"

"Twenty-three years old. Belonged to a fanatical right-wing group and worked out at a kendo club. But hardly a professional assassin, according to the police."

"An *assassin*?"

"It happens. In eighty-nine, one of the right-wing groups tried to terminate the mayor of Nagasaki without due process for simply questioning the late Emperor's responsibility for World War Two. His own party, the Liberal Democrats, kicked the mayor out rather than offend the right wing."

"Who's behind Okamatsu's killing?"

Ready shakes his head. "My friends don't say."

"But they know?"

Ready nods. "Under Japanese law, the police can hold a suspect for twenty-one days before even charging him or letting him talk to a lawyer. Their confession rate is the envy of cops the world over."

Ready gives me his best Dirty Harry smile. "The Japanese police have two dirty little secrets. This first is that anyone they bring in for interrogation tells them whatever they want to know." He pauses for effect.

"And the second?"

"The police rarely act on the information. Especially if it's at all politically sensitive. Hey, they got the killer, literally red-handed. Beyond that, Japanese police don't make waves. Which brings us to the next name on your checklist—Ishii." Ready takes another dramatic pause.

"You know who he is?"

"Possibly Ryoichi Ishii. Think *godfather*, but the Japanese term is *oyabun*. Head of a major Yakuza syndicate. Very senior, very rich. Not only somewhat beyond the police, but . . ." and here Ready vibrates his hand in a gesture to indicate the area where boundaries fade.

"He did time in Sugama Prison after World War Two for unspecified war crimes. Or at least the Japanese police wouldn't tell me what they were. He underwent rehabilitation during the fifties and sixties, solving labor problems for major Japanese corporations."

"What the hell does that mean?"

"He broke strikes. By organizing gangs to break the heads of strikers, Communists, radicals."

"With the quiet sanction of the police and government, I imagine."

"You got the picture."

Something scurries out from under the rock Ready has turn over. "Would this Japanese godfather still be involved in these corporations? Significant stock holdings, for instance?"

"We'll look into it. You have a particular company in mind?"

"The Kuribayashi Electric Industrial group."

"*Kuribayashi.*" There's a strange note in Ready's voice. He cocks his head and looks at me, but hesitates before he speaks. "For one thing, all the Yakuza are involved in *sokaiya*."

"That's the second time I've heard that word."

"A local folk custom. Gangsters buy a share or two of a Japanese blue-chip, then announce they'll attend the annual shareholders' meeting to raise certain embarrassing questions."

"Extortion."

"Not physical threats. But the Japanese avoid any embarrassing confrontation like the plague, so they pay *sokaiya* as the cost of doing business harmoniously. According to my sources at the National Police Agency, most companies pay up to a million a year. That's dollars, not yen."

"And Ishii?"

"He's well beyond that. His stock holdings are in the hundreds of millions, maybe a billion."

"Dollars, not yen?"

Ready nods, then exhales with a sigh of impatience. "So, you want to tell me something I don't know?"

"Okamatsu was going to sanction our—InterNatCom's—acquisition of Japanese electronics companies. Otherwise there might be trade sanctions."

"Is that what this is about?"

"Yep."

Ready whistles softly. "Kuribayashi Electric."

"Essentially, we'd take a controlling interest in several divisions of Phoenix Electronics in exchange for our stock and cash, but it would require reorganization of both companies."

Ready is silent a long time and then, as if his feelings are hurt, says, "That's all you're going to tell me?"

"*That's all?* That's a goddamn national secret. And it's not something this twenty-three-year-old amateur-night ninja would find out. This *true believer*, he was pumped up by somebody."

"Yeah, well the stakes are pretty high. What, six, seven billion, give or take a couple of bil." There is an edge to Ready's voice. "Was this a conspiracy? You're in the movie and TV biz, right? But you go out for the traditional Tokyo business entertainment, and the next day a hostess you were with is found beaten to death and raped. In your hotel bed."

"*Raped?*"

"Yeah, they took their ugly pleasure with her. Ah, the police didn't tell you that."

"No." In my repressed knowledge I knew—from the way she was trussed on the bed, naked, her thighs akimbo and pubis glistening from some violent secretion—but I'm not ready yet to confront that added horror.

"That's why they're pretty confident that it wasn't you. You're not dumb enough to leave your blood type and DNA inside her. But your basic Yakuza asshole is."

I feel the blood drain from my face, and take a deep breath to calm the rage that threatens to boil over.

"You didn't, did you? I mean like the night before? It's important, Peter."

"No."

"I gather she was very pretty."

"She was beautiful. But I didn't."

Ready absorbs that. "Then they'll get a DNA, unless he was practicing safe sex."

"But will the Tokyo police run tests? It's just some hood and a black half-breed whore in their minds."

"Maybe not normally, but they want to either nail you or clear you. And they can establish pretty quick if it was a Caucasian or Asian, just with a pubic hair."

Ready sits silent for a while before he speaks again. "You're not playing straight with me, Mr. Saxon." He gives me a strange reproachful look.

"What's going on?"

He studies me a moment. "I don't know. So not being subtle, I'll lay it out straight. While I was talking to the police, I called another in. I had them look you up. That first time you called from Tokyo, you had some strange questions that implied they might have something on you from back when you were a Sea Scout. So I had them check your file."

"What? The Tokyo police have a file on me?"

"Oh yeah, and it's expanding fast." There is a heavy sarcastic weight to his voice.

"What's in it?"

"The latest entry, of course, is your association with the late Mari Midori, a hostess employed at the Black Rose bar and grill. Your explanation is that she was the daughter of a black serviceman, and you were going to help her find work in the United States."

"An air force man from Tachikawa."

"They don't mention that, but they do go into some detail on your insisting that you had no sexual contact with her. That your presence in Japan was politically sensitive and that whoever killed her and then called the police was trying to embarrass you. Tokyo's finest apparently took what you said quite seriously."

"Does that tell us anything about the source of their tip?"

"It was an anonymous phone call."

"There was a hotel security man watching my room."

"Yes, well he first told police he was feeling sick—bad sushi or something—so he left his watch for a while. Didn't see anything. Apparently he was less than convincing. So he is currently undergoing their twenty-one-day truth cure."

Ready checks a small notebook. "Which brings us to the next item—the genitalia nailed to your door. I'm hurt that you didn't share this exotic incident with me."

"It was like a medical school prank to embarrass me."

"No, it was a very serious warning. But you didn't take it. And now a girl is dead. And whoever did it is in over their heads with nothing much to lose. What the hell did you think when the girl was killed?"

"I thought these Yakuza thugs had gone too far. They had slapped her around before, and she came that morning to warn me. She had a black eye."

"Is it possible it was all an act?"

"She's dead."

"Good point."

Ready studies me as if he's searching for some telltale tick.

"The guy's following me."

"Who?"

"Dragon Hands. The two guys who probably killed her. They were on the bullet train. In the next car. Obviously someone knew I had reservations. They made a move on me, but your sumo wrestler stepped in."

"Did you call the Tokyo police?"

"And say what? A couple of guys are following me who match the description of the guys who beat up a hostess in Tokyo?"

Ready grunts. "You got anything else you're holding out?"

"I think that's it."

"You're a tough guy to work for." He glares at me and flips through pages of his notebook, his index finger scanning lines of indecipherable scribbling. "Nineteen sixty-five," Ready announces, "you were a witness to—I guess you'd call it the sexual mutilation of an American serviceman—one Thomas Cochran, Lieutenant, U.S. Navy—at the Kanko Hotel by—and this I find a fascinating coincidence—a hostess from the same Black Rose bar and grill."

"But I didn't go there on my own this time. I was brought there as a guest by a Kuribayashi exec, who also arranged for Mari Midori to join us."

"You're being set up."

"But for what?"

"Right now, offhand, I'd say a murder."

"But they can't make that stick."

"Maybe they don't care. As you say, maybe they just want to involve you in a lurid sex scandal that will be embarrassing enough to blow the deal."

"I'm just the point man. Besides, it's too obvious. There'd be retaliations from Washington."

"Do they know that?"

"At the highest level, they must. That's why the police are tiptoeing."

"OK, but something else doesn't add up. The police records are now computerized, but they weren't in sixty-five. So someone must have gone back through all the files by hand, picked this up, and then added it. It wouldn't pop out in a random search."

"I wasn't even a principal. Just a witness, questioned and a statement taken. So how would it even show up?"

"The Japanese police file incidents with American servicemen differently, to refer them to the military police or embassy. If you're involved, you're tagged."

He holds my eyes a moment, then glances down again at his notes. Ready is a highly experienced investigator, and the sequence in which he asks questions is important. You save the most important for near the end of the interrogation, when you have the suspect already talking and on the defensive.

"Have you had any contact with this Cochran or the Black Rose who sliced off his jewels?"

"No, I've totally lost touch with him. I tried to contact him after I got out of the navy—wrote him regularly for awhile—but never got any response."

"What about Michiko Kuribayashi?"

I'm out of my chair. *"Who?"*

"The girl you were with at the Kanko Hotel back in sixty-five, according to the police."

"Lilli?"

"She gave her name to the police as Michiko Kuribayashi. Another fascinating coincidence. It just gets curiouser and curiouser."

After Ready leaves I sit in stunned silence, knowing for a certainty for the first time that Lilli is truly close at hand.

But she is a lifetime away. And the pain of that final separation now paralyzes me.

When the grueling Japanese police interrogation was over, there was a navy CID investigation of Cochran's mutilation, but eventually Lilli and I were alone, and the stricken silence was awful.

Finally I said, "How could you tell Junko that story about the prince and the geisha's last night together? You told her that story, huh? The beautiful geisha who cuts the prince's cock off." It was an accusation.

"I did not tell her. It is a famous Japanese love story."

"A *love story,* for chrissakes. Jesus! You're a sick fucking people if that's your idea of a love story."

Lilli was silent, her eyes downcast. Finally she raised her eyes and, as if reading my mind, said in a soft voice, "You are afraid to ever sleep with me again."

And the truth is that I was. I kept seeing those two matched ceremonial samurai knives in the cedar pagoda of her family shrine.

But there was something else on the table. I had received orders. My leg had sufficiently healed, and I was flying back to San Diego on a special charter flight of walking wounded to clear the now needed beds at the Yokosuka navy hospital.

Lilli shook her head. "I would never hurt you. You and I have shared great pain. But it is very strange, I think. My pain has made me more Japanese. Your pain has made you more American. Your navy doctors are right. You will only heal completely in America. And I could never be who I am there."

The true meaning of *sayonara*, Lilli had once taught me, was "If it is so, we must part." With exquisite gentleness and tact she had said *sayonara.*

I pick up the phone and dial Michiko Hara's number. She answers in Japanese, *"Moshi moshi."*

"Lilli, this is Peter. The masquerade is over. I have to talk with you."

There is a sharp intake of breath on the other end of the line. Then she says, "You have the wrong number. There is no Lilli here." And there is the piercing dial tone of a disconnected line.

22

The Death of Lilli

Later that night there is a knock at the door, and a bellhop delivers a hand-written note. It instructs me to take a cab early the next morning to the Daikaku-Ji Temple, north of Kyoto. There I am to ask at the *kimmokaku*, the main gate, for the Roshi Hekiun, who will be expecting me. The note is signed "Lilli."

A six-foot wall of gray-white plaster topped with tiles of baked gray clay surrounds the temple grounds. The main gate is a two-story wooden building in classical Chinese style with a curving sloped tile roof, and a young Japanese monk with a shaved head in a black robe meets me at its huge doors. He bows formally from the waist, a stiff military movement with his hands on his thighs gliding down past his knees.

Within the walls, a great flock of white pigeons carpets the square in front of the temple's main hall, and the birds part slowly with a soft cooing, as if they have not a single fear that we might step on them. The dark pines about the courtyard are pruned and shaped, their growth artfully trained and not left to wanton nature.

The young monk leads me down a pathway roofed in the same baked tile as the gate, through long verandas, silent spaces with rock gardens laid out with stones, moss, shrubs, and precisely raked sand, past a pond with large calico koi, and into an inner walled cloister, finally arriving at a small house with a four-sided sloping roof covered with cypress bark.

The young monk motions for me to remove my shoes, then kneels, eases open the shoji respectfully, makes a small bow, waits until I enter, then repeats the ceremony to close the door, as though I am now on holy ground.

Retreating from the bright sunlight into the cool twilight gloom of the priest's chamber, all I see at first are shadows and shapes. Roshi Hekiun is a looming dark presence on the other side of the room, a hulking figure in black and saffron robes.

"Thank you for coming, Saxon-san." The voice is soft, strangely compelling. Before I can answer, the monk steps from the shadows into the light of a screened window. He is a ghost materializing.

The short black hair and widow's peak at the broad forehead have receded, and the Japanese diet, or perhaps just middle age, have taken a toll on the once handsome, tough Irish face. His flesh is pallid, and in his costume of saffron and black robes Tommy Cochran looks ethereal, not unlike a gaunt, aging bishop.

Tears well in my eyes. Cochran must see them because he says in the same soft voice, "I wondered if you would recognize me."

"Jesus, Tommy, you don't forget the man who saved your life."

"You always exaggerated that."

"How could you disappear like that? What the hell's going on here?"

"I don't know."

"What are you doing here?"

"Oh, that I can answer. But here, let me look at you."

As he comes near, on impulse I throw my arms about him and hug. He accepts the embrace and pats me on the back, as a father might an affectionate child. Then he holds me at arm's length, studying me. "You really look quite well. Being a tycoon apparently nourishes you. I thought it might. You had the instincts and spirit for it."

"What the hell are you talking about?"

He laughs—more of a chuckle really. "Let's go for a walk. It's quite beautiful. The temple was founded by Eisai almost seven hundred years ago. Twenty-two subtemples really. The forest is a park." He leads me outside.

A morning mist still hangs like smoke over the gentle pine-clad mountains to the north, east, and west. Touching my elbow, Cochran strides away from the cloister into the trees.

"We got all your letters, by the way," he says finally. "You were very persistent, considering that I never wrote back. I apologize, but there was nothing I wanted to write about. 'This was a bad day. I was in pain, and I thought all day about killing myself.' Or 'The doctors have given me this plastic tube for a prick so that I can piss.' Dr. Samuels, my confessor and Jewish urologist, saved my gonads so I wouldn't grow breasts and sing soprano. Lilli thought I should write letters like 'We visited the temples in Kamakura today, and the way the light changed in the maple trees was a miracle. A crane flew by, and that was another miracle.' It was years before I could write letters like that, and by then everyone had stopped writing me all those unanswered letters."

It had all been thirty years before. "Lilli?" I say in wonder.

"She's dead. She's not with us any longer," but he says it in a strange way, as if she were a metaphysical concept rather than a woman.

"What happened?"

He smiles gently. He has really developed this beatific smile. "I didn't see any reason not to share your letters with Lilli, since you very tactfully did not mention women. Tact for my condition, that is. But she was really very happy when you wrote that you had passed the Law SATs with high grades, were going to law school in Berkeley."

"But you saw Lilli. What happened to her?"

"We took care of each other, each in our way. She visited me in the hospital. Always bringing flowers, fruit, little gifts. A sort of atone-ment. Always apologizing, as if she was responsible, which was non-sense. Junko—that was the lady who did me in, remember?—was always somewhat crazy. You didn't know that. I think—now that I've gotten to know the Japanese—perhaps that whole generation born during the war are partially crazy."

We are on a path of rough stepping stones, seemingly set at random but always wide enough for two. The rocks are slippery with dew, but Cochran's steps are sure-footed.

"And me, I was suicidal. This Catholic altar boy thought a lot of suicide. Lilli helped me get through all that." Apparently Cochran is going to tell me about Lilli in his own way, like a parable that has its set form, and my impatient questions will not change it.

"I think it was her way of staying close to you. She never talked about it, but she had really loved you. You weren't just another shack-up. And you were our connection, in a way . . ." He smiles again, an ironic, oddly feminine expression. "What incredible patterns our lives and karma weave."

The surrounding mountains, the temples—glimpsed through the pines now spooky with tentacles of morning mist that clung to gray-green branches—Cochran's materialization in his black and saffron robes, all disorient me. The past and present flow and swirl together. "You saved my life."

Cochran gives me a faint smile and nods. "And perhaps, you mine. When you visited me in the hospital, you told Dr. Samuels that. This urologist from New York putting in his time because the navy had paid his way through medical school. He, and the other doctors, saw me as some kind of bawdy joke at first. But after you talked to Samuels, he was quite moved. He talked a lot about the loyalty of men in combat to each other. I think he wanted to share that in some way. He decided I might have gotten the same sort of injury if I had been shot down instead of you. From a piece of shrapnel, the flak. Traumatic castration in combat—that's what he rewrote on the medical record. Apparently it wasn't unusual, especially for grunts who step on antipersonnel mines. And with my Air Medal, I became a disabled hero on paper."

"You *were* a hero."

Cochran dismisses it with a gesture of his hand.

"You weren't there on the ground. You don't know how close it was."

"Well, this hero was still somewhat an embarrassment for the navy and the Japanese police. They wanted to keep things hushed up. The navy, of course, wanted me out. But with an honorable medical discharge. You know us Annapolis ring-knockers. We take care of each other. I didn't want to go back to the States. So I was assigned temporary duty at the American embassy in Tokyo while I was recovering and being processed."

"The American embassy," I repeat. There is a connection here. But Roshi Hekiun is getting to things at his own pace of revelation.

"And when did you become this . . . monk?"

"After my discharge. Lilli took me to a Zen dojo near Tokyo University, to Kamakura on a few weekends, then a pilgrimage to Kyoto. I practiced meditation. I didn't really plan to become a Zen monk. I just thought—a glimpse really—I might find some peace. A path for myself. And after a while I realized that this really was my calling."

He smiles again. "It's a natural for an ex-altar boy and Annapolis man. But I certainly didn't think so at first. There was so much Catholic guilt and repentance, I . . ." He shakes his head and doesn't finish.

"This is the Rinzai sect. That doesn't mean anything to you, but historically it's the path of the samurai warriors. Sword fighting and archery are spiritual disciplines. I teach. I organize seminars. I have something of a following. The sexually wounded gaijin ex-pilot and war hero. I say nothing, and both versions of my wounding—the truth and the now official version—are whispered about. In Japan, both are almost equally romantic, you see."

I laugh. "You're charismatic. I apologize for laughing."

"Don't, it is hilarious. It's the joke of heaven." And Roshi Hekiun laughs and slaps himself.

"What's it like?" I ask.

"What?"

"The years of meditation. Stripping everything away to spirit."

Cochran shakes his head. "I can't explain it. I mean words are nonsense. One thing I can tell you. There's an ecstasy to it." His laugh is a self-mocking chuckle. "Perhaps the only ecstasy I'm capable of, but it's there. After a while, it was one of the lures. In fact, if I still had all my jewels intact, I probably wouldn't have gone after the greater treasure."

He chuckles again, and I wonder from the phrasing if he is translating from something he says often in Japanese.

"Do you still fly?" he asks suddenly.

"No," I say. "Is it like that?"

"Not at all. That's a lot of adolescent RAF poetry. Remember 'touched the face of God' and all that nonsense? It's just a question."

"When was the last time you were in the States?"

Cochran shakes his head. "I've only been back once, briefly, when my father died."

"Don't you think it's time to come home?"

Cochran smiles gently and holds his palms up in a gesture that embraces the pine forest and the surrounding mountains. "This is my home."

I study this strange robed figure, searching for the young warrior I had known. "I never told you something. But if you hadn't made that last gun run, I would be dead. It came down to me hiding in this paddy, up to my eyeballs literally in shit—this pig shit, peasant shit, piss and mud they fertilize the fields with. And then this old farmer with a beat-up rifle came down this path between the paddies." I now tell Cochran the story I had not told him thirty years before. "The Vietnamese troops were close enough to put a bullet in my leg."

The Zen monk who was once Tommy Cochran listens, face expressionless. His head nods slightly in a manner that is Japanese. "The wound and compound fracture got infected from that night soil.

Remember? Even with the best instant navy medical care, I almost lost the leg. The Vietnamese would have killed me right there. But if they didn't, I would have died in an agony of gangrene in some bamboo cage."

"I didn't know that," Cochran says.

"I never told anyone. I mean only one person."

"Your wife."

"No, she wouldn't understand. She would rationalize it, but she really wouldn't understand it."

Cochran is silent, then suddenly says softly, "You told Lilli."

I nod.

"I thought you were just frightened by being shot down."

"I was. But I was more terrified of them cutting off my leg."

"Yes, but you killed a man with your bare hands. And thirty years later, you can still describe each knife thrust and his last breath. And you told all that to Lilli. And of being terrified."

"She told me even worse stories about the war."

"She kept seeing dark things in your letters, and I never knew what she meant until now. She really loved you," he says, as if surprised by this revelation. "She didn't blame you for leaving, of course. She just accepted it, the way the Japanese do."

The wind stirs and whispers through the trees. I notice maples, their dark limbs now budding, scattered between the evergreen pines, as if to some deliberate esthetic pattern. And then it all comes together for me. "You still see her on occasion. As an old friend, confidant, a spiritual advisor even."

He smiles back at me. "Lilli's dead," he states, but his voice neither confirms nor denies what I just said.

I look back at Cochran. "Lilli. Before you were discharged— while you were still on temporary duty at the embassy—you got her a job there."

He says nothing.

"After all, she was a beautiful girl, but everyone knew there was no sexual hanky-panky going on. She was a goddamn angel of mercy as far they were concerned. And educated, spoke and wrote English very well. Her father had been an army officer in World War Two who had done the honorable thing and disemboweled himself on the Palace grounds."

"How long have you known?" Cochran asks quietly.

"Just now. Until last night I thought it was just some mid-life obsession with the past. But I seem to be the only one who didn't know."

"She wanted to change her life. That part involving the Black Rose was totally over, the way the war and the navy were over for both you and me."

He shakes his head. "I am the last man to pretend to understand a woman, especially Lilli. She worked at the Black Rose to support her family and pay for her younger sister's education. But that wasn't all of it. This was a beautiful young woman with deep fears. The war, the fire-bombings, her father's suicide—had all happened to her as a child. Perhaps the only time she felt safe was when she was sleeping with Americans, particularly pilots, or they were courting her. Then *she* was in control. I don't know what the Freudian rationale is here. But she once told me that the time she felt strongest was when you and that marine fought over her in the garbage behind a restaurant."

"It's true."

"Ha!" Cochran laughs in acknowledgment. "But then you came back frightened and crippled."

"And she healed me."

"But when you left—for whatever reason—she wanted to get on with her life in a normal way."

He is silent, then continues, "I said there was a generation of Japanese that are a little crazy. Perhaps you got the best of that craziness, I got the worst."

He shakes his head and smiles broadly, as if confirming something wonderful. "And yet here we are again, bound—we three—by this curious triangle of *giri-ninjo*."

My look must be a question because Cochran explains, "This web of human relationships, lifelong duties and obligations to one another. They governed feudal lords, samurai, and peasants. And they still govern Japanese behavior as strongly today."

The early morning fog blankets the ground and cloaks our legs, making it appear as if Cochran is an apparition who floats alongside me, feet not touching the ground. "But why are you here?" he asks.

"You tell me, Roshi."

"I don't know."

"What does Michiko think?"

"She doesn't know. She only knows what will happen if you recognize her."

"What?"

"She and her husband will be disgraced."

"I won't hurt her."

"No, you won't, because your interests require that. But I wonder what you would do if the circumstances changed."

I have no reply.

"When you insisted that she be your translator with Kuribayashi, and without her husband present, it really tipped the scale."

"She's the only one I can trust. I'm sincere about that. And I didn't really know she was Lilli."

"Yes, but you were willing to endanger her, her husband, her family, just to satisfy your curiosity. And you may now deliberately, or inadvertently, say or do something. She doesn't have either your experience in negotiating or your sang-froid under fire. She is, after all these years, just a Japanese housewife and a mother."

"She is the only one I could trust," I repeat, but in truth I am not at all sure of my motives.

"After all these years, how did you even suspect it was her?"

"Somebody is desperate. You don't understand how desperate they are. They're murderous." I tell Cochran of the genitalia nailed to my hotel room door with a woman's dagger, of being taken to the Black Rose, and the murder of Mari Midori.

He listens patiently, without comment, until I finish. Cochran laughs ruefully. "No wonder Michiko is terrified of what you'll do. In a way you've haven't changed a bit. They throw a blanket of antiaircraft flak at you, and your instinct is to dive closer to the guns and fly so fast they can't get a bead on you."

The rocky path suddenly turns and passes through a garden only of moss, the varieties, from a deep spinach green to pearl gray, craftily cultivated to appear as if they have spored spontaneously under the dense canopy. We emerge into a clearing with a small wooden building just large enough for a shrine and perhaps two or three devotees. About it are small Zen gardens—coarse sand painstakingly raked into patterns of ripples and whirlpools, carefully shaped dwarf trees, a composition of stones.

A low gate separates an outer garden from an inner rock garden, and Cochran motions me through. We both have to stoop to pass under the top post.

Cochran deliberately walks only on the rounded stones that form a path, and I follow him to a stone basin filled with water, across which lies a bamboo dipper. He rinses his hands and mouth and silently invites me to do the same.

Then we sit on a wooden bench a few yards from the entrance to the small building. "This is about a woman's honor," he declares.

I stand up. "A woman's honor! What the hell are you talking about? The Lilli I knew . . ." I don't finish.

"She didn't have her father's luxury of slitting his guts open and leaving his family destitute. She had to survive and support her mother and sister. And she did what she had to do to conquer her own demons. If she had passion, she had no less compassion. For you. And for me. I might not be alive now."

Cochran speaks softly, and yet in the morning stillness of the forest his voice penetrates to the bone. "You say you owe me your life. I will now collect that debt. I want your word that you will protect her *at all costs*."

I start to say something, but Cochran stops me. "*Lilli is dead*. And you will protect Michiko from her ghost. You will lie to your friends, superiors, even your wife. You will commit perjury if you have to."

"Is this what she wants?"

"Yes."

I look about at the ghostly veils of mist still clinging to the dark branches surrounding us. We inhabit a world where the paddies of North Vietnam are as alien as my office in Beverly Hills. "Can the Roshi Hekiun claim a thirty-year-old debt owed Lieutenant Thomas Cochran, USN? Is that a legal question?"

"It's a question of honor."

"*Honor*. Aha, Lieutenant Thomas Cochran, Annapolis graduate, I presume. Here to save the honor of a woman who had, what, passion, guile, vengeance, all that, yes. But honor? What a romantic notion."

I hold up my hand to stop his objection. "But you have my word. I pay my debt to whoever stands here claiming it. I will protect the Lady Hara. Is that formal enough for you? I know in Japan things don't have to be said. Obligations are understood. But I'm just an American lawyer now, and obligations are stated, contracts drawn."

"Why are you angry?"

"This meeting. Your materializing after all these years. What the hell's that about? I feel manipulated, cheated, used. A beautiful young girl who was working her way out of a life of shit she never made has been raped and beaten to death. And I still don't know why, or who's behind it all. Why the hell shouldn't I be angry? But you have my word—my word of *honor*." I hesitate, then say it, "I'll blow off this deal, if that's required."

"Thank you."

"No, don't thank me. Lilli may have saved my life. Certainly my leg." Emotion suddenly rises up from some deep well where it has been hidden away, chokes me, and for the second time that morning tears flood my eyes, and I wipe them away. "I've never even paid the interest on my debts—this *giri-ninjo*. I know that."

Cochran gives me a faint quizzical smile. "After this morning, even if you find yourself alone with Michiko, you will never acknowledge that you ever knew her as anyone other than Mrs. Michiko Hara."

"Why after this morning?"

He glances at the entrance to the building and, following his eyes, I notice a small stone, tied with a rope as though it is a package, set on a larger path stone.

At that moment the shoji slides open. Michiko Hara in a formal flowered kimono kneels at the threshold and bows deeply.

23

One Lifetime—One Meeting

Inchigo ichie. In Japanese it literally means "One lifetime—one meeting."

It encapsulates the Zen of the tea ceremony, for this tiny formal building is, in fact, a ceremonial teahouse.

"Please, I do this for myself. I am so very nervous to meet you now. It is not necessary for you to follow the etiquette of the tea ceremony. That would make me more nervous, I think," Michiko Hara says in a tremulous whisper.

In hand movements as ritualized as a priest performing Mass, she folds a cloth, then ladles hot water from an iron pot heating on charcoal into an undecorated porcelain bowl, rinses it, and wipes the bowl with the cloth in precise circular strokes.

All the while kneeling, she spoons the green tea powder from its box into the porcelain bowl with a bamboo *chashuka* and again draws hot water from the black iron *kama* with the long bamboo ladle—each small gesture according to some exact code—and pours it into the bowl. She whips the tea into a green froth with a whisk of split bamboo. Then she carefully places the tea bowl in front of me with both hands and bows as if making an offering.

I carefully sip the tea. I have no idea what I am doing or what it means, only knowing that in that tea ceremony, and my awkwardness, there is symbolized a whole Japanese universe of meanings that will forever evade me.

I set the tea bowl down on the tatami and smile at her, and at that moment the impact of my vow to Cochran strikes me. *Inchigo ichie.* This is the only meeting in our lifetime in which Lilli and Michiko Hara are to be the same person, when time is a river without banks, and we might acknowledge that we have once been lovers.

"Why am I here, now?" I ask.

Her smile in its poignant mystery transcends years. "Perhaps, without knowing it, I have sent for you."

"Why, after all these years, are you and I meeting again?"

"I don't really know."

"How did my name first come up?"

Michiko at first looks downcast, avoiding my eyes, then actually laughs, and glances at me with a sly expression. "A woman's foolish and romantic curiosity."

I wait.

"My husband asked me to help him do research on American communications companies. With Sony and Matsushita buying studios, and Toshiba investing in Time Warner, he felt that Kuribayashi would be left behind. But Kuribayashi is too small to buy a studio. It must form some sort of partnership in order to prosper."

"He's thinking exactly as I am."

"Yes, he is very clever and far-thinking in business. But many in the company are against such a merger. I had useful experience working at the American embassy. So I helped him with the research and translations. In one report I saw your name."

"My name just popped up?"

"Yes, in a corporate report. I wanted to see your picture. Know more about how you were. Your family. Your career. It was foolish."

"Who did your investigation?"

"There is a business research company in Tokyo."

"And you dealt directly with them?"

"I asked my husband's assistant to request information."

I take a deep breath. "Well, they did their research with terrific Japanese thoroughness."

Michiko Hara looks at me questioningly.

"There is an old Tokyo police record in which I am interviewed as a witness to the sexual mutilation of a fellow navy officer at the Kanko Hotel."

Her response is a low exclamation of breath, "Aaah."

"The girl I was spending the night with—also a witness—a hostess at the Black Rose, gave her name to police as Michiko Kuribayashi."

The blood drains from her face, and for a moment I think she is going to faint.

"You didn't know?"

"No." The word is hardly audible.

"Why did you think I was here?"

Her eyes are wide with astonishment, her voice a whisper. "I thought it was Fate."

She says it with such utter conviction, I cannot challenge it. "Perhaps it is. But Fate is playing her hand in a very subtle way. Who is Kuribayashi's heir apparent?"

"I do not understand?"

"Kuribayashi is—what?—almost eighty years old? Who's going to take his place?"

"It is confused. Yamaguchi, whom you call the chief executive officer, is very ill. That is why he was not at the meeting yesterday."

"And your husband?"

"He is perhaps too young. And many do not like this idea."

"How did you meet him?"

"It is Fate, I think." Again she pronounces the word as if invoking an old Shinto deity.

"How exactly?"

"I worked at the American embassy, and one day Kenji came for help to obtain licenses to use American electronic patents. He worked for Kuribayashi Electric Industrial Company in Kyoto. This is very curious, I think. This is the name of the business my family had during the war."

"The old family business resurrected from the ashes?"

"Yes. After the war, everything was crazy. My father's family were all dead, I thought. We lived with my mother's sister. I did not remember my father's brother."

Her father had disemboweled himself with the specter of the massacre of American POWs over his head. Had his brother then fled to Kyoto, afraid of retaliation from the occupation authorities?

There are, of course, a hundred other questions. How had the old man received his long-lost niece? To how much of the company is she herself heir? But all those questions have one subtle bottom line, immediately read by anyone who has worked as an executive in Hollywood—Kenji Hara had married her and quickly risen to the top in Kuribayashi Electric.

But now Michiko Hara sits pale and drained, as if at any moment she may collapse, the cloth of her kimono spreading on the tatami like a silky liquid that seeps from her shoulders. "I have brought great shame on my husband and uncle," she says.

"Not yet you haven't," I think aloud. "Whoever wants to disgrace your husband and kill this merger—if they had proof that Michiko Hara was once . . . the lover of an American serviceman—who was involved in a sensational scandal—they would have exposed it long before our negotiations got this far. Trust my experience in this."

Michiko looks up at me with anticipation.

"They don't have any proof. All they have is a name on an old Tokyo police record, of a frightened hostess from the Black Rose, who may have given the police a phony name."

"But what if someone from the Black Rose recognizes me?"

"Who are you talking about? Another ex-hostess, a bartender thirty years ago? These places are run by Yakuza hoods. All you have to do is deny it. You worked at the American embassy. You tell me, how would Kuribayashi handle that kind of accusation?"

"The Japanese will do anything to avoid an embarrassing confrontation."

"Right, they want an ugly American to do it for them. And they've now maneuvered the ex-lover to Japan to recognize and expose you, create a scandal. And that would effectively kill any other takeovers by American companies for a while."

"Who would do this?"

"Offhand, I would say about seventy-five percent of Japan. Certainly all the conservative elements that control your business and government. And from our meeting yesterday, I'd bet that would also include your uncle."

Michiko is silent with shame, but then, like an apparition, Lilli surfaces with a teasing smile. "And how did they maneuver my ex-lover to Japan?"

"Get the subtlety of this—whoever set up the negotiations suggested very politely to Greenwald, our chairman, that to ensure harmonious negotiations he should send someone who has spent time in Japan, so that he will not be distracted or disoriented. Someone who is familiar with the technology. And someone who will be comfortable with the formality of Japanese protocol, perhaps has a background as a military officer."

"That does not seem unreasonable."

I nod. "No, it doesn't. In the navy, all our senior officers would probably qualify. At an electronics firm, maybe half of the top executives. But at a Hollywood studio, you're hard-pressed to find one. In this case, Greenwald's former VP of corporate acquisitions and now attorney-at-law perfectly fit the profile. The opposition really did their homework."

Michiko stares at me with puzzlement. "Why are you smiling?"

"Because bringing me here was their big mistake."

"Please, do not get too arrogant."

"No, not because of me personally. They had to escalate the negotiations to this point. And now it has become a real political issue, a crisis between Tokyo and Washington, if the deal doesn't go through. The Japanese can buy American communication companies left and right, but we can't buy theirs. The shit will hit the fan."

"But do they know that?"

"I carefully laid it out for MITI in Tokyo. Your husband is aware of it. And apparently the stakes have been conveyed to your uncle. He is, as we Americans say, between a rock and a hard place."

"You told them that?"

"They called it *gaiatsu*, I believe. Foreign pressure." There is a long silence. We are talking about current business as if by agreement to avoid talking about a past love. But there is an electric charge in the air. Finally I ask, "Does your husband know?"

"I do not think so." She sighs. "Is it not amazing that I have a husband and two children who are almost adults, who do not know who I am? Is it the same for you?"

"Yes."

"You might tell them, I think. In America it is different."

I shake my head. "No. They could never understand. It would all become a story, an anecdote, and that trivializes it. Silence honors it."

The woman who was once Lilli smiles gently. *"Hai."*

"I don't even talk about the war. There're stages you go through. At first I thought about little else—flying through the guns, getting shot down, wounded. I thought—if I survive that, then what the hell is there to be afraid of, right?"

She says nothing.

"Then you get married and have one, two daughters, and in Los Angeles there is suddenly everything to be afraid of. The fact that you've survived the guns of Phuc My Luc no longer has any meaning. No relevance whatever."

The woman who was once Lilli nods again—*"Hai"*—and sighs deeply. "My son and daughter are *shinjinrui*—the new human race.

They have only been rich. They have never known hunger or terror. They do not know what it is to look for your home, where you lived and played with your friends the day before, and now see only ashes, ruins, corpses. To be happy, surrounded by your family one day, and the next day alone, surrounded by the dead and dying. To be so poor we mixed the tiny ration of rice with soybeans, barley, even grass and weeds."

For a moment I have the depressing feeling that I am listening to a dreary old woman grieving about her tragic childhood. Then Lilli looks straight at me. "But if you survive, you are so strong. So strong. That is why, I think, the older Japanese are a little arrogant to Americans now. You can understand this pride, I think. Please, be a little patient."

I am surprised. "Can we still put this thing together . . . ?"

She is hesitant. "I don't know."

"Do you want me to walk away from this?"

This time there is no hesitation. "No. To surrender is a greater disgrace for my husband, I think." Suddenly there is a sly, coquettish smile, as Lilli struggles to emerge.

"What?"

"You never gave me a farewell present."

"What do you want?"

"If you can, give my children this new world."

She looks away, her eyes fixed on nothing in this tearoom, and when she looks back, directly into my eyes, with a poignant smile, in that *inchigo ichie* both Lilli and Michiko Hara speak. "With all the horror that our lives embrace, our dark secret—and I feel no shame of this, only a memory of pleasure—is that we were once lovers."

"But there are people who have killed, and will kill, to expose that." I reach up and for the first time in a quarter-century touch my fingertips to her cheek. "I promise I will protect you." We kneel that way for a moment.

"Oh, Peter, what an extraordinary skeleton in my closet you are.

I was terrified that you would recognize me," she says earnestly, then looks up at me with a mischief that transcends the years. "I would have been heartbroken if you did not. You must not play games like that, Peter."

"It wasn't really fair. You knew, but I didn't. I had to keep guessing."

"I didn't think you would remember me."

"You were unforgettable."

She shakes her head slightly, not rejecting the thought but more in wonder. "I think back sometimes, and it seems like I was an actress playing a role. And I am astonished that I was Lilli."

"I know. I am astonished I was . . ."

"Was it just youth, I wonder?"

"Only part of it. It was the war, history, Fate. It pushes you to some edge. I know other men who look back and are astonished by who they were and what they did."

Then she laughs with delight at some memory—her laughter a familiar, lovely peal that resonates in time. "Oh, Peter, there you were brawling in the garbage cans in Yakitori Alley, over me. Do you remember?"

"It's not something you easily forget."

"Do you remember what you told me later?"

I am silent.

"You said I was Circe, the enchantress in *The Odyssey* who turned men into pigs." And again she laughs with some quiet pleasure. "You inspired me to read *The Odyssey*. You said it was a great classic. And all Western men aspired to be Odysseus."

"I don't remember that part of it, but it sounds like something from a Stanford seminar."

"And what adventure in *The Odyssey* is this, I wonder?"

"Sometimes I think I'm still trying to find my way back from the war."

It is her turn to be silent a moment. "Ah, Peter, we were so young, so beautiful and crazy. The handsome young pilot and Lilli. It is all a dream, I think."

The kimono is a gown of subtle sensuality cut to expose the throat and its dimpled recess, accent the long, graceful ivory line of a Japanese woman's neck to her cheek.

"You're still beautiful," I say. "Time has only made you elegant," and it has. Her smile in its pleasure and flirtatiousness is one that Michiko Hara would never allow herself.

"Ah, Peter, it is not proper to say that a man is still beautiful. But you were once, and now you have fulfilled all the promise of what you might become. The word is *handsome,* but there is much more, I think." There is something breathless in her voice, a palpable tension. Tears fill her eyes, and she looks down quickly.

My trembling fingers reach for her face.

There is an urgent knocking that shakes the door, and she starts. The shoji slides open, and Cochran's pale face looms in. "Men are coming. You must not be seen together."

24

The Attack of Dragon Hands

Michiko and Cochran, the elegantly kimonoed lady tottering on wooden *getas* and the black and ochre robed monk, their long full sleeves fluttering in flight, disappear along the stone path behind the teahouse.

I jog back the way we had come, along the dew-slick rocks that trace the trail down the hills. My foot slips, and as I stagger for balance, there is a guttural shout behind me and I am hit with a stunning blow across my shoulder blades that drives me headlong down the slope onto the rocks.

I break the fall with my hands and push up onto my knees. A stocky Japanese hovers over me, gripping a hardwood kendo sword with both hands, the blunt end inches from my head, his feet braced for another blow.

There is an exchange in Japanese, and a second man materializes out of the pines that bracket the path. It is one of the two that had followed me on the train, the older, beefy thug with the bald scalp and hair tied in a ponytail like an old samurai.

He unsheathes his short sword and motions with the point for me to stand up. I stagger to my feet, watching the kendo swordsman warily. The samurai nods with his head for me to climb back up the path toward the teahouse, and when I hesitate he lightly jabs me with the *wakizashi*. Its point pierces my jacket and draws blood without effort.

"OK, OK." I stumble up the rocks.

There is another brief exchange, and when I glance back, the guy with the kendo stave is trotting down the hill.

The ponytailed thug prods me with the short sword along another path, and I lurch through the pines into a small clearing containing a rock garden and a huge hanging green-copper gong that fronts yet another shrine.

Michiko lies sprawled in the white sand, stripped half naked, her obi ripped off, kimono open to her bared breasts, and her underpants torn off. A guy has her pinned down by the shoulders.

Dragon Hands stands over them with a camera. He waves the camera at me, its long leather strap whipping the air, and smiles with a mouthful of tobacco-stained teeth. "Hey, nice pictures. Wife of Hara-san and big-dick American."

The sight of Michiko terrified and assaulted by the guys who have raped and murdered Mari Midori pours out instant adrenaline. My rage purges all caution, yet flares into its own crazy canniness. I actually smile at Dragon Hands. "Hey, yeah, pictures." I hold out both hands in an expansive, friendly way and step forward as he raises the camera to photograph me.

My kick catches him in the stomach and drives him back three feet. He trips over one of the big granite garden rocks and crashes down, dropping the camera. I charge forward and on the same momentum drive my foot into his face. His head smashes against a rock.

I lunge at the camera, grab it by the long leather strap, and blindly whip it in a wide circle around me. It bangs the ponytail in the chest, and he reels back, ricochets off a tree, back at me, and catches my second two-handed swing of the heavy metal camera full in the face. He screams, throws his hands up, and collapses to his knees. Blood pours between the fingers that cover his face.

The third guy lets go of Michiko, jumps up, and starts to stalk me warily. A big knife materializes in his hand. Suddenly Michiko is on his back, her fingers clawing at his eyes. He grabs at her groping fingers with one hand and awkwardly tries to reach back and stab her with the knife.

I seize the knife hand with my left and drive my right fist into his stomach, as if punching my hand up behind his ribs into his heart. The air goes out of him with a hoarse moan. And then, with an absolute clarity of purpose, I drop down and smash my hand into his scrotum. His retching cry is all the more horrible for being breathless. He collapses at my feet.

I pick up his knife.

"Don't kill him." Michiko stares at me, her eyes distended with fear.

I yank his hair, snapping his head back, and press the blade to his throat. Even the touch of the edge draws blood.

"Please don't kill him," Michiko whispers.

"Tell him if he moves, I'll kill him."

She says something in Japanese.

I move the knife to the back of his neck, and he sprawls face down and lies there.

"Where's Cochran?"

Michiko stands trembling, still half naked. I take off my jacket, slip it around her, and she thrusts her arms into the oversized sleeves.

"Where's Cochran?" I repeat.

She points back in the direction of the teahouse. "They hurt him, I think. I am so sorry. . . . I am so frightened . . ." She suddenly screams.

I spin. The ponytailed samurai is on his feet fumbling for the short sword.

With a great shout, Cochran lurches out of the trees, an apparition with his face painted in blood from a lacerated scalp which now drips over both arms. He drags one leg, poling himself along with a hardwood stave as a crutch. In one motion he rears up and swings the stave in a great arc at the samurai. If the hardwood had been a razor-edged *katana*, it would have decapitated the man. As it is, he sprawls like a sack at my feet.

As though the blow has expended his last bit of strength, Cochran drops to his knees alongside the hanging gong. "Get her out of here," he orders. "She can't be seen here."

I kneel beside Cochran. My immediate fear is that they have stabbed him, but I see no bloody tear in the saffron robes. He looks at me with a dazed expression, eyes slowly coming back into focus.

"They beat him with kendo sticks," Michiko says.

A purpling bruise along his neck extends up into his scalp. Cochran struggles into a sitting position like a man for whom each movement brings a stab of pain. "Get her away from here," he mutters.

"You need help."

". . . your word. Protect her. Your oath."

Michiko kneels and cradles his head.

"No," he insists. "You can't be caught here with him."

There is a wooden mallet hanging from the crossbeam by which the gong is suspended. I seize it and strike the gong, then again. Michiko stares at me with astonished eyes. I hit it again and keep a slow, rhythmic tolling.

Far down the path, I finally spot a group of monks, their long black robes like one dark billowing curtain, hurrying toward us. "Monks are coming," I say.

Cochran is now sitting up, his feet splayed out in front of him. His mouth twists into a smile, and he says something in Japanese, then waves his hand weakly as if to shoo me away. "I'll be all right. Don't let them see her with you."

I grab both blades the thugs have dropped, seize Michiko's hand, and half drag her into the woods, away from the advancing monks.

"This way!" I plunge down a path in the direction Cochran has indicated.

"Maybe other Yakuza," she whispers behind me.

But there is no caution, only adrenaline and anger. I charge through the trees, a short sword in each hand, vaguely conscious that my hands and forearms are covered with blood from Cochran's, the samurai's, and my own wounds. Michiko trots behind me to keep up.

After we are out of sight and earshot, I stop to get my bearings. Michiko stares as if she is as frightened of me as of the Yakuza hoods.

"Two of those men—the one with the ponytail and the one with the dragon tattoos on his hands—they raped and murdered a girl from the Black Rose," I say in as quiet a voice as I can muster under the circumstances. "They followed us from Tokyo."

"Why?"

"I don't know. Whatever game they're playing, it's all gone too far. Now we can identify them." I hold out one of the knives, the handle toward her.

She takes it, not quite sure what she is to do with it. "The camera," she says, holding it out by the strap to me.

I open it, remove the film, and unspool it in a beam of sunlight that stabs through the canopy of pines. I then slice the film into bits with the *wakizashi*. It is like cutting through paper with a honed razor, requiring only a touch of the blade.

She stares at the knife. "Yes, they want to kill us both," Michiko says in a strange, distant voice. "It is to be a murder-suicide of old lovers. Very romantic. Very sensational for all the TV and newspapers. We will become very famous," she says with a strange laugh.

"Then we'd better get the hell out of here."

Crows caw in the tops of the tall pines. We move through the woods on instinct and a vague sense of direction and come out just behind the two-storied *kondo*, the main hall of the temple compound. My car and driver are waiting across the square cloister, just outside the main gate.

"Stay behind me, as if we're not together," I say, "but stay close."

I move close to the *kondo* walls, under the shadow of the extended overhanging sloped roof. The courtyard and cloisters appear deserted, the tiered pagoda at its center empty of attendants, the monks perhaps all drawn by my gonging to Roshi Hekiun's aid. I check behind me to ensure that Michiko is following at a discreet distance, then cross into the brightly sunlit yard toward the main gate, my footsteps crunching on the gravel.

The hood silently materializes from the shadows of the porch surrounding the central pagoda, holding the long hardwood kendo stave in front of him with both hands as if it is a razor-edged *katana*. Even in his fashionably baggy dark designer suit, he moves like a swordsman, dancing to intercept me with a quick sidestep. I circle to the right, and he sidesteps with me, yet floats forward to within striking distance.

I swing the camera up by the strap with my right and whirl it above my head like a bola, threatening him with the short sword in my left. He feints to my left as if to avoid the bola, but suddenly the hardwood sword whips up and across, cutting me right at the wrist with a sharp pain that sends the camera flying across the courtyard.

With a windmilling motion that is a blur, the hardwood sings back over my head and slams down on my left shoulder with a violence that sends an electric shock through my arm and drives me to my knees.

The hardwood swings up again, and I instinctively throw up my right arm to shield the blow to my head. He shouts, a karatelike cry that catches in his throat. The stave drops on my arm with no more punch than a twig and falls to the ground.

The swordsman sinks to his knees, face to face with me, his eyes wide with astonishment. He clutches with his left hand at his right side, just under his arm, and blood flows through his fingers. He stares at it, then back at me, questioning how I managed to do that, and keels over, still clutching his right side, now moaning with pain.

Michiko stands behind him. There is only the slightest smear of blood on the blade she holds. Her slash into his raised armpit had been so swift that neither he nor I saw her coming.

My left arm has no feeling, and my right wrist stabs with pain when I try to push myself to my feet. Michiko helps me up. "My arm might be broken." I wince.

"My car is outside the gate."

"So are more of them. They followed one of us here."

She lets out a breath like a hiss. The fallen swordsman is now watching her. She picks up the short sword I have dropped and, a blade in each hand, stands staring down at him. He scoots along the ground, pushing himself with his feet, to get away from her.

"The roshi's motor scooter," she says after a moment. "He always leaves the key in it."

"I don't think I can drive it."

She looks back at me. "I can. My son has one I drive on holidays," she says in a flat, matter-of-fact way.

We retrace our flight back across the courtyard through the cloisters to Cochran's residence.

"How are we going to get out?"

She points. "There is a *so-man*, a west subgate there."

The grounds are still unusually empty, with no novices or monks about. "Where is everybody?"

"At meditation."

Cochran's motorbike is in a shed behind the building. Michiko stows the *wakizashi* in the case beneath the passenger seat, where she finds a pair of World War II-style aviator goggles. Somewhere in our flight she has refolded her kimono so that it is presentable.

There is feeling and a painful mobility returning to my left arm. The collarbone may not be shattered. I balance precariously on the seat behind her, gripping her jacket with my enfeebled left hand, my right arm with its swelling wrist about her waist.

"Oh, you too big. I only ride with Yuki behind."

"Well, we'd better learn fast."

The motorbike teeters drunkenly as she throttles to speed, and I clutch at her in alarm. But Michiko does not hesitate and accelerates quickly to a stabilizing speed, rolling through the portal of the west gate and navigating backstreets into Kyoto.

The bystanders and passing traffic point and laugh at the big gai-jin clinging to the lady in a billowing kimono and kamikaze goggles piloting a Honda motorbike. I hug her more intimately than is perhaps necessary just to hang on. She finally pulls up near a taxi stand by a train station, and we tumble off the scooter.

She pulls her torn kimono tightly about her, and we stare at one another, oblivious to the politely averted eyes passing by. We are both comically windblown, disheveled, incongruously costumed, and there is nothing to do but laugh at our absurdity.

She abruptly stops laughing. "You must go back to help Roshi Hekiun," she insists.

"We can't go to the police."

"Yes, they want to make a scandal."

We look at each other a long moment. Her eyes shine with tears. I make a circling gesture about us. "There are a dozen wonderful Japanese inns in the hills around us, and we can be lost there. Together. Lost in time for a while."

Her smile is ravishingly poignant. "It is a lovely fantasy." She shakes her head. "My daughter is waiting for me. We return to Tokyo this afternoon."

She takes my hand, presses it to her cheek. "This is good-bye," Michiko says. "We must never meet and talk like this again. It is not fair to my husband or your wife."

I nod.

"Good-bye, Peter."

"Good-bye, Lilli."

She smiles sadly at the name, runs her fingertips along the line of my jaw, then touches my lips.

I move to kiss her, but the gentle pressure of her fingers on my lips holds me off.

"There is an old Japanese poem," she whispers.

"How I envy the maple leaf
Which turns beautiful and then falls."

Then Lilli turns and disappears into a taxi.

25

A Letter from Mari Midori

Ready is staked out in the lobby when I hobble in. He's furious I sneaked out of the hotel that morning without alerting him.

I now hurriedly brief him on what happened at the temple, but I leave out Michiko's presence. Apparently it leaves an unconvincing gap in the narrative.

"It was Dragon Hands and the other guy who followed me from Tokyo and at least three others who attacked Cochran and me."

Ready doesn't say anything when I finish but stares back at me in that flat expressionless cop's glare he has perfected over several decades of interrogating America's Most Wanted and then says in a voice that crackles like the last inch of a fuse, "You're not telling me something, Saxon-san. And the way things are breaking, it could cost you your life. And maybe mine, if I get in the way."

I acknowledge that. "Then I've lost it to repay a debt to people to whom I owe my life. You do what you have to."

Ready looks at me in astonishment, then his voice softens. "This Cochran, this is the same guy in the old Tokyo police report?"

"Yeah."

"And you flew with him in Vietnam?"

I nod. "I would have died of gangrene in a bamboo cage, or worse, if it hadn't been for him covering my ass when I was shot down."

Ready grunts, his deep guttural sound of acknowledgment. "I won't even ask about the lady." He cocks his head. "Well, I'll cover your ass as best I can. But you're sure not making it easy."

"Thank you."

"You have a letter from Japan," Sylvia reports over the transpacific phone from my office in Los Angeles. "Somebody should have saved the postage."

"Who?"

"The stationery is from Rikkyo University. The name says Mari Midori."

"Open it. Read it to me."

It is, after its introductory politeness, the detailed account of the interrogation by the two thugs and their description that I had asked her to write. With her ingrained Japanese sense of duty, she had apparently written it that morning right after she had seen me and before her classes. "Part of it's in Japanese. You want me to have it translated? Elegant handwriting, by the way."

"No, put it right on the fax to me. You have the envelope?"

"It's right here."

"Sylvia, lock it and the letter in my safe after you fax it."

At the hospital I walk in on several stylishly dressed women making cooing solicitous sounds over Cochran. He briefly introduces me in Japanese. They bow, smiling charmingly, and after making more cooing, chirpy noises over Cochran, smile, bow again to me, and still chirping, back out of the hospital room, taking their departure like a covey of exotic partridges.

"I have a certain following," Cochran says. He is propped up on pillows in bed, looking slightly embarrassed. There are small, meticulously rice-paper-wrapped gift boxes like Christmas window displays, flower arrangements, and tiny beribboned baskets of fruit on the dresser and bed table.

"It would appear so."

"Monks have a certain romantic tradition in Japan."

"Is that a fact?"

"Unlike the West, the lady and the monk are a reoccurring theme in legends that have been made into plays, puppet shows, even popular films."

"Even popular films, you say?"

"In *Kiyohime Mandara* a beautiful woman falls in love with a young monk. And when he spurns her, she turns into a snake and burns her lover and then herself with the flame of her passion."

"And this is a popular story in Japan?"

"You're enjoying my little embarrassment."

"Tremendously."

"It would appear that God is sometimes an ironist."

"I've suspected that." I look at Cochran. He is pale and sits very still, as if consciously trying not to move. "How are you?"

"They want to keep me here for observation and tests for a day or two, but I don't have a concussion, and that's good. This guy just beat the hell out of me with a kendo pole. There's a lot of aches and pains, searing pain, actually, and it knocked the wind out of me. I'll be black-and-blue and moving like a ninety-year-old man for a week or two, but there's no permanent damage."

"Yeah, I met the guy with the kendo pole." My left arm is in a sling.

"You're still flying into the guns."

"Under them," I correct. "There's a big difference. And I'm not twenty-five. I acted totally on rage, adrenaline, and impulse."

"Well, you did very well for an old man. I have a clear image of you charging into the woods, a sword in each hand, splattered with blood, and the expression on your face . . ." Cochran shakes his head and actually laughs. "Michiko doesn't know whether to be terrified of you or in awe. You practically beat three guys to death."

"Michiko, you spoke to her. Is she all right?"

"Terribly frightened, worried about you. What you'll do now."

"There were no bodies still around by the time I got back to the temple. Did you call the police?"

"Do you want to? Those guys beat it the hell out of there."

"Two of them killed that girl in Tokyo." I tell him about Mari Midori's letter.

"How can you go to the police now without involving Michiko in a scandal?" he asks.

"I don't know."

Cochran is silent, and when he finally speaks, his voice has a meditative quality, as if he is quietly teaching a seminar. "The Japanese concept of truth is not the same as the Western take," he says. "It's not your material, objective, just-the-facts-ma'am truth. Not impersonal, scientifically measured facts. Truth, here in the East, is an ethic—and it has to do with the integrity of relationships and the individual's obligations." He is silent, studying if I am taking this in.

"Why are you telling me this?"

"It's something to which you should be sensitive if you're going to do business here in Asia. You should know that facts are not the same thing as the truth. Asians, particularly the Japanese, often seem evasive to Westerners. It's because they're seeking what is *the truth* in a particular relationship. It takes into consideration the feelings and consequences to other people. It isn't a matter of politeness, tact, keeping your mouth shut at certain times, or even white lies. Those are all Western concepts. Here in the East, the truth is the way something must be to satisfy your obligations. And spiritually, the truth makes you who you ought to be, and not, in the factual Western perspective, who you are. Do you understand, follow what I'm saying?"

"Michiko Hara is not Lilli."

Cochran, trained in silences, answers with one.

I lean back in the chair, shut my eyes.

Then the man whom I knew as Cochran asks, "Do you know why I saved your ass in our other life?"

"No."

"The time you flew back into the guns to get the film, you could have said your cameras jammed and blown it off. But you didn't. Because we operate in a web of obligations to one another, what the Japanese call *giri-ninjo*. It always exists, but it's stronger, more defined in combat. You had an obligation to the men who made that raid and the ones who would make the next raid. Yours was a very pure, spontaneous act. But you showed me, by example, that my obligation was to protect you with no less courage."

"I didn't even think about it."

"Exactly. You were in a state of *mushin*."

"What's that?"

"Not thinking, no consciousness. It's what the Zen swordsman meditates to attain. To be free of fear, even the desire for victory. He acts intuitively, and that gives him superiority over an opponent who thinks about his actions."

"That was me all right. And I don't know what the hell I'm doing now. I don't even know who's shooting at me. But whoever it is is getting desperate."

"Because you're not backing off."

"They're obsessing on the past, and I'm trying to create the future."

"There is no past, there is no future. They're illusions created by the mind. There is only the present."

I shake my head. "That Zen might work for a monk in meditation, but in my world the past creates us. And our expectations of the future create the work we do today."

"That's right. And it all exists in this instant. That's all that exists. Where is the past that flowed to this moment? Or the future that flows from it? It exists only in your mind."

"Time is a river without banks."

"What's that?"

"The title of a painting by Chagall that my boss covets."

"Ah." the Roshi Hekiun nods.

I look at Cochran. "How are you, really?"

"Beat up. I'm pissing blood, but the doctors say that probably isn't serious. It's painful to move, but I know I'll heal quicker if I get up and around a bit."

"Are you fluent in Japanese?"

"For thirty years I've spoken more Japanese than English."

"I'm going under the guns again, Tommy. Will you fly top cover for me?"

Cochran looks at me quizzically, and for the first time since our reunion I believe I have surprised him.

26

The Web of Obligations

Ready and a Japanese associate named Tanaka drive Cochran and me to Kuribayashi's estate in the suburbs of Kyoto.

At one point the car's mobile phone buzzes, and Tanaka—a stocky man with the blunt, haggard features of a detective who has weathered too many late hours on stakeout—answers it, speaks briefly, then turns to Ready and says something in a soft voice.

Ready is carrying a nondescript hardback briefcase—which I had just assumed held paperwork—but now he dials the combination lock and opens it. He withdraws two 9-millimeter pistols and clips, inserts the clips, and hands a pistol and extra clip to Tanaka.

"What's going on?"

"We're being followed. Four *chimpira* punks in a black Honda."

I look out the rear window, but I can't distinguish anything threatening in the cars behind us on the highway. "How do you know?"

"I've got a backup car following us. They spotted them." He looks back at me. "I think it's time to notify that Inspector Goto in Tokyo."

I nod. "Yeah."

Akira Kuribayashi's mansion is an English manor house, dating back several centuries but considerably remodeled and modernized since then, which now resembles one of the old estates on the North Shore of Long Island. Ready and Tanaka wait outside, discreetly checking the surrounding woods and gardens.

Once inside the main hall, there is no doubt that we are inside a Japanese home. The paneled walls of the entry flow to shoji, inlaid wood floors with oriental rugs to tatami, and—Cochran points out— a trap door in the ceiling leads to the *musha-damari*, the small room where three or four samurai once lay in wait.

The Roshi Hekiun makes a towering, dramatic, almost theatrical figure in his black and saffron robes, the tawny *kesa* of a Zen priest draped over his left shoulder, as he strides into the parlor. He limps in obvious pain, yet the erect, unflinching discipline with which he holds himself, and the calm, stoic expression somehow add to the priestly effect of his appearance. I am counting on it.

Kuribayashi, Ozu, and Matsu Yurikawa of MITI are waiting for us. Despite his efforts to retain an impassive poker face, Yurikawa is startled by our battered appearance. "What has happened?"

"Your office apparently failed to inform me that my original contact, Matami Okamatsu, has been assassinated . . . and that my own life is in danger."

"We never—"

"Please." I hold up my hand to interrupt him. "A young lady to whom Mr. Ozu here introduced me has been brutally murdered. And Roshi Hekiun and I were attacked in the sanctuary of his temple yesterday." I pause, allowing Ozu time to translate for Kuribayashi, and glance at Cochran, who nods to confirm that Ozu is translating straight.

"My own security people accompanied me here this morning. The large American outside is a former senior official with our Federal Bureau of Investigation—who has considerable contacts with your National Police and the Tokyo Metropolitan Police." I speak deliberately in a low, nonconfrontational voice, as if deeply hurt and saddened rather than angry.

From the manner in which Yurikawa looks from me to Kuribayashi, he is hearing this for the first time, but the old man looks levelly at me without any emotion whatever, only blinking slightly.

"We have evidence in a handwritten letter from the dead girl that a Yakuza *oyabun* is involved in all this." I hand the fax of the letter from Mari Midori to Ozu. "What is your relationship with Ryoichi Ishii?"

Ozu's eyes widen and dart from me to Kuribayashi, looking for instructions.

The MITI bureaucrat, Yurikawa, breaks the silence. "Ryoichi Ishii is the chairman of one of the largest syndicates—what you Americans call a godfather."

Something Ruff 'n Ready had said suddenly computes. "How many shares of Kuribayashi Electric does he control?"

Yurikawa defers to the older man with a bow of his head, as though he too is interested in the answer.

With a graceful wave of his hand, Kuribayashi invites Cochran and me to sit down. A couch and several chairs are arranged about a low table. The real negotiations have now apparently begun.

A Monet landscape hangs on a paneled wall that stands at right angles to a large window opening onto the garden outside, as if the Monet reflects the lusher, sunnier summer image of the garden. Although the house had, in fact, been built centuries before, it appears the spartan room has been deliberately constructed as a salon for the Monet. The window with a sliding aluminum frame is new, and the garden in the Monet with its mottled sunshine, rampant greenery, and rambling vines is almost barbaric by contrast with the meticulously landscaped Japanese garden outside that is framed by the window. Kuribayashi watches me look from the Monet to the window and back. I make a small smile of appreciation, but neither of us says anything.

"When Kuribayashi-san was rebuilding the company and constructing new electronics factories during the fifties and sixties," Ozu recites, "Ishii-san was very useful."

"Useful?"

Ozu and the old man have an exchange in Japanese. "In controlling the Communist unions and breaking strikes. The company was in
debt, short of cash, so Ishii-san was often paid for his services in shares
of Kuribayashi Electric. Over the years his personal holdings and the
shares his syndicate owns have increased. They now total about one-
point-five million shares." Kuribayashi is trying to scare me off.

"Do you pay Ishii extortion and protection—what do you call
it?—to avoid confrontations at shareholders' meetings?"

"*Sokaiya*. It is a common practice," Yurikawa answers, as if none
of this is a revelation to him.

"Is it also common practice to attempt to murder American businessmen?" I ask Yurikawa. "And their spiritual advisors?"

This grabs everybody's attention. "Why do you think that the
men who attacked you yesterday were of Ishii-san's"—he gropes for a
word here—"family?"

"Roshi Hekiun and I can personally identify two of his little
pricks—what's the Yakuza expression?—*chimpira*." I motion to the fax
that Ozu still clutches. "They are the two described in the letter, who
killed the girl."

There is an exchange in Japanese. "Kuribayashi-san asks, 'What
will you do with this information?'" Ozu relays.

"Give it to the Tokyo police investigating the girl's death."

"Will that not embarrass you?"

"I have nothing to be embarrassed about. She wrote to me
because I offered to help find her a job in the United States. Also with
possible citizenship."

"You are very generous." The derision is in Ozu's flat tone, not his
words.

"She was the daughter of a U.S. serviceman. But I wasn't helping
her only out of generosity. She was a tall, strikingly beautiful girl, and
Japanese—whether or not you consider a half-black Japanese. She
spoke English well and was about to graduate from Rikkyo University
in economics. With a few years of business experience in the United

States, I thought she'd make a strong, loyal asset." I smile at Kuri-bayashi. "Especially if this partnership is completed."

The old man nods. "That is very far-sighted."

"Considerably more far-sighted than Ryoichi Ishii. His little pricks also raped the girl, leaving their blood type and DNA inside her. I can give the Tokyo police a rather complete description, and if they are only half as tough and efficient as I am told they are, they will pick them up . . . and break them."

"This is a common criminal matter," Yurikawa dismisses it. "Gangsters killing a hostess in a cabaret."

"Is it? These two have followed me since I arrived in Tokyo, even before Ozu-san took me to that particular nightclub. And right after the murder, someone called the police to inform them that I had spent the night with the girl—which I hadn't. Then they followed me to Kyoto and attacked me in a secluded Zen monastery. If it had not been for the intervention of my old friend and comrade here, they would have killed me." I have deliberately kept Michiko out of the story.

I glance at Cochran, then turn to Yurikawa. "Now we discover that these gangsters—as you describe them—are Yakuza with considerable holdings in Kuribayashi Electric. And their activities—as Kuribayashi-san has explained—in strike-breaking and smashing Communist unions in the past have had tacit government approval. This is a very unpleasant business." I shake my head, my voice heavy with regret. "It is a scandal that surely can bring about all the disastrous trade difficulties between our two countries that we discussed in Tokyo."

I wait for Ozu's translation to catch up. "There is one thing that does not add up: why this . . . this old associate . . . would go to these great risks to kill this deal. The Yakuza's main interest is money, and their holdings would greatly increase in value. They would make a great deal of money."

"Perhaps Ishii-san is a true believer. That only the Japanese should own Japanese companies."

Ozu's translation does not capture the irony in the old man's eyes, but I look back at him and say nothing, a long period of eloquent silence in which I sit comfortably waiting for the old man to realize that I know—without his knowing why, because the answer lies in the distant past, a half-century ago really, and I am sworn not to reveal that.

It is Yurikawa who speaks first. "Perhaps Kuribayashi-san and I might confer on this matter."

Cochran, who has been silent until now, suddenly stands. "We have been admiring your gardens. We would like the opportunity to see them."

Yurikawa seizes Cochran's lead. "Mr. Ozu, please show Roshi Hekiun and Mr. Saxon the gardens."

As we exit, I turn on Cochran. "Why the hell did you pull me out here to stare at the bonsai?"

"You're heading for a confrontation with the old man. Your voice is calm and cool, but there's a real rage churning underneath. Even Yurikawa felt it. He's trying to help you."

"He's trying to avoid a trade war."

"For whatever reason, he's dealing with the present. Both you and Kuribayashi are in the past."

Ozu emerges from the house. He smiles unctuously at Cochran. "Mr. Kuribayashi likes very much the gardens at Daikaku-Ji."

"Yes"—Cochran nods pleasantly and looks about—"they are very beautiful." He turns back to Ozu. "How did you know I am from Daikaku-Ji?"

Behind the thick lenses, Ozu's eyes are suddenly wary and dart from Cochran to me.

I shake my head. "I never mentioned it either. The Yakuza who attacked Roshi Hekiun and me there followed me to Kyoto. They were waiting for Mrs. Hara and me at the Tokyo station. They knew exactly what bullet train to catch and were in the next car. Mrs. Hara's and my reservations were made by your office."

I point at Ozu. "You should not get involved with criminal activities, Mr. Ozu. You're not very experienced at them."

Ozu is stricken. "I did not know——"

I interrupt him. "Mr. Ozu, I think very highly of you. You are a very loyal, conscientious man, a good soldier."

Ozu is puzzled but nods eagerly. "Yes, thank you very——"

"No, please let me finish. I know you would never do anything without consulting with Mr. Kuribayashi and getting his approval."

I speak in my confiding attorney's tone. "Please let us be open and truthful. You never went to the Tokyo police, as I asked you to, did you? You saw me with the girl Mari Midori that morning when you came to take me to the Tsukuba research center. And you sent those two thugs back to question her."

Ozu only blinks rapidly behind the thick lenses.

"This is a case of murder, Mr. Ozu, and the attempted murder of Roshi Hekiun and me. With very serious international repercussions. But you personally could spend the rest of your life in prison."

Here I shake my head gravely, then again take a confiding tone. "I understand the police can hold you for twenty-one days for questioning before letting you confer with a lawyer. And they are very rough. Brutal. Shall I give the Tokyo police your name?"

There is now fear in his eyes, and it boils off of him in a stinking sweat. "I must talk with Kuribayashi——"

"*No!* You must talk to *me. Now!*" I give him his opening. "Why did you have Mrs. Hara and me followed?"

He leans toward me as he takes the bait. "Mr. Saxon, I also think very highly of you. You say to me be open, be truthful. We have men follow you because we believe you know Mrs. Hara long time. Perhaps you will bring dishonor to Kuribayashi family."

"I don't understand why you would think this."

"Mrs. Hara did very much research about you. She says this research is for her husband. But she wants to know more than business. She asks questions about your navy background, your wife, your children. These are women's questions."

I nod and indicate Cochran. "They were Roshi Hekiun's questions."

"Roshi Hekiun?" Cochran's presence has had both Ozu and Kuribayashi off balance since we entered. I don't know how much they know.

"He flew with me in Vietnam. He was wounded and assigned duty at the American embassy in Tokyo while recovering. As you know, Mrs. Hara also worked there, and they became good friends. The nature of the Roshi's wounds do not allow sexual relations with women. Their friendship was chaste. In fact, it is Mrs. Hara who first introduced him to Zen Buddhism and brought him to visit the temples here in Kyoto."

I turn to Cochran. "Why don't you explain it to Mr. Ozu in Japanese so that there's no misunderstanding. Especially how, when my name first came up in the research, Michiko-san recognized me as your old comrade and, as a very generous favor, researched that personal information about me for your benefit. To see if it might be comfortable for two old friends to meet again."

Cochran talks in a low, rumbling voice, occasionally bobbing his head toward me as if acknowledging confirmation, although I haven't a clue what he is saying. Ozu looks grave, glancing at me from under hooded, perplexed brows.

When Cochran apparently finishes his explanation, Ozu nods his head in a strange, almost formal bow, turns to me with an odd expectant expression, and says, "This is very interesting, Mr. Saxon. But I have a report from the Tokyo police from the year nineteen sixty-five that tells of a hostess from the Black Rose who cut off the sex organs of an American navy officer. There are two witnesses. His friend Lieutenant Peter Saxon and a girlfriend from the Black Rose who have sex in the next room. This girlfriend is Michiko Kuribayashi." There is something arrogant and triumphant in his voice and expression.

"No, her name was Lilli, and she is dead. But you're right, Mr. Ozu, I was involved in a terrible incident in Tokyo thirty years ago."

Cochran starts to say something, but I cut him off. "Remember,

I'm a lawyer. This is my turf." I let out a deep exasperated breath. "What I remember of it was a great deal of chaos, blood, screaming. The girl was hysterical. The police didn't speak English very well, if at all. They were very confused. And I remember some bizarre story . . . Wait. Where did you see this record? In the police files? Do you have a copy of it?"

"It is in Japanese, yes. I have a copy."

"But *you* didn't get it from the police. An *associate* did."

Ozu's hesitation is the answer.

"And these associates are tied to the same Yakuza who extorts millions from Kuribayashi for . . . what's the word?"

"*Sokaiya.*"

"And what did you pay them after they brought you these *counterfeit* police records?"

"Counterfeit?"

"Are they blackmailing you with them?"

"The police records are counterfeit?" He looks to Cochran as if for confirmation.

Cochran speaks in Japanese, and the color totally drains from Ozu's face.

"I told you that the girl's name was Lilli, and she is dead."

"Please, you know this. You give me her real name and family."

"Why? So you can send Yakuza thugs to question and terrorize them. The same goons who killed Mari Midori? Not on your life. The question here is not whether I give you the name and family of a woman for whom I once had a great deal of affection. The question is whether I give *your* name to the Tokyo police. And perhaps the press, just to make sure the police do their job."

"The scandal," Ozu whispers.

"It would certainly end my relationship with Kuribayashi Electric. And honestly, I don't want to do that. I have worked too hard to build this. Destroying all that to punish you is simply not worth it. So please, Mr. Ozu, be the loyal and good staff officer once again and relay to Kuribayashi-san everything—and I mean everything—we have discussed."

Ozu shoots me a look of great fear. Oozing a reeking sweat like shame itself, he bows and hurries off, breaking into a stilted jog, back to the house.

"What the hell did you tell him?"

"I said these men were a black filthy pool who reflected back what Ozu wanted to see," the Roshi Hekiun answers.

"True enough. But we're only killing the messenger."

Cochran is silent. Everyone in Japan converses in silences.

"The old man is behind it all."

"Even he's just a messenger."

"For whom?"

"Japan."

"No, that's too easy. Too cryptic." I glare at Cochran. "He's willing to sacrifice his own niece to break this deal."

"You're still angry," Cochran says. "Normally that's your own concern. But your anger endangers Michiko if you confront her uncle—the man who controls her husband's and family's future."

"Then what do I do now?"

"What you came here to do?"

"And how do I accomplish that?"

"Don't offend Kuribayashi. When possible, be silent. And give him an opportunity to retain, if not his honor, then at least his dignity."

Now I'm silent.

"All these events did not happen in a vacuum," Cochran says softly. "This isn't America, Pete. Events don't happen according to the rampant will, whim, or ego of one individual. Kuribayashi—whatever he may be guilty of—operates in a complex web of obligations and duties. After thirty years I still don't fully understand them."

We stand near a wide pond edged with ferns, moss, and sculptured rocks. At the far end a pair of swans glide through the lotus pads, deliberately avoiding us. There is a ripple and a flash of gold as a large koi briefly stirs the surface.

"Look around this garden," Cochran says, following my eyes. "A mountain is a stone, an ocean an artfully rippled patch of sand. The shoreline of a continent is the graceful curve of that stone bridge spanning a pool with koi. The whole world has been abstracted to just a few strokes refined centuries ago."

The pond seems at first glance dark, murky, but staring down into it there is a crystal clarity to the water that reveals schools of slender gold and white carp flashing against the black pebbles that line the bottom.

After a while Kuribayashi, alone, emerges from the house and trudges slowly across the manicured lawn toward Cochran and me, as if his frail frame can scarcely move under the weight he carries. There is a tenuousness to Kuribayashi's movements that I have not observed before in the limited area of the conference room and his salon. He addresses Cochran in Japanese.

"We will speak privately here. I am to be the translator," Cochran says.

The old man studies Cochran for some time before he speaks again. "He says that this is very painful for him."

I say nothing.

"It was never his intention to hurt either you or me or this young lady in Tokyo. The Yakuza are criminals, and it is very difficult dealing with them. Sometimes the bosses act with honor, sometimes not, but the common criminals, the little pricks you spoke of—I'm freely translating here—are often crazy. They have no discipline. They lie, they threaten, they beat people to extort more money. They even kill to protect themselves. I did not wish this to happen. I am shamed by it, and I beg your forgiveness."

"Yeah, well, good help is hard to get everywhere these days." I look the old man straight in the eye. Kuribayashi is letting himself off the hook too easily, and if I let him wiggle free, the deal is still blown. "Roshi Hekiun counsels me that we must forget the past and live only in the present."

I wait for Cochran to finish translating. "But I believe that is possible only for a Zen master. You and I must come to some peace with the past. With our history."

The secret of controlling the translation is to talk in short takes so that Cochran with his artful tact does not anticipate me.

"But you have a deep *kenbei* against me, against my mission here." Cochran looks at me with surprise at my use of the Japanese word for their gut hatred of Americans.

"This you share with Ryoichi Ishii, who I understand spent some time in prison for war crimes after World War Two. Perhaps because of your shared *kenbei*, the Yakuza felt they had license to do these shameful things."

The old man does not back down a millimeter but holds my eyes without blinking. "You are very well informed."

"My investigator—the ex-FBI guy outside—has access to government records dating back to the occupation."

Kuribayashi purses his lower lip and nods with an expression of being impressed. But the real records to which I have had access were Lilli's traumatic memories of her father's death.

"But let's talk business, because there are great stakes involved here."

"*Hai.*"

"There is an older faction within your company that is against this merger. But there is another, younger faction that believes our partnership will make Kuribayashi stronger. Increase the value of the company, expand you into new markets, and leapfrog you into twenty-first century communications. And they are right.

"And MITI is pressuring your management to prevent U.S. trade sanctions. And they are also right."

I turn to Cochran. "But Kuribayashi-san's pain is justified. This company is the phoenix he has built from the ashes of American bombs."

I wait for the translation. "I understand that he would rather cut his guts out than sell part of it to Americans. . . .

"I can even understand, perhaps, his wanting to murder me. . . .

"But he was willing to disgrace and sacrifice his niece, his brother's daughter"—I am about to say "his heir" but instead say—"his only living family, in this *kenbei*. . . ."

There is a glare of warning and alarm in Cochran's eyes. As with Michiko, I have no way of knowing what Cochran is translating—what is being filtered—and I am dependent on the goodwill of the translator. Cochran has already defined truth as he interprets it, and he is now the medium through which Kuribayashi and I communicate, undoubtedly transforming what we actually say to what we need to say and understand.

"He thought she had already disgraced herself," Cochran translates.

"How?"

Kuribayashi suddenly looks confused at the question. "Please understand that my parents, my precious wife and son, were burned to death by American planes."

A Japanese would not say that. It is too brutal, too personal, too rude. But Cochran, knowing my secrets, translates it into those words, knowing they will cut to the soul.

The old man speaks in a voice little louder than a whisper. There is a moment when Cochran, despite his stoic Zen calm, visibly pales.

"What?"

He is silent.

"What?" I repeat.

"Don't get angry."

"At what?"

"Kuribayashi. He said that when he was a young man, the women carried daggers to kill themselves rather than allow Americans to dishonor them."

Rather than anger, my first impulse is to laugh, but in the presence of Cochran's own dreadful mutilation, only a long silence is appropriate.

"It was unforgivable, abhorrent to him, great shame to his family, when he was told that his niece—the daughter of his brother, who had died in the war—was the whore of Americans," Cochran continues.

"I don't think he said that."

"He used a polite word that meant something like 'consort,' but that's what he meant in his heart."

"Hai," I agree. I remember now what Lilli once told me. This is the man who fifty years ago handed out cyanide pills to the women in his factory to preserve their honor from American troops. His own brother, an army officer, after the surrender, committed seppuku on the Imperial Palace grounds.

"This is enormously painful for him," Cochran says. "The Japanese avoid any confrontation at all costs. That's why Yurikawa and Ozu have been sent away, so as not to witness his shame. Everything hinges on what you say to him."

"Yeah." His is a generation that once forced hundreds of thousands of Chinese, Filipino, Korean, Dutch, and Indonesian women into sexual slavery at gunpoint but continues to deny it out of a sense of propriety. Yet in defeat, they condemned their own daughters for consorting with Americans. To say that the first tragedies were half a century ago and my affair a generation later is meaningless. To Kuribayashi, Michiko and her family, even myself, time is that river without banks that threatens to drown us all. And yet the old man now looks at me as if I have some great truth to share with him.

"You know what to tell him," I say. "Just what we told Ozu. The measure of truth is not the facts but our obligations to others. Isn't that what you said?" At the end of the day Cochran is right—the truth is our debt to those we love.

"You're still angry."

"Hell yes." I shake my head. "But just tell him what he needs to hear."

"This isn't about business, is it?"

"No, it isn't business at all."

"*Good.* Honor will be damn well satisfied then."

Cochran and Kuribayashi talk in gentle voices for a long time, Kuribayashi nodding his head in agreement. "*Hai, hai.*" Then Cochran begins translating back into English, as much to underline the points for Kuribayashi as to inform me.

"Because I have known you as a young man with whom I flew in combat in Vietnam, I can vouch for your honor and integrity as few other men can. These qualities are very important in a negotiation such as this. There have been so many misunderstandings in the past."

Then Cochran speaks directly to me before he translates. "We discussed the serious criminal matters. All this by thugs employed by Ryoichi Ishii, who reported to Mr. Ozu. Ozu is the whipping boy here, to avoid a direct confrontation between you and Kuribayashi."

"What would I do without you?"

Cochran gives me a small smile, then again addresses Kuribayashi at length in Japanese.

"There is a great price to be paid for all this. I reminded Kuribayashi-san that you and I are warriors, and we don't demand this lightly."

The old man bows to me, accepting the obligation. There is something terribly feeble in his stance now, as if a vital sinew has been severed. But since that sinew is hate, I cannot summon up a great deal of compassion for his weakness. Before, he had appeared as tough and gnarled as an old weathered cypress, but now I see death lurking in his frailty, his deeply lined face and sallow skin. He does not have long.

"Tell Kuribayashi-san that I cannot ask him to forget his pain. He, his brother, my father, and your father fought a war with great horrors and brutality. You, I, Hara, and Michiko inherited that world, but now our children have come of age. I ask him to allow Hara-san to do what is best for his children,"—I make a rapid calculation here—"the grandson and granddaughter of Kuribayashi's own brother."

I follow the flow of Cochran's translation, and the reference to Michiko's kids brings a slight smile to the old man's lips. He again nods and bows solemnly, accepting this new obligation.

27

Flight to Paris

Cochran and I sit on a porch of cedar wood and contemplate the sun setting over the higher mountains to the west.

Below us, amid the centuries-old temples, tour buses unload reverent crowds of camera-wielding tourists and classrooms of students, and a recording—now scratched and staticky from use—on the public-address speakers urges the arrivals to have a spiritual experience.

"He doesn't have long to live. It's cancer," Cochran says.

I wonder exactly what Kuribayashi has told him, but I had seen an advancing death in the old man. "That's probably why he was so desperate."

Cochran smiles at me, and there is nothing ironic in his smile. "You will create a great empire. But I wonder, if it had not been in your business interests, if you would have protected Michiko."

"Out of friendship, please give me the benefit of the doubt."

"Yes," he says without hesitation.

Perhaps because of the mystical setting or his black and saffron cleric's robes, I want Cochran to think well of me. "This *is* about business, money, and power," I say. "And ninety percent, possibly more, of what we do turns out to be pap with the label of entertainment. But with it we've somehow set up a global communications network beyond the control of any government in a dangerous, increasingly fragmenting world. If that ultimately doesn't serve the common good, it's because there's no common good to serve. And I can't look at my own daughters and believe that."

"But you still believe it's an extraordinary coincidence that you're here?"

"Yes."

Cochran laughs softly. "You wire the entire world for bits of electronic impulses beamed up to satellites in space that now convey all information—entire libraries, pictures, voices, music, motion pictures, even human emotions—and yet you don't believe love and passion have the power to influence events."

"You were also instrumental," I suggest.

"I only did what I had to do to protect Michiko . . . because I love her."

The sun sinks behind the distant mountains, and we sit in silence in a shimmering twilight that casts no shadows.

"Meet me in Paris tomorrow."

"What? What the hell is this all about?" Joan asks, but there is excitement in her voice.

"A celebration."

"You pulled it off. We're going to be scillionaires."

"Not yet. There are backbreaking details to work out. And more shit's going to hit the fan here in Japan than I knew existed. But Kuribayashi has agreed in principle."

"Then why are you going to Paris?"

"It's a long story. But they bought me a first-class ticket to replace reservations I said I canceled. And now I have to use it to maintain credibility."

"Aha! The old I'm-flying-to-Paris-in-two-days-so-we'd-better-get-this-negotiation-on-track gambit."

"You've got it."

"Who's supposed to be in Paris?"

"Euro-Media. André Benoit."

"The chain-smoker with receding gums who told me I looked like Catherine Deneuve."

"I don't remember that."

"Are you really going to see him?"

"Maybe for dinner. But I don't want to have to fake too much, so I'll cut it short."

"Well, say hello. You know I can't just take off and leave for Paris on a day's notice. I'll take a rain check."

"No rain checks. Once I get back it's going to be eighteen-hour days putting this bitch together. Even weekends. With the time and day differential, our Sunday is their Monday. It's Paris now or never."

There is silence on the other end of the transpacific beam, and I can envision Joan biting her lower lip.

"I have nothing to wear in Paris."

"You can go shopping there."

"Oh, well then."

Hara accompanies me in the limousine to Narita Airport. "Please, we will not discuss business. My English is not very good, and there will be misunderstanding."

"Your English is fine. It's my Japanese that is nonexistent." Ozu is absent.

What, I wonder, does Hara know of the intrigues that have swirled about his wife and me? "Will you be traveling to the States often?"

"Oh yes, I think so. This new organization, this is my responsibility." His career is on the line. I sense a sticky filament in the web of my new obligations snake out and ensnare me.

"Will your wife be coming?"

"I don't think so. Maybe when we are old and retired, we will take cruise ship to United States."

"A cruise ship?"

"Yes, she does not like to fly. Airplanes make great fear."

"The bombing raids on Tokyo?"

Hara looks surprised by my knowledge.

I stammer to explain. "Kuribayashi-san, her uncle, mentioned to me that he had built Phoenix Electronics up from the ashes. Many of the family had died in the air raids."

"Yes, always great fear of airplanes. Always, I think. That is why you take bullet train to Kyoto." He says it as an apology.

Lilli is dead, but Michiko Hara still bears the fire scars of her childhood.

There is, of course, unfinished business. Ozu identified Dragon Hands and the samurai to Inspector Goto of the Tokyo Metropolitan Police. They were immediately picked up, interrogated, blood samples extracted, and will be charged with the murder of Mari Midori.

Whatever they may reveal to the police about the relationship between Kuribayashi and their *oyabun* I will never know. They each have their own web of obligations that has spun for a half-century.

There are, as Rufus Ready once briefed me, two secrets. The first is that no one—not the toughest—stands up under the Tokyo police interrogation. The second is that the police seldom act on the information if it is politically sensitive.

I have never revealed the letter Mari wrote me naming the Yakuza *oyabun* Ryoichi Ishii—at best, it is hearsay, legally not evidence—nor have Cochran and I reported the attack at the monastery. Either risks involving Michiko Hara, and yet in our silence we weave our own webs that snare Kuribayashi and Ishii.

Ozu has disappeared, at least from my view, but I will have need of him. A considerable sum of money must pass from Kuribayashi and the *oyabun* to Mari Midori's mother, and a continuing scholarship for the descendants of American servicemen and Japanese mothers will be set up in her name. In death, Mari has spun her own web.

As we sit in the first-class lounge sipping tea, Hara offers, "My son, Hiroshi, he thinks maybe go graduate school of business in United States."

"A very good idea. Bring him for a visit. He's a good-looking boy. My daughters will be happy to show him around Stanford or USC. And I have contacts at Harvard. I can arrange for written recommendations that will get the schools' attention."

"Thank you very much." The way Hara says it and bows his head implies that this is a favor that he will probably accept. I have spun my own filament of *giri-ninjo*.

The public address speaker announces the JAL flight to Paris.

At the security check-in, I turn to Hara. "We're going to make this work, you and I," I say, and I offer him my hand.

An escalator carries me up to the departure concourse. A psychic pressure, like a delicate touch on the hackles of my neck, causes me to turn around.

A multitiered structure of marble stairways and balconies overlooks the upper and lower concourse. There, on one of the balconies, Michiko Hara stands watching me.

She holds my eyes, as if she has knowingly commanded my attention, a faint *triste* smile playing on her lips. She does not wave, nor does her smile broaden into some cheery expression of good-bye, but she stands silent, unmoving, her eyes fixed on mine, until the crowded escalator mounts to the upper concourse and the unceasing stream of travelers carries me out of her sight.

On board the Boeing 744, I lean back and shut my eyes, something I had not done as I worked on my way from LA to Tokyo.

Cochran, of course, is right. Our passions do influence events and make things happen beyond any odds of probability, although not always the way we might will them.

In Kyoto, sitting on that mountain, he had asked, "Will you be coming back to Japan?"

"Yes, I expect so."

"While you are wiring the world for sight and sound—more information and entertainment than anyone could possibly absorb—you might set aside some time to come here and sit in silence."

"In silence?"

"Yes."

About us I heard the stir of the wind in the pines, but nothing more. "Yes, perhaps I will."

I shut my eyes, not to nap but to probe now for that stillness.

Flying west, Paris is about equidistant between Los Angeles and Tokyo. It would be an adventure, perhaps even enlightening, to hop from Tokyo to Hong Kong to Bangkok to Calcutta to Karachi to Athens to Paris, and if I took such a flight, crossing the Gulf of Tonkin and North Vietnam, my soul might be pierced with deep mystical insight. Perhaps not.

But Japan Airlines in their efficiency has this direct polar flight that spans the featureless steppes of Russia, pacing the sun, and I descend into Paris in time to meet my wife for cocktails on the same afternoon I have left Tokyo.

ACKNOWLEDGMENTS

The word *fiction* in its Latin root means a shaping or molding, in the case of this novel a dramatic shaping of contemporary realities that go back 50 years.

The events of the World War II flashbacks of this fiction are a matter of public record from the transcripts of the Yokohama war crimes trials to numerous nonfiction accounts of the bombing of Tokyo. The best overall history of those events and their background I have read to date is *The Fall of Japan* by William Craig, published by The Dial Press in 1967.

A generation after World War II I served as an officer aboard the aircraft carrier USS *Midway* on a Far East tour during which we operated out of Yokosuka, Japan. Through the years shipmates and friends have shared their stories with me. Of particular note were personal accounts of the first raids over North Vietnam. Many years later, while working on this book, I again verified certain details, but the individuals declined any formal acknowledgment.

Capt. Ronald Morse of the Navy Office of Information—West checked the accuracy of the early drafts of these sequences in the book. But I later added details which I had independently confirmed. They are fictions, but I did not make them up.

Concerning the contemporary wheelings and dealings of this fiction, at various times I have worked in various capacities in motion pictures and TV, at one time as a VP of ABC Pictures. I mentioned this specific experience because two of my contemporaries at the time have since become major media moguls, by any definition of those words. All this and the firsthand anecdotes of friends and business associates invests this fiction.

I might note that I live in the Toluca Lake area of Los Angeles, which is flanked by two major studios which at one time were taken over by Japanese electronic companies. Matsushita has since sold its controlling interest in Universal, and Sony has now bought and occupied the former MGM lot—where I once had an office—and moved their Columbia Pictures there.

During the work on this novel, I frequently freelanced for *Variety* writing special reports. Although no specific material from *Variety* is incorporated here, I was in continual contact with people ranging from technicians to CEO's involved with motion pictures, television, and the new technologies. That experience also enriches this fiction, and I am grateful to Peter Bart, editor-in-chief; Steve Gaydos, managing editor special reports; and Peter Pryor, the former editor.

There are producers and executives—still associated with Japanese media interests—who have read the manuscript and made valuable commentaries. They have requested not to be acknowledged by name, but I am no less appreciative of their insights.

I am indebted to the following:

Todd Mittleman, currently an executive with Honda Trading, who through the years has related his experiences as a teacher in Japan, a translator for university scientists, an official at the Japanese consulate, and his perceptions enrich this narrative.

Jim Biggs of the Zen Mountain Center shared his personal experiences in a monastery in Japan. He was uncommonly generous with rare books and videos, and then reviewed the manuscript with a keen editorial eye.

Rev. Shohaku Okumura, director of the Soto Zen education center, briefed me on finer points of language and names.

Nariko Galloway lived through the times and places of this novel as a girl growing up in Tokyo in the aftermath of World War II, then as a young woman in Yokosuka during the Vietnam War, and now as an agent with Japan Travel Bureau. She read the manuscript, corrected my faulty Japanese, then gave me the wonderful gift of affirming that even from her totally different perspective I had somehow gotten it right.

There are four individuals to whom I am deeply grateful for being instrumental in bringing this book to print:

Scott Waxman, my literary agent, proved to be a sensitive editor in addition to being a very able dealmaker.

Richard Shepherd, my representative for movie and television in Los Angeles who has headed two major studios, shared his insights with me, and it was his initial enthusiasm that propelled the manuscript.

Allison McCabe, my very capable associate editor at Harper-Collins, first read and championed the manuscript.

And, ultimately, Lawrence Peel Ashmead, executive editor and vice president of HarperCollins, made the key decisions and transformed an unedited manuscript into a handsome novel.